the
GIRL
BEHIND
the
GLASS

SPELLBOUND CHRONICLES:
DARK FAIRYTALES RETOLD

APRIL GRACE

Copyright © 2022 by April Grace
All rights reserved.

No part of this book may be reproduced in any form or by any electronic or mechanical means, including information storage and retrieval systems, without written permission from the author, except for the use of brief quotations in a book review.

Cover Design by Josephine Blake at Covers & Cupcakes, coversandcupcakes.com

Developmental Editing by Katie Wismer at Ahimsa Press, katiewismer.com

Map artwork commissioned by Abigail M Hair, instagram.com/authorabigailmhair

Character artwork commissioned by Athena Bliss, twitter.com/AthenaBliss4

Chapter headings artwork by Bobby P Art, instagram.com/bobbyp_1980_art/

Formatting by Julia Scott at Evenstar Books, evenstarbooks.com

(eBook) 9781739911461
(Paperback) 9781739911447
(Audiobook) 9781739911454
(Hardback) 9781739911478

Because this book has a strong maternal theme - with sisters, mothers, grandmothers and witches alike – it is dedicated to Nanny, Nanna and Mum. May both of my beloved grandmothers rest in peace. I know you're cheering us all on from above.

Mum, thank you for everything you do for us. There may be an evil mother in this story, but just know that she isn't based on you. Love you.

WINDSPELL
OCEANWELL
CRANWICK
WINTER FOREST
WINTER CAVES
ICEFALL
BLOSSOMHEART

PART ONE

THE CURSED & THE LONELY

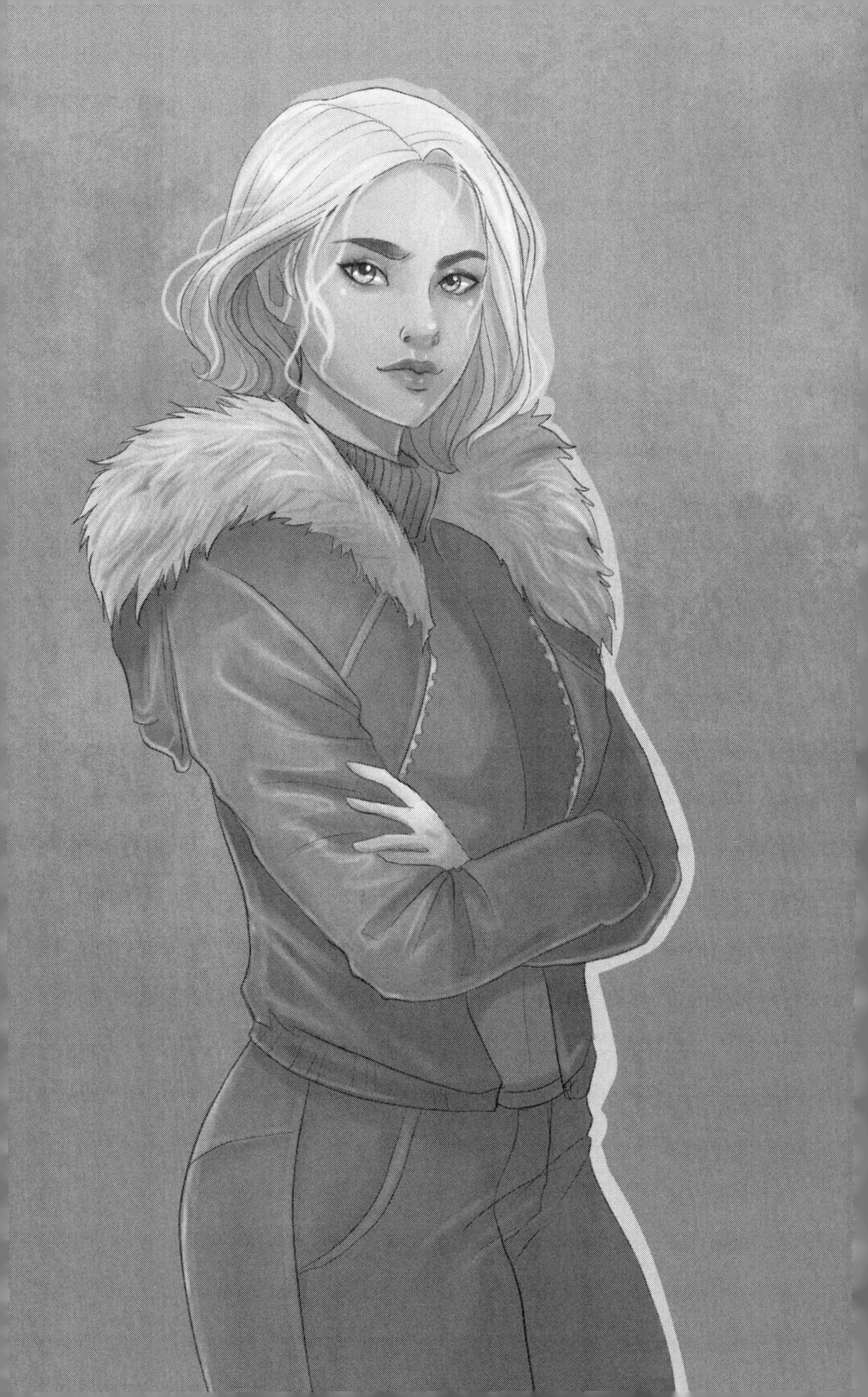

1

WINNIE

I NEVER MEANT TO KILL THE WITCH.
She appeared at the wrong time. She charged forward, along with an endless stream of her magical sisters and their Enforcers, the police force that did most of their dirty work for them. The Enforcers imprisoned people, orchestrated lashings and public punishments, and kept the city in order.

But sometimes, like Brulle, the witches preferred to teach people their lessons themselves. I couldn't have known that because she was an elderly witch, she already had a number of health issues that left her close to death. In my defence, I shoved her away. She fell to the ground and then she was gone.

Just like that.

More on her later. This awful day began with Cranwick's Pride Festival and a night of protests that would change the course of history for our city forever. I mean, it wasn't strange to see so many people together. The streets were usually busy, full of people laughing and shopping. Cranwick was the kind of place where you were never bored because there was always something to do.

The perfect utopia, or so one would think. Although it might have looked pretty on the outside, it was a living nightmare. There was no way in or out of Cranwick. That was its curse. There were no visible doors, only strange mirror portals that were known to be well guarded by the Enforcers. There was also a wall that stretched like a snake all the way around the city, built with little towers and well-hidden walkways for them to peer down at us from above, scrutinising our every move and forever eliminating any possible threats to their world.

All on behalf of the witches they worked for.

Cranwick, the Mirror Village.

Cranwick, a beautiful prison.

Imagine living in a dystopian world where your day-to-day life was monitored and controlled by ancient witches, all because a previous mayor from centuries ago decided to kill one of their own. Not fun, right? As you can probably imagine, the people weren't happy about it. The protesters were well within their rights to fight against the way our world was run, and I understood that more than anyone as the daughter of Cranwick's mayor.

My parents and I lived in a decent sized house right in the centre of the city, with my cousin and best friend right next door. My life revolved around school, my books and the few friends I had. But Barchester and I were inseparable. It was the first time that he and his friends had successfully managed to drag me along to the Pride Festival they attended every year without fail. I'd finally taken the bait and chosen to go. Not that I was ever against going, but there had always been something else more important happening for me at the time. School trips, summer days away with Mum and Dad, or piles and piles of homework assignments that I was unable to get away from.

Besides, his friends were *his,* not mine. They were mostly loud, proud, and only too happy to share their beliefs with everyone they met.

It was *meant* to be a good day, but I'd already been reminded of the witches' force when I was leaving my house that morning. An elderly man had collapsed after a small altercation with a few Enforcers in the city square outside the largest clothing store, *Reflective*. Then another man, middle aged and probably capable of standing up for himself, had been arrested for breaking curfew and trying to feed a homeless woman and her dog with a piece of bread from one of their food trolleys that had been left to waste. A few people rushed over to help him, but he was quickly whisked away and placed into the back of one of their vans.

At the time, I was too much of a coward to say anything to stop it, and honestly, it'd left me in a foul mood. It wasn't a great start to the day that Barchester had been looking forward to for months.

So many thoughts rushed into my head. What kind of a world are they running? People can't even help each other without facing arrest? All right, technically he's stolen from them, but his intentions were the most important thing, right? Or, they should be.

No, control, that was all they wanted. For the people to be silent, and complacent.

Obedient.

I tried to be positive as we set off for the square, where a large stage had been set up along with a space for people to drink and dance. One of Barchester's favourite drag queens paraded across the stage, wearing the highest pair of rainbow heels I'd ever seen, dressed in a blue velvet gown covered with sequins. Charcoal lined her eyes, and a sparkling tiara was nestled in above the fringe of her dark, waist-length wig. I had to appreciate the art form, even as someone who wasn't typically an expert on drag queens. I could never do my makeup like that.

My cousin linked his fingers through mine and together we began to dance and sing along to the music. He and his friends laughed excitedly, pushing themselves closer to the stage. 'Dance with me, Winnie.' *Sweet Sherry* was performing a rendition of Cranwick's next big hit, *Sway,* and the crowd were going wild for it. I tried to look like I was having fun, even if I wasn't. But it did start to ease my mood a little. I studied his friends closely as they cheered and danced along with Barchester.

Fletcher was typically draped in black dresses that made her look like some kind of vampire, but today her dark hair and long-sleeved silk dress was highlighted with a large pansexual flag, a little silver tiara was perched above her black fringe, rainbows were painted beneath her eyes, and silken fairy wings poked out over her shoulders. She was probably my favourite member of his friendship group, always welcoming and kind to me. 'I'm so glad there's no witches here to watch us today!' she cried as she danced along with the music.

'Of course they're here, we're just ignoring them,' Luna answered with a bottle of blackcurrant flavoured cider in her hands.

'Damn straight,' her twin sister agreed, swigging on her own bottle of rum.

The Raven twins, Luna and Lyrah, were petite identical twins with blue hair and a constant bubbling energy, known to shout about their views on feminism and equality. They were tiny, and could have passed for actual fairies, but they weren't to be messed with. They both wore bisexual flags like mine, and matching pastel pink dresses with knee high Doc Martens boots in silver. I was always stunned by Barchester's stylish friends. They were so cool.

Too cool for me, probably. Maybe that was why I wasn't fully comfortable being myself around them.

Bran was the most mysterious, always silent except when it came to Barchester. The two were close, and somehow, I knew my cousin saw a side of him that the rest wouldn't. The way he looked at him was probably the same way I did, but for different reasons. Barchester was my family, but Bran ... there was something else going on there. I'd sensed it for a while, whether it was reciprocated or not. Perhaps he loved Barchester but was too afraid to tell him.

They were a good group, just not the type I would have expected to meet with every week. But I was happy that my best friend had friends who he shared common interests with.

What I hadn't told Barchester was that I had my own plans for the day. There was something that had been bothering me recently, and I hadn't yet plucked up the courage to tell him about it. For a few weeks now I'd been watching my mother sneaking around the house at night in fancy clothes – ballgowns – as if she were going to a costume party or having some kind of *affair*.

If it was an affair, I knew I couldn't tell him. She was as much of a mother to him as she was to me, since his own mother had practically abandoned him when he was small, due to struggles with bipolar and depression. He knew it wasn't her fault that she was sick, and that she loved him, but for years, she'd refused to get the help she needed. I also knew it all hurt him more than he would openly admit.

And perhaps I was a coward, but I loved him too much to break his heart like that. But today would be the day I discovered the truth. I only hoped that, one day, I would finally find the courage to tell him what I found.

We attended a few more events throughout the day, comedy and music events, and we even played some games at the fayre and won ourselves a few cool prizes. The timing was perfect. While they were busy shooting plastic ducks, collecting cuddly toys and comparing them with each other, I slipped away and ran past the crowd, beyond the chanting and dancing people, through the festival doors and back into the chaotic streets of Cranwick. I hoped he wouldn't be annoyed that I'd left, but this had been a long time coming.

Once again, I passed through the crowds of shoppers and diners, taking in the usual chaos of the big city. Cranwick might have been labelled as the Mirror Village by our ancestors, but it was far from a village now. It was a lively world, or so it seemed on the outside. And Dad, like his father and his father before him, held the power over it all. One day it would be my responsibility to control the treasury and attend countless boring meetings every day in order to keep our society going, all under the scrutiny of the Enforcers of course.

We had no true power here, they just wanted to make us feel like we did, to stop us from rebelling or striking out at their kind. To keep us in line.

I'd always dreaded the day I would take my father's place. It would be the day I lost my freedom. But it was my birthright, and there was nothing I could do about it. In the meantime I decided to make the most of my time away from home. I relished in the sound of chatter and gossip. People rushed in and out of the little boutiques and patisseries, and long queues lined the doors, waiting for the next big designer item.

I knew if I was lucky, I would catch Mum at her favourite coffee shop, and follow her wherever she chose to go next. I'd overheard her speaking of plans to officially talk with the witches once her work meetings were finished the following day, the Pride Day. It was strange that she was talking to someone since Dad hadn't even been home, yet and there was no one else around. I'd snuck in through the window, determined to catch her and whoever she was talking to. She was alone, and yet she was speaking *through* the mirror in the hall. And someone had answered, a deep and hollow voice, that told her to meet them in the city at midday.

I moved quickly through the streets, knowing she was a fast walker, and scanned every shop from the windows. It felt like an eternity as I searched, until finally there she was, her phone to her ear as she ordered a sandwich and a coffee from *Deniro's* before scurrying toward the nearby cluster of government buildings. She was dressed in her usual work uniform: a slim-fitting black dress with long sleeves and a skirt that bounced around her knees, her mass of dark hair falling down her back as she moved.

As the wife of Cranwick's mayor, she had some responsibilities, since so much fell on Dad's shoulders. I often wondered if my future spouse would agree just as willingly to a life like that, or if they would run? The thought caused a shudder to crawl up my spine. This wasn't the future I wanted for myself.

I swore then that once I was done learning everything Mum was up to, I would bargain with the witches and find a way out of this damned place.

She turned down a narrow street, instead heading for my father's sky tower, a place for meetings away from the government spaces where everything was always chaotic. When she entered, I waited a few minutes before following, climbing the enormous staircase that always caused my muscles to burn until my body was drenched with sweat.

She was at a desk in one of the meeting rooms when I found her, facing an oval mirror with a golden frame on the opposite wall. Making sure she hadn't noticed me, I walked around the lobby, staring through the glass side of the building that gave a view of the city below. From up here, you could see everything. The grand wall that surrounded it, and the snow topped trees beyond, covering the road leading to the Winter kingdom on the other side. Further down you could see the mountains of the Autumn kingdom. I could only imagine the rest of the world that awaited me if I ever found a way to escape. I'd been up here a few times during Dad's meetings, and a few times with Barchester as well. So this wasn't my first rodeo, but it *was* the first time sneaking around after Mum like this.

I peered through the hole in the door of her meeting room and tried to listen. Like last night, she was speaking to someone in the mirror. A witch? *But what is so secretive that meant she needs to be here alone?* I wondered.

'Leraia Braxton,' the voice was saying, deep and rough with age. 'You are late.' The face was too far away to see clearly, but I could just see a shroud of white curly hair and a large, freckled nose. She had to have been hundreds of years old, at least.

Unable to help myself, a shudder left my body cold; the typical reaction to seeing one of the witches face to face. I tried to avoid them as much as I could, by staying out of trouble, and not drawing attention to myself, but sometimes there was no escaping them. They often came over to speak to Mum and Dad, with an Enforcer or two nearby.

They always gave me the creeps.

'I'm sorry, Brulle, I've had a busy day and it was harder than normal to get away.'

The voice was stern as the witch answered, 'Make sure it doesn't happen again. This whole situation you're in relies on you staying committed.'

Committed to what? What situation is my mother in? I thought to myself. She'd always been a highly valued member of her community, and unlike Barchester and I, was proud to be loyal to Cranwick and everything the witches stood for. She outwardly refused to tell me what exactly those beliefs were, which frustrated me even more, because from my perspective they only seemed to care about themselves, and that gave me no reason to be loyal to them.

'Of course, Brulle, I promise that it won't.' This was the first time I'd actually heard my usually calm and collected mother talking with a nervous tremor in her voice.

'Good. Now, you will leave tomorrow night. The king is ready for you, and everything is in place.' There was something so eerie about the way she spoke. Perhaps it was because the witches we saw in the square were always so silent and mysterious.

That shudder pushed through me once again. So many questions were spinning inside my mind. *Where is she going? What king is ... ready for her?* This was all completely nuts, and I wasn't sure what to think.

'But I'm not ... I haven't told Winnella yet.' For the first time, my mother stumbled through her words, and they weren't sinking in. 'Please, Brulle, it's not time yet.'

'Then you are not committed. Your husband will remain sick, and he will eventually die. Your daughter will take his place as mayor, and you will live the rest of your days in our state prison for breaking the rules of your contract.'

I was in shock at the witch's words. My father wasn't sick! They couldn't do that to my father, to our family.

'No!' Mum cried, and I saw tears rolling down her face. Heard the desperation in her trembling voice. Never had I seen her looking so *weak*. 'I will do it. I will go.'

'See that you do. We have already allowed this engagement with the king to go on for three years, and that is long enough, Leraia. The king is growing impatient.'

With that, the mirror went black, and Mum crumpled forward onto her desk, sobbing, and slamming her fists against its wooden surface. It was only as I left the tower, afraid she'd leave that room and find me here, that the shock started to wear off and everything the witch had said began to hit me.

My mother was engaged to a king and had been for *three* years. She was leaving tomorrow night, clearly under the spell of an agreement she'd made with the witches, to marry this king. She would become a queen, but of what kingdom, I didn't know.

My father was sick, of what illness I also didn't know, and if my mother didn't leave us, he would die.

I didn't understand how the witches could do this to our family, it wasn't fair. As I stormed down those steps, my blood began to boil. I didn't know how my father had ended up sick, why neither of them had told me the truth, or why my mother had made an arrangement like that, but I was going to find the witches who were responsible and do something about it ... Something.

But by the time I got to the bottom, I just slumped on the bottom step with my head in my hands, the tears streaming down my face. What could I do to end a deal like that?

Nothing.

Because they would always control us and destroy our lives with their cruel rules.

Feeling like a failure, I wiped my face with my sleeves and went back out onto the streets. I didn't want to go home, but I also didn't feel like returning to the festival. I decided to go somewhere to collect my thoughts and make a plan to confront my parents about the secrets I'd uncovered. That place was the fountain outside *Elders*, my favourite second-hand bookshop. Could there ever be a more charming place?

I was on my way there when I noticed a commotion in the city square. Little did I know that I was walking out of the frying pan and into the fire. The noise and commotion pulled me from my thoughts as I headed through the square.

There was a large protest going on, a peaceful one with chanting and singing. I'd heard the rumours, of course, about the first city-wide fight against the witches' power. Many had been attempted before, but they were always quickly shut down, the organisers never to be seen again. This time, it seemed the word had finally spread further than they could have anticipated. I would be lying if I said I hadn't considered joining the fight this time, but I also knew that these things never ended well.

The witches didn't want peace: only control.

By now, Barchester and his friends were close by, and my cousin came running over, the rainbow flag still draped over his shoulders. His white suit-shirt was ruffled and creased, no doubt from too much dancing and pole-grinding. The thought did make me smile, but it faded a little as he said, 'Where did you disappear to, Winnie?' But there was no chance to answer because his friends began to move toward the protesters, trying to get a better look, and we were forced to follow.

'This won't end well,' Fletcher whispered, voicing my earlier thought, as we headed through the crowd.

The others whispered to Barchester behind me, glancing my way as if they were afraid I might overhear and tell my father something they'd said in front of me. I was used to people not trusting me or wanting to be my friend because of who my father was. Barchester, as my father's nephew, had the same problem sometimes, but this felt fresh, and their mistrust stung. They clearly didn't know me very well at all if they thought I would snitch on them like that.

'What can we do?' said Fletcher.

'Not much,' said Barchester.

All around us, signs were held overhead as people sang, chanted, and swayed. There was no aggression, but still the Enforcers approached, circled the residents in the square and began spreading tear gas, trails of smoke bursting from the canisters in their hands. The air reeked of the thick substance, and it lingered in my throat, choking me and the others as it seeped into our lungs the closer we got to the crowd.

Horror clouded the atmosphere as others screamed and tried to run, or clambered over each other to get out of the area. Nearby shoppers fled with their children close to their sides, afraid they would become a victim of the chaos, despite not being a part of the day's fateful events.

One by one people around us began to drop to the floor like flies, unconscious, then were swiftly hauled away by cloaked, leather-clad Enforcers. Signs fell, showing various messages that displayed their hopes and wishes for a more peaceful city.

For a democracy.

Enforcers dressed head to toe in black gathered them all up and broke them into pieces. I watched cardboard and paper fritter to the ground like the autumn leaves.

We want our city back!

We need a better world. We need peace!

No more witches, no more imprisonment!

I could only watch, in desperation, with my leather jacket over my nose, as a mousey-haired little boy was almost apprehended by a large Enforcer. All the child had done was cross the line between the protesters and the Enforcers, probably curious and wanting to get a better look at them. The boy's broad-shouldered father shoved himself forward to stop them and handed him to a woman I could only presume was his mother, who stood there frightened like a deer caught in the headlights as the Enforcers silently approached her husband. 'Run!' he screamed as the Enforcer reached for the boy again.

The boy's mother screamed and fled with tears streaming down her face. She darted away, only to smack into another line of other Enforcers, who began to drag them off. There were thousands of people here. Did they really intend to arrest every one of them?

Those screams broke my heart, and made my knees weak. I might not have had the courage to do something earlier, but I couldn't stay silent forever. I needed to do *something*. 'You have to stop this!' I screamed, running to stand beside the boy's father, who was now on his knees, sobbing hysterically as his wife and son were stolen away. One by one, people began to stare, but I ignored them. 'No one is trying to hurt anyone. They're just standing up for their beliefs!'

The Enforcers looked upon me with surprise, sudden recognition dawning. They approached me, circling and observing me with scrutiny.

One Enforcer in particular came forward and placed a hand on my shoulder, and I recognised her large freckled nose and the wiry hair that fell around her face. It dawned on me then, that this wasn't one of the witch's brutal guards, after all, but one of the witches themselves.

Brulle, the witch from the mirror.

Suddenly I was filled with rage, not only seeing the young family before me but the happily married couple at my house that she'd broken apart. Thinking of their heartbroken faces, I shoved hard at her chest, screaming, 'You destroyed my parents. You sent my mother away, you ... ,' with tears rolling down my face as my voice trailed off.

A line of other witches surrounded Brulle as she fell back, two Enforcers also striding forward to help her to her feet, but they weren't fast enough.

The elderly witch slumped to the floor, knocking her head against the concrete, and then her eyes fluttered closed. They checked her pulse, but she was clearly gone. I fell to my knees, guilt, despair, and fear all rolling together into one huge ball of emotions.

It had only taken one little push, and I had ended her life.

'Winnie, no!' Barchester cried as he tried to lead me toward the others who'd now started to flee, but I tore myself away from him.

Just as a hand clamped down over my shoulder, and another took hold of my mouth. One of the usually silent witches leaned in close and whispered in my ear, 'My, my, Winnella Braxton. Look what trouble you've gotten your dear father into.'

Then a piece of cloth covered my face, and the blackness quickly took me.

WINNIE

The Roth witches weren't bluffing.

They apprehended me, knocked me out with some kind of gas, probably so I couldn't cause any more trouble for them, and brought me home.

Now, my father would be the one to suffer the consequences of my actions. He didn't need to say a word as the countless bruises on his face, neck and arms spoke for him. As did the small crowd of witches standing in our living room, speaking amongst themselves and ignoring Dad's terrified pleas for the punishment to end. Through the glass window in the door, I could see Dad struggling to move without crying out in pain; his left eye was swollen shut. His mousey brown curls fell around his face, and hid some of the bruising, but only glimpses of it.

Barchester and I tried to push through from the dining room, but we were helpless. Mum was blocking us, not wanting us to see my father in this state, her pretty face streaked with tears. I had always thought she loved and admired the witches as she would never speak a bad word against them, and always seemed to follow them willingly, but perhaps she was just as afraid as everyone else.

When Barchester and I were first returned to my house, Mum was furious and distraught that I'd chosen to confront the witches, her face red with rage. But she remained silent until they left, the vicious creatures having reminded my parents that if I ever defied them again, I would be taken away.

Her silence had only brought me back to the sky tower, and I was brutally brought back to the moment when her secrets were revealed. How dare she stay quiet while Dad continued to be beaten? How dare she stop us from breaking our way in there and forcing those witches to leave him alone? She was terrified of the witches, that much was clear now, and she wasn't brave enough to do something about it. Her complicated deal with the witch I'd killed was making it harder for her to fight them. I couldn't blame her for being afraid, but this had been going on for too long. Surely she should have tried to do something by now.

It was Dad who'd saved me from a beating, or worse. 'My daughter is a sweet girl, and she will be a great leader one day,' he insisted when they tried to steal me away after his punishment ended. But surely it was hopeless. I'd *killed* one of them, the same way a previous mayor had before he'd thrown our city into an endless curse. 'She has much to learn before she becomes your mayor, but I promise I will teach her. She will be reminded of the error of her ways.'

Even when he faced such pain, he still chose to defend my honour, while Mum just watched the commotion silently with a stern expression on her face. The witches must have believed that a psychological punishment would have made more of an impact on me, because eventually they left with their Enforcers in tow. Well, they would have been right. If they'd beaten me like that, I would have kept fighting them purely out of defiance. But I couldn't bear to see my father hurt anymore, especially if he was as sick as Mum had claimed.

I wondered if the people in the square were given the same treatment. Somehow, I doubted it. I'd been given the mayor's daughter's privilege. It was at that moment that I swore I would break Cranwick down, one day, single-handedly or not. I would find a way to defy the witches and destroy the cruel world they'd created.

Only when they left did Mum finally speak up, letting us into the room, 'You stupid child. You knew the risks to our family, and to your father, but you still got involved. You should have come straight home.' Her sea-grey eyes were hard as she stared at me, her arms folded over her chest. Disappointment radiated off her in waves.

Hot anger boiled my blood. How dare she be so ignorant? 'Mum, people were taken and hurt. You weren't there to see it. They separated a baby from his mother and father! How could I have been silent after something like that?'

As the question burst from my lips, I realised what a fool I'd been before that, how timid, and frightened. How could I have stood back and done nothing when the middle-aged man was attacked in the square, after trying to feed a poor woman and her dog?

But that was just the way of our world, wasn't it? It was terrifying. Who would stand up against a witch when they could chant a spell that would stop your heart in a blink? When they separated people from their families every day, just for insulting one of their kind?

Fear stopped people from *choosing* to act.

I had spent most of my life trying to hide from them. But now I was in the limelight, and it had made me realise that if no one ignored their fear and decided to be brave, we would be beneath the thumb of these witches forever.

Perhaps I would be the first to try.

'You *know* the witches, Winnella, and the dangers we face every day.' Mum wasn't wrong, even I had to admit that. 'How could you be so selfish?' She glanced at Barchester, who was still standing helplessly in the corner of the room, his fear leaving him silently trembling. 'Barchester said nothing. You should be more like your cousin.'

'It wasn't Winnie's fault,' Barchester cut in. 'She was just trying to help people. And the fallen witch, well Winnie was angry, although I know it doesn't excuse her killing one of their own.' His gaze lowered to the floor, and he didn't look up for some time after that. He wasn't the confrontational type, nor had he ever dared to argue with either of my parents.

I reached out and laced my fingers through his, hoping to comfort my best friend. I'd never seen him so afraid. 'Barchester was just scared, Mum. But I'm not. I mean, in that moment, all I wanted to do was help all of those people, I –'

'And you will, one day, when you become Cranwick's mayor. I know you care, child. But you're going about it the wrong way.' My mother's gaze softened as she spoke, and she reached out and cupped my chin in her hand. Her eyes were warm as she peered down at me. It transformed her features, and she no longer looked as stern.

'No.' The word only caused her eyes to widen. But she wasn't listening to me, not really. After everything she had been hiding from us, I could now see that she thought only of herself and her own fears and beliefs. Perhaps she wasn't selfish, exactly, but ... self-focused. 'So many things have to change before I can lead Cranwick like that, Mum. I won't be their little puppet on a string like Dad. I have to make a real *difference*.' As those words left my lips, I realised my mistake. I didn't want to hurt my father, but they were true.

Her eyes darkened suddenly, the scowl returned and she hissed, 'How dare you speak about your father like that, after all he has done for you?' As quickly as her face had relaxed, it had now reddened with her rage. My mother was hot-headed, and there would be no pleasing her.

But how could I apologise for my words if I had meant them? I would be lying to myself if I did, so I said quietly, 'It's true though, isn't it? Not by any fault of his own, I know. But he can only do so much.'

Control the treasury, to a point.

Negotiate peace talks with the four kingdoms and their rulers, to a point.

Work with the witches, but only to a point.

Everything he did was restricted, and he never tried to argue with their word. He always did as he was told. Now I knew it was because he was just as scared as Mum, not just for himself but for his family. Perhaps Mum was right, and I had been thinking only of myself. But as Barchester said, I was only trying to help people. In a world like this, no one I loved would ever win. Everything needed to change.

Dad winced, but deep down I knew he agreed with me and that my words weren't about him and his character, but more about the circumstances he'd been born into and how he'd chosen to deal with them responsibly, with kindness, for the sake of his people and his family. 'Let it go, Leraia,' he said, sitting up carefully. 'Winnie has learned her lesson.'

'I wish I could say I agree with you on that, Farn, but I don't,' said Mum, turning on me again with a sharp glare that pierced right through me. 'Go home, Barchester. Winnie needs an early night to think over the consequences of her actions.'

🍎

Barchester didn't go home. He left through the door so that she would have thought he had, but he climbed back in through my bedroom window as he did so often. If Mum was still angry with me, she wouldn't come to my room tonight and find him.

She'd be giving me the silent treatment, which was always enough of a punishment on its own. But it brought its own perks with it, like the fact that it made it a lot easier for me to sneak around. She would probably have a heart attack if she knew the amount of times we'd slipped out through my window and paid nightly visits to Dad's sky towers, where the view was always stunning. There was nothing like looking out at the backdrop of the vibrant city skyscrapers lit with colour, the cool wind whipping against our skin as we stood beneath a black sky full of dotted silver stars.

I wished we could have been there at that moment, but there was something more important to focus on. Fear drummed through me as I sat my cousin down on the edge of my bed and faced him. Why did it feel so warm in my bedroom all of a sudden? Claustrophobic. It was as if my small single bed, my little reading nook, my writing desk and bookshelves might cave in and crush me. I wasn't used to feeling this way, and I didn't like it. This room had always been my sanctuary, but now it seemed that Mum's lies were hidden everywhere, waiting to be discovered.

Never mind not wanting to save Barchester's feelings, he needed to know the truth about Mum. 'I have to tell you something, but I want you to promise me that it won't change anything about how you see my family.'

My cousin stared back at me, wide-eyed. I hoped he would keep an open mind about everything I was going to say. Perhaps it wasn't the best timing after everything that had happened, but there was no keeping my mouth shut now that the words were out. Besides, how could I continue to keep something like this from my best friend? It needed to be done.

A plan had begun to form inside my mind over the last few hours, one that I hoped would stop my mum leaving us. But I wasn't sure I was strong enough to do it all alone. I peered into the face of my best friend, the boy I loved like a brother, and realised it would help to have someone to share the burden with.

He reached for my hand, and his eyes were solemn as he said, 'Winnie, you know you can tell me anything.'

Unsure how to say the words, I paused for a moment before telling him about Mum's behaviour and the conversation I'd overheard in the sky tower.

His eyes were wide like saucers, and his mouth dropped open. 'Winnie, I can't believe she would do something like that.' He seemed to be processing my words for a while, but then he said, 'But clearly she's being controlled by the witches, right? She shouldn't have hidden it from you, but perhaps she feels trapped.' We were both silent for a while after that. Then, after some time, he said, 'What are we going to do?'

He didn't know how much those words meant to me. Glad he was on my side, I answered, 'I think I have a plan to stop her from going. Would you like to help me?'

'Of course I would.'

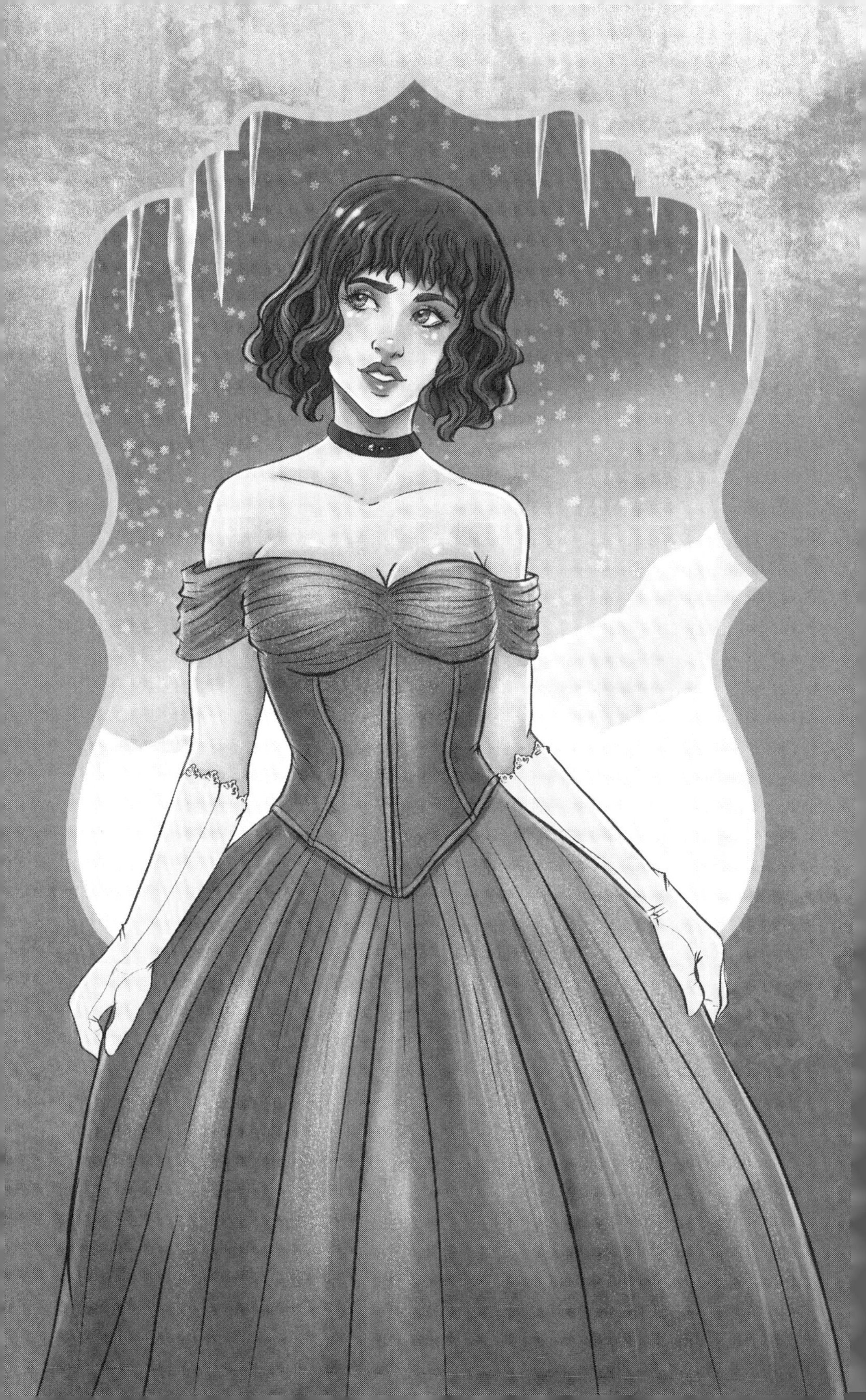

3

FROST

NEVER HAD THERE BEEN A MORE BEAUTIFUL LIAR than the one sneaking through my father's palace halls, her footsteps closely followed by the pitter-patter of my own heels against the stone floor.

I would be lying if I said it was the first time I had watched my soon-to-be stepmother snaking through the darkness once everyone else had gone to sleep, but I could only hope it would be the last. I saw the swish of her blood-red skirts and the toss of dark hair that fell down her back in gentle curls, just before she disappeared down a hallway several metres ahead of me.

The gown clinging to her elegant frame had once belonged to my mother, the late Queen Rosa Winter. Scarlet dresses in bright silks were my mother's favourites, and mine. Mine, simply because they made me think of my mother. Hers, because they made her feel bold. That was what she had always told me as a child. She liked to feel that every eye in the room was on her, but not just for her beauty. My mother had spent her life being underestimated by those around her. She had not spoken much of the family she came from, but I knew she had been the eldest daughter in a large family of girls, and that she had always been the most timid.

So she had stepped into her role as queen, welcoming her new family into her heart with kindness and sincerity. My mother had been adored by all who knew her.

Meanwhile, Princess Leraia was a stranger from a faraway kingdom. But my father, Icefall's lonely and hopelessly misunderstood king, clearly knew her far better. His fiancée would arrive most evenings when the meetings were finished for the day, and then shut herself away in Father's rooms each night so they could spend their evenings together and strengthen their courtship.

But over the last week or so, I had come to realise how good at sneaking around she actually was. She would leave his rooms in the middle of the night, no doubt having slipped a sleeping concoction into his drink first. For three years, it had been this way. Whenever the subject of their eventual wedding was brought up, her reluctance to actually marry my father was made clear, and I could not help but be suspicious.

There was something else at play here. I did not trust her, nor did I believe I ever could. At night, it was as if the entire palace was under her spell. Spellbound, and silent.

Now, I knew better, and I was onto her. Where was she going tonight? She was moving at a fast pace, glancing around as if she feared she was being followed. She was. Unfortunately for her, as a child of the Winter palace, I knew all of the best little places to become invisible. The small towers that stood tall in the centre of the palace, and their entrances and exits. The dungeons, the hidden passages in every bedroom, and the dimly lit tunnels leading out of the building beyond the servants' quarters.

I may have only been a princess for now, but I had always been the queen of Hide and Seek. Years of my childhood had been spent escaping the stern clutches of the servants and kitchen staff, only to later be scolded by my parents when I was supposed to be sitting through a lesson or dressing for a ball. She did not stand a chance evading me.

Her gray-blue eyes were piercing in the dimmed light of the tunnel as she turned, the flaming torch above her reflecting the flicker of orange in them. I could see why Father would be enthralled by her beauty, but I only wished he would see her falseness, that I could prove it to him in some way.

She was heading for the small tower at the back of the palace, close to the servants' quarters, no doubt because it was rarely used by the king or any of his council members. Turning once more, she slipped through the doors and snuck up the endless staircase that led to the highest point of the palace, somewhere she could no longer be seen.

As she moved, I lingered closely behind, bracing myself for the steep steps that would leave me breathless. When I finally made it to the top, she was in a tiny room that only contained a bed and a small wooden chest with a few clothing items. This room was rarely used. It was only given to visitors who were seen as less noble. It was well hidden, so that those visitors would not enter the main areas of the palace without permission. It had once been my mother's painting room, because, 'The view of the Winter kingdom is simply beautiful,' she had said. You could see the white-painted trees of the Winter Forest from here, and the river beyond. Somewhere in the distance was the Autumn kingdom, and the other kingdoms beyond it.

Tears stung my eyes as I remembered my mother working here, her easel set up by the large window, but nothing of her remained here anymore.

Princess Leraia was staring at the gold-coated mirror on the wall. Intricate golden swirls encircled the glass. It was not a mirror that I recognised. Could she have brought it here, and if so, why? Perhaps she had sought out the room for her own keeping. But there were plenty of bedrooms in the palace that were more suited to a princess who would soon marry the king. It did not make sense. Only as I looked closer did I realise that the glass in this mirror could have been painted black because there was no reflection staring back at her. My father's bride stood up, and a face appeared on the mirror's surface. Matted locks of white hair surrounded a large nose, deep wrinkled skin and a pair of dark eyes. It could not be possible that she was speaking to a ... witch? Could it?

'Hello Leraia,' said the figure in the mirror, refusing to grant the princess her title, which was unheard of in any of the four kingdoms. Surely, they should have named her appropriately? Doubts began to creep in under my skin, at the thought that she might not be who she claimed she was. 'I see that you made it. How close are you to breaking the king's spell over Icefall and revealing his true nature to his people? You must –'

The princess's tone held an unexpected desperation as she interrupted, 'Restore his kingdom to one of peace, yes I know.' Her lips were pursed with clear frustration, and a sigh burst from her lips before she continued, 'The wedding is in two days as we agreed, Dina, but I have done everything you asked of me, so let me go. Rid me of this ... contract. Please.'

So, it was true. She did not want to marry my father, and it sounded like she may have been forced into the arrangement. But that did not excuse her coldness toward me.

'And let your husband die?' said the witch, her lips spreading into an amused smile. Practically, a smirk. 'Leave the king, his daughter and his people to starve, all because of your selfishness?'

Husband? What a lying creature she was, deceiving my father into marrying her.

I was close to storming in there and taking her scrawny neck into my hands myself when she began to speak again, 'I don't want to hurt either of them. I just want my life to be the way it was before, in Cranwick, with my husband and daughter. I was a fool to come to you trickster witches.'

She had a daughter and a husband back home, wherever home was. My father meant nothing to her, and in turn, neither would I. I had never expected her to replace my mother when she took her place as queen – no one ever could do that – but perhaps I had been hoping for ... something else, because the disappointment that lingered within me stung.

The witch laughed in Leraia's face. It made her uglier than before, which I did not believe was possible. 'Then be a fool, woman. You made your grave, now lie in it.'

Then she was gone, leaving Leraia kicking the chest of drawers, tearing out clothes in her rage and throwing them to the floor. Leraia stormed out of the tower, missing me by only a breath. My new stepmother was already married, and she had a *daughter*. Curiosity took over, and I could not help but wonder who this daughter was, how old she was, or what she was like. Did she look like her mother?

Leraia had been lying to my father for three years, pushing their arrangement off for as long as she possibly could, until the witches were left with no choice but to give her an ultimatum. Her husband was sick, and she had made this deal with the witches to find a way to heal him. Was she even a princess? Did she even have the riches to repair our kingdom?

Monster.

No matter her reasoning, she was cruel for keeping my father in the dark like that. He was the type to help people in need, despite his reputation. He had withdrawn himself from the other royals and nobles since my mother's death five years ago, and they all thought him bitter, except for my friend Prince Hugo's parents, the king and queen of Windspell, the Autumn kingdom. I did not understand the secrecy. I knew my father would have offered to find a potion for her husband if she had asked, without needing to do what she did.

She snuck away, and I went after her. I planned on following her through the palace, determined to know what her next move was, when Prince Hugo found me. I could not tell him what was happening, so I let him lead me away to the palace gardens, our favourite meeting place. 'I missed you, Frosty,' he breathed, and took my hand.

A sigh left my lips as we walked together, and I felt like a fool since I had forgotten we were meeting. There was so much that my best friend did not know. Where would I even begin?

In the palace gardens, on his favourite picnic blanket, I could almost forget that in only two days my father would marry a stranger. It was peaceful here; trees blanketed with soft white snow surrounded the palace of the winter kingdom. The sky was a sheet of black sprinkled with stars as my best friend and I laid there, staring upward into the pretty night, with our fingers intertwined. Snow continued to fall, but that did not matter to us. It was picturesque, and it was *our* place.

We had spent many evenings here after I had suffered through long and exhausting days attending palace meetings, day trips through the kingdom, and other social events, but it was in these gardens that I was always comforted by the presence of my best friend and my late mother's glass statue. It dawned on me that this was probably the last time we would be able to spend our nights like this, since tomorrow we would be occupied with my father's wedding preparations, which, unfortunately, reminded me that soon after he was married, I would be shipped off to the Autumn kingdom like some kind of prized goat. I was to become my best friend's *happy* little trophy wife.

I decided we should just make the most of the moment, play games, laugh, and distract ourselves from everything that was about to happen. But it was hard when Hugo was feeling sentimental. Over the next hour, he told me of his plans to take me to his kingdom. I think he was excited for our future together, but I did not feel the same, and I was not sure how to let him down softly. Hugo was my best friend, the Autumn prince, and my betrothed all in one. He was handsome with kind brown eyes, full lips that were always smiling or laughing, and dark blonde curls that often sat in a tousled mess around his ears.

Perhaps in another world, I might have fallen for him, but we had spent so much time together as children that I could not see him as anything more than a brother. I supposed my father was not against me spending time with Hugo alone, since I had been betrothed to him since we were barely six months old. Perhaps Father thought we were merely strengthening our bond before the wedding. But then again, I had never told my father of my friendship with Hugo, or how I felt about anything else.

In fact, over the last few years, I had barely spoken to my father at all. Especially not about my feelings toward my new stepmother. Princess Leraia Braxton was a mystery from a faraway kingdom, whom my father refused to tell me anything about. Icefall would soon have a new queen on its throne, and I would have a new stepmother, one who had made no effort to speak to her future stepdaughter during her time in our palace. She must have really loved my father to cast me out of his world like that.

After that night, however, it seemed I knew why: she was an impostor.

But there in our favourite place, my best friend and I could forget about everything, if only for a short time. I wished I could scoop this moment up into a bottle and hold onto it forever. But Hugo stared at the floor, his cheeks reddening as he struggled to meet my eyes. My stomach twisted with dread, wondering what he was about to say. I could see the cogs working in his mind, and sensed that something big was coming. 'Frost, can we … practice? I have never kissed a girl, and I want to know that I am going to do it right.'

There it was. I would have thought that such a handsome boy would already have skills in that department, but then perhaps his strict parents had warned him away from more casual greetings with other girls since his future was already planned out. I did not know how to tell him that kissing him was the last thing on my mind. 'Hugo, I … ,' my voice trailed off as I realised I was unsure of what to say.

He ran a hand through his curls, his mouth set in a firm line and his gaze falling to the ground as he took in my rejection. 'I am sorry, I do not know why I asked.'

Guilt filled my chest. How would I explain how I felt about him without hurting him? He would always hold a place in my heart, just not in the way he clearly hoped. 'No, you just took me by surprise, that is all.'

'You do not feel the same for me, do you?' His eyes were full of hurt as they met mine again, and it broke my heart. 'I have loved you for years, Frost, but I think I have always sensed that the feeling is not mutual. I suppose I was afraid to hear you confirm this as the truth, so I never asked, but now we are nearing our wedding and I must know.' A single tear rolled down his cheek, but he wiped it away with the sleeve of his cloak. 'I have been such a fool.'

'I am so sorry, Hugo. You have always been my friend, but I just do not feel that way about you.' I knew the words would hurt him, but they were true. He moved to his feet and began to walk away but I stopped him. 'Remember, Hugo, we are to be married, and my feelings may change over time.' There was no way I would give him false hope, but I also needed him to feel better. The thought of losing him sent icy shivers through me.

It was hopeless. I knew he did not believe me. He shook his head and headed for the palace. 'I understand, Frost. I will see you tomorrow.'

'Hugo, come back? We can still talk things through.' I knelt before the frozen fountain, staring at my reflection and wishing for a way to fix this.

He refused to hear me, and stalked away.

I decided to give him space. Hugo had always been sensitive, and I had always known how he felt about me. He had never been subtle when expressing his devotion.

A small part of me wished my own feelings matched his already, because it would make the future so much easier. I wished I did not have to be so cold to tell him how I felt. Because if I was not careful, I knew I would lose both my father and my best friend, and then I would be truly alone in the world.

At that moment, I knew I needed to find a way to stop my father from marrying this monster.

4

FROST

THERE WAS NO BETTER WAY TO END A BETROTHAL than a letter declaring a fear of commitment.

I would be lying if I said my conversation with Hugo in the gardens had not inspired the idea. Placing ink to paper, I tried to picture myself from my stepmother's perspective, planned out everything I wanted to say in my mind, and began to write.

Dearest James Winter, devoted king of Icefall,

I am sorry to break your heart by writing this, but I fear I have overstayed my welcome in your palace for far too long. I am afraid my heart is not brave enough to leave my kingdom, let alone my sick father. I have not told you of his illness or anything else of my life back home, at least anything truthful, and now, I realise I owe you honesty.

THE GIRL BEHIND THE GLASS

There were a few questions I had to ask my father's council about in order to authenticate the letter. Of course, I had to do this subtly, by asking the council members that taught me the ways of the kingdom, who trusted me, and knew I enjoyed confiding in them. They would not betray my trust. They told me of Cranwick, the Mirror Village that my stepmother had come from. Some of the lies *Princess Leraia* made my father believe, were of her sick father, dead mother, and the poor treasury of her made-up kingdom.

I could use these lies to my advantage, and her own deceit against her. I carried on, feeling satisfied in the thought that I would make a difference to my father's life.

I am afraid I have much to confess. I am not who you have always believed me to be. I have a daughter back home; she is sixteen and I miss her dearly. Not only that, but my kingdom is false: it does not exist. I am from Cranwick, the Mirror Village. No one in your kingdom seems to believe is real.

I never wanted to marry you, and I fear that my feelings still have not changed. You are too good for me, my dear. Be happy, and find someone who will truly benefit your people, because it is not me. I am sorry to have led you astray.

I carried on with some more of her lies before finishing up with her name and real title as the already married spouse of the mayor of Cranwick.

WINNIE

I<small>F MY MOTHER COULD TALK TO THE WITCHES</small> through their magical portals, so could I.

It probably wasn't the best timing to try something like that, but I was quickly running out of options. My mother would leave to marry a king soon if I didn't stop her. I'm sure she was shaking in her boots at the thought of it, oblivious to the fact that I knew her little secret.

With Barchester hiding in the dining room and my parents working in their office, I took a deep breath and calmed my thoughts, preparing myself for what I was going to say. All night, my cousin and I had agonised over a plan, but found ourselves limited. I was practically a criminal, about to plead my way out of my sentence. I could only think of one thing to do, and it included being bold, audacious, and proud. I had to do it, or I might lose my mother forever.

Desperate times called for desperate measures, wasn't that the saying? Well, it was true. If my mother wasn't going to tell me that she was leaving, or about the deal she'd made, I would take matters into my own hands.

'Hello?' I said into the mirror in the hall, the one I'd seen Mum use before. When there was no answer, I made another attempt, 'Hello, dear witches?'

After a few more tries, a face finally appeared. Wiry hair like Brulle's sat around a thin neck and a deathly pale, heavily wrinkled face. She frowned as she took me in. 'What is the matter, child? It's early, and you are disturbing our beauty sleep.'

She wasn't wrong, it was only 6am, an hour or so before Barchester and I would have had to get ready to leave for school, if we were going. Which we weren't. Still, her words struck a chord, and I couldn't help the laughter that burst from my lips before realising her expression remained blank. 'Oh, you're serious. Erm, sorry.'

She stared back at me with a hard gaze, her frown deepening. 'Well?' she said finally, irritation clear in her tone. 'What is it that you want?'

This was it, the moment I had been waiting for. 'I want to give myself to the witches – as an apprentice, or assistant – in return for a potion that will heal my father's sickness.'

As I said, *limited options*. I was happy to give myself up for the sake of my family, but I knew I would get out of there eventually, and it would mean that nothing else at home would have to change. Mum and Dad could stay happily married, while I …

Well, I'd soon find my way. Maybe I would even enjoy being a witch's apprentice. It couldn't be too hard, preparing spells and herbs like some kind of scientist's technician. 'You may have my cousin Barchester as your next mayor, and I will have a new purpose, to learn new enchantments and train with the witches. It'll be a dream come true.'

To my horror, she began to laugh, a wild cackle that shook the house, and I swore I even heard Barchester wince from the other room, no doubt jumping out of his skin with fright. 'You have thought this through,' she said after she finally stopped laughing. 'Unfortunately, you have missed a few important details. Your mother has a deal in place, and everything is set in stone. It appears you have discovered her truth, clever child. She's leaving you, and that will not change. The sooner you accept that, the better.'

Her dark eyes seemed to become bolder still as she went on, 'Your father's sickness is not normal in your world, although perhaps it is common among mayors. It is simply caused by a dark and ancient magic that is contained in certain spells, draining your life source. Reflective magic, child. Being a mayor has begun to kill him. An antidote to this poison can be found in the Winter Caves, and your mother is going to find it.' She seemed to think her words through before continuing, 'As for you, even if you made a great apprentice, it's not possible because we only employ blood relatives. The same for our mayors. And all of that, and we would have to forget the fact that you killed one of our kind. Why would we employ a murderer?'

'But you'll happily keep me as your future mayor? And Barchester isn't an eligible heir ...'

'Exactly, you are the current mayor's closest blood relative. And, child, we have our reasons for keeping you around, believe me. You have no idea what is coming. There is a much bigger journey ahead of you.' With that, the witch smiled. 'Stay out of trouble, Winnie.'

What was she talking about? I couldn't wrap my head around anything she said. Then she was gone in a blink, only my reflection staring back at me again.

Well, that was useless. Time for plan B.

'Barchester, bring me the chair. We're going to make sure there is no way for her to leave!'

I would go to the Winter kingdom myself if it meant saving my father's life. Marriage was a permanent thing, and she loved my father. She didn't have to do this. There was always another way, and I would make sure of it.

My cousin came in, carrying one of the dining room chairs, his face pale, no doubt with shock at what he saw.

'Prepare for seven years of bad luck.' I took it from him, told him to back away and swung all four wooden legs into the glass, watching with satisfaction as it shattered, falling to the ground in thousands of little pieces.

'I'll find the other mirrors,' Barchester said, with a hammer in hand, and ran upstairs.

'When you're done, we'll go to the sky tower as well,' I called out. We would smash every mirror there, and any other mirror we saw nearby.

This had to work. My life in Cranwick was counting on it. Dad needed to get better, and there was no way I was letting Mum leave Cranwick. I didn't care what the witches said.

Then we would find a better way to heal my father's sickness.

🍎

Our plan didn't work.

The house was quiet when Barchester and I finally passed Dad's study that night, creeping through the dimly lit hall and heading for Mum and Dad's bedroom. Somehow, every mirror in the house had been replaced. Mum must have come home from work early and found them broken, panicked, and bought some new ones.

But that didn't mean it was over.

There were no sounds coming from the bedroom, so Mum must have been in bed.

Before she could come down and stop me, I quickly removed the mirror from the hallway wall and hauled it upstairs to my room, slipping it beneath my bed and pulling the duvet down to cover it.

Then I returned to the door of the study where I heard typing, and knew Dad was probably busy talking to his officials about government business. The witches' punishment would have put more pressure on him than ever. I had never really paid any interest to his work, because he was always occupied so I tended to avoid his study altogether unless he called on me directly, and that was usually only because he wanted to teach me something, or show me off to his colleagues as Cranwick's next mayor, but that didn't happen very often.

We went to my bedroom to read and listen to music for a while, and talk quietly about everything that had happened today. Waiting, silently, for the moment when everything changed.

A couple of hours later, the sound of hurried footsteps appeared on the landing outside my room. I stared through the gap in the door and there was Mum. She was more beautiful than I'd ever seen her, with her long black curls falling down over her navy-blue gown, her soft features powdered and plumped, and her blue eyes appearing bolder beneath her heavy winged eyeliner.

My mother, soon to be a queen.

We listened for a while before following her down the stairs, where I could hear voices. So she'd either snuck someone into the house or Dad was actually with her this time. Barchester's eyes were wide with awe as we leaned closer to the door in the dining room, trying to hear what they were saying, and hoping to catch something important.

'I will come back to you both,' Mum was telling Dad, this time not in a whisper, although she continued to look around as if fearing that I was listening.

My heart was in my throat. This was it. It was actually happening, and she was preparing to leave us.

When they headed for the door and almost spotted me, I darted backward, but she turned to face Dad and just missed me. 'I promise you, love, I'm only doing this for you to be safe and healthy, to get you the medicines you need, and for us all to be together again.'

There was the truth, just as she believed it. I staggered backward, almost falling into Barchester's arms. It almost felt unreal, like a dream, or a nightmare. I knew everything, but now it was actually happening, and I was going to puke. She was leaving, and I knew she was doing a heroic thing by trying to save Dad, but I still couldn't get past the fact that she was actually *leaving* us.

I peered through the glass panel in the door, trying to get a closer look at their faces. I couldn't breathe. I'd never seen Dad look so exhausted as he reached for Mum's hand and said, 'There is another way, Leraia, you don't need to go.'

Damn right, she didn't.

He struggled to speak through his staggered breathing, and I wanted to run over and help him. But something within halted my steps. Maybe it was the fear in his eyes, or the frustration in Mum's, or maybe deep down I knew it wouldn't change anything. She was still going to leave us, and he would still end up broken. 'You don't have to marry him.'

Mum released a heavy sigh. 'You're not well enough to go anywhere, Farn. You must stay here with Winnella and get better for all of us. This is temporary, I promise.'

Temporary? Marriage wasn't temporary, not when it was right. Tears stung my eyes as I drank in Dad's pale complexion, and his frail and exhausted form. I'd never seen him like this. A sudden frown set across his brow, and his eyes burned with anger. My heart was glass, and it was breaking into pieces.

'You fell in love with him, didn't you? You might have been doing this for me at first, but now ... ,' his voice trailed off as he erupted into a sequence of violent, chest-heaving coughs.

I knew it wasn't true. The witches had forced her into this contract, and she was unable to break out of it. It wasn't her fault. Okay, she was a liar, but she'd also been thrown into an impossible situation.

She reached out her hand to stroke his cheek, but he flinched and pulled away from her. I didn't miss the hurt in her eyes. 'I did no such thing, Farn! I can't believe you could even accuse me of that. Everything I have done on the other side of that glass has been for you and our girl.'

I pushed the dining room door open, my chest tightening and making it difficult to breathe as they laid eyes on me and I sobbed. 'You weren't even going to say goodbye, were you?'

Mum's eyes filled with emotion as she said, 'Sweetheart, what are you doing out of bed?' There was something unspoken there as she looked at me, something that didn't make sense to me. It could have been sadness or even heartbreak, or perhaps it was grief for the daughter she would soon be leaving, but what I saw was shame.

'I could ask you the same thing.' I couldn't help myself as my gaze looked her up and down. 'You were so quick to tell me I was wrong for acting in a way that got Dad hurt, but look at you now.'

It felt like she was rejecting us, and it made me want to scream.

Mentally, I saw her back off. The guilt that flashed behind her eyes, and made her hesitate. 'Winnella, go to bed.' It was like she wanted to avoid the question because she didn't know how to be truthful with me. It had always been this way for us. She never knew how to have those conversations, the heartbreaking ones that were actually important, so there was often an underlying tension in our home.

Sometimes, it couldn't be avoided, so we just left it. At others, there were screaming contests. Things would never be perfect here, but I still didn't want them to change. She loved me, and I loved her. I didn't want her to leave; it wasn't fair.

It was impossible to hold back the tears that rolled down my face. Staring into her eyes, suddenly everything clicked into place. 'You were just going to disappear in the middle of the night. You're going to the Winter kingdom, aren't you?'

Tears rolled down her face, but she was smiling through them. 'I have a plan, darling. I will get us all out of this cursed village.' She ran her hand over my hair, then leaned down and planted a kiss on my forehead, as if my accusations were nothing but a few childish fears. 'Look after your father. He will need you.'

I crashed into her, and tried to pull her closer to me, but she almost knocked into Dad as she moved backward. He merely laughed and caught her, but she instantly pulled away. 'You need to be more careful, Winnella. You almost made me hurt your father.'

'*You* are going to hurt him, Mum, by marrying someone else.'

'Winnie,' Dad whispered, reaching for me with a sadness in his eyes that only made me hate the witches who'd cursed her more. 'Go back to bed, sweetheart.'

'How could I sleep, knowing she's leaving? Mum, please don't do this to us. We will work things out together, we will find an antidote together, we will be a family.' I didn't know what we would do, but any plan we made together would be better than her running off in the middle of the night like this.

'How much of our conversation did you hear?' she asked. When I didn't answer, she hung her head and walked back into the hall, where she stood before the tallest mirror in our house, the one that showed off most of her glistening gown, and her reflection from her head to her knees.

We followed her, and I remembered her conversation with the witches through the mirrors, and it became clear to me what she was going to do. The way their portals worked. 'Mum, please don't go.' The tears fell harder and faster as I struggled to contain my sobs. Barchester leaned into me, and wrapped his arms around me.

Was it true? Had she really fallen for this king, or was she just as much of a victim of the witches' power as the rest of us? The line between truth and reality seemed blurred, and frankly, it was exhausting.

But she shouldn't have even had to go to the Winter kingdom in the first place, and that was the heartbreaking part.

The witches had broken our family.

She reached forward, delicately placed her arm through the mirror's surface. I watched with awe as coloured lights swirled around the sleeve of her gown, and then I quickly grabbed her other arm and tugged her against me. Gently, she stroked my hair away from my face, and planted a kiss on my forehead. 'I love you, Winnella. I'm so sorry. Remember who you are. My ticket to the ball ... ,' she spoke the words from my childhood favourite story-time expression.

Usually, I would have fallen for her trick, and I would have finished them, 'The fairest of them all.'

But this was no typical, sentimental moment between mother and daughter. I could say nothing, too stunned to speak as she turned from me, let go of my hair and dived through the mirror, leaving me, Barchester and my father behind.

6

FROST

THE MORNING SUN WAS SHINING DOWN over the roses and sunflowers that graced Mother's tombstone. The reds and yellows that marked her grave, along with the paintings and little glass statues and written letters, filled my heart with peace that blossomed every day.

I always visited her early in the morning, and just before bed. Being here made me feel closer to her, like she had not really left me. Her death, five years ago, had left a void in my heart that could never be filled. But, kneeling before it, I could pretend she was right here with me, as if she were listening, and somehow I knew she always was. Wherever she was, I would remember her.

It was a day that should have been perfect for a wedding. But the tension I had felt when Prince Hugo walked away from me had only festered into a monstrous thing. Along with the fact that my father clearly had not received his letter because the preparations for the wedding had thrown the palace into a place of chaos.

I knew I would spend the day feeling solemn.

Icefall was a beautiful kingdom, and it always had been. Father was kind, even if the rumours often told otherwise. I had always dreamed of one day taking his place as its queen. But now ... I began to dread the moment Leraia would enter our home, *my* home, and take the place in my father's life that should only have been meant for my mother.

Here lies Her Majesty, Queen Rosa Esmerelda Winter of Icefall. Beloved queen, wife and mother. May she always be remembered as the queen of our hearts.

I took out a new letter, one that detailed all of my thoughts and emotions over the last few weeks, and delicately slipped it underneath the edge of the glass casing that shielded her grave from the snow. Right next to the previous month's one.

I had caught the servants reading a few of my little notes, always wiping a tear from their faces as they left, but I did not mind. There was something calming in the thought that my messages brought others some kind of hope. And they were gentle with her grave, so I had no issue with it.

I was always careful to consider people's feelings as I wrote them, but I was *always* honest. This one, more so. I did not care if Father read this and blew up with rage. Because my feelings were just as valid as his, and they needed to be said.

I read over the first few lines again before tucking the paper into its place. Today was the right moment for this.

Dear Mother,

I miss you more than anything. The last few days have been incredibly hard, and I am struggling to cope with the secrets and lies that this palace conceals. Father has not spoken to me for weeks; he is spending much more time confined to his rooms or busying himself with palace meetings.

I am done with this place. I love him, and I will always love Icefall, but his ignorance makes me want to run away and never come back.

In other writings, I was more cautious in how I presented my feelings, knowing they could be read by anyone. But in this moment, I truly did not care. I just wanted to get them out, and to say them to the one person I loved and missed the most in the world. Not only that, but this letter explained things I had never said to anyone. Not even Prince Hugo.

I left Mother's grave and headed under the stone arch, into a different section of the gardens where the statues seemed to whisper amongst each other as the wind blew between them. I sat down on the bench beside the glass copies of our kingdom's past – that I knew were supposed to resemble icicles – and imagined a day where it was just Father and I for the rest of our lives. I had always dreamed of fantasies that would never come true, as if the thought might bring them to life.

But, three years ago, Father told me our world was crumbling, our alliances with other kingdoms were fading, and that Icefall would suffer without Leraia's riches. So he had spent those three years courting her. He had fallen in love with some version of her that I had never seen, and then asked her to marry him. Or perhaps he had only done it out of convenience. I feared I would never know.

Now the day had come for our kingdom to benefit, for our world to heal. Or so it seemed in Father's eyes. It was once difficult to believe that he had even wanted to meet Leraia, but now it seemed that she was everything to him. More so than me.

The statue of my mother gazed down upon me and not for the first time, I held her glass hand. I wrapped my arm around her ice-cold waist and felt comfort in her cold embrace. It was different here, alone with her beneath the sunshine, than on mine and Prince Hugo's evenings.

'Frost!' the familiar voice burst through the gardens, interrupting my moment of calm. The prince came running through the once still air, wearing a beaming smile. He wore his soldier's uniform, a light brown jacket with black cotton cuffs and steel buttons lining the middle. He had slicked back his curls, and there was a new brightness in his eyes. He looked handsome, and I had to do a double take. This was no longer the best friend I had always known. This was someone entirely new. 'I am so pleased to see you.'

I wished I could say I felt the same, but I was not ready to see *anyone* today, not even my best friend. I would be nothing but a ball of nerves all day, ready to burst at any moment. That was not his fault, but he would be the first to receive my solemn mood. Unfortunately for him. 'What do you want, Hugo? I would like to be alone right now.'

He chuckled, and although a flicker of irritation stirred beneath my skin, I was relieved that he was no longer upset with me after our conversation. 'Oh, lighten up, Frosty.' His laughter only sent the fear already churning in my stomach spiralling, but it reminded me that this was my best friend I was speaking to. 'You are going to be fine.' He wrapped his arms around my middle, but I pushed him away, too overwhelmed to want to be touched. 'Frost, what is the matter?'

He knew what was bothering me, but he did not know of my attempt to stop Father's wedding, and how I had failed. And I knew how he would judge me if I told him the truth. He would believe I was trying to take my father's happiness away from him, and a chance at a safe future away from my kingdom. But would he ever believe me if I told him of Leraia's deceit? He would certainly think me a fool. 'What do you think, Hugo? My father is getting married today. I am going to lose him.'

The prince offered me a wide smile. 'You are not losing him; he will always love you. But he needs love in his life, too.'

I released a heavy sigh. 'He has me. That should be enough.' That much should have been obvious, that his only daughter held more value in his life than his future wife. A woman who had betrayed him, and played him as if he were a pawn. The only love in his heart should belong to my mother and me.

'It will all be alright, Frost. I promise. You have me, and my family. You have the people of Icefall. Things with your father will become peaceful again, in time, I am certain of it.'

He would not understand, so I realised I would have to let it go for now. 'Very well, Hugo. I know you are correct; I am just ... not in the right state of mind this morning. Could you give me some time alone with my mother?'

He glanced between her statue and I, and cast me a sad smile, the same one I was used to from him and everyone else in the palace. Grief was a difficult thing to face for many people, as who would want to be around someone who was always in a depressive state? Well, I imagined that was what many of them were thinking when they saw me. But, for five years now, I had been completely alone.

'Of course, Frost. I will come and find you later on, or you can meet me after dinner if you wish.' He bowed and walked swiftly back into the palace, leaving me standing there, thinking happy thoughts, of times when Mother was still alive, and things were better than ever before. Her grave and her statue were not the same, but I was grateful for the comfort they brought me on days like today.

I took some time with her, and imagined she was offering me her words of wisdom, laughing with me over the past, and then with my head held high, headed into the palace and down the hall to the ballroom where the guests had begun to gather. The guard at the door announced my entrance and everyone turned to face me, the room falling silent as the women offered curtsies, and the men bowed.

Nobles draped in silk and velvet gowns danced and talked with each other, holding little flutes of champagne, eyes darting around the ballroom with intrigue as the ceremony grew closer. I strode down the central aisle, between the tables that had been set up for the nobles to eat and socialise, decorated with little buckets filled with ice-blue roses, and across the wide floor for the evening's dance. Smaller statues that resembled those in the gardens were scattered through the room.

When I paid them little attention, the guests began to speak and laugh amongst themselves again.

The ceremony was to begin in the throne room in twenty minutes. Very soon, my life would change. I would be lying if I said I felt ready for any of it.

My gown was a bright red, an old gem of Mother's that I had always loved. One of my maids had suggested that I wear it today, and I had agreed. It could not have been more fitting: red was the perfect colour to describe how devastating today would be for me. To top it off, my maids had straightened my short black hair, plumped up my dark fringe over my brow, painted my lips red and spread a powder over my cheeks that gave me a pale complexion that made me appear ill. But that was fine with me. No one would expect anything from me today. There were two thick black wings over my eyes, accentuating the blue in them. I wore Mother's wedding and engagement rings on a chain over my throat, and listened to the people as the excited chatter spread through the air.

The ceremony itself would take place in the throne room, and then we would come back here to dance and eat and embrace the dawn of a new future.

Well, the nobles might be celebrating, but I certainly would not be.

Very rarely were the four kingdoms brought together like this, so it was a bizarre sight to see everyone laughing. King Arder and Queen Ira of Oceanwell, the Summer kingdom, were relishing in the sunshine, taking walks in the garden with their daughters, Princess Piper and Princess Martha. I could see them through the ballroom window, pointing out the different flowers and admiring the statues. Where was their son, Prince Harwin? Their heir, the eldest of their children, had not been seen in our palace since he was small. Perhaps he had more important matters to address back home, or he was truly lost. Queen Ira's plum-coloured velvet gown covered her feet entirely, making her appear as if she were walking on air. Her daughters were carefully preened with brown hair falling in ringlets around their chins, and their gowns matched their mother's.

The kingdom of Oceanwell was our biggest enemy, the one that had caused the most issues for my father. There were even rumours that they may have ordered my mother's death, but they were rumours that Father refused to listen to. Because knowing that Mother had been killed was far too painful a thought for him, and not one that he wished to acknowledge.

We always avoided the king and queen of the Summer kingdom, but here they were, acting like everything was fine. Even though they had cast countless attacks on our palace over the last few years, and Father was almost assassinated by a guard from an unknown kingdom. All because our kingdom guarded the key to the Roth witches' power: because our kingdom contained the door to reach the source their magic came from.

All kingdoms would have loved to control the Roth witches and their power because their magic was so strong. Four kingdoms surrounded the caves that led to their mines where their magic was stored, but our kingdom was right next to it. Heavily guarded by Roth witches, of course, but we were closest to it, and we had always had the best relationship with the witches themselves, meaning they even trusted us with their magic where it suited them. For that reason, our kingdom's security was the strongest. Our people were happy and could access their magic for a small price, but usually, only if it benefited the witches.

But no other kingdoms held the key.

Queen Arabella and King Danver of Blossomheart, the Spring kingdom, danced with their daughter Princess Artemia, in the centre of the ballroom. The Spring princess seemed a little more timid than the others, although I believed she was a few years older than most, but her mother continued to spin her around and she soon joined the steps, her golden hair falling down her back as she turned. She wore a pale pink ballgown that shimmered with little beads, and a small tiara over her full fringe. She was the image of her mother, sharing a smile. She and I had walked together in the gardens a few times, laughing about the other nobles. I would not go so far as to call her a friend, but she was kind and loved to talk and gossip when the opportunity arose. Her father twirled her around and dipped her down, leaving her laughing.

The Spring kingdom was probably our closest ally when it came to our issues with the Summer king and queen. The queen had hosted us in her palace a few times over the years, so Princess Artemia and I had shared several slices of cakes and the odd chocolate fondant when our parents were not looking. Somehow I knew if we ever got into trouble, I could go to them, and they would help me.

Today was the first time in a few years where our allies and our enemies would be brought together for a wedding. The atmosphere was vibrant with excitement and joy, people whispering about watching the king of Icefall taking a new wife only five years after my mother's murder. Father would not see it that way, as her death had been made to appear as a suicide with her body hanging from a rope beside her bedroom window. But there was something off about that image for me. Father had refused to let me enter the bedroom to spare me the sight, but even a second's glimpse was triggering enough. My mother was happy, and she had so much love in her life. She was always there to provide for us.

She would never do that to me.

Since her death, the other kingdoms had distanced themselves from us. Only slightly, as we were invited to less events, but it was noticeable, and I know it affected my father. Mother was always the more active party in the kingdom, attending many more meetings and socialising with the other nobles and royals. Father was a little more withdrawn, which was probably why they had cast him out and stirred rumours of him being cold and even cruel. But that was not my father at all. He was a good man,

THE GIRL BEHIND THE GLASS

but his abandonment had only made me lose trust in him, and I could not help but wonder what his intentions were with the new queen now. Did he truly love her, or was he doing it all for the sake of Icefall's finances?

He caught sight of me and came storming over, only for his path to be blocked by Prince Hugo's mother. Queen Aura hurried over to greet me and wrapped me up in her arms, and I was thankful for the diversion as I did not feel ready to speak to my father right now. When he saw I was preoccupied, he sighed heavily and walked away. I watched him go before turning to face the king and queen of Windspell, who had been more like a mother and father to me in recent years than my own father.

'Oh Frost, my dear, you look magnificent.' Queen Aura's eyes were warm, and the same rich brown as her son's. She wore a sky-blue gown in a shining silk with a heart shaped bodice, and a silver locket at her throat. Her light brown hair was curled and sat in short waves over her shoulders. She was petite, her height exaggerated slightly by the blade sharp heels on her feet.

Beside her was Hugo's father, King Archibald. 'Keep your head up, Princess Frost. You are strong, and you will get through this day with pride, just as we planned.' Where Queen Aura was shorter, her husband was tall with a wide and heavily muscled build. His dark hair fell down over his chest, and his slanted eyes were kind like Hugo's. He was a wonderful storyteller and an even greater king, welcoming and fair, but there was a strength to him that meant you would not want to mess with him. Even the white cotton of his shirt could not hide the dark tattoos that covered his arms.

I knew Prince Hugo looked up to his father, and I could not blame him for that. 'Thank you, both. I am well, I promise. Just a big day, that is all.'

The Autumn king placed a hand on my shoulder. 'We are right here with you.'

As we broke away, my father seized his opportunity. 'Frost!' he called out, and grasped my shoulders. 'I am so happy to see you.' Only last night I had knocked on his door, and he had slammed it in my face. But his blue eyes were soft as he said, 'I am so nervous, can you tell?' His body trembled when he spoke. I nodded my head, unsure of what to say. 'Almost as nervous as when I married your mother.' He laughed and ran a hand through his white-blonde hair. There were circles beneath his blue eyes, which made it clear that he had been having trouble sleeping. 'You look beautiful.'

Rage was bubbling beneath my skin; I was unable to help myself. It was almost laughable that he was now giving me his undivided attention. Where was that focus during the three years of his engagement? 'Thank you Father,' I said solemnly, running my hands over Mother's red gown.

'Are you alright?' he asked sheepishly, as if he truly cared. As if he sensed that I was upset with him, but did not know how to ask the question directly.

The concern he was showing me now was so scarce that I did not know how to feel, but hot tears rushed to the surface. I blinked them back, forcing myself to be calm and remember where I was. Perhaps I was a coward, but I did not dare to say how I truly felt. To admit everything I had heard his bride say about him. So I did what I would later wish I had not: I lied, 'I am fine, Father. You will do well, too.'

He laughed softly. For someone who presented such an icy exterior to the rest of the world, my father was one of the kindest people I knew. 'Thank you, my love. I am glad you are alright, and I appreciate you being here with me today. I know it has been hard for you.'

He believed he knew how hard it had been for me, but the truth was he had not truly bothered to look past his daily meetings and his courtship with Leraia enough to see me. To see how much I was struggling. He was just like the rest of the kingdom in that respect. Why comfort your only child after the loss of her mother, when you could just throw yourself into your duties and forget that such grief even existed?

My gaze lowered as hot tears rolled down my cheeks, but I wiped them quickly away before facing him again. He gathered me into his arms, his expression full of love and sympathy. Something I had not seen from him for almost five years.

'Your stepmother should be here any moment. I suppose I should get ready.'

'I love you, Father.' The tears rolled down my face as my heart swelled with the sudden emotion. For a moment the anger I felt toward him dissipated. How I had missed holding him like that, drinking in his smile and hearing him tell me how much he cared.

'Oh, Frost. I love you, too.' He kissed my cheek, and then I watched him head out of the ballroom, toward the throne room where the ceremony would soon begin. Where he would walk up the aisle, wearing his army captain uniform. The uniform of a king on his wedding day.

Soon enough, the nobles filed out of the ballroom and into the throne room where two long rows had been set up, decorated with white and blue roses. Like the ballroom, statues lined the space. I took my seat at the front of the row on the left-hand side, beside Hugo and his parents. Beneath the enormous stained-glass windows that portrayed stories of Icefall's past. Light burst through them, painting the room in a multitude of bright colours: the perfect moment for such a *wonderful* ceremony.

Hugo slipped his hand into mine and squeezed it gently, as if he could feel me trembling. 'I am right here, Frosty,' he whispered. 'You have nothing to fear.' His words were sweet, but unfortunately they were far from the truth, and I think even he knew it. The world was changing, starting today.

I saw it as the other nobles took their seats in the aisles. As Father waited by the altar for his bride, and as she appeared, wearing a long white gown in the finest silks, her dark hair braided back into a neat bun with blue roses woven through the little tiara on her head. White and blue roses were her favourite, clearly, but they were also my mother's. White and blue roses adorned my mother's grave, and the flower bed beneath her statue in the gardens. How could Father have agreed to a wedding like this, one that imitated my mother's life in the palace?

Leraia had been to the palace countless times, so there was no way this was a coincidence. She knew perfectly well what she was doing, and I was onto her. Was there more to this impostor who had found herself trapped in a marriage she did not want? Such imitation implied jealousy, which gave the impression that she was more than what she seemed.

On the outside she was beautiful, but I was yet to truly determine her character. Princess Leraia of a faraway kingdom. A peaceful kingdom filled with riches, as Father had told me. Leraia, this woman who had taken my father from me. Leraia, not a princess. Leraia, a mother and a wife.

Leraia, the impostor.

My new stepmother cast me a wide smile as she passed me.

I chose not to return it.

7

WINNIE

It didn't matter the cause, I would bring my mother home, and stop her from marrying the Winter king. Because she didn't belong there with him.

She was *ours*.

Before Dad or Barchester could follow or try to stop me, I reached a hand through the mirror, feeling a warmth spreading over my skin before I took the plunge and dived headfirst toward my reflection. I watched as the twinkling light from both worlds shimmered around me, and sent a shiver crawling up my spine. Soon enough, I would be right beside my mother in the Winter kingdom.

I inhaled slowly, found my feet, and opened my eyes. The ground was dark but steady beneath my feet, and I could stand up fully without toppling over.

But Mum was nowhere to be seen, and at first I thought I was alone in a dark space. Then, when I peered around, the flames from a nearby fireplace bathed the room in a soft light. I was in some kind of cabin room, the type you might expect to see in the mountains. The slightest hint of smoke lingered in the air. A small armchair sat before it, with blood red cotton-woven cushions, upon a large bearskin rug.

A few metres away sat a small steel basin, and a bed with thick woollen blankets spread over the carved wooden frame. Suddenly, I felt like I'd travelled back in time, or fallen into some kind of storybook. This cabin was nothing like my home in Cranwick. What other explanation could there be?

But, then ... What was I talking about? I had just thrown myself *through* a mirror, hoping to end up in the Winter palace, where my mother was about to marry a *king*. Nothing about this situation was normal.

Taking a deep breath and forcing my mind to clear, I took another look around. Around me, against the walls, were rows of ceiling-high shelves holding books, large and ancient looking tomes bound in leather. Other shelves contained large glass jars which stored small animals, plants and ... body parts. Red muscle, and rich pink skin, like something out of a science lab. Gross. There was also a musty smell in the air, like the stench of earth and mould.

What was this place?

A hooded figure was sitting in an armchair by the fire, leaning over a book. Around them, strange paintings were hung on the walls, their images portraying dark abstract shapes and images that didn't make sense. Somewhere in the distance, someone was laughing. No, cackling.

I turned around, my heart suddenly racing, and tried to search for my mother. But as I faced the mirror I'd stepped through, I only caught sight of my own reflection, still wearing my leather jacket and jeans with my ankle high boots, my dishevelled dark blonde hair falling around my face in light curls that rested at my shoulders. 'Mum?' I called out, waiting for them to look up and reveal their face. My mother's face, I hoped. 'Is that you, Mum?'

The hooded figure finally glanced up and caught my eye, then slipped the hood down, but it wasn't Mum. It was an old woman with dirty white hair, deep brown eyes and wrinkled, sagging skin, and a large mole on her chin. She opened her mouth and smiled a little, revealing a set of blackened and broken teeth, some of which were missing. She reminded me of the elderly witches who often came to visit my parents on urgent business. She reminded me of Brulle, the witch I had accidentally killed. I couldn't help myself; I scrunched up my face in disgust. 'Who are you? I'm looking for my mother ...'

The old woman cackled again, the sound bursting from her throat, deep and rasping like a dying animal. 'Stop panicking, child. Your mother is exactly where she needs to be.'

What the hell was that supposed to mean? A frown creased my brow, and I probably appeared terrified as I demanded, 'Where is she?'

'Well, that question has already been answered for you, hasn't it, child?' She laughed again. 'Why do you bother to ask questions you already know the answer to?'

A sigh burst from my lips. 'Fine, why am I here then? Wherever I am?' Clearly, the desperation and need to find my mother had temporarily clouded my judgement. I *knew* how the mirrors worked, should have anticipated that leaving Cranwick wouldn't have been that simple. They were never going to let me leave, even through a mirror. 'I followed her through the ... to the –'

The woman smiled, which caused a grimace, and her words only confirmed my thoughts. 'Does this look like a pretty palace to you? Silly child.'

The witches wanted Mum to go to Icefall, so she had a good enough reason to slip through their portals. But I ... didn't. Besides, they probably knew of my attempts to stop her leaving, so I wouldn't exactly be their favourite person to allow through to the other world. And they wanted me to be their next mayor, so in their eyes I should never leave Cranwick.

But they didn't know how determined I could be when there was a goal I needed to see through to the end. Or how far I would go to bring her home. 'But my mother is marrying the Winter king ... I have to end this; I have to go –'

The witch's smile became a grin, clearly satisfied that I was beginning to understand the meaning behind her words. 'She was only allowed to leave because it was agreed with my sisters and I that she would bring back a healing potion for Cranwick's mayor.'

'I know this, but I –'

'Listen to me, child. When we began to see benefits for Icefall, the only kingdom that has ever truly valued us witches as people just like them, not just bodies containing the magic they clearly wanted, the marriage between your mother and King James was set into motion. Your mother could heal her husband, and we could save Icefall from its downfall, killing two birds with one stone, so to speak. But our arrangements are always set in stone, and cannot be changed.'

Bitter laughter burst from my lips before I could stop it. 'But if you could just magic up some treasures or money for Mum to give this king, to pretend she was a fancy princess from a faraway kingdom, why couldn't you just do that on your own to save Icefall? Why did you need my mother? It isn't fair that things have to be this way ...'

A slim smile spread across her lips, but there was a sadness behind her eyes that I hadn't expected to see. 'Everything has a price, Winnella. We cannot use magic for no reason, or even for the sake of ourselves. My sisters and I have a goddess that we worship, Goddess Urda, who tells us that everything we put out into the world must one day be returned. Even sunflowers, beautiful as they are, must one day die. An eye for an eye, a tooth for a tooth. We must not act in selfishness, or in vain.' She glanced around the room. 'We heal the sick for a small price, or we give people riches if they give us something in return. Nothing comes without a sacrifice in this world, child.'

Was this why the people of Cranwick were cursed? Because one of their people had been killed by one of ours, in vain, centuries ago, now our people were forced to live forever under their thumb. It didn't seem right, but it suggested a reason for their way of thinking. But the desperation was still heavy in my chest, and I refused to end this now. 'I don't have much time. I have to go to her.'

Her grin faded, and her dark eyes were suddenly filled with something like disappointment. Her lip curled downwards. 'Did you hear a word of anything I just said? This arrangement cannot be altered. Do you really wish to stop her from healing your father?'

For a moment she'd seemed sincere, like she wished to help but knew there was nothing she could do, but now the wild cackling had returned, revealing her true nature. She clasped her bony, wrinkled hands together as if she hadn't expected any of this, but it was still a game to her. 'I will call you Wicked, by my own name. Wicked Winnie, how does that sound? It's a little tacky, isn't it? No, just Wicked will do.'

She was quite literally the wicked witch. How ironic. 'No, I don't want her to stop that, at all ... But it's not fair that she has to leave us, that she has to hurt my father and break his heart ...'

Something like sympathy appeared on the witch's face, but it flickered and returned to an amused smile just as quickly. 'I told you, Wicked. She is where she needs to be. She will heal your father, and all will be well in Cranwick. But if you wish to follow her, sacrifices must be made. Your mother offered her heart to me, so what will *you* give me, Wicked?'

I staggered forward. 'That is not my name!' I paused, realising once again that my emotions had taken over. 'She gave you what?'

'I told you; she gave me her heart.' She sighed heavily, as if my questions were frustrating, then held out a jar filled with a red, beating heart.

I screamed, the shrill sound breaking every glass surface in the room. Her jars and mirrors all fell to the ground in thousands of tiny pieces.

The organs the jars contained also hit the ground, until a girl appeared from a door I hadn't seen open and ran around the space, gathering them up. She seemed to be around fourteen or fifteen and wore a small cotton dress, and her dark hair was tied into braids.

'Well, that's your way home destroyed, unless you decide to sacrifice something you love to me,' said the old witch, Wicked, pulling the child closer.

The girl peered up at me through her emerald green eyes. She didn't run away or even appear frightened. Perhaps she was used to the old witch having regular visitors. If this was where the residents of Cranwick ended up when we tried to escape, then I supposed it was possible that I wasn't their first.

'Let me see what I can take from you.' Wicked paused in thought before continuing, 'Your mother's heart brought her to me. She was insistent on finding a way to heal your father, and now she lives without it. What do you love the most in this world, Wicked?'

Mum, Dad, and my cousin Barchester. Our terrier, Coco. And, my fantasy books, of course. But there was no way I was going to give her any of those things. 'My name is Winnie.'

The witch raised an eyebrow and laughed softly. 'Perhaps you would gift me your name.'

My frustration building, I yelled, 'I will give you nothing. Now, take me to the Winter kingdom!' She thought she had me under her spell, but she wasn't going to win this. I would get my mother back, and find a way to heal my father, and all would be well in our city. At least, until the day I could finally leave and make my own way in this wretched world.

She tapped her chin with a long and pointed fingernail, deep in thought. The smirk on her face told me that she was going to say something I wouldn't like. My heart plummeted as the dread crept in. 'Very well, Wicked. If you have no reason to go, you have no reason to ever return to Cranwick. Icefall will become your new home, where you will live as a measly servant while your mother prances around her new palace as a powerful queen. As you wish, child –'

'No! Okay, I'll give you something. Just let me have a reason to bring my mother back, please.' Damned witch, trapping me with her magical words. She would pay for this one day. Even if I couldn't stop her now, I would come back and make her regret doing this to me.

She grinned widely, a true witch in every sense of the word. A trickster, and a manipulator. 'Very well, child.'

Anything I gave her; I could surely get back with enough time if I were smart enough to outwit this witch. 'Alright, witch. I will give you my name.' Since she seemed so determined to have it. Besides, it was just a name, only used to identify me. 'It's the one that that connects me to my father. To the world, I have always been Winnella, but to Dad, I am Winnie. But if I do, you must guarantee my safe trip to Icefall and my safe return home with my mother.'

There was a strange glint in the witch's eye before she said, 'It is a deal, Wicked. Safe travels!'

'What will you do with it when –'

But I didn't finish speaking because in that instant, I felt myself flying – no, falling – through light and water and air all at once. It was the strangest feeling, like I was still, yet moving through a dark tunnel while wrapped in a colourful stream of light.

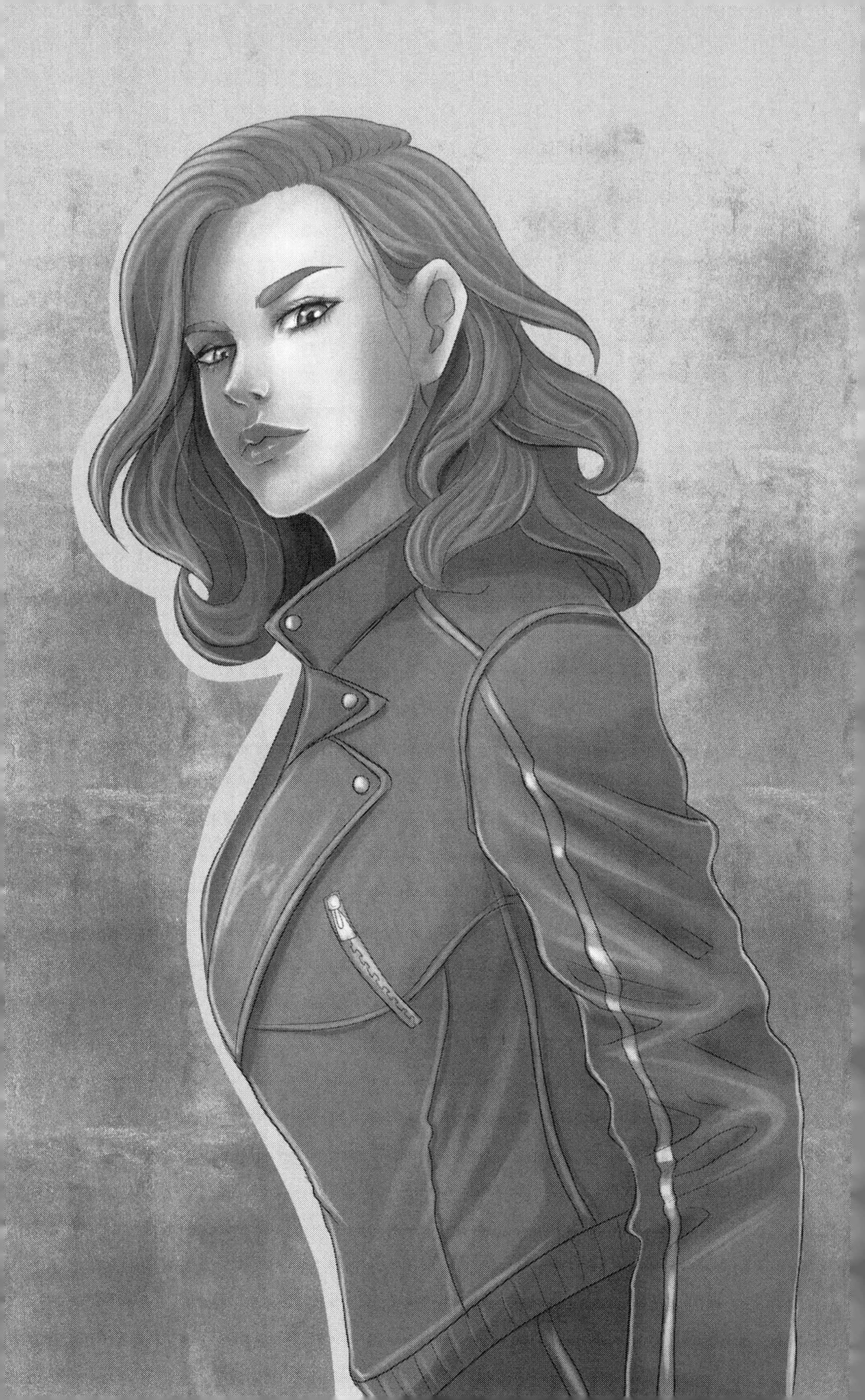

8

WICKED

'Winnella, what are you doing here?'

Light and colour faded, and the world spun around me as I *landed* on my backside somewhere new and bright, on a bed of snow. It was almost blinding, the sun shining down on snow-blanketed hills. My leather over coat suddenly wasn't enough to keep me warm. I realised I had no idea where I was. My surroundings were like something out of a fantasy story; sky-high mountains seemed to circle the hill I was standing on, the snow making them appear brighter and higher.

Behind me was an enormous stone building with a huge entrance, glistening stained-glass windows and small arched towers that seemed to reach into the sky. It didn't take long to realise that I *did* know this place, but it was absolutely ridiculous that I was here, and I swore I was dreaming.

This was the palace of Icefall, the Winter kingdom. But what was I doing here, wearing these strange clothes, my hair much shorter, and painted a sun kissed *gold?* Where was my long auburn hair, my dozen rings and bangles and my leather trousers? I glanced around, running a hand over my face and examining parts of me that no longer seemed real. My fingernails were painted a pale sky blue, meaning my usual black tips had disappeared.

What was happening to me, and who in Roth was Winnella?

The woman who'd called out to me was now storming over, wearing a floor-length gown with a heart-shaped bodice in white cotton, and intricate lace sleeves decorated with small flowers and ice flakes.

A *bridal* gown.

Her long dark hair was braided back behind her head, and she cast everyone who passed her a gentle smile. She was beautiful, but she was a stranger to me. 'Winnella?' she said again, and reached out a hand to stroke a strand of hair away from my face. 'Why are you here? I told you not to follow me, it could be dangerous for you here.'

Brushing her hand away, I snapped, 'I don't know who you are, or why you keep calling me Winnella, but I'd like you to stop because that is *not* my name.'

The woman threw her arms around me, and I stumbled backward, confused, before shoving her off. Various emotions flickered across her face at once. There was anger, elation, and then a silent desperation, although I couldn't understand it. 'Of course, it's Winnie. I'm sorry, my love. You should have stayed home with your father. He needs you.' She stood back and smiled upon me.

I didn't know what to think – her words weren't sinking in. My mind was a blur, nothing remained but colours and images that passed too quickly. Memories? I couldn't make sense of it, and the world began to spin.

When I didn't respond, she studied me more closely, analysing every inch of my face before saying, 'You had to sacrifice something to the witch, didn't you?' She ran a hand along my brow. 'What did you give her? Tell me, sweetheart.'

Something wasn't right here. The last thing I remembered was being at the farm with my uncle and my twelve sisters. No, *escaping* the farm with my twelve sisters, and escaping our uncle, the abusive brute who wanted us to labour ourselves until we dropped. Apparently when you were often away on important government trips, the next best thing for a guardian for your thirteen young and fiery witches was a lonely farm owner who wasn't technically of any relation, but used to be our mother's best friend's husband. Not quite an uncle, but about as close as you could get.

Of course, our parents didn't know how he treated us because he always presented himself as the doting uncle who cared for us as if we were his own children. Most of us were of the age where we could care for ourselves, so it wouldn't be long until we could leave this place and find our own way in the world.

But the woman's words confirmed the truth to me. I was no longer a witch, but I was somehow inside the body of a stupid girl who'd made a sacrifice to one of our Elders. But for what reason? There were so many questions racing through my mind at once that my vision blurred, and my head began to ache. All I could say was, 'My name isn't Winnella ...'

The woman's blue eyes were solemn as she stared into mine, wrapped an arm around my shoulders and pulled me close. Then, before I could think of running for the snowy hills, she slipped her arm through mine and pulled me into the palace.

We wove through the halls with the woman leading me forward despite my own mind screaming at me to tear myself away and leave. I supposed a larger part of me was curious about how I'd ended up here in this girl's scrawny body, and where the rest of me was. As much as I hated to admit it, this woman might just be the key.

Still, the stubborn part of me was about to tell her where to shove it when a servant passed the woman and I with a trolley full of shining silk fabrics. Gowns, fit for a ball.

Wonderful. Just what I needed right now.

'Your Grace,' she said. 'Are you ready? The ceremony is due to begin in ten minutes.'

Ceremony?

How could I have missed such details? This woman was wearing a wedding gown, and the servants called her *Your Grace*. She was marrying King James Winter of Icefall. This woman would soon be Icefall's *queen*. And she seemed adamant that she was my ... this girl's mother. How had I ended up here? I was surely the last person who should have found myself in this building, in this body.

But here we were.

'Yes, yes,' said the woman in response to the servant's question. The servant curtsied and stalked slowly away, eyeing me closely. When she was gone, the soon—to-be Winter queen whispered, 'We have to get you home to your father. But first, Winnie, tell me what you gave the witch.'

I tried to push her off me, but she was holding me in a vice-like grip. 'Who?' I frowned as I tried to collect my thoughts. But although the lights that clearly brought me here had faded away, I still struggled to remember anything that had happened between being at the farm, and ending up in the snow outside the Winter palace. What a mess. 'I still have no idea what you're talking about.'

Her mouth dropped open. 'You don't remember your father?' Tears rolled down her face and threatened to ruin her beautiful bridal makeup. 'Do you know who *I* am, Winnella?'

Swallowing, I shook my head. 'And I told you, that is not my name.'

She released a whimper. Desperation darkened her blue eyes, and twisted her features. Her lips were set into a firm line in clear frustration. 'I am your mother, Leraia Braxton, and your father is Farn Braxton, Mayor of Cranwick. You gave away your memories?'

Cranwick, the cursed Mirror Village. The witches had cursed its people over two centuries ago, and they had remained trapped within its wall ever since. Good. Witch killers and their descendants deserved to have their comeuppance.

Leraia. The name stirred something in my mind, uncovered a memory, perhaps, before flickering and quickly fading away. I still didn't know this woman, and I would be a fool to try to convince myself otherwise. My mind was blank, containing only remnants of my own past, and there was clearly nothing I could say that would answer her endless list of questions. 'I don't remember.'

A single tear rolled down her face. But the devastation was clear in her eyes and in the way she wrapped her arms around herself as she whispered, 'Winnella ...'

'My name is Wicked.' Frustration stirred in my chest, and I ran a hand through my hair, which wasn't *really* my hair. How many times would I have to tell this woman that I wasn't her daughter before she listened to me? She was oblivious. But I was beginning to piece this girl's story together, bit by bit. She'd made a sacrifice to the Elders and given away her memories, and ended up ... here.

But why?

And how did I still have my consciousness if my body was gone?

'Wicked?' She staggered backward, clutching her chest. 'Oh goodness, it's happening ...'

'You are not my mother. I would know if you were – I would *feel* it.'

'Years ago, the witches told me that one day I'd lose my first-born to them. I had a still born a few months before you came along, so I always assumed his death was the curse she was referring to. She called you Wicked, didn't she?' she paused before adding, 'She called me that, too, when I went to see her.

'You gave her your name, and with it, your identity. The witches, unfortunately, require a great sacrifice. You might think they're doing it for their own benefit, but really it's because they have to appease their goddess, Urda, Goddess of the Skies. They have their own set of rules to follow, and who better to sacrifice than those who must break their rules? You killed one of their witches, so you must … Gods, Winnella. What are we going to do?'

This woman, Leraia, and her daughter had both found themselves cursed by the Elders of Roth, and perhaps it was for the best if they were foolish enough to fall for such tricks. But her words only confirmed that she would be my best way out of this girl's body, and to help me find my sisters again. I missed them dearly, and I would find them soon, even if it meant I needed to pretend to be someone I wasn't to get there.

I decided I would play along for a while, and see where I ended up. But slowly, a new plan began to form in my mind. 'Alright, maybe we can help each other get out of this mess. I'll get my body back, and you'll have your daughter again.'

Her eyes seemed to assess me as she stared back, drinking in every detail. 'Alright, come with me. Perhaps you are right, whoever you are.'

'I told you, I am Wicked.'

'Yes, but I don't know *who* you truly are, on the inside. Right now, you look like my daughter, so you will have to play the game for a while.' She gestured to the closest servant. 'Please find a gown for my daughter and inform them that I will be a little late.' The servant looked her up and down, so she added, 'I wasn't aware that my daughter was coming.'

'To your wedding?' the servant's eyes seemed to read. But she quickly said, 'Yes, of course, Your Grace.' And then the servant scurried off to do the woman's beckoning.

For her wedding, in a palace. I was about to watch the Winter king take a new wife, and she believed I was her daughter. But she was also beginning to accept that there was a new consciousness inside the girl, and had begun addressing me as such.

What a mess I had found myself in.

Leraia narrowed her eyes, a tear rolling down her cheek as she said,

'I will not lose you if you are in there, Winnella. We will get through this together, I promise.' She stared hard at me, and seemed to recompose herself. 'As for you, Wicked, we will have to become allies, won't we?'

I knew what she wasn't saying: Until you disappear, and I have my daughter back.

Could I blame her for feeling that way? Of course not. But I didn't enjoy the realisation that I would soon be discarded as if I were nothing. But I would have myself back, when that time came. My own body, and mind, all wrapped safely together. 'I'm not so sure, Leraia ...'

I frowned as the memories of what had happened at the witch's house came unbidden to mind. Even if they weren't technically *my* memories, I felt them as if they were real. As if I'd been there to experience them. It was as if the shock of the enchantment was beginning to wear off now, my thoughts clearing a little more with each moment that passed. Or Winnella's thoughts? 'The witch told me Leraia gave her heart away ... ,' I said, my voice trailing off.

'Of course she told you that,' she said. A sigh left her lips, and she reached out to take a loose strand of hair between her fingers, before realising what she'd done. She tore her hand back quickly, as if she were afraid I might bite it. It was only more proof of her realisation that I was a stranger to her.

'But she showed me the heart ... in a jar?'

She pinched her nose between the bridge of her thumb and forefinger. She either felt such frustration deep within, or she was a wonderful actress. "No, darling. That was probably someone else's. The witches crave meetings like ours. They cannot thrive without taking sacrifices from people who require their support. Look, I gave her my ability to love romantically. I cannot love your father or this king, but I can save them both.'

It was impossible to know what to believe with my head so muddled up, full of Winnella's memories, and my own.

She inhaled sharply before continuing, 'I was given a title, riches, and the place to find a healing potion to end your father's ... the mayor's curse. But I also grew fond of the Winter king – he is far kinder than others make him appear. I couldn't fall in love with him, but I value his friendship. He understands my curse. He knows I will be helping him, and Mayor Farn. He will be healed, and the Winter kingdom will thrive again – both men will be satisfied.'

The king knew who she really was, and yet he was still going through with the wedding? Didn't that make him a fool? Things were finally beginning to make sense again, allowing the rage and frustration to break through, the fog over my mind slowly fading away and making everything clearer.

But one question came to mind: 'Satisfied?' What she was saying was ridiculous, but I could understand why she'd bargained this way. She knew there was nothing to be gained for herself, but she was willing to do it all to help those she cared for. Or was that part of her plan all along, to become the powerful queen of Icefall? Perhaps there was more to her than we could see. 'Will *you* ever be satisfied, Leraia?'

She ignored my question, and asked back, 'What did you ask for?'

'Safe trip here, safe return home.'

'Oh! You should have asked for more, done more! You're getting barely anything, and now she owns you.' She pulled me against her, stroking my hair. 'Don't worry, darling. Everything will be just fine. I will make this right.'

Leraia led me to a small room in the servants' corridor where a maid was stitching gowns.

I barely registered anything they were saying as they measured every inch of my form and tried out various sizes on me before the maid gave up and left the room. 'Not good enough,' she muttered, glancing around at the rail full of colourful gowns. 'Too big, too small, or not dazzling enough for a royal wedding. Wait here,' she called out as she left. 'Thankfully for you, I have a plan.'

Honestly, I didn't care what they dressed me in as I wasn't even the type to wear sparkling and shimmering gowns, but clearly I didn't have a choice anyway. Not if I wanted to get out of this place.

'That is no way to speak to your future queen,' said Leraia, her tone startling me. That was the voice she used when I'd taken one of her necklaces or when Barchester and I had been out for too long, not to speak to a maid in a palace. It was beginning to dawn on me why I was actually here, and everything that was now at stake. Leraia was here to marry the king.

She was going to be a *queen*.

But how did I know any of that?

For a moment, I had understood her and where she'd come from, but I had never set foot in Cranwick. Could Winnie's conscience be peeking through into my mind?

No, that wasn't fair. If I couldn't keep my own body, I wasn't going to give away my mind as well. She would just have to stay hidden for a while longer, at least until I got my own form back.

'You have a good salary here, and your family are well provided for back home, yes?' said Leraia, shooting the maid a glare.

The maid nodded her head quickly with wide and fearful eyes. Leraia's stare deepened as she settled her eyes on the maid. 'Very well. You will apologise this instant, and you will find the perfect dress for my daughter, or you will leave the palace at dawn, and you and your family will be left to fend for yourselves. Am I understood?'

The maid's eyes darkened with something like rage, but she scurried out of the room. 'Yes, of course, Your Grace. I do apologise.' I didn't miss the scornful glare she offered the future queen before she left.

Did every palace attendant think the same of Leraia? Her behaviour made me wonder if she'd given up more than her ability to love romantically, after all.

Especially when she turned back to me.

Her blood was obviously still boiling when she said, 'That may have seemed harsh to you, Winnella, but I have learned not to tolerate their disrespect. They will only value my presence here as the wife of their king if I set the boundary.'

'You must be careful, Your Grace,' I said slowly. 'Not everyone will agree with your methods.'

If she acted too rashly, she'd get herself into more trouble than I think she would be able to deal with. Besides, she was overestimating her own skill here. She would have to think about how she dealt with the people here very carefully.

Boundary, or threats? Respect, or fear? They were very different things.

9

FROST

CHAOS HAD CREPT ITS WAY INTO MY HOME, and now I was nothing more than a prisoner with a heartless stepmother and a father who would abandon me for the sake of his new alliance.

The future of our kingdom, my kingdom, was now here, and there was nothing I could do about it.

I felt Father glance in my direction before the red-coated minister led him and Leraia through the proceedings, but my stare remained fixed on the floor ahead. At my side, Prince Hugo squeezed my hand, and I allowed my mind to wander as they answered the minister's demands.

Are you committed to this marriage?

The false smile she wore as she answered made me want to retch. 'Yes, of course, I love my husband,' she said.

Are you committed to this kingdom?

You could have heard a pin drop in the throne room as she spoke, with clear delight in her eyes. 'I give my life for Icefall, as His Majesty always has.'

And of course, countless other questions of the same nature. My patience was wearing thin, so I was relieved when the minister finally asked, 'Do you, Princess Leraia Cara Braxton, take His Majesty King James Winter as your devoted and loving husband for as long as you both shall live?'

Princess Leraia was staring lovingly into Father's eyes. But that was all a lie as well. Three years was a long time for an engagement like this one. Leraia had been putting off the wedding for as long as she could, but now her time was up.

Their hands were linked together, and the minister looked upon them both warmly, although I saw that his smile did not meet his eyes. Even the servants around Leraia seemed weary of her, like they knew just as well as me that there was someone under the surface that they could not trust. She was polite when she needed to be, but there was a sternness to her smile and expression that made me anxious.

Not only was she a liar and an impostor, but her façade was sickly sweet. She was trying too hard to be like us. As if she truly felt she belonged.

'I do,' she said, with a smile stretching across her lips.

I watched the way Father smiled at those words, at her commitment to him. He seemed nervous as he ran a hand through his white blonde hair. Nervous to align his life with this woman's, just as he had been when he married my mother all of those years ago. But I feared this time, it was for very different reasons. He was blind in loving Leraia – he was the only one that did not seem to see it. Or perhaps he did, but simply did not care.

'And do you, Your Majesty King James Winter, take Her Grace, Princess Leraia Cara Braxton to be your devoted and loving wife for as long as you both shall live?'

'I do.' As he said the words, he caught my gaze and held it, but I looked away.

The rest of the ceremony passed agonisingly slowly, with Father and Leraia staring sickeningly into each other's eyes, a sight that twisted my stomach into knots because it was not real. They each spoke their vows, promising to support each other both in sickness and in health, and in our kingdom.

But I could not stop watching my stepmother and the girl in the opposite front row aisle, wearing a pastel pink gown that was clearly mine. The daughter Leraia had mentioned was here, but how? Had she not chosen to leave her behind?

When the ceremony was over, a crown was placed onto Leraia's head, and she was told to recite Icefall's rite of passage before being declared as our queen. It was yet another ceremony that seemed to last forever. Then guests were directed back to the ballroom, where tables were being set up close to the entrance from the kitchens, and the floor was cleared for everyone to dance and drink as they pleased.

Father came over as this was happening, with his new wife following behind like some kind of lost puppy. I had been happy to see him, but my hope fizzled out when she arrived. Father seemed to notice because he said, 'You should make sure Winnella is alright,' and cast her a loving smile. 'We will speak soon. I need a moment with my daughter.'

'Of course, my love.' She curtsied and stalked off to find the girl.

I folded my arms over my chest, glaring at her back as she scurried away. 'She would barely give you five minutes alone.'

He laughed softly, and reached for my hand. 'Frost, the ceremony just ended. Give her some credit.' He spun me around, and I felt like a child in my father's arms again, enjoying ballroom dances with my parents.

Tears stung my eyes at the thought of Mother holding me like that, and I was forced to blink them back. To be strong. But it was so hard to do that when everything in this ballroom – the white and blue roses, the huge stained-glass windows, and the nobles speaking contentedly amongst themselves – reminded me of her.

Oblivious to my distress, Father held my hand in his own and began, 'So, how did you find the –'

'What if she does not deserve credit?' I interrupted, my frustration seeping into my voice. I knew he would be disappointed at my words, but I was unable to help myself. 'What if she is not good enough for you? I tried to be happy for you, but I cannot stand it any longer. I do not trust her, Father.'

There they were, my feelings out in the open.

I was right; his disappointment was clear on his face and in the heavy sigh he released, which caused a heavy feeling of guilt to fall upon my chest, but I refused to hide my feelings from him. But perhaps Prince Hugo was correct after all – perhaps I only thought of myself.

The concern was clear in his creased brow. 'You barely know her, Frost.'

'But that's my entire point, Father. You have been seeing each other for three years but you have never introduced her to me, nor has she ever said a word to my face. I have barely seen you since you have been together. I already lost my mother. How could you do that to me?'

He shook his head and let out a sigh, pinching the bridge of his nose between his thumb and forefinger as if my words were giving him a headache. 'And you only choose to tell me how you feel on my wedding day, after the ceremony has already ended?'

'What other chance have I had?' There was so much desperation in my heart, a full aching in my chest, that there was no way I could keep it in now. 'Besides, I doubt my feelings would have changed your mind.'

He was quiet for some time, the regret clear in his eyes. His gaze was solemn when he finally said, 'I am sorry, Frost. I fell in love with her, so perhaps I was blind to you.'

Perhaps? No, no. How could he have been so ignorant? So oblivious to his only daughter's suffering? That was the last straw for me. There was no going back now, the damage was done.

It was too late.

But I would not let this end here. Before I could change my mind, I began to spill everything I had heard Leraia say to the witch in that mirror, how I had been chasing her around to find out more information about her because I could not bear the thought of losing him like that. I waited for him to gape back at me with a horrified expression or shout me down in rage, but instead I watched the knowing, and the realisation, dawn behind his eyes.

Then came the anger, and it radiated from him in waves. 'It was you. You wrote the letter from my wife, to try to end my marriage …' My silence had told him everything, because he ran a hand through his hair, and he could no longer look at me. 'Do you know how stupid you have been? How long I have waited for her to finally accept my hand in marriage? You could have ruined everything.'

'But clearly I have not.' Boiling anger burned inside my chest, but I ignored it and spun away from him. 'Have a wonderful life together, Father. I wish you a happy marriage, and I hope the kingdom prospers from your matrimony.'

It was a curt and tactical response, the type only given by a princess who had been trained in royal courtesy. But perhaps a selfish part of me hoped it would hurt him as much as his rejection had hurt me.

Like knives in my chest, he had pierced my heart over and over for years now. I did not wish to upset him, truly, but I was still so *angry*.

'Your plan failed, child, because I already knew everything she was hiding.' His words made me turn slowly back, and I faced my father to find tears rolling down his face. He appeared solemn, and somehow more beautiful than ever before.

My gaze softened. How I had missed him talking to me like this, and showing his love. It was far too easy to be cold when you must learn to contain your emotions every day for the sake of your people, but now I could see, even through my rage, how much he cared.

'I knew for some time, and after a while I came to accept it because I ... I still wanted to marry her. But not only that, I knew she would be good for us, Frost. Good for our people, for our kingdom. Princess or not, her agreement with the witches had its benefits. But by then, I had already fallen for her, and even in her deceit, I understood her.'

'Good for you, Father. I am glad.'

How stupid he had been, to risk our kingdom like that. I was glad he was happy, even if I did not quite believe it myself, but could he not see how much of a fool he had been? If the council heard of how he had deceived them by continuing with this marriage, even when he knew it was wrong, they would end us all. A new ruler would be appointed, one of their own design. But of course, he had not been thinking of the potential damage his actions might cause. He had been thinking only of himself and his love for this woman.

I stormed out of the ballroom, unable to take any more of this conversation. Dipped down the steps and raced toward the gardens, taking deep breaths, and praying I would find comfort in my mother's statue. I headed through the little floral arch, toward the section where the royal statues stood proudly, thinking only of my mother and her beautiful glass face.

Horror rippled in my veins when I found Queen Leraia and her daughter gazing up at it. The sight set my blood on fire, and it was all I could do not to run over there and tell them to back off. But as I approached slowly, I saw them whispering, and my interest was piqued. I hid behind a rosebush; certain they could not see me.

'Are you alright, Winnella?' my stepmother was asking her daughter. 'I know it's all quite scary right now, but I'm here. We will get through this together.'

'I still don't understand,' said Winnella, running a delicate hand along her hairline. 'My head feels clearer now, like the first part of the enchantment has worn off, but my memories don't match the life you say we have always led. It's like the witch added new fears and thoughts in me that I don't recognise. It's hard to know what is clear, as those memories don't even feel real or right to me even though my heart tells me they are mine.'

My stepmother stroked her daughter's blonde hair away from her face, wearing an expression that could only be concern. 'We will have to visit the witch, and get her to erase the enchantment.'

The Roth witches were not to be messed with. My father and I knew that first hand. What had these two imbeciles gotten themselves into?

Winnella's eyes were wide and full of fear. 'But what if she just wants to take something else from us? She already took your ability to love romantically, and my name. What else could she want?'

She had bargained her way into my father's heart without the ability to love romantically.

The more I heard from these impostors, the more my rage blossomed inside me. She truly was cruel. How dare she deceive him and break his heart like that? In doing so, she had torn him away from me, and broken mine, as well. But if her daughter had lost her name, had she also lost her identity? The Roth witches were sneaky, and there was no bargaining with them.

Everything came with a price.

If these bastards were in this for the long haul, they were stuck here with us. If there was no getting them away from the witches, there was no way I would ever be rid of them. Wherever they came from, I needed them to go home and never trouble my kingdom or my father again. Because liars and selfish, greedy people were not welcome here.

I needed a plan, one that would help me get them permanently removed.

Leraia frowned, but wrapped an arm around her daughter's shoulders as if hoping to provide comfort. So she could be loving where it suited her, just not to her stepdaughter. 'I will not let her trick us again. We will confront her together on our way back to Cranwick –'

I chose that moment to step out from behind the rosebush. 'Cranwick is the Mirror Village, Stepmother. It is a place of myth, of storybooks, it is not real.' I knew full well from what I had heard from her conversation in the mirror that it did exist, but the princess she thought I was would have been oblivious and naïve, so that was the part I would happily play to find another way to end her scheming and have them both sent back home.

The queen curtsied and said softly, 'Oh, Princess Frost. I am sorry, I did not see you there. Were we speaking offensively? Cranwick is very real indeed, or it is in the kingdom I come from. Stepdaughter, meet my daughter, Winnella.'

The girl nodded and curtsied. She stared at me, wearing an expression that seemed nervous or afraid. Perhaps, both. 'It is good to meet you, Your Highness.' The girl smiled, although it did not meet her eyes. She was watching me with a strange expression, as if she were not expecting to even be here among royalty.

'This is your mother's statue, Frost?' said my stepmother, taking my mother's glass hand.

The image boiled my blood, but I held back the urge to shove her away from it hard, and smiled politely. 'Yes, Stepmother. Being close to her brings me peace.'

And seeing you so close to her makes me want to punch you, I thought at the same time.

'Please, call me Mother if you like.' She offered me her hand, and I had to force myself not to pull away in disgust at her audacity. Her eyes were filled with warmth as she drank me in, but I did not believe it was real for one moment. 'I understand that it has been hard for you these last few years. But you have a friend in me, dear girl. I will gladly be your new mother if you will let me.'

I did not miss the look of confusion in her daughter's eyes, then.

I offered the queen a nod, although I wanted to tell them both to leave my mother's statue alone, and give me silence out here with her statue. My real mother, and my only one. 'You and Father could have talked to me, you know? I was never granted the opportunity to get to know you.'

I wished there was a way I could confront them both, but I also knew I needed to be smart about this. Acting impulsively would only take away any opportunity I might have to find out what they were really doing here.

I saw Winnella watching her with awe-filled eyes as she said, 'Honestly, I sensed that you did not like me, and I was not sure how to be around you. I suppose I was afraid. I am sorry, Princess Frost.'

'I only did not like or trust you because I had no way of knowing you. I still do not. But we are acquainted now.' I offered her my finest smile. She did not need to know of everything I knew about her just yet. At least, until my father told her about our argument, which I was certain that he would. 'You should both and go and enjoy the celebrations.'

They curtsied and walked away, and as they went I promised myself I would watch them very closely, and make sure to learn more about the Mirror Village of Cranwick.

10

WICKED

The late queen's glass statue seemed to be looking down on me with a scornful glare.

I mean if she were, I probably wouldn't blame her as I was merely an outsider. To everyone else, I was the new stepsister of her daughter, but on the inside I was a Roth witch. God, what a mess.

Leraia was up to no good. She snuck off while I was transfixed by her new husband's ex-wife's glass copy. Even *that* was a mouthful. From the sudden urge I had to slip away and find her, it seemed that Winnie had expected her mother to stay with her in this palace. She'd followed her here, after all.

But the woman clearly had plans of her own.

What had the girl been thinking when she followed her mother here? Surely she would have known how hopeless her little mission was. But I also knew that the new queen had been coming to this place for three years, so she would have learned many of its little crevices and secrets by now.

I started with the ballroom, scanning the wide space that was slightly intimidating in its size. Everyone else would have, no doubt, thought the same. So it was time to become invisible, and learn more about the royal life the woman had thrown herself into headfirst. To see the world through her eyes, if I could.

I walked beyond the buffet table with its colourful little cupcakes and sandwiches containing various meats and salads, and it was a challenge not to become distracted by the luscious smells or the thought of chocolate on my tongue ... Shaking myself off, I turned my face instead to the high ceilings decorated with paintings and tapestries that told stories of Icefall's history. War, bloodshed, and tragic devastation. And of course, the odd celebration.

Many years ago, Icefall had fought the three other kingdoms in their homeland and the previous king had slayed their rulers, leaving the other lands barren until King James Winter later took the throne and restored peace between the kingdoms, even helping to appoint three new rulers. He didn't want to be known as the king slayer like his father, King Wilhelm Winter. He was still very much the cruel king, but maybe there was more to him.

He'd granted the other current rulers their new positions when they were all young. If he had not worked with the councils to find them and give them their rule, they would not be here like this. Ruling their kingdoms; sharing the festivities with their spouses and children. No one knew where he'd found them, and that was the mystery. Perhaps this was why many of them feared him. Perhaps they thought he would one day become his father. I saw this in the way they were looking at him with fearful stares, as if they were afraid he could explode at any moment.

But a few of them were also observing him with interest, as if they believed him to be more than the rumours described.

But he wasn't my reason for being here. The queen was my way out of this place, so I had to find her and use her to get out of this palace in one piece. I moved quickly, passing gown to gown, watching the dancers with fascination as they enjoyed their celebration. I was probably the only one here who wasn't revelling in the freedom of the food and music, swaying and swishing my skirts to the sound of the nearby lyre, and loving being watched by the many arrogant and brooding men across the dancefloor.

But maybe I was wrong, I thought, when I noticed the young Winter princess studying the guests with clear dismay behind her icy blue eyes. Winnella's new stepsister slipped around the room with a smile plastered on her face. The beauty curtsied to everyone who passed her, but her stare remained fixed on her father and his new wife. She seemed lonely.

Seeing her pressed me into action, and I shot from the ballroom once I caught sight of the king and his new wife through the window, walking through the gardens arm in arm. They were a beautiful couple, there was no denying it, but you could also take their solemn expressions as a sign that today wasn't a pleasant occasion for all.

'Damn right it's not pleasant, my mother is marrying another man!' a thought slipped into my mind, intrusive and unwanted. Where had it come from? It couldn't be ... her ... breaking through into my conscious mind, could it? *'Get out of my head, witch. You've already taken over my body, the least you could do is go away and let me work through this mess in peace.'*

Well, I supposed that confirmed it.

Best to ignore it, I thought, and hope it would leave me alone. Because although it might be her body I was trapped in, my consciousness was evidently much stronger than hers. So it would just have to stay that way until I could get the hell out of here, permanently. Then she could do whatever the hell she wanted with her body and mind.

'No chance, Wicked. You're stuck in my body, which means you're stuck with me.'

And whose fault was that? Clearly not mine.

Although, my own curiosity began to take over and I asked her inside my mind, or hers, whoever it belonged to, *'How long have you been here, watching my every move? And why haven't you made your ... presence clear earlier?'*

'I've been here since you appeared in my head outside the palace, but I haven't been able to communicate until now. It feels like there's a wall between us, and I've only just managed to push through it to give you a piece of my mind. Literally.'

'Ha, I see what you did there. Alright, looks like we've gotta get on with this. But you can go back behind your wall, thank you very much. I don't need you here right now.' And then I focused hard, and found the wall she was speaking of, so I slammed against it with force. I heard her screams as she became nothing but a silent observer again. I couldn't help but feel a sliver of satisfaction when she didn't appear again after that.

There we were, alone at last.

I was almost at the door to the gardens when a voice called out from behind me, 'I have not seen you here before, have I?' The girl beside me could have been sculpted by the goddess herself. She was beautiful, with a thick fringe over her brow and golden hair that fell down her back, curling at the ends. She wore a pale pink gown with long sleeves and a tight bodice, and a small silver tiara on her head. If I wasn't mistaken, this was Princess Artemia Spring of Blossomheart, daughter and heir of King Danver and Queen Arabella.

'No, I doubt you have.'

She was staring at me with a strange expression, eyes widening with surprise and ... awe, as if I were from another world altogether and she were fascinated by the thought. I wasn't sure how I felt about that. Her brow lifted slightly in a sign of curiosity. 'May I ask your name?'

At least she was polite, unlike some of these scowling nobles. They all seemed like nasty pieces of work, especially the king and queen of Oceanwell, who smiled in everyone's faces and then uttered brutal words as they walked away. King Arder was a scrawny man with a permanent frown on his brow, and Queen Ira's smile was very clearly faked. Their twin daughters Piper and Martha wore the same stern, scrutinising bitch stares as they passed the other nobles. They reminded me of the girls at my old school, when Mother made the foolish decision to put my sisters and I through a mainstream school. They were the type to bully others to make themselves feel more powerful.

Windspell's rulers, King Archibald and Queen Aura, seemed fair. They practically glided around the room, giving the nobles kind smiles and laughing at their jokes. Nobles passed them regularly, holding little flutes of champagne and sharing stories that made the royals smile. Their daughter, Princess Aurelia and their son Prince Hugo, seemed to relish in their parents' popularity. They danced together before moving around the room and greeting others, but Prince Hugo's stare always returned to Icefall's princess, Princess Frost.

'You may, it is … ,' but although I'd agreed to give her my name, I couldn't seem to find the words to actually say it, and my voice trailed off as I glanced around the room, studying all of the other royals and waiting for the opportune moment to slip away from this conversation and go to the king and queen.

My eyes must have glazed over because the Spring princess prompted, 'Am I sending you to sleep?' She laughed gently, and her gaze followed mine. 'I apologise, I will let you enjoy the –'

'Go!' Winnie's inner voice pushed through again. 'Leave her, now. She's just distracting us from what we're supposed to be doing.'

'There is no us about this. Don't tell me what to do, I can't rush out or I'll look like a toad,' I snapped back before focusing on the princess again. How had I found myself in this situation? It was becoming far messier than I could have anticipated. 'No, no. There is a lot going on, I'm a little …'

'Overwhelmed?' the Spring princess finished for me with a smile.

That was the understatement of the century.

But her blue eyes were warm and kind, and I found myself laughing with her. 'Yes, I suppose you could say so. My name is Winnella.'

'No it isn't!' Winnie snapped.

'You know damn well I can't tell her it's Wicked, so just be quiet.'

'You're insufferable.'

I heard her huffing inside my mind, and I almost laughed. This was becoming ridiculous, and I couldn't wait to go and give those Elder witches a piece of my own mind. *'And you're irritating. But it looks like there's nothing we can do about any of this until we find the witches that cursed you, so let's just ... try to work together?'* I couldn't believe I was actually trying to reason with this stubborn daughter of the queen, but clearly I didn't have much of a choice.

'It is very good to meet you. I am Princess Artemia of Blossomheart.' The princess reached for my hand, and I placed it into hers. Could she read my inner frustration on my face? It must have been almost comical. 'So, what brought you to Icefall, Winnella?'

I shrugged. 'My mother married the king.'

'Imaginative,' Winnie muttered.

I ignored her and fixed my gaze on the princess, whose hand flew to her chest as her mouth dropped open. 'Goodness, Winnella. You are a princess of Icefall now.' She stared at me for a moment, clearly processing the information. 'Where did you come from? Is your old kingdom very far away?'

'It is quite a distance, yes.' Running through a brief explanation of the story Leraia had told me to stick to before she slipped away, I saw the surprise and awe as it appeared on her face.

The plan was simple in Leraia's eyes: persuade them she was the princess of a kingdom called Selyn; the daughter of a rich king called Natticus Spyfall – a stupid name if you asked me – a distant cousin of the Roth witches' leader. It was nuts, in my mind. But the king had apparently spent one of their three years courting believing she was who she said she was.

At least, until he'd caught her in her lies, and she was forced to reveal everything. Surprisingly, after the shock had worn off, the king appreciated her honesty and allowed the alliance, and eventually the fake wedding, to continue. The benefits for his kingdom were far too worth it.

'So you have come a long way. How does it feel to be here in a new kingdom? A new home?'

This wasn't my home, nor would it ever be. But to play the part, I nodded and cast her a smile. She didn't need to know what was really going on inside, nor did anyone else. 'Strange, but I am optimistic that the alliance between our kingdoms will be a useful one, and help us all.'

'Of course. But that seems to me like a rather tactful answer. How do you *really* feel about it all?' There was a strange glint in the Spring princess's eye when she said those words, like she knew there was something I wasn't telling her. But she was broaching dangerous territory if she was trying to make me speak badly of the kingdom I'd fallen into. Not that any of it – true or false as it may be – was her business.

I refused to satiate her petty need for gossip.

Instead, I curtsied and said goodbye, but she stopped me with her hand raised. 'However you are feeling, Winnella, I can understand. Please, just be careful of the Summer king and queen if you stumble upon them. They are vicious, and determined to see Icefall crumble.'

I followed her gaze to the laughing royals. 'I will evaluate their actions for myself, but thank you, Princess Artemia. Have a good night.'

Because of her endless questions, I'd lost sight of the queen.

Behind me suddenly, I heard footsteps and a voice calling my name. I turned to face the Winter king, who was now coming toward me. Luck clearly wasn't in my favour tonight when it came to speaking with Leraia, but perhaps I had found the next best thing. Maybe the king could give me some answers. He probably wouldn't know the specifics of Leraia's deal with the witches, but he might know something. He led me away from the Spring princess, linking an arm through mine.

'Be careful what you say to him. Remember, we need to get my mother home. Don't ruin that for me!' Winnie cried inside my mind.

'By the goddess, you're a ray of sunshine, aren't you? I know. But your mother isn't what I'm here for, remember. I am looking out for number one.'

'You're stuck in my head, and seem to have control over my body as well. What do you expect?'

I couldn't help but chuckle inside, but was forced to turn back to the king, who was now watching me with interest.

'I hope my dear Artemia is looking after you, sweetheart,' he said. 'She is one of the kindest young ladies I have had the pleasure of meeting. Be wary of the others, they like to talk about things they do not understand.' His stare flickered to the Summer royals, and their queen turned and locked eyes with him. He lingered there for a few seconds before returning to me. So much history they must have shared.

I tugged my arm back, slightly alarmed. 'What makes them say such bitter things about you, Your Majesty?'

His eyes burned with something hot, like white rage. 'I have spent a lot of time in my palace observing the other rulers from a distance. Many believe, because of my father's cruelty, that I killed my wife, the late queen. But I would never, ever hurt my dear Rosa. She was everything to me, and my daughter more so.'

'That's heartbreaking,' Winnie whispered.

The king's gaze softened. 'But you and your mother need not fear me. I would never act in such a way that makes you feel unsafe.' He wrapped an arm around my shoulders. 'I am glad you are here, although I know it was not in your mother's plans.' He stroked a stray hair back from my face, and tucked it behind my ear. 'I know everything about Cranwick, your father and the curse. He will be cured, and my kingdom restored with the treasures that the Roth witches gave her during her bargain. In both of our worlds, there will be peace as a result of this unity. And in time, I will find a way to end the curse on Cranwick, so you will be free. Your father and his people, too.'

Tears welled in my eyes. Winnie's doing, no doubt. I couldn't believe what I was hearing. This king, who I'd only ever heard terrifying tales about, was willing to help end her village's curse. It was actually quite sweet. 'Hearing you promise that means the world to me, Your Majesty. Thank you.'

'I can't believe he would do that for me,' Winnie whispered, her voice trembling with emotion.

The king laughed softly. 'You have gained a second home, it seems. You are not a prisoner, of course, so please do not feel forced, but you are always welcome here with us, and I hope you remember that.'

'Thank you, Your Majesty.' Even I couldn't help but be touched by his words, and knew I was speaking on behalf of the tearful girl in my head.

'You are most welcome, my dear.' He gathered me closer. 'Shall we introduce you to some more of our friends?'

'I think I'd like to go back to my room, actually. Being here is quite ... exhausting.' As was juggling two voices at once, but he didn't need to hear about that.

But he also didn't need to know that I didn't intend to go to my room at all, but to carry on hunting for the new Winter queen instead.

'I think that is understandable.' He peered around at the nobles closest to him. A few shiny dresses swished past, but I wasn't sure if I'd been told who they were or not. There were far too many people here to know for sure. 'Ah, Princess Aurelia? Might I ask for a favour, please?'

Dread coursed through me at the thought of meeting yet another nosy princess, but there was something warm about the girl that appeared before us, her deep brown eyes and wide smile. Long brown hair fell down to her waist in light curls, and she wore a shimmering golden dress that clung to her small frame but floated at her feet.

'Of course, Your Majesty,' she answered.

'This is my stepdaughter, Winnella. Will you show her around the palace for me before taking her back to her room? Do make her feel welcome for me.'

'I would be happy to, Your Majesty.'

The king turned his kind gaze on me again and offered me a curt smile. 'Thank you. Winnella, I will leave you in the gentle hands of Princess Aurelia Autumn. She is the princess of Windspell.'

The daughter of King Archibald and Queen Aura Autumn, and the younger sister of Prince Hugo. It was all so much to digest. So many names and faces to learn and remember that I wasn't sure I would ever hold it all in.

So Princess Aurelia whisked me away, down the long corridors toward the royal suites, pointing out the servants' quarters and the Guard House. 'I would be terrified if I were you,' she said suddenly, sounding far too much like Princess Artemia. 'I am sure you know your mother well, but something does not seem quite ... right with her. No one here trusts her. She seems to think she is respected, but she needs to watch her tongue. Every kingdom here is out for themselves, but some of us have our loyalties, and the Winter kingdom is not exactly popular.'

'I've noticed that. But what rumours surround King James? Because all I've heard are negative things, but he seems kind and sincere to me.'

Like he mentioned, people thought he'd killed his wife. I'd even heard some servants saying he'd assaulted Princess Artemia's mother many years ago. But were these false truths being spread to cover up their own behaviour? To put the blame on someone who already presented a cold exterior to the world simply because it was easy?

'He is a good king, and I fear your mother is not good enough for him. I am sorry to say it, but that is how many of us feel.'

Those words hit me like a blow to the gut. I knew Leraia's behaviour wasn't likely to be accepted here, but this was a strange confirmation of that truth. I knew my mother as kind and welcoming, a blessing for

Barchester, Dad and I to spend time with. Although I knew her deal with the witches and her even being here was wrong, she was still the mother I had always loved. So to hear them speak of her that way, it cut me deeply inside. But, once again, those thoughts were Winnie's consciousness taking over. 'I should go.'

I headed for my room, or the place I was sure it was in, but she stopped me, grabbing my wrist. I tore my arm away, but her grip was too strong. I was getting sick of people doing that.

Winnie was growing stronger inside, pushing past *my* conscience and taking control of herself. I didn't like it, because it wouldn't be long before I was thrown aside. And what would become of me then?

Before she could slip in again, I pushed and shoved her back behind that wall, but this time I felt her force, fighting against mine.

One mind against the other.

And she was winning.

Princess Aurelia's eyes flickered with something like confusion as if she could see my mind contorting inside, as if she could sense my mental frustration along with Winnie's. But still she offered me a wary gaze and said, 'Be careful of King James and Princess Frost. They are not the bitter and cold rulers they appear to be, but with your mother around they may not take kindly to you in private. Imagine your conversation with the king just now as a façade. Because he always has a hidden motive, believe me.'

'You're wrong,' Winnie screamed, and in that moment I sensed my downfall. Sensed her forcing me away, down and down into a mental tunnel.

The last thing I heard before I slid away was, *'You're wrong, I just know it.'*

11

FROST

HER MAJESTY MIGHT HAVE BELIEVED SHE WAS INVISIBLE in the palace, sneaking through the dark halls at night with a torch in her hand, but I knew better.

Careful to look around and ahead of me, I inched forward, avoiding my father's men and keeping my gaze level on my stepmother's silk skirts. Her gown swayed at her feet as she hurried through the lower halls of the palace, the light in her hand casting shadows over her face and neck, making her appear both beautiful and terrifying.

I could appreciate her pretty face and see why my father had fallen for her. But her icy nature made her ugly. To me, she was no dazzling queen, but a ruthless monster.

Winnella was no longer with her, and I presumed she had gone back to her room since by now it was getting late. Leraia glanced around her before entering, as if she feared she was being followed. How would she react when she realised that her new husband's only daughter was following her, suspicious of her every move? Only time would tell.

By now, most of the guests had begun to disperse and leave in their carriages. so the grounds were quiet, leaving more room for the new queen to sneak around. But her behaviour would not go unnoticed. Not by me, at least. I would use her secrets against her, and she would be banished from the kingdom and sent back to Cranwick where she would be forced to spend the rest of her miserable life, isolated and alone.

She headed through the Guard Halls, the guards stationed there forced to bow to their new queen. I lingered closely behind.

When I passed them, their eyes widened with surprise. 'Princess Frost,' said Marcus, bowing to me. I was not afraid to admit that he was my favourite of my father's guards; he was warm and welcoming, but I also loved that he could pack a good punch and would not treat me like a weak princess whenever I wished to fight. In fact, he and his brothers had been training me in combat and self-defence for a few years now. I trusted them more than any of the personal guards my father had appointed to my room. 'Is anything troubling you? We don't see you down here very often anymore.' He laughed, no doubt remembering the years I had spent here as a child.

'Of course not, gentlemen. Just making sure my stepmother does not get lost in this maze of a palace,' I answered with a grin, also remembering those days.

While my mother and father were adamant that I should be learning the responsibilities of a future monarch, I had always been less enthusiastic about the idea. My feet would often lead me down here, where I would stay for hours, observing the guards, stealing their weapons and trying to persuade them to teach me. Let us just say I was always good at getting what I wanted.

No one would ever remember me as the soft little princess who could not defend herself if the palace suffered an attack. With my father's reputation as the ice-cold Winter king, this was probably for the best.

You never knew what could happen. I listened to their words as I hurried after the new queen. All those years of sneaking around the palace had also taught me to listen, and with exceptional hearing.

'What is she doing?'

'She doesn't trust Her Majesty then, either.'

It was a relief to hear that I was not the only one who did not approve of the queen.

She crept beyond the Guard House toward the servants' quarters where she slipped into the kitchens, offering curt smiles to every servant she passed. I did not miss the look of disdain they passed each other when she turned away from them, clear suspicion and fear in the eyes of the servants I so admired.

The people of Icefall were good and compassionate, but we were known to be stubborn, and we could always sense a liar. Except for my father, in his moment of weakness of loving my stepmother, it seemed. But it was one of the many things that had always drawn me to conversations with the palace's attendants. How I adored asking them about their busy schedules, and wishing them well.

This was something I had earned from both my mother and my father. If the other kingdoms spoke ill of Icefall's monarchy, our own people would certainly argue their opinions.

Leraia requested two glasses of red wine, but the servants were not expecting her. Two of them staggered backward into the Head Cook's enormous bowl of soup, knocking it over and spilling the hot liquid onto the floor. I hung back behind the doorframe as the loud, plump, and ancient Head Cook, Madame Vespa Butcher, began slapping the servants with her oven mitt while the queen just observed the commotion with a giant smirk on her lips. 'You silly fools!' Madam Butcher cried. 'Clean this up now, or you will spend the night here scrubbing the floors!'

It was impossible not to laugh at the look of shock and dismay on the servants' faces as the old woman chased them around the kitchens. Still, it was hardly their fault, and I felt guilty for laughing.

Madame Butcher answered to no one, not even the king. Father loved her food, and she had been around since he was a child, so I knew she brought him some comfort, but I also knew she made him nervous. Honestly, she terrified me. But it was also clear to see why she was so respected here.

But Leraia seemed to think she could slip in here and tell the cook what to do. She truly believed that just because she was now the queen, the people of Icefall would bow to her every whim. She would learn her lesson soon, because she was gravely mistaken.

As Madame Butcher poured the glasses for her and batted her out of the kitchen, Leraia strolled toward the royal suites, wearing a satisfied smile. The maids and cooks whispered insults behind her back. A queen must earn the respect of her people, but that would not happen overnight.

Or at all, if I had anything to do with it.

I was not entirely sure what my plan would be yet, but I just knew I needed to get her and her troublesome daughter out of my palace, and out of my father's life.

She walked, with both glasses in her hands, slipped into Father's room and did not come out again.

I waited there for some time, planning my next move. If she was only there to find a drink for herself and Father, why was she so concerned about being followed? She was up to something, and I was going to find out what it was.

The door slammed open, and I hid myself against the wall around the corner as she staggered out, breathless, and almost collapsed on the floor. She strode away from the room and down the hall. I followed quickly, careful to shield myself from her view. Looking around her again, out of sight of the guards at their door, she reached into her cloak pocket brought out a small clear coloured pouch containing a strange white powder. Some kind of drug?

THE GIRL BEHIND THE GLASS

Then, inhaling sharply, my stepmother raised her chin and, pushing the pouch back into her pocket, went back into the room. I walked after her, but lingered near the door, nodding to the guards stationed there.

'Can we help you, Your Highness?' said one of them, Pietyr, I thought his name was.

'I am fine, thank you. Has my father gone to bed?' I asked, and hoped he would think I wished to check up on him before I retired to my own room for the night.

Pietyr looked into the room for me. 'I believe he has, Your Highness.'

'Thank you, Pietyr.' Peering through the glass panel, I saw that he was right. The two glasses of wine were placed delicately on the bedside table. Leraia leaned over Father and planted a kiss upon his brow. I pressed my ear against the door, hoping to hear what they were saying.

'I love you, King James Winter,' she said, her voice muffled by the wood. 'I have been so fortunate to have spent the last three years at your side, but now you must go.' She wiped the tears away quickly. Her complexion paled as her smile became a wide grin, a sight that twisted my stomach into knots.

Suddenly, everything made sense.

The powder, and the wine.

Horror coiled through my blood as the reality of what she was going to do here dawned on me.

All of that drivel about her marrying my father to save her sick husband and return home to her daughter – they were rotten lies. What did her daughter truly mean to her?

She had married my father for his kingdom, for his power, and now she was going to *kill* him.

I had to stop her.

The first place I ran to was the Guard House, where I was ready to tell them everything she was planning and watch them hunt her down, swords blazing, but there were no soldiers there in attendance.

They must have been positioned around the palace, on extra guard in case of an attack from the other kingdoms. A coronation would always leave a kingdom vulnerable, after all, as a new ruler might not be so accustomed to dealing with such political issues.

But they needed to realise that in this case, the true danger already laid within the palace. If we did not stop her, we would lose our king tonight. I had already lost my mother. I could not lose my father, too.

It was obvious what I had to do next, where I would have to go. I practically fled back to his rooms, nodding to his guards and entering quietly, and was relieved when the queen was nowhere to be seen.

Striding to his bedside, I whispered frantically, 'Wake up, Father. We have to get you out of here.' There was no way I would be able to lift him on my own. I called for one of the guards at the door. Pietyr and his fellow guard were gone, now replaced by two female guards I had never seen before. 'Help me, please! I believe my father has been drugged. My stepmother has ...'

'It's alright, Your Highness,' the guard replied, blank-faced. Her hair was braided back, but two long strands hung close to her ears. She wore leather trousers and a cloak over a corseted leather shirt. She was beautiful, but I had never seen her before. She must have been new to the Royal Guard. Not to mention that female guards were rare in Icefall, because usually women were busy attending to household duties, and it was much harder for them to gain entry into the army or the Royal Guard. What was going on? 'The king is just deep in slumber. He has had a big day.'

'No, no, I saw my stepmother –'

'You should go and rest. I will call for my brother to escort you to your rooms.'

It was hopeless. They would not believe me, and they refused to do anything, which meant I was on my own.

'Have you secured the grounds?' my stepmother's voice echoed through the hall, and I heard her heels clanking against the marble floors as she approached.

With my heart thudding in my chest, I slipped back into my father's room and closed the door. The guards had been watching me closely, and honestly, it made me wonder if they were even my father's. Perhaps she had brought her own soldiers here, men and women with loyalty to her only. I slid down against the door, my breathing coming in slow and shallow as I reminded myself to be silent, and to listen.

'Yes, Your Majesty, but you must be careful,' a voice said from some distance away. One of her cronies, here to do her bidding. She must have brought her own guards here, and they knew where I was. 'The princess is wary of you and your plans. She believes you have drugged her father.'

Laughter pierced the stillness, the sound twisting my gut. The echoing laughter of a woman who had tried to kill her husband on her wedding night. 'Well, she would be correct. Where is she?'

Soon, she would find me, and it would be over. But not if I had anything to do with it.

Acting quickly, I tugged at Father's writing desk and shoved it hard against the door. My heart began to race as the wooden frame trembled behind it, meaning the false guards knew I was inside and would have alerted the queen to my presence.

Well, I was fortunate in the fact that she did not know every part of the palace yet. There were various tunnels leading the royal suites to the longer exits of the palace via the Guard House, especially the king and queen's bedroom. You could only access these tunnels if you knew where to look, meaning I hoped she would not be able to intercept me now.

Father's breathing was shallow, his chest rising and falling slowly. It was all I could do to hope I was not too late. The glasses were still full, so that was something. Perhaps she had gone to get more poison, or more wine. Whatever it was, I would save him before she broke her way in.

I stood before the two glasses, drained them into the basin and watched the bubbles float away. Then I replaced them with the bottle of wine I had brought with me, and quickly shoved open the concealed entrance to the dark tunnel. From there, I hauled my father out of his bed and onto the floor. If only I had something to push him on. 'Sorry, Father, this might be a rough journey for you if you wake up.'

But, by the way the door was shaking now, it was clear that I had no choice.

At least it was only a short walk to the Guard House, so I told myself I could do this. Hauling him up by his arms, I dragged him a few feet into the tunnel before gently placing him down onto the stone ground and shutting the wooden door behind us, the sweat already pooling on my head due to the warmth in the lower parts of the palace.

Then, taking a deep breath and readying my limbs for the straining of pulling a man who was far bigger than me, I began to move him down the tunnel, step by step. I was no dainty princess, and I had practiced various types of combat with Marcus and his brother Ryan and the other soldiers, so I was probably far stronger than the other princesses, but pulling his deadweight was a challenge. I was exhausted by the time I reached the guards' training quarters.

Leaving my father on the ground, I found Ryan, Marcus's brother, and called for him. He was kind, with warm eyes and a contagious smile. 'Princess, how can we help you?'

'I need a favour, Ryan,' I said breathlessly. He only needed to look down to realise what had happened. 'The queen ... she tried to ... my father ... help me, please.'

'Sit down, Your Highness. Get your breath back.' He gathered me into an armchair in the communal area of the guards' residential quarters. His resemblance to his brother was obvious, the soft brown eyes and the small dimples in his cheeks. They shared the same mousey brown hair that fell around their ears in small curls. Their features were almost identical, and they might have been twins if not for their differing frames, Marcus's thin limbs and Ryan's muscular shoulders.

Best of all: they were both kind. They were always there to listen, and to help me escape my daily responsibilities whenever I needed a short release. I knew I could rely on them today, as well. 'Marcus, I need you. Lienus, Titus, Cassius, I need your help. But with the ultimate secrecy.'

All at once, the guards crowded their king and began carrying him into a bedroom, where they laid him out on a bed. Marcus checked his pulse, and Ryan whispered words that had my heart thundering in my chest, 'Is he gone?'

I could not breathe. Could not think, could not move. This could not be happening.

'No, he is still with us, but his pulse is faint,' said Ryan. Those words filled me with relief, and eventually the panic attack passed. 'What happened, Your Highness?'

I rushed through everything I had heard the queen say, the way the guards had refused to help me, and described them in detail when they asked what they looked like, telling me that they had not met or heard of them. This only confirmed my suspicion that the queen had brought guards of her own to the palace, although how she had done so was another thing altogether.

'We will get through this, Your Highness,' said Ryan softly, offering me his hand.

'My brother is right. Your father will survive this,' Marcus agreed.

'Is that so?' the voice that appeared behind me set my pulse racing again, my heart hammering in my chest. When I turned around, there she was, the woman that had married my father for his power and status, and poisoned him for his throne. At her wedding, she had seemed almost timid, as if she were afraid of me. But now, she peered down at me from her high horse with a serpent-like smile. 'Hello, Princess. It appears that we have much to discuss.'

12

WINNIE

Darkness surrounds me.

I'm sure I'm in the witch's cabin again because I can hear the same cackling from before, but I can't see anything. I stumble into something soft, and yet solid. Velvet cushions, and a thick wooden frame beneath them. A bed of some kind? I'm on the carpet, so I move carefully to my feet and inhale deeply, only to be hit by the strong scent of ... lavender, like my mother's favourite perfume. It's comforting, and I find myself warming to it, relishing in the reminder of home.

The sound of heavy breathing appears from somewhere nearby. Then a hollow voice says, 'Wicked,' in a tone that contains nothing but malice. Instantly, I'm pulled away from the house I shared with my parents and brought back into this ... darkness. 'Where are you?' the voice asks, and it seems to be coming from another room. It's not in front of me or behind me, but it's close. Too close.

But my name isn't Wicked, so it isn't me they're searching for. Is this

Wicked somewhere nearby, and does this mean I am in danger?

A torchlight flickers nearby, painting the room in a shroud of golden light and revealing a wide bed, the one I fell into, and shelves full of leather-cased books. A basin sits in the corner.

As the intruder calls out again, I slip beneath the bed, the fear inside me causing my body to tremble. 'Wicked?' they call out. 'I know you're here.'

My breathing is shallow as I hide, praying to every possible god that I will not be found.

'You have been ignoring your curse, Wicked,' the elderly voice says as the woman – no, the witch – appears in the doorway. I can see the toe of her brown leather boot, and hear her feet crunching against the floor. 'Using the name you sacrificed to me, even though it no longer belongs to you.'

As those words begin to sink in, my mind clears. The sacrifice I made when I arrived in her cabin after stepping through the mirror, my arrival in Icefall and ... the young witch taking over my mind.

But I'd taken it back, hadn't I? Is that why I'm here, and why she is chasing me? Because I didn't stick to her agreement.

She cackles, a deep and hollow sound that shakes the room. She stands over the bed, and I continue to tremble, hating her with everything in me. 'It seems that my enchantments do not hold you down for long. Well, perhaps I must use a stronger spell.' She looms over me with a knife in her hands, and tears me out from beneath the bed. I'm kicking and screaming for someone to come and save me. But it's just me and the witch. She lifts the knife. 'I will teach you a lesson, Wicked.'

A shrill scream bursts from my throat as the knife begins to turn and fall, blade first, toward my face.

Sweat drenched my sheets, and I woke up screaming in the bed in my royal suite, my entire body soaked and trembling with terror. There was the chaise lounge, and the wide window revealing the busy courtyard full of royals and nobles, celebrating the king's wedding. There was the large bed with silk sheets, the little en suite, the writing desk and the shelves overflowing with books.

It was just a nightmare, my mind's way of processing everything that had happened since Mum left. Since we'd stepped through the mirror and entered the Winter kingdom. It was nothing but a silly dream. I inhaled, calming myself as I realised I wasn't dead or impaled. I was still in the Icefall palace, and my mother was married and ... my mother was married to the Winter king. The reality struck me like a blade to the throat.

She was now the queen of Icefall.

A sudden dizziness overwhelmed me, and I sat up slowly, reminding myself of where I was, and *who* I was. The dream was only a warning from the witch, although a terrifying one, but I was alive. I was Winnie Braxton, and I was safe. My head felt light again, and stars swam before my vision.

Before another thought could appear, I blacked out.

When I woke again, I wasn't alone. It was still dark outside, so it must still have been the night of the wedding. When had I fallen asleep?

My head was still clear of the witch's consciousness, and no more of her memories had materialised yet, but there was my mother, perched at the end of my bed and watching me with a curious expression. She was dressed in one of her fine gowns, a nightdress with white and blue lace, and her dark hair had fallen down over her chest in light waves. She was as stunning as I'd ever seen her.

But there was something ... different about her now, and I couldn't work it out. A strange glint in her dark blue eyes, as a satisfied grin settled on her lips. 'Winnella, darling, you're awake,' she whispered, leaning forward and planting a kiss on my cheek. 'Very good. You are going to help me with something.'

I sat up slowly, rubbing my eyes, sleep making it hard to wake up properly and concentrate on everything she was saying. 'What is it, Mum?'

Her smile was wide, a strange knowing in it that made me feel a bit sick. I knew that look. She was planning something, and fear crept through me at the thought that I would soon discover what it was. 'How far would you go to be happy, Winnella? What would you do to get back to your father, and be safe and well?'

Seriously? What kind of a question was that? My gaze fell to the floor, and I was suddenly unable to meet her intense stare. 'Why, Mum? What do you want from me? Because all I want is for us to go home together and be a happy family again.'

Those were my dreams, but I wasn't a fool, and I sensed, by the wild look on her face, that we were well past that now. Our family would never be the same again.

What tricks did she still have up her sleeve?

She waved a hand around at the room, gesturing at the grandness of my new bed, my other smaller pieces of furniture like the writing desk, the wide view of the grounds and the snow-kissed hills beyond. The room that was double the size of my bedroom back home. 'Very soon, this kingdom will be ours. *Ours,* not just mine, dearest. His Majesty has almost expired, and his time here is almost up. As for his only heir, well, you could take her place, if you wanted to.'

If I could scramble back through the headboard of my bed, I would have done it. Horror, white-hot, burned in my chest as I realised what she'd done. The king, and his daughter, Princess Frost. All of those lies spread to leave my father, to heal his sickness and marry this king, and this was how their story had ended. She was urging me to join her and become her *heir.*

My mother was evil.

Her eyes were fixed on mine as she said, 'I would rather not kill the child myself, but you ... you may wish to prove your loyalty to me, Winnella.' She even had the audacity to smile. She knew exactly what she was doing here. 'How did it feel when you killed the witch? Didn't you taste that honey sweet revenge? You could have all that again, and more, if you do this for me.'

I couldn't have come from her. This monster wasn't my mother. 'No, I refuse. Killing that witch was an accident, and you know that!' Where had all of this cruelty come from?

Lying to Dad and marrying the king was one thing, but this was a whole other ballgame. She thought she could take the king's place, that I'd take the princess's, and then we could run off together and play happy families as queen and princess. This was madness. She was off her rocker. No way.

She laughed softly before she said, 'I know you didn't mean it, but didn't it feel good, my love?'

'No, it didn't! I have never felt so ... disgusting. So ashamed, and so *dirty*. I wouldn't wish that feeling upon my worst enemy. How can you speak of *killing* someone so calmly and laugh about it?'

She ran her fingers through my blonde hair, but I flinched and smacked her hand away. Her smile faded instantly, and her eyes darkened. 'That feeling will pass, my love. But I'm afraid I wasn't asking. You have no choice. You will do this for me, and perhaps you will even come to *enjoy* it.' She laughed as my wrists were bound in chains that seemed to have materialised out of nowhere.

Like magic.

'How did you do that?' She had never done anything like that before, at least not before my eyes. She was a stranger, and it stung, knowing that she wasn't who she said she was. That she had been lying to me, my whole life, it seemed. 'I don't know who you are anymore.'

She just winked. 'Never mind that. Come along, sweetheart. We have a kingdom to take.' She reached out to stroke a strand of hair away from my face, but I flinched. Her smile faded and her features contorted in rage at my rejection.

'I want to go home,' I said softly, although deep down I think I knew I never would. This journey had been a waste of time. Bringing her home would only cause us more pain. So, what now? Wishing would get me nowhere, but still I found myself hissing, 'I wish I had never followed you through that mirror.'

'This is your home now, Winnella. Ours.' She was watching me with a saddened expression now, her smugness having faded. There was a sincerity in her eyes, as if the façade of playing this strong and powerful woman had worn her down, and now she had opened herself up and was showing her true emotions. My words had hurt her.

Good. She deserved to feel all of the pain and hurt she had brought upon me and my father. Not to mention the king and his daughter, and the kingdom of Icefall. I would have to work on finding the potion for him, and ending Cranwick's curse. But for now, everything was too complicated. 'Never.' I struggled against the restraints, and made it clear that I would never commit to her barbaric plans.

I would always love my mother, but how could I go along with such cruelty? She wanted me to kill the princess for her, after she'd already killed the king. But if she thought I would become the heartless creature that she was, she didn't know me at all.

And she certainly wasn't the mother I had always known and loved. She truly was a stranger.

13

FROST

MY SHOULDER MUSCLES BURNED, my gut twisted with fear and rage, and I felt dizzy, as if I might pass out at any moment. But those symptoms were nothing in comparison to the ache in my heart as I knelt beside my father, who was now unconscious on the throne room floor.

To the pain inside me as my stepmother stared down at us from my father's high throne, smirking, like this was all just a game. And as much as I did not wish to admit it, she was winning. Good for her.

My father was one of the few good things left in my life, and she wanted to take him away from me.

She truly was a monster.

But she just smiled as she peered around at the wide room that she had stolen from my father, the brutal satisfaction clear on her face. Her daughter, Winnella, knelt below her throne, eyes lowered to the ground as if she were afraid to look up and face her mother or any of her guards.

When I gripped my father's cotton shirt, I found that the wound was still fresh. What could I do? No matter how many times I tried to shake him, kiss his cheek or stroke his hair, he did not wake. It was as if he was truly gone. But I could not bear the thought of that, so I slipped my fingers through his, held them tightly in my own, and hoped we would get out of this.

'How does it feel, Princess, to lose everything?' the queen said proudly, gesturing at my father. The mask she had worn at the wedding had been ripped away now, and she no longer held a false smile. She was her true self in this moment, it seemed. A completely different person to the one I had seen in the ballroom only hours ago. 'You did not want me to marry your father, did you?'

'You were reluctant to marry him,' I snarled. 'And as if *you* lost everything! You had a family, a husband and a daughter. You had a life, and yet *you* decided to throw it all away.' I did not miss the way the girl's eyes flickered to me before falling back down again. She was clearly as terrified of her mother as I was. But I refused to be that timid.

The queen cast me a knowing glare. 'Not everything is crystal clear, child. Yes, I had a family, but I also had a husband who was sick and dying, and a daughter who was, for some time, blissfully unaware of that fact.'

Tears shone in the girl's eyes, but she wiped them quickly away with a sleeve.

'I had the chance to make things right, so I took it. But things do not always turn out as we hope they will. But you have already discovered that, haven't you, child? You tried to stop my wedding, but you failed.' She gestured a hand at her daughter and said, 'She tried to stop me leaving Cranwick, but she failed. You both would have taken all of this from me.' She glanced around the room, eyes wild. She was living in a dream world. She was insane, and I would have her thrown into an asylum by the time I was finished with her. 'But now it is mine.'

'This is not your kingdom, Stepmother,' I growled. 'And it never will be. Your daughter was right to stop you. You should both have stayed in your pathetic, cursed little village. You should never have come here!'

Her laughter echoed through the throne room. 'You are showing your true colours now, aren't you, Princess? You are just as fiery as your mother.'

If my blood was not bubbling over before, which it was, that would have done it. My body began to tremble when those words appeared, and kept repeating themselves over and over in my head. 'You knew my mother?' How was it possible, if this woman had spent her life in the cursed Mirror Village?

No, there was no way. She was just trying to get into my head.

She chose that moment to step down from the dais, passing her daughter and gently patting her head, making the girl wince, before coming to stand over me.

Behind her, Winnella was trembling, her eyes frantically searching the room. She wanted to act, I realised, but she was terrified. She needed to get her act together soon if she was going to do something.

I attempted to move to my feet, but the queen's guards forced me back to my knees. Her dark blue eyes pierced through mine as she leered over me, her voice echoing through the room as she said, 'It doesn't matter if I knew her or not, child. Your father has told me plenty, as have your weak little palace servants. Her ghost still lingers in this palace, her presence is in every hidden corner. Her statue shining in the gardens. How could I not have heard of the beautiful and kindhearted Queen Rosa Winter? They all love the late queen; she is all they seem to talk about. But when I am finished with them, Princess, I promise they will love me more.'

Despite myself, laughter burst from my lips. She must have been dreaming if she thought she could ever live up to my mother's reign. 'You are delirious.'

She did not answer, but a sharp pain stung my cheek, bringing tears to my eyes. She had slapped me hard across the face, her blade-like nails scraping my skin. Only then did she say, 'You would do well not to insult me, child.'

Then, in a flash, everything changed.

Winnella rose to her feet and placed a hand on her mother's shoulder, eyes widening as her mother turned to face her. Then, she spat in her mother's face. Shoved her hard in the chest, taking her by surprise. Then she stood over her mother with a defiant glare contorting her features. 'Let her go, Mother,' she cried, shaking against her restraints just as I realised she was chained to an iron bar at the base of the throne.

'And me, too. I don't belong here. You're not my mum anymore. I want to go home.' Her voice trembled, making her sound small and frail like a child or a small animal.

But she had stood up to her mother, tried to make her release the both of us, despite the fear that had made her silent. That had taken courage that I had not thought she possessed before. Impressive.

The queen only cackled again, and her guards helped her to her feet. 'I am afraid I cannot let that happen, Winnella. You had your chance to be my heir, and eventually I will wear you down. But for now, I suppose I will have to do things differently. You have left me with no choice.'

The queen lifted her hands, and her men brought forward a steel cage on wheels, and when the queen inclined her head, they released Winnella from the base of the throne and shoved her into the cage. I was forced to watch as they rolled her to one side of the room, with the girl inside screaming and clutching the bars.

How barbaric. Something very dark must have been rotting inside my stepmother for her to treat her own daughter like that.

Then a new cage was brought forward, and the guards began to approach me. But instead of pushing me into it as I expected them to, they tore my father's limp form away from me, more guards storming forward to haul me back as I fought to stop them. But they threw him into the cage and took him from me.

'No, Father!' When he was gone, I ran before the queen and charged at her, slipping my knife out of my boot.

But the very moment I faced her, I was blasted backwards by an invisible force, and thrown across the room.

As if by *magic*.

When the guards brought me back to my knees, the queen nodded silently and my stomach twisted with dread. The guards restrained me no matter how many times I bit, slapped and kicked at them. It did not matter what I did or how strong I thought I was, it would never be enough against her enchanted soldiers.

A magical, evil queen.

But she had one final surprise in store for me: Ryan was dragged into the throne room, his face bloodied, and with one eye swollen shut. This sight was the last straw, and I pounced on the queen.

But the guards swarmed me in an instant, and I was unable to get close enough.

The queen stared at me, eyes full of wicked delight. 'I will not kill you, Princess. In fact, I am rather enjoying this little game we are playing.'

She peered down at me as she strode over to Ryan, took his head into her hands with her bony fingers prying his hair, and tore a jewel-studded dagger out of the side of her boot. From her cage, Winnella's eyes widened with horror as she studied the blade, wondering how long her mother could have been hiding such a beautiful weapon.

'Three strikes and you're out?' said the queen with a dark grin, her teeth glinting in the light.

Ryan grunted, and I whimpered as she swiped the knife hard across his throat, and my friend crumpled to the floor. His blood soaked her hands, and in the same instant it began pooling around him.

But the queen did not cry out or let any sign of regret play out across her features. She simply looked down at her blood-drenched fingers and laughed. 'That will teach you not to play me, won't it? Strike one.' Then her eyes grew large as they settled on mine again with a hard stare.

'That was strike two! You taking my father was the first!' I growled. My hands gripped her gown and I pulled her toward me, seeing red with rage. I scraped my knife over her chest, watching with satisfaction at the stream of blood that poured through the rip I had created.

Strike one.

Before I could move again, her knife was at my throat and her hand pulled at my hair. 'You have ten seconds to run, child, before I change my mind and send my guards after you. Do not try to go after your father, because if you do, you will find yourself alongside my daughter, a pretty bird trapped inside a cage. I suggest you go, quickly.' She released me and I fell to the floor.

I clambered backwards, thinking only of my father and Ryan as I ran from the room, leaving Icefall, and my father behind.

Part Two

The Fragile, the Fierce & the Muted

14

WINNIE

Never had I felt more like a coward than I did in that throne room, frozen still and unable to confront my mother about her cruelty.

Now, look where it had gotten me: knee deep in urine and excrement in the dungeons at the base of the Winter palace. I had let my father down. The reason we were here in the first place was to find him a potion that would end his sickness, but I'd been so caught up in everything that had been going on in the palace, that I'd barely given him any thought.

I was a terrible daughter.

And I had let myself down, ending up hauled away by my mother's enchanted guards. Was she a witch all of this time? That would just be another thing she had refused to tell me.

But, somehow, that didn't feel right. Her magic appeared to be coming from a different source altogether. There was something strange about it, a confidence I had seen in her when she taunted the princess. When she performed her magic, it was like she'd been doing it for *forever*.

I should have acted sooner, told my mother I would work with her, if only so I could stop her before she killed that boy on the royal guard or ordered her men to leave the unconscious king at my feet.

Here he was, a brutal reminder of everything my mother had already done to destroy this kingdom. No matter how many times I tried to wake him, he wouldn't open his eyes.

Not only that, but the poor, grieving soldier, Ryan's brother, and the others, were all crammed into the cell beside mine. I could hear them talking, breathing heavily and sobbing, making me feel more helpless than ever.

What we needed now was an escape plan. God, when had my life become an adventure story? 'Boys?' I hissed through the metal grating between my cell and theirs. 'Guards?'

There was no answer, but my cell door opened and the guard behind it poked his head in and snapped, 'No talking!' before slamming it shut again.

How had the others not been scolded for that?

How unfair.

'Ignore the guard, we have to get out of here,' an unwelcome yet familiar voice appeared inside my head. Was I going insane down here, or was that Wicked? *'It's me, Wicked, you fool.'*

Well, that answered that. Now, of all times, was when she chose to pop up again? Could this get any worse? Somehow, I doubted it.

'Things can always get worse, Winnie. Don't talk like that.'

'Get the hell out of my head!'

'Stop being a child, and take advantage of the fact that you have someone else to scheme your grand exit plan with.'

As much as I hated to admit it, she was correct. The more the merrier? Oh, it was useless.

'Damn right I am. Now, think positively, no more feeling sorry for yourself.'

Who did she think she was, my mother? Although, honestly, anyone would have been a better replacement than the murderess in the throne room.

But if she would stop telling me what to do, maybe I could concentrate. I peered through the grating, and found the boys clustered together in the neighbouring cell. One of them was holding his arm close to his chest as if it were broken, and a few of them had eyes that were swollen or bloodied like they'd been beaten. Ryan, the boy my mother had killed in the throne room, was lying in the corner of their cell as a reminder, no doubt, of their new position in the palace.

We were all as lost as each other. Maybe we could work together, and even find the princess as well. That was one of the things I'd heard his brother mention as I was dragged into this cell with the king.

She had let the princess go as some kind of game. Because every evil queen in the fairytale books loved having a little princess to torment.

'Get a move on,' Wicked admonished. 'Don't you want to get out of here? And they do, too.'

'Of course I do. Alright, alright.' I scanned the cell, and the space outside it. There were three stocky, bored looking guards armed to the teeth behind the cell doors, and a door at the end of the hall, no doubt the one that led to the higher floors of the palace.

One that would lead us out of it. Maybe? It was hard to tell in this maze of a building. 'Hey, Marcus,' I whispered through the grating, praying that the guards wouldn't shove their heads into my cell to tell me to be quiet again. This time, to my relief, they didn't hear me, but the trapped guards did. One by one, they lifted their heads to the grating, but it was Ryan's brother that I wanted.

'Do you have any spare weapons?' Perhaps I was clinging to hope, and I didn't know if I would even be able to hurt another person like that, but we needed something at least for self-defence, and they must have a small blade that we could use. All I had was an unconscious king and a few hairpins.

'Are you mad?' Marcus snapped. 'If we did, do you think we'd be in here?'

'Sorry...' How rude. But the boy had just lost his brother, so I supposed I should give him the benefit of the doubt.

'I have something, Marcus,' whispered one of the guards beside him. 'Managed to smuggle this in.'

'Titus, you genius,' Marcus said. He took the knife from his friend and twisted it in the light. The wooden handle was carved with pretty patterns, although it probably meant more to the guard than that. They all revealed another knife which was engraved, and a few paper notes. 'How about you, queen monster's girl? Anything useful?'

Queen monster's girl? Was he serious? I prepared an answer, ready to give him a piece of my mind.

But before he could say another word or I could snap back, one of the guards pushed their door open and growled, 'What is going on in here? Better not be talking!' If he saw their weapons, they were screwed. But to my relief, Titus had managed to slide them out of sight. The guard pushed forward, grabbed Marcus by his shoulders, hissing, 'Answer me!' Then when the boy said nothing, he let him go. 'Unless you want to end up like your brother, be quiet.' He locked the door again and went off to find his fellow guardsmen.

I held up the hairpins, letting my braid fall, and began searching the king's clothing, cursing myself for not doing so sooner. *'You've not been much help so far, Wicked,'* I cursed the witch inwardly. *'Make yourself useful, won't you?'* The king had a small knife on his person, which I was sorry to take, but I hoped he could eventually forgive me under the circumstances.

I held it up so the boys could see it, then worked on the door with the hairpins, and slowly unlocked it, leaving it closed. As soon as the coast was clear, I would make my escape.

'Help them,' said the witch, ignoring my comments and choosing to

boss me around again. *'Give them the hairpins.'*

'That was next on my list, don't you worry.' Something occurred to me then. 'You're a witch? Know any good sleeping spells?'

'Against mage soldiers? No way. My memory isn't exactly what it used to be right now, but even if it was, I wouldn't –'

'Please, Wicked, there must be something *you can do.'* I heard her sigh as it echoed through my brain, a sound that made me shudder inside. 'Marcus,' I whispered, handing him the pins through the grating while she filled me in on her limited store of spells that she could recite from memory. She would have to tell me her spells and I would repeat them, which might be awkward as I could barely speak my own language without becoming tongue tied, but it was progress.

Her idea made better sense than mine, of sending the guards to sleep. But we had a plan in motion, and that was all that mattered. I quickly told the boys what Wicked had said, and then watched them unlock their cell door as I had done with mine.

The queen's guards returned to their post, and we waited. As I recited the spell from Wicked, word by word, they began to file out of the dungeons, one by one, every one of them hearing the queen's voice calling to them, requesting assistance in the upper floors of the palace. It didn't matter that there was no one left to supervise their prisoners. They were transfixed, as if possessed.

It was strictly genius on Wicked's part. But it wouldn't be long before the queen noticed we were gone, so we needed to move quickly.

We left our cells quietly, and slipped out into the night. The guards hauled the king through the snow, and together we headed for the Winter Forest, the boys taking turns to carry the sleeping king between them.

We walked for some time, the guards seemingly unfazed by the eerie stillness of the forest before us, as they entered a clearing a short distance away, crickets chirping in the trees and birds piercing the silence.

It was only then that I realised my sleeveless gown wouldn't be enough to keep me warm in the cold night air, and I began to shiver. One of the boys, Titus, kindly removed his thick cloak and wrapped it around my shoulders, leaving himself frozen in only a thin cotton shirt. He kept moving, muscles tensing as they continued to carry the king.

'Thank you,' I whispered. 'But I don't want you to be cold … ,' my voice trailed off as I realised I didn't know what to say in response to his compassion. The only people who had ever been so kind to me were Dad, Barchester and … my mother. A shudder overwhelmed me again, but this time it wasn't from the freezing weather.

'Don't worry, Princess,' he said coolly, before turning away again. 'I'm more accustomed to the cold than you clearly are.'

'I'm not a –'

He chuckled, his dark hair falling into his eyes as we continued to move. 'Your mother is a queen, isn't she?' His eyes were a pale blue, like ice. His features were thin and narrow, his lips full. He could have been carved by the Roth witches' goddess herself. They all could have. But his kindness, in particular, made him handsome.

The others seemed less inclined to speak to me unless they had to, especially Marcus. I slunk down into myself, unsure of what else to say. Titus was right that my mother was a queen, but I didn't feel comfortable calling myself a princess while the real princess was out there somewhere, lost and afraid of her future without her home.

But I didn't need to answer the question anyway because the moment we stopped for the boys to catch their breath, they turned on me.

One by one, the questions came.

'How in Icefall did you do that?' Marcus cried.

'Are you a witch? A sorceress like your mother?' said Titus.

'How can we trust you now?' said Lienus, running a hand frustratedly through his sandy blonde hair. His green eyes were wild with fear and confusion, just like the rest of them. 'You might turn out to be just like her. What if you're secretly working for her?'

'I might ask you the same. You all used to be the king's guards, didn't you? Well, how do *I* know you haven't been taken over by my mother? How do I know that any of *you* aren't working against *me?*'

Their silence told me everything I wanted to know. They were so quick to judge me because I wasn't one of them, and because I was the daughter of the cruel queen, but none of them had stopped to think about how *they* might appear to *me*.

Worst of all, they were all staring at me like I had grown another head, eyes full of suspicion and fear. But they didn't know what was really happening inside my mind. I couldn't blame them for being confused, but how would I even begin to explain what had happened back there?

That I had a witch's conscience in my mind?

That a curse had, for the first time, become our saving grace.

So, let them judge me. They knew nothing yet, but soon they would learn just how wrong they were.

'What do you mean, how can you trust me? I just saved your arses, didn't I?'

'Not my brother, though,' said Marcus.

That stung. A low blow. Even if Wicked's magic was my own, how could I have helped Ryan without my mother killing me, too? Clearly the woman wasn't so opposed to killing children, after all.

'You could have saved him then, worked your magic charm on the throne room,' said Marcus, but this time there were tears rolling down his face.

The feeling of hurt within me faded slightly. He was just grieving; he didn't mean to take it out on me. It wasn't personal. But I wasn't going to be disrespected. I didn't need them. Snow began to fall as I walked away from the ungrateful bastards, only to stop when I remembered they still had the king. 'Wow. You're all welcome, by the way.'

'You're right, I'm sorry,' said Marcus, his words making me turn around and stop in my tracks. 'That was cruel of me. Thank you for getting us out of there, however you did it.' He smiled softly. 'I suppose it's hard to trust what you don't understand.'

Despite myself, I laughed darkly, the irony comical. 'Believe me, I know. But don't worry, I'm no witch. Although ... '

'Although?' he pressed.

'It's a long story,' I said. If I told them the truth, there was a chance we would be here all night.

He let out a laugh, and the others joined him. 'Come on, you can explain while we search for the princess. She has to be out here somewhere.'

'He's cute, but don't go getting distracted now,' said Wicked. She was right, but flirting with some boy soldiers was the last thing on my mind right now. There was far too much at stake.

'Shut up, Wicked, I'm not into boys.' Well, perhaps that was a lie. I wasn't *only* into boys.

Wicked's inner voice contained what could only be a sly edge as she said, 'Never mind that. You've had your time to shine, Princess, now it's my turn.'

I was sure then that if I could see her right now, she would have a huge smirk on her face, and I didn't like that thought one little bit. *'What do you mean?'*

No, no, no. She couldn't be considering pushing me back down into that mental tunnel again. She wouldn't do that to me, would she?

Who was I kidding? Of course she would.

I had done exactly the same thing to her.

'Farewell, Princess.'

'No!' Before I could say another word, or try to take control of my own mind, she cast me aside and I found myself spiralling, falling, down, down, down.

Then she locked the door, and I was trapped inside my own mind once more.

15

WICKED

FINALLY, MY MIND WAS PEACEFUL AND QUIET.

No more mental battles, debates or arguments to distract me from our plans. Because, by the goddess, that girl could overthink an orange into an apple. She was far too slow, too easily preoccupied with her own emotions. But me, I would get the job done without all of the dramatics.

Our first task had been to escape the dungeons, and that much we had done.

She would try to find the princess, while I would search for the witch who had cursed me and make her pay. Leave Winnie and Princess Frost to save the kingdom, or whatever they chose to do. I would find Princess Frost if it helped me pacify Winnie for a while longer.

So I set off through the snow, with the unconscious king and his boy soldiers at my side. Icefall wasn't my problem, nor was the queen sitting on its throne, but the witch was. Specifically, the Elder witch who'd cursed

Winnie and brought us together.

For what reason? I truly hoped this wasn't intentional on the witch's part, simply a big misunderstanding. One that she would soon rectify.

'You seem different, Winnie,' said one of the boys, Marcus, their leader. 'I'm sorry if we were rude to you before ... are you alright?' Was I dreaming or was he actually looking at this girl with affection in his eyes? Maybe she hadn't noticed in her naivety, but to me it was obvious. I sure didn't miss the way his gaze flickered to my – her – lips.

Great, more emotions to get in the way of our purpose. Not happening. 'Just dandy,' I snapped, turning away from him and striding on ahead.

He eyed me suspiciously, and his brothers soon followed suit, as they had when they'd first witnessed my use of magic in the dungeons. 'Alright. Well, let us know if you need anything.'

'Why, because I'm a woman? I don't need you, or anyone else,' I hissed, quickening my pace. 'Now, hurry.' We stormed through the snow, deeper into The Winter Forest, which was rumoured to contain many dangers like wolves and other vicious beasts. But the cold was the worst killer. You wouldn't survive for long without the appropriate resources. And this stupid little gown wasn't going to do me any favours, even with the cloak I'd been offered, which meant I would have to find shelter very soon.

'If you don't need us, we may as well split off,' said Marcus, forcing me to spin back around to face him. 'We don't need you, either.'

'Don't be silly. We're not here to make friends, but we can all help each other.'

He laughed, but he was still watching me with suspicion, casting glances at the other boys as if he hoped they might agree with him that I was acting rashly. 'Very well, Winnella. We'll work together until we find her.'

'It's Winnie.' Because I wasn't about to explain that I wasn't really her when it would only cost us valuable time.

On the other side of the clearing, through the white-blanketed trees, was a flicker of dark brown hair and the flash of a sparkling red ballgown. Not exactly the type of gown you'd want to be wearing out here, alone in the forest.

I tore through the snow, over frozen twigs and thorns, the tail of my dress snagging on the bushes as I scraped past them. I ran after her, the snow's surface so cold against my ankles that it burned.

Tears streamed down the princess's face as she bounded through the darkness, her screams for her father disturbing the night's peaceful silence. All I could do was watch her, hesitantly at first, harbouring no patience for her tears, but then softening when I remembered everything she'd lost, and wishing there was some way I could help. Winnie's influence, no doubt, those pesky emotions peeking through.

The king was here with us now, safe and alive, and Princess Frost didn't even know it. But how long did he have before the icy cold overtook him, or the queen returned to finish what she'd begun?

The princess fell onto the snow in a heap, and I lingered in the distance, just observing her. I had never seen anyone so helpless, and I felt the same, knowing there was nothing I could do to take her pain away. I sank down against the tree I leaned on, and peered around at the beauty that surrounded me, as if to find a distraction or a way out of this mess.

The Winter Forest was more beautiful than I could have ever imagined. Frozen ice clung to the tree branches, while soft snow covered every rock and patch of grass on the ground. Many had fallen here, vulnerable to the cold and unknown dangers lurking in the night. And yet here I was, chasing this foolish princess in the middle of the night, like an idiot.

'What are you doing? Go and get her,' Marcus said, kneeling closely behind me, the others somewhere nearby. 'We don't want her to freeze out here, do we?'

I had told Winnie to move quickly so perhaps I would be a fool to admonish this guard for doing the same, but I also didn't want to rush over to the princess and scare her off. 'Just thinking it through,' I snapped. 'Where do you plan to take her once she's on our side? To set up a bed in one of the nearby trees, where a wolf could pick at our bones? No, thank you.'

His soft laughter lingered close to my ear. 'Lucky for you, we have somewhere we can all go.' He glanced around the forest, staring thoughtfully into the distance, but his gaze gave away no sign of where this mysterious location would be.

Eyes widening in surprise, I said, 'And you didn't think to mention that before? Do enlighten me, soldier boy.'

'You haven't told us how you got us all out of the dungeons yet, so don't be such a hypocrite,' he argued, but there was a hint of amusement in his tone. He seemed to flip between suspicion and being amused by my words. Perhaps this was as much of a game to him as it was to the queen.

'Fine,' I said quickly. 'I'll explain soon.'

As he began to tell us where he planned to take the princess and her unconscious father, hope appeared like a light in my heart.

It triggered something: a sudden memory, vivid as a night's dream. Perhaps the exhaustion was making me more prone to hallucinations, or the witch's enchantment still lingered inside. Either way, there was no escaping the images as they came.

I was lying on the ground, practically buried in the snow with a bearskin coat wrapped around my shoulders.

Seeing my original form was quite a shock to the system. I had almost forgotten what I actually looked like. It was like looking at an old painting of myself. I was a fair bit taller than Winnie. My auburn hair fell in a long braid to my waist, and I wore thick leather trousers with a full-sleeved cotton shirt and knee-high boots, my typical uniform as my sisters and I were well travelled, and it always helped to be able to breathe as we moved. No pretty corsets for us.

A tall figure approached me, staring down at me with his piercing blue eyes, raven hair falling in light curls around his chin.. 'Wake up, Wicked,' he said softly, before leaning down to brush his soft lips against mine. 'Has the headache gone away yet?'

It was as if I was watching the memory from far away, but I was also feeling everything: the pounding in my skull, that passionate kiss, the warmth of the bearskin coat against my skin, and the burning love and desire for this hunter. His eyes were filled with warmth.

'Hello, Wicked?' he said again. 'I asked you a question.'

'Sorry. I'm a little tired, Greyson.' Greyson Marks: the name came to mind in a flash. My betrothed. We had been engaged for three years. He was the leader of the Ajanid Clan of Mages, a clan of powerful spellcasters, and honestly I was a little shocked that I'd managed to forget about him. The witch truly had messed with my memories, and probably Winnie's as well. 'What's happening?' I murmured, more to myself.

The memory continued with Greyson leaning in to kiss me again. Then he pulled me to my feet as we caught sight of a girl running through the snow, dressed in a silk white gown. Her pale pink hair was braided back, but loose strands fell wildly at her shoulders as she fled. Her thin shoulders and pale feet were bare. They were in the frozen forest, where I was in this moment.

They chased the girl and caught hold of her, although she was obviously freezing and terrified. They plunged her face down into the snow, ignoring her screams. Who was she, and why were they hunting her like this?

'Come on Wicked, here is your time to show me who you are,' said Greyson, still pinning the girl down. She kicked, screamed and thrashed. I watched myself as if from a distance as I leaned over the girl and conjured power in my mind.

The girl still fought, but then she began to change. Before Wicked now, the girl became a porcelain doll, unable to move.

'Wicked, why would you do such a thing?' Inside my head, Winnie's voice echoed, her words causing my stomach to twist with shame and regret.

Her question remained unanswered, and I forced her deeper down in the back of my head. Soon, I would be strong enough that she wouldn't resurface again.

'You did it,' said Greyson with a smile. 'You are finally rid of your nemesis.'

My voice was mine, but it didn't seem like the words were coming from my lips as I snarled and said, 'She did have it coming to her, though, didn't she? Poor little Autumn princess, scheming against my coven, trying to turn us all into frogs. At least she looks pretty in porcelain.'

'What good will that do us?' said the mage clan leader.

My memory-self even gasped as Greyson rammed the hilt of his sword into the Autumn princess's porcelain body, causing the remnants of her to shatter.

16

WINNIE

Wicked thought she was strong, but she wasn't strong enough to keep me down forever.

That memory must have done something to her, *weakened* her, because it had been easy to take control again. As much as she didn't want to admit it, we really did have to work together. I didn't want her in my head, but clearly I was stuck with her.

We had broken out of the dungeons for god's sake, surely she could see we were more powerful as a pair. She clearly didn't care for anything or anyone but herself, and her only goal was to get her body back, while mine were more important: to find the antidote to my father's sickness, and to find the poor grieving princess and help her so she wouldn't be lost and alone in the forest for any longer.

My mother had wanted me to kill the princess, but I was determined to defy her and flip her plan for Icefall on its head. If I was trapped here, I would at least try to make use of my time before I went home.

'Where is this shelter you speak of?' I asked Marcus as we trailed endlessly through the dark forest. My fingers were numb with the cold, and my body trembled. 'We must be getting closer by now.'

'Don't worry, it's just through this clearing,' Marcus reassured me, still oblivious to the warzone inside my head. 'We have to stop the princess from going off course.' I followed his gaze through the trees, searching once again for a flash of a bloodred ballgown, but she'd vanished from sight. 'Although, it looks like she already has. She must have gone that way.' He pointed downward at a set of markings in the snow. He was right; her footprints revealed her path.

We followed them quickly, faces pink and lips chapped with the bitter night air. 'You still haven't told me how you know of this place we're going to,' I said quietly, still deep in my thoughts.

'You'll see, soon. It's a cabin, an outhouse of sorts, for the king's men to stay in when we are travelling beyond the palace gates. It's cosy, with a fire to warm ourselves and some extra clothes and weapons. You'll like it.' He seemed optimistic, and I supposed it was better than nothing.

'Well, thank you.' I hoped this wasn't the first time I'd shown him my gratitude, because without him, I would have been lost and alone in the snow, just like the princess. Wicked's stubbornness wasn't exactly helping matters.

He laughed. 'You're welcome, Princess.'

I'd already been through this with Titus, but now Marcus thought it was just as funny. But it was irritating to be on the receiving end of it. 'Please stop calling me that.'

He held his hands up and chuckled again, as if he'd found some amusement in my irritation. 'Very well, Pr ... Winnie.'

Sometime later, we finally found the princess. She was standing before an icy lake, and she'd gathered her skirts around her ankles as she considered the gentle steps she would have to take to cross it. There was no other route to the clearing on the other side of the forest, and it seemed that she knew it. 'Princess Frost!' I cried, approaching her carefully while the others lingered behind.

She spun around when she heard her name, and her gaze met mine. 'You,' she said, her eyes widening in disbelief. The look was followed by a defiance that I would never have expected from her.

Weren't princesses supposed to be dainty and gentle? But then, she had lost everything. Her father, her kingdom, her home. Could I really blame her for feeling this way? Of course not.

"What are you doing?' she demanded. 'Why did you follow me here?'

It was almost impossible to find the words to describe what we were all doing here, after we'd escaped the dungeons, other than to start with the truth. 'You ran, Princess. We were imprisoned, but we managed to escape. We came to tell you that your father ... he is ...' Right here with us, unconscious but alive. The words were there on my tongue, but they refused to leave my lips.

'Dead. My father is dead, or if not then he will be very soon, and I have no future, and I ... I do not know why I am even talking to you about this, as you would not understand.' She began to move again, picking up her skirts and quickly travelling across the frozen lake with ease, like this was something she'd done a thousand times.

Either she was extremely brave, or a fool. Or maybe both. But she was still the princess, and we still had her father lying at our feet, and we were here to help her if we could.

Still, I was less than confident. But I crawled on my hands and knees, for maybe fifteen feet, slowly ... slowly ... because what other choice did I have? Because it was the right thing to do.

I kept going, tried to climb quickly as she made it to the other side and began to run. 'I do understand, Princess Frost,' I cried. 'I mean, my parents aren't dead like your mother is, but I have ... everything has changed for my family, too.'

To my surprise, she turned back again. 'That is probably for the best after what she did in the throne room! My father's throne room.' Her anger festered into something wild, but then softened as a new understanding began to settle. She hesitated for a moment before continuing, 'You said, dead like my mother is. Not my father. You do not believe my father is dead?' She took a step toward me, eyeing me as closely as she could from the other side of the lake. 'Tell me what you know!'

What was wrong with me? I couldn't even find the words to tell her what had happened since she'd left the palace. 'We will show you, I promise. Come with us.'

She stared at me as if she thought I was mad. But it was impossible to blame her for thinking so. Both my mother and I had broken into her kingdom with witch's tricks and false promises, and she'd lost everything. That was reason enough? She didn't move, but her confusion continued to radiate off her in waves. 'Who is we?' Her gaze searched the space, but she was unable to see the boys or her father's unconscious form from where she was standing. 'And, come with you? Why in Icefall would I do that?'

This was going terribly. I was still stuck on this bloody lake, and the princess clearly hated me.

I couldn't blame her for it, of course, but it still ... sucked. If I was honest, I didn't even know why. It wasn't like we were friends. I supposed it was the guilt creeping in, of knowing that my mother had ruined her life, and I wished I could be the one to fix everything. 'We have a cabin nearby, it belongs to some of your father's guards. We were going to take you there, so you could see your ... father.'

'Who is we?' she repeated. By now, her pale complexion had reddened with anger and frustration. But tears were also sliding down her face, and they kept coming. 'My father? Tell me what you are talking about!'

A breathy sigh left my lips, but I called out, 'Marcus?' to the clearing where the soldiers were waiting patiently for me to speak to the princess. He'd wanted to speak to her, but so soon after his brother's death, and the death of her friend, I reminded him that she was hurting enough already. That maybe we should get her to the cabin first, and then we could tell her everything. But clearly, she wasn't going to come with us as willingly as that. We might have to just tell her first, to make it clear that we were on her side.

As these thoughts were spinning around my head, the desperation inside me growing more with each moment that passed, something cracked beneath my right knee. 'Oh, no!' I cried out as the ice cracked further, piece by piece. The boys came running over, all three of them wearing the same frantic expression as I held myself still, my heart pounding like a drum in my chest. I was quickly losing time, and someone needed to do something. 'No!'

My scream pierced the air as the ice beneath me broke, forcing me into the freezing cold water.

The cold stole the air from my lungs as I began to sink deeper and deeper ...

🍎

Stars shone before my eyes, and my chest burned. Nausea forced my body to convulse, as shivers coursed through me.

My clothes stank of dirty water, and the taste of it remained in my throat. But some of it filled my mouth and made me heave all over again. Gross.

There was no way of knowing how long I had been under for. But I glanced upward to find someone patting my cheek. I was lying on the snow now, not the ice. I coughed and retched a stream of icy water and bile, and still I struggled to breathe. I was wrapped in a bearskin coat, and surrounded by coated figures. I looked into the face of ... Greyson Marks. It was the man from my dream, or Wicked's memory, I supposed, although now he was several decades older and with wrinkled skin and short white hair. But those eyes, they clearly belonged to him.

At his side were Princess Frost and the elderly witch. All I could focus on was the witch as she stared down at me with a pair of piercing blue, almost black eyes. 'Wicked,' I said, slowly trying to sit up as I came to the realisation that I must have been dreaming.

Maybe even hallucinating, as a side-effect of the icy lake water in my system. Nothing made sense.

Worse, the princess was staring at me like she wished she could cut off my head with a blunt-edged knife. 'I should have let you drown,' she said, leaning forward so that she was staring right into my face. 'You should be dead like my father.'

'Then, why didn't you leave me to die?' I said, retching between coughs. The combination of water and bile in my mouth tasted like acid. Disgusting. I wanted every last bit of it gone.

'These two showed up,' said Princess Frost, gesturing to the witch and her companion and laughing bitterly, 'practically out of nowhere, and basically begged to me to haul you out of the water. Thanks to you, I am drenched.' She shook herself off, hugging the witch's bearskin coat tighter around herself. It reminded me that if we didn't find shelter soon, we were at risk of dying from hypothermia.

I sat up slowly, but the witch pushed me back down. 'No, rest. Drink this.' She passed me a flask, and I sipped warm water, feeling relief as it heated me inside.

It was a start. It calmed me, and helped me find the words to begin saying how I felt. 'I'm sorry for what my mother did to you, I really am. I promise you; I had no idea what she was planning.'

Perhaps the latter was a little white lie, because I had known why she was coming to Icefall, but how could I have known of the magic she possessed or her plans to murder her new husband for his crown? My life really had become something out of one of my fantasy books, and I wasn't sure how I felt about that.

Despite the fact that she'd saved my life, the princess's eyes were still full of suspicion. 'You were there at the wedding, and after. You were there when he almost ... '

If she wasn't going to believe me, I supposed I would have to prove it. 'Princess Frost, I was going to wait until we reached the cabin to tell you everything, because I didn't want to overwhelm you, but your father isn't dead. He was a big part of our escape plan. Your guard friends helped me ...'

Marcus and the others brought her unconscious father forward, and my heart broke all over again as she crumpled in the snow, wrapping her arms around him and planting kisses on his forehead and cheeks. Then, as she threw herself into Marcus's arms, and embraced each of the young guards with tears rolling down her face.

'Why did you not just tell me that back there?' she cried. Laughter broke out across the forest at her words. We could have saved ourselves a whole lot of trouble, and maybe I wouldn't have almost died as well. 'Thank you, Winnella.'

'I wanted to tell you at the right moment, not like this ... you're welcome, Princess.' I glanced around, but she'd disappeared. 'And thank you for saving me back there.' I wanted to thank Greyson and Wicked as well, but they were also gone.

They had vanished as quickly as they had come, as if they were never there at all.

Leaving me wondering if it was all a dream.

17

FROST

It may have seemed that because the Winter kingdom was my home, I should have known it like the back of my hand. I knew the inside of my palace well, because I had spent my childhood exploring its hidden passages, but perhaps I should have memorised the streets of Icefall so I would know where to go if I ever found myself lost.

But what good was map knowledge when you could never leave the palace unattended? It was not that I was trapped, and in the happier days of my early life, we would take regular trips out through the palace gates, to the Winter Mountains and the Winter Caves beyond.

We would parade through the streets in carriages, and the people would throw flowers and sing songs of love and light.

Icefall had been a beloved kingdom, once.

But the day my mother died, everything changed. My lessons were increased, meaning I was left with barely any time to rest and spend time with my father. But it seemed that our precious evening dinners together were no longer important to him because my invitations were always declined.

He also seemed to shut the people out, and busied himself with meetings with his advisors and generals. This meant that, in turn, other kingdoms began to close their gates to us as well.

We were no longer invited to weddings and other celebrations, nobles and servants spread word about the cold king, and resources that had always been shared evenly between the four kingdoms were not available to us anymore. My beautiful mother had been the connection between the four kingdoms, the ray of light in an otherwise dark world, so of course when she was gone, that light faded.

Our kingdom's treasury began to dim, and with it, my father's loving and happy heart. In the five years that passed, he had become a ghost, casting me away from him and only speaking to me through the palace staff.

And then he had worked hard, day and night, to find a way to heal our broken kingdom. An alliance and a dowry would be the only way through. He would marry, and when that day came, I would be sent off to Windspell to become Prince Hugo's bride. That had been our plan for a long time, but now everything had changed again.

I ran without looking back. A stillness had settled in the air, which only made the icy maze ahead of me seem far eerier. I fled through the trees that seemed endless, and walked for hours as my world crashed and burned around me. If I could get lost here, what good would my people have?

Not to mention that an impostor was sitting upon my father's throne, which should now have been passed down to me. It was not clear if her daughter still followed, or why she had even come after me in the first place.

Perhaps the queen had sent her to kill me, and yet I had just saved her from drowning. But as the ice broke beneath Winnella's body and she cried out for help, all I thought of was Father's limp form as he was carried away from me.

A selfish part of me had wished to watch her die to get back at her mother. But then the guilt had crept into my chest, so I crawled carefully across the ice and tugged her out of the water, knowing that leaving her there would only have made me a monster like Leraia herself. So I pulled her from danger, and laid her down on the snow.

'I'm sorry, Frost,' she said, eyes widening as she stared up at the sky. 'I didn't know what my mother had planned, I promise.' Her voice held a sincerity, and I knew she felt guilty for everything her mother had done.

But those words just tightened their grip around my heart. 'I should have left you here to die,' I told her before bolting away. I left her on the soft ground, which was far better than the icy lake. She would find her way from here eventually. Her mother had killed my father; I owed her nothing.

She claimed he was alive, but I refused to believe it. Gratitude had spread within, until I saw the way his eyes refused to open even when I kissed his cheek. If he was alive, he would not be for long, and I could not bear the heartache of waiting for it to happen.

Perhaps she truly wished to help me, but our loyalties were not aligned. She may not be her mother, but she was her *blood,* and there was a chance that she may soon become her. That was not my father in Marcus's arms, and perhaps it was not even the guards I knew and loved so well at all.

Perhaps Winnella had conjured up these hallucinations to make me follow her. She must have been a magical being, just like her mother. It seemed the cold was affecting my judgement.

I collapsed again in the snow, the exhaustion and the bitter wind finally overwhelming me completely. I must have fallen asleep or passed out because sometime later I woke in a warm bed beside an open fire. A thick woollen robe was wrapped around my shoulders, and there was a bowl of hot soup on a small table at my bedside.

'You're awake,' said a familiar voice. Winnella's voice. She was wrapped up in a robe of her own. I backed away from her as she attempted to bring a spoonful of soup to my lips. 'It's alright, I'm not going to poison you.' I shoved the bowl away a bit too roughly, spilling it down the skirt of her dress. 'Ouch, that's hot!' She sighed, the gap in her robe revealing the gown from the ball. I was still wearing mine as well. A breathy sigh left her lips, and then she stared at me for a moment before a frown creased her brow.

She turned around and began to remove the gown, and changed quickly into a soft navy-blue shirt and some leather trousers, throwing the dress into the basin by the fire. 'Look, I know the witch told you to save me but –'

So many questions came to mind as she said those words, but I settled on one: 'What witch? What are you talking about?' I peered around the cabin, confused, wondering where she was getting these silly ideas from. I had saved her life, but she really thought some *witch* had forced me to. Clearly, it was not just me that was hallucinating as a result of the cold. 'I did that. There was no witch.'

'You didn't see the witch and the mage? Wicked and Greyson?' Winnella's voice tore me from my thoughts. Her eyes were wide with fear and confusion. 'Okay, I must have been dreaming ... ,' she seemed to consider this thought for a moment before adding softly, 'Well, I figured you saved my life in the lake so I should probably return the favour by not leaving you outside the cottage to freeze to death.' She smiled, but I did not return it.

I merely stared back at her with an endless amount of questions brewing inside. 'Well, it seems we are even, then.'

'Exactly,' she said. She retrieved a bucket of hot water from beside the stove, poured it into the basin and began to scrub the gown, but the stain remained. She looked around her at her surroundings with wide eyes as she said, 'This place is homely though, right?'

I narrowed my eyes, my anger rising slightly. She was ridiculous. 'Are you really trying to make small talk with me right now?'

She laughed, a smile curving her lips before her gaze fell downward again. It lit up her face, and for the first time she seemed less anxious. Not that I truly cared. 'I suppose I was hoping to ease the tension a little.'

'Ease the tension? Winnella –'

'Call me Winnie.'

Winnie was a shortened version of her name, a nickname, and nicknames were for friends and family only. People who shared a close relationship. Winnella and I were not friends, and although by marital law we were stepsisters, we were not family. Not after everything her mother had done. My hands became clenched fists at my sides as I said, '*Winnella,* your mother took everything from me, and you want to *ease the tension?*'

I climbed out of bed quickly, searched the room for my cloak and boots which were hanging on a rail beside my bed. Looking around, I saw there were six other beds just like this one. So this was either the guards' cabin she had spoken of, or they had just walked into some cabin in the middle of the forest.

Either way, it did not belong to her. 'Look, there's a mirror over there, so off you go.' It was a large one, hanging on the wall beside the basin, with golden edges engraved with detailed swirls. 'Back to Cranwick, right now.' The quicker she was out of my sight, the better.

She gasped, her eyes widening in horror. 'You don't understand, Princess Frost. I can't go back to Cranwick without my mother. It was part of the deal with the witch.'

I released a sigh, remembering the queen's words back in the gardens. 'Safe trip, safe return.' This was all such a mess, and I only wished the nightmare would be over. I never wanted to see either of their faces ever again, but it seemed things were far more complicated than that now.

'Yes.' Tears rolled down her face. Our conversation must have stirred something within her, and her emotions came loose. Once she started, she was unable to stop. 'I came here just to get my mother back,' she said between sobs. 'Dad is sick, and Mum was supposed to find the potion that would heal him. If I go back now, if I don't find a cure for him, I'll have come here for nothing.'

Her problems were nothing in comparison to my own. Her mother may have killed my father, but Winnella was not innocent. If she had not followed the queen and set off her rage, and made her poison him, this would not have happened. My eyes flashed with rage, and the words burst from my lips before I could stop them, 'Perhaps you should lose your father. Then you would know how it feels.'

Her hand sprung to her cheek as if I had slapped her. 'Princess, I told you by the lake that your father is alive. In fact, look over there and you'll see that he is awake. You don't truly mean any of it, you're just angry. I can tell you are kind.' She sighed. 'You really didn't see the witch.'

'I do not know what you are talking about.' Remembering her words about my father, I crossed the cabin to the beds and found a familiar figure lying in the one closest to the little window. He was awake, and glancing around the room as if *he* thought he was seeing things.

I had heard rumours of the tricks the Winter Forest could play on your mind, but had never thought I would see them with my own eyes. Beasts in the night, fairies singing in the trees at dawn, and witches hosting seances in the middle of the night. But they were just rumours, stories told to scare small children into good behaviour. Or, were they?

'Frost, is that you? Where are we?' his voice was soft and gentle, not the proud and regal father and king I had always known and loved.

I ran to him, and knelt before his bed. Tears streamed as I laid my head against his chest, and he began stroking my hair. 'Father, I thought you were dead,' I sobbed. 'I thought she ... I missed you so much. I thought I had lost you.'

'Oh, my darling Frost, we are together now.' He peered around the cabin, and I followed his gaze, taking in the warm fire, the seven beds and the basin. He kissed my knuckles, and ran his hands through my hair, tucking a few of the loose strands behind my ear. 'How brave you have been, I am so proud of you.' On the wall were rows and rows of armour and weaponry, and he was studying them intently as he spoke. 'Forgive me if I seem distracted, my love. I have not seen this place for many years. This cabin belongs to Harlow and his brothers, yes?'

I did not know enough to answer, so I remained silent, but he laughed as the guards came over and introduced themselves as newer members of his Royal Guard, recently out of training. Marcus explained their journey here, and their escape from his murderous wife.

'Well, you have saved us,' said my father. 'You have shown so much bravery and honour, so you will be climbing the ranks very quickly, lads.'

'Thank you, Your Majesty,' said Marcus softly. Behind him I could see Lienus and Titus watching them speaking with hopeful stares.

'You carried me all this way? I do apologise if I was dead weight.' My father's humour was shining through once again, even after his near death, and it warmed my heart. 'Winnella, dearest. Come here.' He gestured for my stepsister to come forward, and held her hand within his own. 'I hear you have been very frightened. I am so sorry for everything you have been going through, and it must all be very confusing for you right now. Please know that I care for you, my dear. Your mother's actions have not changed the way I see you as my stepdaughter. Alright?'

Fresh tears glistened in Winnella's eyes as she said, 'Thank you, Your Majesty.' She held his gaze, but seemed to gather herself for a moment. She cast a glance in my direction, and guilt crept into my chest at the thought that her mother's actions had not affected how he saw her, but they had for me. And that, even so, Winnella had still treated me with kindness. I remained silent as she said, 'I think I have to tell you both something important about my mother.'

'Do go on,' said Father softly, and patiently.

Even I was curious to know what it was that she had to say.

'Before she went, she said she was going to Icefall to marry you, and I came after her. I found myself in the house of a witch called Wicked, who told me I must sacrifice something I loved to go onto the Winter kingdom.'

'Your name,' I said, wondering where she was going with this, since I knew she was aware that we both knew her mother's secrets.

The tears had stopped rolling down her face, but now she wore a sad expression as she recounted everything that had happened before she came to Icefall. The version I had heard in the gardens had been watered down and less descriptive, but this time I felt the emotion within her. 'Yes. She told me my mother sacrificed her heart, and that she now lives without it. But when I saw Mum, she denied it and said she'd given away the ability to love romantically.

'I believed her because I love her, and I wanted to, even though the witch showed me the jar containing a beating heart.' She ran a hand through her short hair and sighed frustratedly. 'I suppose I hoped that maybe it belonged to someone else. That my mother would never have done that. Now, looking back, I know that was foolish of me. But after you left, and we thought she had killed you, Your Majesty, I saw that the witch was right all along. She really did give her heart away. It makes so much more sense that way, doesn't it?'

Things were starting to become clearer, but it did not change anything between us. We were not the sisters as she seemed to want us to be. Or even friends.

We were enemies. 'Your mother is heartless?' I asked all the same. Even though I had heard her words, and I knew what they meant, they were not sinking in fully.

'Literally so, yes. In loving Dad enough to want to heal him, she gave everything away.'

I clenched my fists, forcing my father to wrap his fingers around my own. 'So that was why she tried to kill my father. She cannot love.' Because she was no longer human: she had become something else entirely. A creature who possessed no emotion, and no empathy at all. No heart.

A monster.

'She said she wanted the kingdom all to herself. I'm so sorry, Frost.'

I began to understand her predicament. Her mother had become ruthless and cruel through the witch's curse. In that way, I knew Winnella had lost her mother just like I had almost lost my father. But the difference between them was that her mother's decisions had led to her demise, while my father was an innocent and grieving king who only wanted the best for his people.

We were not the same.

18

WINNIE

When the following morning arrived, Princess Frost was still a firework that was about to go off.

She'd been through so much in such a short amount of time, the destruction all committed by my mother's hands, so it was understandable. But her obvious hatred for me still stung, probably because I was forced to watch her laughing with the guards.

I didn't even know why it affected me so much, because we weren't even friends. In fact, before my arrival in Icefall, we'd been strangers. But I had quickly come to realise that the cold created awful hallucinations. I'd imagined the witch and her beloved for god's sake, so perhaps it was affecting my emotional state as well.

Not to mention being homesick away from my father and cousin, and coming to terms with my mother's betrayal. There were so many more important things at stake here, like bringing a healing potion home to my father to cure his sickness, and taking my mother home. Because, as much as I may have wanted to abandon her here, the arrangement I'd made with the witch wouldn't allow me to leave without her.

I was truly stuck in Icefall.

But perhaps the princess knew a way to the Winter Caves, where I would find the enchanted water that would heal my father. She was my way out of this, and if I needed to use her to find it, then so be it. Desperate times called for desperate measures.

'Marcus, grab us some weapons and meet me outside,' said Princess Frost. Her eyes were burning with a new fire as she ran out into the snow, leaving them watching her with the same baffled expressions.

Like me, she was now dressed in leather trousers, a silk shirt and a thick cloak that was twice the size of her. It hadn't taken long for me to realise that these clothes probably belonged to the guards who lived here. We were wearing men's clothes. But at least they were comfortable, I supposed, and they allowed us to move freely than the gowns. They also kept out the cold far better.

'I would like you to train me, just like you and Ryan used to.' The mention of his brother's name seemed to affect him because he said nothing, only stared back wide-eyed.

'Your Highness, I'm not sure that's such a good idea,' said Lienus.

'What if you –' Titus said, but was interrupted by the princess.

'I was not speaking to either of you. I was speaking to Marcus.' Her brow furrowed as she waited for her answer, but none came. She ran back, grabbed a sword off the wall and lifted it. But she returned it when it was too heavy. Then she picked out a smaller sword, and swung it around a few times. It seemed to fit better, and a wide grin crossed her lips.

I didn't miss Marcus's smile. There would be no telling her no when she looked at him like that. I was quickly learning that the princess could be persuasive when she needed to be, and it wasn't even because of her title or her powerful father. Despite her sullen nature, there was a charm to her that made the boy soldiers fall at her feet.

'Please, Marcus?' she persisted. 'I need something to throw all of this energy into.'

'Me, too.' If you couldn't beat them, join them! She turned to look at me and laughed, but I just shrugged. Her eyes were like saucers, maybe wondering if I was crazy to want to go along with her plans to learn to fight. Maybe I was, but it wasn't like I was leaving this place anytime soon. Maybe the fresh air would do me some good. 'What? I'm as stuck in this world as you are, aren't I? Might as well learn to defend myself.'

Marcus heaved a sigh, but of course he relented to Her Highness. 'Alright. We'll eat first, though. I need some grub.' As if agreeing with him, his stomach grumbled loudly, making everyone laugh.

Not for the first time, I was reminded of how wild my situation had become. Soldiers, a princess, and a *king*. I had to pinch myself to remember that this wasn't some strange dream.

Princess Frost grinned, her face lighting up for the first time since we'd come here. A sudden hope settled over the atmosphere of the cabin. It was strange how much her sullen mood had affected us all, and how much happier we all were now that she was feeling better. 'Thank you, Marcus.'

As we ate our meal of leftover rice and pheasant – a meal for posh people, really – a new memory appeared like a flash.

I was running, and something was chasing me.

'Get back here, you little rat!' a voice screamed as I bounded through the courtyard of my uncle's farm, small stones sliding beneath my feet. 'You will not get away with your thievery this time. Your father might spoil you girls rotten, but while you are on my farm, you will work!' Uncle Burgess, the bulk of a man with enormous hands and a shiny bald head, snarled. He wasn't one to be messed with.

But I'd always loved to tease him, move his stock around, dirty his farm animals and take the horses out for night rides so they would be too exhausted to work during the day. My sisters and I were working on his farm, clearing muck out of the stables and caring for the animals, but all we wanted to do was play.

Mother and Father were away taking care of some important Roth witch business, so here we were, forced to work. Our mother was an Elder for the Roth witches, meaning she was regularly needed with her coven. It didn't leave much time for caring for her thirteen daughters. But our uncle had earned himself thirteen extra farm hands, all between the ages of ten and twenty. A good working age, in our uncle's eyes.

But Uncle Burgess would soon learn not to fool with thirteen young witches. After all, most of us were only just coming into our abilities, and that made us ambitious, and for some, slightly reckless. The punishments were coming in thick and fast, and we were sick of them, so we'd started to mess around. Stealing food from the storage closet, jewellery from his late wife's bedroom cabinets, and sending the animals running laps around the farm all at once. Watching him chasing them down one by one had all of us in hysterics.

Especially the pig, the way he chased it, covered head to toe in slop. That would be a sight I wouldn't forget any time soon. I'd stolen some clothes from his wardrobe and carefully dressed a few of the pigs in them, and he'd had the last of it.

We were forced to scrub the toilets until they shone. But we made a run for it, and were soon planning on finding our way home, even if our parents weren't due back until next week. But his farm hands had caught us searching through his rooms, and we'd been given fifty lashes each, so we were sore and exhausted. It was definitely time to leave.

His bear like dog chased us down, quickly finding us in the courtyard but we were too fast. We stole one of his trucks, and we were on our way, with me taking hold of the wheel and feeling the power of my new driving licence in my hands.

Nothing could stop us now.

The memory vanished as quickly as it had come. For the first time, I began to see more of the witch who was trapped inside my head, and I'd be lying if I said I didn't find her interesting. She was feisty, brave and a thief, but I was fascinated.

Although, it would be great if I could find a way to get her out of my head.

We began our training session in the clearing only a few metres away from the cabin.

Princess Frost was full of energy, her anger fuelling her quick strides. Marcus was determined not to force us to fight each other, in case she killed me in her rage toward my mother, no doubt, so I dealt hand to hand combat against Lienus while Princess Frost repeatedly knocked Titus down. I couldn't help but laugh each time he fell. Her spirit, and the skills she already possessed, were impressive. Although, I did believe that her rage had a lot to do with it.

But, as you could probably imagine, with this being my first ever lesson in physical combat, I sucked. I lost count of the amount of times Marcus had to pull me up off my arse. I mean, at least the snow beneath me was soft, so I couldn't complain too much. But as it poured around us, and we became a group of walking snowmen, I found myself frozen. My muscles were stiff from the cold, making it uncomfortable to walk.

We went on like that for some time. Hours, probably, or it felt that long. But somehow, the adrenaline seemed to warm my bones. Princess Frost demanded to use a larger sword and a crossbow on separate occasions, although fortunately for Titus, Marcus reminded her that it was better for us to learn the basics first.

'I already know the basics,' Princess Frost hissed, her sour mood returning with her frustration. 'It is not my fault that she does not.'

'Sorry for holding you back,' I said, and couldn't hold back the laughter when it came. The storybooks depicted princesses as calm and collected, always maintaining their emotions and remaining polite and sophisticated in any situation. This princess was far from that. It was apparent to me now that in reality, these stories were not so simple.

The king watched from the doorway of the cabin with a proud smile as we trained, cheering us on and at other times, reminding us to be careful. One day, maybe there would even be a family of her own, one that didn't involve evil stepmothers and a stepsister she clearly despised. But now I was getting ahead of myself. I wish I could say that happiness would continue, but like most fairy stories, sometimes those moments must come to an end.

We kept training until Marcus and his brothers suddenly marched us back inside the cabin. 'Everybody, go!' His gaze scanned the forest, and it was soon clear why he'd been so afraid. Some distance away, the sound of hooves grinding against stone could be heard.

Then they came into view. Dark armour was draped over the riders and their horses, and their leader shouted orders to his men as they searched. Their horses weren't coated with the king's crest of blue and silver, two adjoining swords piercing the top of a snowflake. Now, their silk coats were designed with a new one in gold and white: a delicate hand with black dagger-sharp fingernails tightly clutching a golden heart.

Which was ironic, considering that my mother no longer possessed one.

Princess Frost's smile faded, and horror dawned on us all as we crammed ourselves back into the guards' cabin, quickly blocking the doors and windows with wooden boards and cotton bedsheets, every one of us silently holding our breath.

We hid beneath the beds, and the guards all blocked the princess and the king, clutching long swords against their chests in case the queen's men stormed in here. I was certain that you could hear every heart in the room slamming against our chests as we waited for it all to pass over.

How quickly Princess Frost's moment of happiness had slipped away.

19

FROST

Terror formed a fist around my heart.

The queen's men were nearby, which meant they would soon find us.

If any of my father's men remained as captives in the palace, they may have told the queen's cronies of the small cabin in the forest that they would often use as an outhouse. Tightly closed mouths could often be opened with the right methods.

If the queen's guards had already been led here, where else could we go? I suddenly wished I had attended more of Father's day trips out of Icefall.

Marellia, Icefall's capital, and the outer cities and villages beyond, should have been explored by our carriages.

We all remained silent for some time, too afraid to move or even breathe in case we were heard. It was hopeless. We were training ourselves in physical combat, but for what? It would be impossible to defeat an army of *magical* warriors. It was like taking a teapot to a sword fight. We would be greatly unequipped. This meant there was a decision I must make. Although, honestly, perhaps I had already made it. 'Father, I am sorry, but I must go.'

If the queen wanted me, she could have me if it meant my friends would be safe. My father, too. They were precious to me, so I would protect them any way I could. It was the only sacrifice I was willing to make.

Tears welled in Father's eyes as he said, 'No, Frost. It is too dangerous.' He wore a solemn expression as he pleaded with me. 'I will not lose you.'

Weaving my fingers through his and planting a kiss on his cheek, I said, 'I love you, Father.' The tears in my eyes matched his own. It should not have been this way, but priorities were important. 'Hiding out here will do us no good. We have to defeat her. Please, trust me.'

His breathing was heavy, broken up by harsh sobs as he trembled for me. My father had always been a stern man, but he had never shied away from showing his emotions with Mother and me. Even so, I had never seen him this way. It hurt my heart to watch, and guilt slithered through my veins, leaving me ice cold and shivering. 'No, Frost. I am afraid for you ...' He was strong, but I must be stronger. He needed me now.

I would do this for him, and for Icefall. 'You must understand, Father. You will be safe here where they can care for you. When all of this blows over, and I end her, I will come back to you. I promise.' It made sense. I had been a fool to not see it so clearly before.

Sitting still like this would do nothing while there was an evil queen on my father's throne.

Planting a kiss on his cheek, I reached for the door and walked out into the forest.

20

WINNIE

WITH TEARS ROLLING DOWN HER FACE, Princess Frost wrapped her cloak around her shoulders and fled, barely allowing herself time to pull on her boots before placing her feet down onto the snow.

We'd been training for hours, and by now it was growing dark, but she didn't even want to wait until the morning to leave. Her father pleaded with her to stay, and Marcus and the others tried to persuade her otherwise, but her mind was clearly set. She was leaving, no doubt so she could run off to the palace to defeat the queen all by herself.

A stupid decision if you asked me.

'Princess,' I called after her. 'You don't have to do this alone.' How could I help her if she refused to let me? She needed to see that we weren't really enemies, and that I was as cursed and alone as she was. Besides, who knew what dangers lurked in the forest? Wolves, bears, wildcats, or worse? She'd left me with no choice, yet again, because there was no way I was going to leave her on her own out there. 'Princess Frost!' I cried as she sped through the trees, and followed quickly, batting off tree branches and stumbling on the uneven ground as snow continued to fall around me. 'Princess, come back!'

She turned for an instant and bellowed, 'Do not follow me,' before darting off through the trees.

Quickening my pace, I yelled, 'You said that last time,' through my shallow and uneven breaths, wiping snow off my face before it could slip into my mouth, and wishing I'd put in more steps on Mum's treadmill.

The princess didn't seem bothered by the weather conditions. Perhaps she was used to them, having spent so much time in her fancy palace gardens. 'Please, Princess Frost, we can help each other. You're only risking yourself out here. It's almost midnight!'

'As if you care! Leave me alone, Winnella.'

I didn't move. Even when I'd helped her, even when I'd been working alongside her guard-friends to escape the palace, she still didn't believe we were on the same side. Or maybe she was just too stubborn to actually let people get close to her, out of fear of losing someone else. I supposed that made more sense. But it still sucked.

'Winnella, I am warning you, if you come near me, I will –' Her threat was cut off by a piercing scream, one that came from her own lips.

There was something in front of her, a terrifying creature with black silky fur streaked with golden stripes. Its large and rounded head sloped down into a wide, arched back and long legs as thick as tree bark. It prowled toward her, opening its mouth to reveal a set of sharp teeth.

A shudder rushed through me as I imagined the kind of claws that were hiding beneath all of that fur. My breath caught in my throat as I hurtled after the princess.

She backed further away from the beast, her eyes wide with terror. She stepped backward slowly as the creature hissed at her feet, lowering itself onto its haunches and preparing to pounce. With eyes wide like saucers, the princess peered behind her, searching for a way out as the creature approached.

But she'd reached the end of the forest, and behind her were only the raging waves of the fast river that led to a mighty waterfall. 'No, Princess Frost!' I cried, but her name barely left my lips as the reality dawned on me that she was either going to drown in the river, or be eaten by a strange feline beast.

As if things weren't already weird enough.

She edged closer to the water, while the creature approached more quickly with every step.

Cursing to myself, I glanced around for something I could use. Something long and sharp, maybe. But I wasn't that lucky. All I had were a few large rocks. I held one over my head, inhaled a sharp breath and aimed, sending it crashing into the creature's back.

It turned its head, giving the princess a spare moment to focus. She screamed, and in that moment, threw herself backward into the river and found herself being dragged toward the waterfall. A sob burst from my throat, but there was no time to find out if she was alright because the creature settled its golden eyes on me. It stalked toward me, and snarled through a panther like snout, those long silver teeth protruding from its mouth.

Great, so the thing was chasing me, but all I had to defend myself were a few small rocks. I threw one after the other, causing the beast to whimper a little, but the attacks only seemed to anger it further.

'*Foolish child,*' a voice appeared in my mind, deep and ancient like it came from stone itself. And it definitely wasn't Wicked's this time. The creature was looking right at me, reading me. '*If you would just listen and stop throwing stones, perhaps we might help each other.*'

These hallucinations were just plain weird. First I'd imagined Elder Wicked and Greyson by the lake, and now …

'This is no hallucination, child,' said the voice, those eyes boring through me. 'Your step-sister would not listen to me, but you … you are special, Wicked.'

A sharp laugh escaped my lips. I turned and ran, but the creature barrelled after me and pinned me to the snow, saliva dripping onto my face as it held me down. I thrashed, pushed and kicked, but I was trapped.

'You are a friend of our elder's. Wicked, are you not?' the creature snarled. 'You contain something ... else as well. A new ... form inside.'

'It's a long story, and my name isn't Wicked. It's Winnie. What the hell are you, and what do you want with me and Princess Frost?' This couldn't be happening. I was dreaming, or suffering some kind of vision, or maybe I was in one of Wicked's memories again.

'We wish, simply, to protect you, Wicked. As for what we are, I am surprised you do not already know.' I didn't answer because I was far too focused on trying to weasel a way out from under the beast without being stomped on, scratched or bitten, so it continued, *'We are the ancient Guardians of the House of Roth.'*

As much as I knew of them, they were the mythological beasts known to guard the Roth witches, consuming wandering souls who made their way past their gates, or any who came to harm the witches. In other words, they were supposed to just be a story made to scare small children into behaving. But they were known only in stories of legend, and I had never seen one even lingering close to Cranwick, where there were plenty of witches to go around.

'I am here to take the princess home.'

'What do you mean, you're taking her home? She doesn't belong with you, she's –'

'She is a Roth witch, child, even if she doesn't yet know it. Her mother rules the House of Roth, and has seen the unrest that has befallen her kingdom, so she has asked me to bring her home.'

Princess Frost was a witch? But that didn't make sense. There were so many questions spinning through my head at that thought. Wouldn't she have learned magic, or *felt* it somehow? She wouldn't be ... normal.

She would be just like the witches in Cranwick. Frightening, and spooky. Different.

But she was just a sad princess who'd suffered far too much grief in her life.

Another question struck me harder: 'But Princess Frost's mother is dead ...'

'Yes, child. Exactly. Queen Rosa of Icefall now reigns over the spirit realm.' Those golden eyes were fixed on mine, piercing into my soul. Perhaps it thought I was an idiot for not understanding. I felt like one in that moment. *'Her mother wishes only for her to be safe and cared for, but she is alone in Icefall. There is nothing left for her there.'*

'You're wrong. Her father is alive, and she has ... she has her friends. There has to be another way.' Even with her mother's good intentions, I couldn't let this happen. She was my only way out of Icefall. Besides, did her mother really want her only daughter to die so soon? That didn't seem right.

Princess Frost had so much more to do, to defeat the queen and restore peace to her kingdom, and live. And she still needed to help me heal my father. 'Tell them I will help her. I will care for her as if she were own my sister. Because I cannot leave my mother to destroy her like she did to the king, I will not stand for it.'

'But she is still a stranger to you, child,' said the beast, although those eyes now held a strange knowing, like they had expected my words all along. *'We sensed that you might say so.'* To my surprise, it bowed, and seemed to smile through its long snout and wide jaw. *'You are everything we knew you would be, Winnie.'* It inched closer. Before I could say another word, it nuzzled its head against my leg. But it wasn't a pet, and the gesture just forced a shiver to crawl through me, so I shoved it off me. *'We will be watching you, child. Protect our princess at all costs. If you should need to call for me, I will be here. Call for Vencin, and I will appear.'*

And then it slipped through a curtain of light and vanished as if it had never been there at all, leaving me wondering the hell what had just happened.

It had tried to speak to Princess Frost but she'd refused to listen. Had it told her that her late mother was a witch? Did she even know the truth about her mother's heritage? She'd ran, but I couldn't blame her for it. The creature *was* horrifying to stumble upon.

What a strange thought: Queen Rosa was a witch who now ruled their spiritual realm.

The princess still had a full life left to live, and clearly Vencin had known it too, or he wouldn't have left me to rescue her.

Could they really have been expecting me?

Now, I had to find the princess, because I had essentially promised her mother that I would, through the strange messenger cat. I would do my best to fulfill this promise, if not for the good of the princess herself but for Icefall. My legs couldn't move quickly enough as I charged through the snow.

I stopped when I saw the river.

The current was so fast. Had the princess survived the fall? I couldn't help the thought that rushed to mind then: if she hadn't, this would all be for nothing.

No, I needed to think positively.

I set off across the dark path to the end of the river, and stared down the cliff face at the waterfall and the rock pool below.

There, some distance away, was a small frame with short raven hair and wide, terrified eyes.

She was so close to the edge, but there was still hope yet.

21

FROST

Who knew this forest would be such a maze?

My first thought had been to run, and make my way back to the palace, but the night's darkness had led me down a different path, leaving me lost and more afraid than before. Then I was running through the forest like something was chasing me.

Snow-covered leaves fell through the air, and I was forced to shove them off as they blasted themselves against my face and neck. Birds sang in the trees, and somewhere close by, a beast howled.

With shivers coursing through my body – as a result of both the cold and the fear of wondering what creatures I could run into – I kept going until I reached the end of the line, where I stumbled upon a wide river with a fast current that led to a raging waterfall.

There was nowhere else to go.

Forcing myself to think clearly, I turned back the way I had come, and headed for the cabin where Winnella had tucked me into bed. Not because I wanted to return, but because I hoped there might be others, or perhaps even a way out of this forest.

With tears dripping down my face, I darted through the trees. One way after the other, and then back on myself when I realised I was lost. Everything looked the same, and I could not remember for the life of me which route I had taken on my way here. I collapsed in the snow, heartbroken and seething with rage at the way my life had turned out. Nothing would be the same again.

But I had to keep moving. Dwelling on these tragedies would only send me deeper into a sinking hole that I would never be able to get out of.

I took a deep breath, pulled myself quickly to my feet and headed back for the river, hoping for a new way out of this wretched mess. Then I would return to the palace and take down my stepmother myself.

But as I turned around, I realised that this time I was not alone. There was a cat-like creature standing before me, preparing to pounce. Its large body was curved and lean like a wildcat, with short black fur engraved with golden streaks. Enormous fangs protruded from a wide jaw, and it padded toward me on feet that were almost as big as tree roots.

'*Princess Frost, come with me, your mother wishes to bring you home.*' The hollow voice that spoke within my mind was rough and ancient, and the sound sent a shudder up my spine.

I would not have believed what was happening if it was not for that stare. Somehow I knew it was speaking to me inside my mind. Fresh tears welled at the thought of my mother, but I blinked them back hard. I refused to wait around and let the thing eat me.

This was simply a hallucination, a symptom of the bitter cold.

I took a step backward, inhaled a sharp deep breath and threw myself into the river.

Perhaps, as an afterthought, that was not the best idea. The water was colder than the air on my skin, and it chilled me to the bone. The current was far too fast. I sank deep under the water a few times before breaking the surface again.

Not to mention that I was now heading for a high and mighty waterfall.

I thought I could hear Winnella speaking quietly then, but I may well have been dreaming. The voice that spoke seemed to know the person they were speaking to, but the sound was muffled, and there was no one else around besides the strange panther-like beast. She was not hearing it in her head too, was she? But what was odd was that it knew who I was, as if it had read my every thought when it appeared in my head.

Stars. If this was what my life had now come to, I truly was screwed.

As I floated downstream, I tried to think happy thoughts, to imagine Mother's face and Father's gentle embraces, but there was not much happiness left for me to picture now that my kingdom was gone.

Perhaps it was better for the waterfall to take me, too. At least that way, I would soon be with my mother again.

What a depressing thought.

What I needed now was to think positively, get home and take my kingdom back. As that thought seeped in, I saw the end of the line. I was mere seconds away from falling down the waterfall to my death if I did not do something. Survival instincts kicked in and I reached for the edge of the river, swimming quickly toward the riverbed and praying I would find something that would save me.

Tears stung my eyes as reality dawned, but I kept swimming, fighting and kicking.

'Princess!' a voice cried, one that was both familiar and unrecognisable with my foggy thoughts. My gaze followed, and found Winnella staring down at me from the side of the river, holding her hand out to me. 'Take my hand!'

Unfortunately, she was my only hope. She was irritating and persistent and refused to leave me alone, but she *was* offering to save my life, *again*, so she was all I had. I threw out my hand and hoped for the best.

She gripped my sleeve and hauled me closer, but I soon lost touch and fell quickly downward toward that waterfall. Holding my breath, I waited for the end to come.

All hope was lost.

Then I opened my eyes, and a glimmer of light rose within me again. A tree had fallen across the river, creating a kind of bridge.

As I floated toward it, I threw my hands upward and clung on for dear life.

22

WINNIE

W<small>E WERE SO CLOSE,</small> but she'd slipped out of reach and then she was gone, speeding toward the end of that river and over the waterfall.

Or, so I had thought.

Hanging from a fallen tree log before the edge, was the tear-faced princess. Hope blossomed within me then. Good fortune was in our favour, and we would have to make the most of it.

As I ran along the riverbed, I searched for something I could use as a rope, something to reel her in. But there was nothing. I tore off my cloak and fled for the end of the line, knowing she wouldn't have the strength to hold on for too long.

Then I twisted my cloak up tight so it formed a sort of makeshift rope – a rubbish one at that – and held it out, shouting, 'Grab hold!' But she was too far away. 'Swim along the tree a little, and use it as a kind of rail!'

Her eyes were wide with terror. 'It is too far, Winnella!' she cried between sobs. 'I am losing time ...' There would be no consoling her now as the tears rolled down her face and her expression became more contorted with her discomfort. Not unless I could do something to help her.

'Focus!' I yelled back, and was filled with relief when she began to inch closer. But I knew I couldn't get in with her or we'd both be lost to the current. But I would use everything I had to save her. 'Can you pull yourself up onto the tree?'

Then a thought dawned, one that terrified me to no end, but I had to do it. For Queen Rosa, and for Princess Frost and my father, and for the good of both Cranwick and Icefall.

The princess screamed as I scrambled onto the end of the fallen tree and began to scoot closer, pulling her up with me. But she was too scared to move, and I feared that if one of us fell, we would take the other down. We were truly stuck.

'Please, Winnie,' she whispered, with terror-filled eyes. After spending hours watching her swinging swords and kicking down the soldiers outside the cabin, seeing her so frightened was a shock. 'I do not think I can do it.'

Then it sank in that she'd called me Winnie. That might have seemed like nothing to some, but to me it sounded like trust. It only fuelled me further, creating a new surge of energy in my chest. I hauled her up beside me, and then I started to slide backward, pulling her along with me. 'Slowly,' I reminded her. 'This way. You can do it.'

She started to crawl toward me along the log, and refused to look down. Her whole body trembled as she moved. 'Would this be a good moment to tell you that I am terrified of heights?'

Although it probably went against some moral rule, I found myself laughing. 'No, this is possibly the worst moment you could have chosen in the history of time. Not long left, keep going.'

Despite herself, she laughed, and her smile lit up her entire face. 'You are ridiculous.'

My grin quickly matched hers. 'And you are defying gravity right now!'

'Do not make me laugh, or I will fall!' she whispered frantically, but the distraction seemed to be helping because she was close to me now, and almost at the edge of the river.

'Little bird, ease your way, sing to me and brighten the day. Leave your troubles behind and start afresh, close your weary eyes and lay your head to rest.'

'What are you doing?' she said, the confusion brewing on her face, but she wasn't frowning anymore. She was fully smiling now. 'Singing me a lullaby? Are you ill in the head, Winnie?'

I shrugged, simply glad it was working. 'They always calmed me down, and that was one of my old favourites.'

Something in her expression softened, and her eyes filled with tears as she said, 'Mine, too. Mother used to sing it to me when I was little. Thank you.'

'You're welcome. You're almost there.' With a little help, she made it back to the riverbed, and we stared awkwardly at each other for some time, until she threw her arms around my shoulders. 'Don't you think running off was a tad ... irrational?'

She eyed me nervously. 'I could not help myself. When I knew the queen's men were close by, I had to leave. I still think I need to, but perhaps I rushed my decision. I want to go back to the cabin, but I fear what will happen to my father if the queen's men do find us.' The words that followed weren't exactly surprising, but they made me smile all the same: 'I hope this does not give you the wrong idea; we are still not friends, but I do appreciate you saving my life. Let us go home.'

A breathy laugh escaped before I could stop it. If only she knew how much that meant to me. 'I can live with that. So you actually like the cabin now, then?'

She gave me a playful shove. 'Do not push your luck.'

Back in the cabin, we were seated together before a warm fire. The soldiers didn't seem to be around, so perhaps they had gone looking for us.

Princess Frost was curled up in an armchair, while I had spread out every book I'd found on a large woollen rug and was slowly scanning the pages for something interesting. A good story to keep my mind occupied, or even some pretty artwork.

The princess was clearly feeling sentimental, because she asked countless questions about why I had gathered her into the cabin and followed her when she ran away, distracting me from my reading. She wanted to know why I was being so kind to her, especially when she'd been so cold to me already.

She was right; she had been cruel, but honestly, I should have expected it. Multiple times now I had considered the thought that deep down she knew that my mother's actions weren't my own, but she'd needed something or someone to pour her resentment into, and I'd become the perfect target.

As soon as we returned to the cabin, Princess Frost threw herself into her father's arms and apologised over and over, telling him she never should have run off on her own like that. Then she was forced to explain everything that had happened in the river, and her father only held her and stroked her hair while she cried, telling her that all was forgiven.

After some time the two of us talked a little, and I told her about my strange memories with the witches and the awful curse that had left me feeling trapped and alone. My eyes were swimming with tears as I told her everything. 'I saw the witch not long before you saved me by the lake, and after. They were toying with an Autumn princess. I think the witch has been trying to show me her past memories. When I saw you, you said the witch told you to save me.'

A frown creased her brow. She wrapped the woollen dressing gown more tightly around herself, pulling it right up to her neck. 'You gave her your name, so she took your identity with it?'

She was finally beginning to understand what was happening to me. I couldn't help but feel relieved, knowing that even if we weren't friends or even allies in this situation, I was no longer alone. 'Yes. Now it seems she's messing with my head as there are parts of me that have been starting to remember again. I don't know how. Maybe she knows she made a mistake and is trying to confuse me again now that I've been getting my mind back.'

Was that rage in her eyes? Rage, this time, in defence of me. It was the last thing I would have expected from her. 'I think I would like a word with this witch,' she said.

'What are you saying?' I asked, hope suddenly filling my chest at the thought that things between us were improving.

A slim smile creased her lips. 'I will help you, Stepsister.'

This was progress. My chest suddenly felt lighter. With the princess on my side, I would be back to my father with his healing antidote in no time.

If only that feeling had lasted.

But the door creaked open, forcing the princess to run from the chair and duck beneath one of the seven beds in fear. The rest of us quickly followed. 'Hide.'

She crawled back out when the boy appeared. He had a petite but muscled build, soft features, warm eyes and short hair that curled around his ears. He wore some kind of soldier's uniform, so he clearly held some authority, but he seemed quite young. Maybe even mine and Princess Frost's age. And she seemed to know him, very well, in fact. She ran over and leapt into his arms, and smiled as he embraced her. There was so much love in his eyes as he held her in his arms.

'Hugo!' she said. 'What are you doing here?'

He was at the ball, I realised. Prince Hugo, her best friend. Her fiancé. I watched them embrace, and smiled. The princess still had someone she cared about. Despite their engagement, the way she looked at him was like how a girl looked at her brother. It was the way I looked at Barchester.

But this prince ... the way he stared at her was ... different. He loved her, and it was unrequited. How heartbreaking that would be for him, when they eventually married and she couldn't give him what he obviously wanted.

Even so, it wasn't any of my business. They had their own issues to deal with, and I had mine. I reached out and offered the boy my hand. 'Hi, I'm –'

'Winnie,' said Princess Frost, taking me by surprise. I definitely didn't expect her to say that again. 'Hugo, this is my stepsister.'

'You are the daughter of the evil queen.' The Autumn prince inched closer, and came to stand before the princess in a defensive stance even when she pushed him away. She tried speaking calmly with him, but he protested. 'Frost, she is not on your side. What are you doing with her?'

Who did he think he was, her fierce and mighty protector? If he thought he could bully me, he was wrong. 'I'm Winnie, daughter of a woman who literally gave her heart away to a trickster witch to save her sick husband. Yes, she married Princess Frost's father and became heartless, but her actions have nothing to do with mine, as your princess is quickly learning. Even His Majesty said so himself.'

I didn't miss the flash of amusement in Princess Frost's eyes then. It seemed I was slowly rubbing off on her. Gone was the stern daughter of the monarch, and her true colours were starting to peek through. Her softer side was slowly coming out. I had the impression that she didn't let her guard down very often anymore. But who could blame her? She'd been through so much pain and loss in such a short amount of time. And she was much stronger than she knew, even I could see that now.

Still, it appeared there would be no fooling the moody prince who had staked his claim over her. Her beloved, her best friend and her knight in shining armour, or so he hoped. 'I do not trust you,' he snarled as he stormed forward, and sneered down at me.

If he was trying to intimate me with his height, it wasn't working. He wasn't much taller than me, and I only needed to look upward slightly to stare hard into his face.

Princess Frost shoved him back again, and blocked his path to me before he could do something he might later regret.

'I heard everything that happened,' he said, as if he thought he was the biggest threat of all.

I laughed hard in his face, and watched his sneer become a scowl. Behind him, the princess watched our conversation the way she would a tennis match: her gaze shooting back and forth between us in quick succession. 'I get it, you are protecting your princess. But I'm not going to hurt her like my mother did. The way I see it, my mother is as sick as my father, but in a different way. *Mentally,* perhaps. She thought she was doing the right thing. Not that I owe either of you an explanation, but I just want you to understand that we are on the same side here.'

Princess Frost took him aside, as if fearing he might attack me if she didn't. 'I am sorry,' he said when she'd finished explaining, and shook my hand. 'You saved her life. You are not your mother's mistakes, Winnie. Please consider my sincerest apology.'

A prince had never apologised to me before. Suddenly, I felt a little warm beneath the collar. 'Thank you.'

He laughed, but his attention was quickly diverted to the princess again. He took both of her hands in his, and planted kisses across her knuckles. 'My beloved, we are together again. Let us go and defeat this heartless sorceress.'

Princess Frost glanced in my direction before returning her gaze to the prince. I didn't miss the hint of annoyance that appeared in her eyes before quickly disappearing. 'No, not you,' she said firmly. 'That is for

Winnie and me to do.'

Was that admiration I read in her expression as she glanced over at me? It was one thing that she might be beginning to trust me, but to want to work with me to defeat my mother ... that was something else entirely. That was special. Disappointment radiated off the prince in waves, but hope began to sing in my heart.

Still, he clearly wanted to be the big, bad boy here and save the princess from eternal ruin, even if she wasn't having it herself. 'Well, I wish to assist –'

Pass the popcorn. This prince was clearly devoted to the princess of Icefall. Betrothed, even. He talked like a cheesy Prince, and honestly, all I could do was cringe. Because real life wasn't supposed to be like that.

'Hugo –'

'Frosty –'

Frosty? What was she, a breakfast cereal? This prince couldn't be any more of a cliché if he tried.

Princess Frost sighed and slipped her hands out of his, and let them fall by her sides. 'Very well, Hugo, but please do not get in the way.'

'I would not dream of it.'

Unable to help myself, I snorted. He was definitely going to get in the way. I had the feeling that he was going to be the biggest pain in the arse known to Icefall. What a joy.

'Your Majesty, I cannot believe you are here,' he said, crossing the cabin to the armchair where the king had been watching us patiently. He gently took the king's hand and shook it. 'I am glad to see that you are safe.'

The king offered him a grand smile. 'Prince Hugo, I am glad you are here as well. How did you find us?' It was an important question, and I heard what he was really asking: if *he'd* found us, how easy would it be for the queen's men to find us as well? Were we safe here, especially the king and princess?

Prince Hugo stood taller, squaring out his shoulders confidently as he answered, 'I have been searching for the princess all day.' I had the sudden feeling that he may have sniffed out her scent like a doting little puppy, and grimaced. But I also couldn't help but laugh to myself at the thought. 'I fear the queen has been drawing closer to the cabin, but I sent her men off track.'

That wasn't really what the king had asked, but anything he could do to tell the king how he'd saved his life, he would do it. Arrogant bastard.

Well, at least he was good for something. But I was beginning to see why the princess hadn't fallen for him in the same way that he clearly had for her. He was handsome, sure, but there was no *substance* to him. Nothing that I could see, at least. But there was definitely a strong temper beneath his charm, one that he struggled to control when it came to his beloved princess. Delightful.

'We do appreciate that, Prince Hugo,' said the king through gritted teeth.

Perhaps he'd sensed it as well.

'Thank you, Hugo,' said Princess Frost, and hugged him again.

'You are most welcome, Frost.'

As if this day couldn't get any more bizarre, the door slammed open again, and we turned to face five young warriors bearing swords and shields. Soldiers from the king's army. Now my mother's, I supposed.

They stormed over and began firing questions at us like they were part of the Roth witching army. 'Who are you?' said the one at the front, clearly their leader. He wore a soldier's uniform like Prince Hugo's, but this one held the original crest of Icefall over the chest. 'Wait, that's Prince Hugo and Princess Frost, and a servant. And, oh, Your Majesty.'

They gathered around to greet their king, who explained everything we were doing here.

But there was only word that stuck out to me: a servant? Was he serious?

The soldiers came over to greet us. 'Princess, it is good to finally make your –'

But the princess had other ideas as she quickly grabbed my wrist and tugged me against her chest. We didn't hear the rest because we dived through the closest mirror. I would never get used to the feeling of falling through the Roth witches' mirror portals.

I imagined it would feel similar to stepping through a ghost's shadowed form, or hurtling through time. A shroud of colours wrapped themselves around us, and it felt like I was flying through a narrow tunnel, but the journey itself lasted only seconds.

Then a chill crawled up my spine as I found myself back in the witch's house. There she was before the fire, the sound of her laughter echoing through the room. She also wasn't alone this time; the entire coven seemed to be crammed into it. There were twelve other elderly witches with the same white hair and wrinkled skin, the same stern expressions. But there were also a few younger witches and some children scattered around.

This was the witching community right here, and we'd taken them by surprise.

'Well, well,' said Wicked, turning around to face us. 'It appears that we have some royal visitors. How exciting.'

'Are you going to turn them into porcelain, Grandmother?' said one of the younger girls, clearly recalling the custom that was so well spoken of here. Or perhaps the witch was just toying with me as she had on the icy lake, if she was really there at all. 'Or, what about stone?'

'Come on girls, this is clearly a task for your grandmother. You all have some spellcasting homework to catch up on, don't you?' She pulled the girls away and the others shortly followed, leaving four witches; three elderly, including the one who'd cursed me, and one young witch. 'We will resume the coven meeting in an hour,' said the leader to the rest of her coven, who turned back to nod in confirmation before continuing on their way through a door at the back.

After they left, the leader stepped forward and cupped Princess Frost's chin in her long and bony fingers before releasing her. 'How may I help you, princesses? Princeling?'

I frowned, the reality of the name she'd given dawning on me suddenly. It wasn't the first time someone had called me that, but it was the first time I had been called a princess by the witch who'd cursed me. I still wasn't growing used to it, and I wasn't sure I ever would. 'I'm not a –'

She merely frowned at me. 'Is your mother not the Winter queen, child?'

'By marriage, only, and surely even that ended when she tried to murder the king. But yes.' There wasn't much else I could say to that.

'Then I believe that qualifies you.' She laughed a deep witch's cackle, which shouldn't have been surprising, but it still shook me to my core every time.

Was it true? Was I really a princess?

'Now, what has brought the three of you here to me?' She focused on me. 'Your evil mother made an attempt on the king's life, yes?'

'Tried to,' Princess Frost snarled.

The witch considered us with a thoughtful expression. 'Does she know he is still alive? And, for how long?'

'How dare you speak about my father like that, witch!' Princess Frost snapped.

The witch considered the princess with a thoughtful stare. 'You must have come here for a reason. Tell me what it is that you want.'

She wasn't wrong. I was still yet to know why the princess had quickly dragged me through the mirror and into the witch's home. She must have known what she was doing, and where we would end up. But she hadn't yet told me.

'I want magic, the right amount to be able to defeat the queen.' She held her voice firm, squared her shoulders and met the witch's gaze with a piercing stare.

How would I tell her what the creature by the river had told me? Princess Frost's mother was a witch, which meant that she was one, too. But she didn't know, and I had no idea how to bring it up. She would probably collapse in shock, and then I would have to scoop her up and drag her back to the soldier's cabin. If we even found a way out of here.

What a mess.

But honestly, what was hilarious was the prince's face as this entire conversation was happening. The princess wanted magic, and the prince didn't know what to do with that information.

If you could have seen the shocked expression on his face, you probably would have laughed. His jaw hit the floor, and his eyes were wide like something out of a strange cartoon.

The witch cackled, ignoring him. 'If only it were that simple, child. Only those who are born with enchanted souls can learn and practice using such spells. But I see that you are desperate, and desperate people will give anything to win. So what would you give, little princess?'

How would I tell Princess Frost what Vencin had told me of her, that she was the daughter of a witch queen? She already possessed magic of her own, and didn't need this witch or her tricks. Besides, shouldn't the witch be able to sense that she had a fellow witch in her midst? It made no sense.

Only a moment ago, the princess had been watching the witch with a desperate expression. Now, tears rolled down the princess's face as she said, 'If it is so impossible, what difference would my desperation make? You want me to sell me away for a deal that will not even be successful in the end? She has taken my kingdom from me, witch, and she will come back for my father's life soon, and no doubt for mine as well. Because her men were close by, so it will not be long before she finds us.'

So that was why she was here. She was desperate. Running away had failed, and now she was determined to find a new way to defeat the queen. 'Don't make any deals with her,' I whispered, shaking her arm and hoping she would remember that I was still under the witch's curse, and she was only going to put us both into more trouble if she did something she might later regret.

'I was not planning on it, Winnie. But I have to go ahead with –'

'I sense a connection,' the witch cut in, her impatience evident as she scrutinised us all closely. 'You have become friends. Perhaps I may help you both.' She laughed as she glanced between Princess Frost and me. 'Have you been paying attention to my lessons, Wicked? Have you learned anything from my memories yet?'

How patronising. She thought she could mess with me, but she was wrong. Ignoring her question, I said, 'I don't understand. Why would you do such a thing?'

'Truthfully, at first, I enjoyed playing with you. It brought back some memories of my youth.'

I remembered the images I'd seen of her tormenting the princesses, and grimaced.

She went on, 'But then when I told my sisters of your visit to my cottage, and how I had cursed you, they painted me a picture of a dream that one of the oracles had seen. Two princesses coming together, related only by marriage, and destroying the cruel sorceress queen. There is more to this picture, but I cannot see it.' She peered around her, as if sensing something or someone that wasn't there. 'Honestly, you both intrigue me. I fear this mage queen may have placed a spell over my mind, for my head is usually so clear. I see nothing but smoke and mirrors when I look at the two of you. So, I must unravel the story.'

Could a mage sorceress really cast such spells over such a powerful

Elder witch? It must be strong magic indeed. Who was my mother, and where did she really come from?

'Her name isn't –' Prince Hugo said, but was immediately cut off by the witch.

The thoughtful smile had disappeared as soon as her story ended. Her gaze fell on me again, but still she spoke to the prince. 'I believe the girl has still been using the name Winnie, even though it no longer belongs to her.' She laughed darkly, and this time she spoke to me, 'That is twice I have taken it from you now, and yet you seem unaffected by my magic. Maybe it is because of your mother.'

This witch was ridiculous, but I refused to be bullied. 'Or maybe you're just not as good of a witch as you thought you were!'

The witch's eyes turned an icy blue. 'Of course I was always going to leave a tiny part of you inside, or you would go completely mad!' She laughed darkly, the sound echoing through the room.

Great, so I had triggered a nerve.

'Perhaps I should take it all away from you, and then I'll have to deal with the little princess as well.'

That didn't sound good. Fear suddenly caused my heart to race. If she did that, there would only be the witch trapped inside my mind, and there would be nothing left of me. 'Please don't do this.'

She seemed to consider this, but then said, 'I trust my oracles enough to know that their dreams often happen no matter how we try to stop them.'

Fear drummed through me at the thought of losing the progress I'd made with the princess. I'd finally found a way to work with her to destroy everything my mother had done, and we hadn't even created our plan to stop her yet.

Then there was the case of travelling to the Winter Caves to find the enchanted water for my father. There was still so much left that we needed to do. 'No, please! Witch, I gave you my name to grant me a safe trip to Icefall and a safer return to Cranwick with my mother, and with Dad's healing potion. Your part of the bargain hasn't even been fulfilled, yet you want me to give you every piece of me? How is that fair?'

The witch merely cackled again. 'Then perhaps, next time you will know better than to make deals with my coven.' She laughed as the darkness overwhelmed me. 'Sleep tight, Wicked. I'm sure I can make use of your soul.'

23

FROST

We had come to the witch's home for a reason, with Winnie and Hugo showing more reluctance to my protesting, but look where it had gotten us.

It was all my fault. She would sleep for now, the witch had said. When she woke, she would be just a shell of her old self, fully so, this time. She would not know who we were or what had happened since she had come here, meaning that all of her own memories – even the ones from when there was only a piece of her left – would vanish.

I wondered then if this was a part of the witch's plan all along, to interfere with my kingdom. She had tricked Winnie's mother into giving her heart away, which could have led to my father's death if Winnie and my friends had not stopped her.

'Frost, be careful,' Hugo whispered as I approached the witch.

But thunder crashed through my veins. How dare she do this to us, play with us as if we were only toys? Surely that was almost as cruel as what the queen had done.

Except, it was a different kind of malice.

You might call me impulsive, but clearly Winnie had an influence over me unlike any other. We were not close enough to say we were friends, but she had saved my life now, twice and counting, and I had rescued her from that frozen lake. Before, I probably would have pushed her in myself.

Something about her and her stubborn nature had weaselled its way into my heart.

Honestly, I was far from used to the feeling of caring for someone other than my mother's ghost, my father and my best friend. But it appeared that I must become accustomed to it, or return to being lonely forever.

No one wanted that.

Vengeance became a new and clear purpose in my mind as I fixed my gaze on the witch again, feeling Hugo's eyes on the back of my neck as I stormed forward. This witch had forced my stepsister to give away her name and very soul, after all.

She was the true villain here, and her name was *Wicked*. How ironic.

She was watching me now with a slightly sadistic smile on her face. 'What do you want the most in the world, Frost? Do you want to marry this prince and live happily ever after?'

She must have been humouring me, because that was a question with a very clear answer even for the most naïve of eyes. 'Is it not obvious? I want my father to be safe, my kingdom restored to peace and ... I want you to leave my stepsister alone. She has done nothing wrong.'

Speaking the words had made them ring true for me. Since our arrival in the forest I had been finding excuses to hate her, to blame her for her mother's choices, when all along, she had been as much the victim as I was.

The more I l had learned of Winnie and her determination to help me, and watching her argue back with Hugo, the more I understood her. There was a higher power at play here, and Winnie was not a part of that, nor was her mother. Well, they had been foolish enough to fall for their tricks, but it was this witch that knew what she was doing. She was the one in control, and yet it was all nothing but a game to her.

'Frost, if she hurt her like that, she could easily do the same to you. We should go back to the cabin,' Hugo warned me from over my shoulder, his voice barely above a whisper.

But somehow I sensed that she had heard him, as there was a new glint in her eyes. They were dark and yet full of a bright and twinkling enthusiasm. 'Look, Princess Frost, do you know the reason why I called her Wicked in the first place?'

I had the vaguest feeling that Winnie had mentioned this conversation to me recently, but I could not remember what exactly had been said. My head was spinning with this conversation, a new ache spreading through my chest, my body overwhelmed by shivers.

She wanted to keep talking in riddles, and probably trick me and Hugo as well. No, thank you. I saw right through her façade. She was vicious and dangerous, trying to appear as an ancient woman with far more than a sprinkle of magic in her blood. 'Because you wished to manipulate her.'

'No, it was because she said she wanted to stop her mother from finding a healing potion for her sick father. Because I saw a piece of myself in her.'

She really thought she was doing Winnie a favour. What a low life she was, playing with people's lives and desires like that. Tricking them into sacrificing parts of themselves for her own personal gain. Disgust crept under my skin, and lingered in my bones. 'She just wanted her mother back, she did not want her to leave her, which is why she followed her here in the first place. She is nothing like you, she is soft and kind.'

For a while I had been blind to Winnie's feelings, but then I remembered the hallucinations she had suffered, the way she thought I was following the orders of a younger version of the witch and her mage boyfriend. And after that, I was sure there had been more. This witch had messed her up inside, placed her own consciousness into her mind, and that would not be easily forgiven. 'You wanted to show her that she was like you, so you gave her more of yourself,' I said.

The witch's mouth dropped open and her eyes widened. This was evidently a new revelation to her. 'Oh, you know about that?'

'Frost,' Hugo whispered again in a warning tone. 'Be careful.'

Ignoring him, with my arms folded over my chest, I answered, 'Yes, she told me everything you did to her.'

'Frost,' said Hugo again. 'We have to go.'

'No, Hugo, I must do this. My kingdom is counting on it.'

A new wicked smile spread across the witch's lips, like she was planning something. 'In that case, I suppose I'd better be rid of you as well, should you choose to interfere with my plans for her.' She continued to study me closely, plotting my demise with each passing second.

I was such a fool. I had felt so brave before, confident to stand up to this trickster witch and demand that she give me a piece of her powerful magic. But I had forgotten the main issue: that she possessed no loyalty to my crown or any other. The Roth witches were their own people. But she had the ability to bring any form of torture down on me, and there was no way I could stop her once she began.

'No, you cannot!' Her words had left me flustered, and there was nothing left for me to do but stumble through my words. 'I mean ... what do you mean by that?'

She grinned, revealing her broken teeth. 'Either you can give me your soul, or that of one of your little friends.' In the mirror behind her, she played out a series of moving images of Marcus and Titus, still swinging swords at each other in the snow outside the cabin. Marcus was winning their practice fight, not failing to knock the guard off his feet on several occasions.

My heart began to pound. Were they safe? Was my father? These questions raced through my head as I considered what to do next. 'In exchange for what, exactly? You owe me. The others were able to ask for something in return.'

'Your freedom, of course.' She cackled, a true witch.

What a fool I had been. How naïve, and blind to the power this witch possessed. 'We should never have come here, Hugo.'

The sarcasm in my best friend's voice was now clear as he scooped Winnie up into his arms. 'No, really?' He headed for the mirror we had entered through, hauling my unconscious stepsister up over his shoulders like the hero I would never have expected. 'I am sorry to say that I told you so.'

Heat spread through my cheeks as I watched him, and little butterflies twisted in my belly. This was not the Hugo I knew, the little boy who had played spy games with me. This was Hugo the prince, my fiancé. Everything was changing too quickly, causing the world to crash and fall around me.

What was happening to me?

'Come on, Frost!' he cried.

But before he could reach for me, the witch shoved him through the glass. A scream tore from his throat as he fell into the shroud of colour with my stepsister's unconscious form over his shoulder.

The witch beamed, and drank me in as I considered following him, eyes flickering between her and the void he had just crashed through.

All without me.

Wicked said, 'Oh, he is going to have quite a surprise! We control the portals. We may just have a little fun with them!'

I dreaded to think what exactly she was planning. 'What is wrong with you? Why are you doing this to us?' When the witch only let out a hollow laugh in response, I ran after Hugo, hoping to fall through the portal again, only to slam hard and fast into the glass, shattering it into hundreds of tiny pieces.

A searing pain sliced my skin, and I yelled out in agony as I spotted a shard of glass in my bicep. Tearing it slowly from my body, I cried out as my skin burned with the sting of the blade and a stream of blood poured down my arm.

'Will people please stop shattering the mirrors?' said one of Wicked's many sisters. She had appeared from a door at the back of the cabin that no doubt led to a bedroom or another area for the witches to gather. She was tall and slim in stature, her features similar to Wicked's, although far narrower. She collected the shards with a cloth covering her slender hands and left the room.

Wicked merely smiled as if her sister had not spoken. 'Now, Frost. What is it that you want the most in the world?'

I found a much smaller shard above my right knee and slowly picked it out, and yelped as it scraped through the skin of my fingertip. I did not answer.

'I will give you your kingdom back and let you return safely if you do one thing for me.'

I shook my head, knowing this would not end well. But still I said, 'How will you do that? There is nothing left in Icefall that is mine to control.'

She raised a hand, twirling her fingers around, and offered me a grin. 'I have my ways, child. You need not worry about the smaller details. But you will promise to silence your precious Wicked, and make sure she does not speak of the memories I have given her, ever. If she does, she will die. She may return to Cranwick safely, as long as she is silent.'

That did not seem quite so bad. But why was it so detrimental to the witch's reputation for Winnie to speak to others of her curse? Wicked did not seem like the type to care of what others thought of her. She seemed only to think of herself. 'What is the catch?'

By the look in her eyes, I could see she was satisfied with the thought that she had now reeled me in. But she would soon know how wrong she was.

'There is none. You will merely slaughter the queen and have your kingdom back. Wicked will be safe, and so will her village.'

With an eyebrow slightly raised, I shot back, 'You speak like I will be doing all of the work for very little benefit,' and staggered backward into an armchair. I supposed I should not have been surprised. I wanted my kingdom back, but was I prepared to go that far for it? Could I do that to Winnie? She seemed to hold the same hatred toward the queen that I did, but Leraia was still Winnie's mother. 'No, I will not kill her mother, that is ...'

A day ago, I would not have hesitated, but getting to know Winnie seemed to have made things more complex, and I felt stuck. More stuck than I had ever been before.

A sigh burst from Wicked's lips as if she were already becoming sick of the conversation. 'The girl will not remember her mother, anyway. She will only have my memories.'

I could only repeat the same question I had asked her before, along with another: 'Why are you doing this? How does this benefit you?'

There were so many things about their bargain, and Winnie's curse, that I would never understand. Pure sadism? Revenge. Vengeance against ... someone in my kingdom?

The possibilities were endless.

'I have my reasons, child. Not that they are any of your business.'

That could mean anything. 'You cannot do this to her. You cannot.'

She smiled wickedly. 'I think you will see that I already have.'

Frustration coursed through me, becoming a raging thing as I insisted, 'But, why? What is so special about Winnie that makes you feel like you must give her your own traits and memories? Why have you chosen to take her soul?'

It must have had something to do with the oracle's vision that she had spoken of before. There was something else she had not told us, because there were far too many answers left open.

What did she want with us?

'Wicked will be very useful to me for many reasons, but she must not spread word of my magic or those who care for and respect me will not see me the same. All will be revealed in time, but not yet.'

She stepped closer, and rested a hand on my shoulder. 'I was lying earlier when I said that everything I saw about you and Wicked was blurred.

'I have witches in my coven who have seen your futures, and they are bright. But I have been warned that I must hold her close, and if that means I must steal her soul, so be it. For the meantime, you will have my power as your guide. I may not be able to give you my magic, but I can give you something just as valuable. My knowledge of spells, and my experience, of which there is plenty. Believe me child, I am no monster. I only wish to help you.'

Questions swarmed. Our futures. Her power. What in Icefall was she talking about?

Could she have been speaking of her younger self and the memories she had shown Winnie inside her mind? *I* did not have the young witch battling it out for my consciousness, but I was already exhausted.

It only reminded me that I needed to find Winnie and Hugo, and continue training with the guards. Perhaps her guidance would be valuable, and we could use it to weave our way through this new and dangerous world.

'Now, child, we must set you on your journey.' She pressed a dagger into my hands. 'You will kill her with this. The blade is carved from mage stone, the only thing that will kill her.'

Mage stone. Where was Winnie when I needed her? We could have looked it up together in her books, discovered what was so important about it. But it was hopeless, because I refused to do that to her anyway.

I would never use it. Of course I wanted her off my throne, and out of my kingdom, but there had to be another way. 'No, I will not.'

That cruel smile appeared on her lips again, and she tore the dagger from my grasp. Disappointment flickered in her expression. 'Very well, I shall turn you into a donkey. Stand back and prepare to look like an ass.'

'No, no ... ' She looked at me then with wide eyes, so I carried on and reached for the blade. 'Very well. I will do it, I will silence Winnie.'

There was a glint in Wicked's eye as she said, 'Very good. But until I am certain that you can be trusted, I am afraid I must silence you as well.'

'What do you mean by ... ,' I tried to say the final word, but even though my mouth moved, I could not hear myself speak. My voice was gone. She had literally silenced me. What else did she have up the sleeves of her cloak?

If that was an ability of hers, could she not have done the same to Winnie? She should not have needed me to do it. But perhaps that was all just another part of her big plan.

'Off you go, little princess.' She pulled out a long mirror from a cupboard against the wall. 'Back to your kingdom you go.'

But where had the others gone? I could not ask her; I was unable to say a word.

Wicked tapped the mirror while her sisters laughed at me. 'Or would you rather be a donkey?' she said, forming a grin.

Seeing no other choice, I stepped through the mirror.

24

WICKED

'I F YOU'RE GOING TO STEAL FROM ME, YOU WILL PAY!' my uncle snapped, eyes practically bulging out of his head with rage as he looked upon my sisters and me.

Then he dragged us all, wrists bound, toward the dark and choking cellar he often used as his dungeon cell. Here we would be left close to starvation in punishment for defying him. Even a single word out of place could have us sent down here for whippings or lashings. If he was in one of his rotten moods, there was no escaping his sadism.

Yet, to others, he was an angel, a great brother and friend. Even to our parents he was seen as kind and caring, and always there to take us in when our parents needed to take a trip to one of the neighbouring kingdoms for official business.

My mother was Falcon, the ultimate leader of Roth. She was rarely ever around, always busy orchestrating negotiations between the four kingdoms and the witches, giving out our magical services for a high price. In some ways, you might say it was a business. My father, Alman, blindly followed my mother everywhere she went. My mother wasn't the type to be tested, even by her children or her husband. She was a powerful woman with little patience for others' complaining or need for sympathy or pity.

But her position meant they were always occupied, so my twelve sisters and I were used to fending for ourselves. We would escape tonight, and be just fine. Maybe even find a small lodge to stay in until our parents returned for us. Or, we would go to Greyson and ask for help from the Ajanid clan.

It probably wouldn't be the best choice to ask our enemies for help, but what choice did we have?

My beloved Greyson was one of his best warriors, and he loved me and cared for my sisters dearly. He would help us. 'We will get out of here,' I reminded my sisters. 'Hang tight and be strong.'

But hope was fading as my uncle kicked me to the bottom of the steps, forcing me to land face-first on my hands and knees. I cried out as the fall stole the air from my lungs.

'Wicked!' my smallest sister Seager called out, her young voice shaking with her fear and emotion. 'Are you alright? We can't see you.'

She was right. It was pitch-black down here, and all I could see were the boxes containing bottles of age-old wine and the open door that led to the pantry with the food storage. It didn't seem to be empty this time. At least if he was trapping us down here, we wouldn't go hungry. Silver linings were all we could hope for.

'Shut up!' my uncle hissed.

I scrambled forward into the cellar as one of my sisters yelled in pain, and then little Seager was right beside me, crying into the collar of her cotton shirt. I pulled her against my chest and held onto her tightly.

'I should never have brought you here, you lying thieves. Stay down there forever for all I care.'

'What a loving uncle you are,' Lunar snarled, but her sudden shriek told me that he might have hit her. 'When we get out of here, we will tell our mother everything you have done, and she will turn you into rat soup.'

My little sister, always the sharpest with her tongue. She was the second oldest, where I was the first, and was always there at my side to back me up when I had to protest for the care of the little ones.

There were thirteen of us in total: me, Lunar, Marthy, Vielle, Sara, Corani, Everly, Hera, Heaven, Alis, Crescent, Mora and Seager, all of us with different personalities and traits. Some were timid, like the four little ones, while Lunar and Marthy and I could always hold down a verbal battle with little help. I supposed we got that from our mother.

Our uncle's laughter echoed through the cellar as he approached, making my blood boil as he dragged the little ones down the steps and threw them to the ground, one by one. 'Vermin, that is all you are to me. Your mother is a whore for having so many of you. Thirteen daughters, better her than me, I'll say. But you do make for some good labour.'

'What do we do?' said Mora quietly after he left, slamming the door shut behind him. 'I'm scared, Wicked.'

She wasn't alone, as the others nodded their small heads in response. 'Remember what Mother always told us?' I reminded them. 'She's glad she has this much love to go around. Her lucky number thirteen.'

Because what might be considered unfortunate to most was a blessing in my mother's eyes. She might have only said those words in the early days when Lunar and I were small, but it was exactly the sprinkle of hope for my sisters right now, so it felt right.

What we needed now was a miracle, and an escape plan. Or both at once if we were truly lucky.

The memory came as a series of images that were still raw and painful because they had happened only a few nights ago. My uncle's dark eyes seared through my vision and would remain locked in my mind forever.

The feeling of his meaty fingers gripping my wrist, the smell of cigarettes and liquor lingering on his breath, and the stench of his unwashed body hitting my nostrils as he leered over me.

Despite the flash of reality being close to home, I had the vaguest sense of de Ja 'Vu, like I was somewhere I recognised but had never been to before.

Maybe one of Marthy's paintings had revealed the place to me. There was no recollection of yesterday or the day before, as my head was a blur.

The air was peaceful, the sky a bright morning blue, which was calming despite the birds screaming above the trees. Murmuring an enchantment in my head that I hoped would quell the noise, I tried to sit up slowly and realised I was lying on the snowy ground outside some kind of forest cabin.

I could only have been in Icefall. But my limbs felt heavy and awkward, like they weren't fully attached. Taking that and the sensitivity to noise as a sign of exhaustion, I slipped back down and glanced around, searching my surroundings for something familiar. But there were no signs of my sisters or my wretched uncle anywhere.

Had we finally managed to break away from his farm? I didn't know where my sisters were, but right now I was trapped. Frozen still, and far too tired to move. Tired, or hallucinating. Perhaps this was all a strange dream, and my sisters and I had escaped the farm and were on our way to our new hideout in the hills beyond the northern border.

There were other witches there. Very soon we would be safe, and ... it took a few minutes to realise that the birds were still singing loudly, a high-pitched chirping that was almost equivalent to a hammer smacking against the fleshy edge of my brain. Why weren't they stopping? I knew I was feeling dazed, but my enchantments were usually faultless.

Taking a deep breath, I tried again.

All I ask is for a bit of peace and calm,

Settle the sky and quell the storm.

Nothing. Something was wrong with my magic, and that wasn't normal.

Rubbing my head, I sat up slowly and peered around. I soon realised I wasn't alone. There was a boy crouched low some distance away, watching me like I was some kind of alien thing.

He seemed familiar somehow, but I couldn't remember where I'd seen him before. He wore a soldier's uniform with the crest of Windspell over the chest, two adjacent swords through the top of an autumnal brown leaf. His eyes were warm and angled in such a way that only made them seem more familiar. His mouth dropped open, and those eyes were wide as saucers.

'Who are you, soldier?' When he didn't answer, I pressed, 'Hello? Don't you have a tongue?'

He reached out a hand as if he wanted to touch me, then pulled it away as if he'd realised he might be crossing a boundary. 'You're ... glass ... Winnie, look at your arms ... your face ... '

Glass? This boy was talking in riddles, and he seemed to think my name was Winnie. There must have been something seriously wrong with his head. I mocked his stuttering, my frustration growing. 'Uh ... uh ... What are you talking about? And who is Winnie?'

He gulped and pointed at my hand which was probably completely ... glass.

My arm was a transparent silvery blue, smooth and ice cold to the touch. I grabbed at my face, my legs and the top of my head, only to feel the same cold surface. Well, that explained why my body had felt so heavy when I'd tried to move.

No, this was all wrong. I *was* dreaming, and at any moment I'd wake up and everything would be normal again.

But when I opened my eyes, nothing had changed at all. I'd been transformed into a statue, only one that could still talk and ... walk, presumably, although I hadn't attempted that yet.

The boy's eyes were panicked, and clearly frantic. 'Where is Frost? We need to find her. She will know what to do.'

Confusion brewed within me. 'Princess Frost of Icefall? What does she have to do with me being a glass statue? Also, you still haven't told me your damned name!' And it was driving me insane that he was still so familiar, a face I had definitely seen somewhere before ...

He stared back at me with a hard expression. 'You really don't remember, do you?'

'Are you thick? Remember what?'

He shook his head. 'You are quite rude. But very well, I am Prince Hugo of the Autumn kingdom of Windspell.'

That explained why he was so familiar, as my family were closely acquainted with the Autumn royals through noble connections. But if he was such an important royal, why had my mind blocked him out? Worse, why wasn't my magic working? And why was my body made of *glass* of all things? It all made such little sense that I wanted to scream.

'My betrothed, Princess Frost of Icefall, travelled to the house of the witches who made you ... this way.' He paused, then told me how Winnie, this girl I'd never heard of, had journeyed there to bring back her mother but had been cursed with a witch's soul in return.

He claimed that I was walking in Winnie's mind, and still trapped inside her body, but now he presumed I was left with only my own memories inside. Everything about Winnie's mind – her memories, personality, thoughts and even her soul – had been taken from her body.

Now, there was only me.

Stars, what a mess.

No, I was definitely hallucinating.

Prince Hugo also said Princess Frost and Winnie – me – had fixed their – our – issues right before the witch's visit. 'I think she must have been tricked. We must find her.' He looked me over, studying every inch of my glass frame and wondering, as I was, if I would break the very moment I tried to walk. 'Do you want me to carry you?'

Peering down at my glass frame, I wasn't sure what to say. Surely the spell that had been cast over me would be powerful enough to protect me from such details, but there was no way of knowing for certain. But who wouldn't want to milk a little attention from a prince when granted the opportunity? 'I'm afraid so, handsome. I'm a little fragile.'

He laughed like it was the worst joke he'd ever heard, but couldn't help himself. His eyes met the floor as if he were embarrassed. 'Statues don't usually flirt with me like this, but I must admit that I am flattered,' he cleared his throat before adding, 'although you would do well to remember that I am betrothed.'

'Sure, princey. Whatever you say.' A breathy laugh brushed past my lips. 'I'll bet they don't talk, either. And who says I'm flirting?'

He lifted me into his arms, and I wrapped my own around his shoulders, although he was still laughing. 'You are the heaviest statue I have ever held.'

A snort escaped before I was able to stop it. 'You carry many statues, then?' He was shorter than most of the princes I'd met, but he clearly wasn't a stranger to combat. If he wasn't carrying statues, he'd definitely held something just as large. 'And that's not very charming of you, Prince Hugo.'

He sighed and shook his head, his handsome face contorting with his confusion. The amusement was gone, replaced by something more serious. 'Tell me then, witch.' He settled me down onto the snow and I struggled to lift my glass legs onto the soft surface. 'Who *are* you?'

'You!' Before I had time to answer, we were interrupted by five armed warriors coming from inside the cottage we'd come from. These soldiers were far larger than Prince Hugo, and they all wore the same angry expressions. 'You were the ones sleeping in our –' he paused, as if finally seeing me for the first time, and his words changed their direction. 'Your skin, it's ... '

'Glass, yes,' I said, not wanting to go over it again. 'It's complicated.'

'Frost!' the prince cried.

The girl had just been shoved through the cottage door, and the prince was now gathering her into his arms. So this was the princess he cared for so much, his betrothed. She was beautiful, with a petite form, and shoulder-length dark hair with a full fringe above her brow. Her eyes were a sky blue, the kind that pierced right through you.

All of these royals seemed to have been carved by the goddess herself, with every little hair and each curved feature in its place.

The soldier pressed his sword to the prince's chin and lifted his head. 'Royals,' he said, turning to his brothers. 'What should we do with 'em?'

'Oh, not me,' I said as Prince Hugo and Princess Frost were dragged rather forcefully into the cottage. 'I'm just a witch.'

'Witch?' said the soldier standing behind their leader. He studied me carefully, as closely as the prince had before. 'What did you do, get yourself caught under an enchantment of your own?'

I smiled to myself, thinking over everything Prince Hugo had told me about their time in the witch's house. 'Well, now that you mention it, that's exactly what happened.'

Princess Frost seemed to notice me for the first time as they were thrown onto the carpet and held as captives in this strange cabin. Her eyes were wide as she drank me in. Seeing her friend like this would have been a shock to the system. She probably thought she was dreaming.

They didn't push me around, though. I thought they were honestly a little scared to shatter me. Who would have wanted to cause such a mess, all of that glass everywhere? A sudden laughter left my lips at the dark humour that was suddenly coming out of me.

We were in a small and dirty lounging area that contained only a few basic items – bookshelves full of leather-backed titles, a wash basin, a stove and seven beds for seven soldiers. Warriors, or whatever they wanted to call themselves. The only thing that came to mind then, was why would a graceful princess want to stay in a place belonging to seven men?

But then, desperate times often called for desperate measures.

Prince Hugo sighed, noticing the way the princess was gazing at me and said, 'The witch changed her, Frost. She's gone.'

I sighed heavily. 'No, I'm right here.'

A frown curved his brow, and he pinched his nose between his thumb and forefinger. '*You* are, but our friend is not.'

'What were you doing in our cabin?' their leader asked, running a hand through his sandy blonde hair and peering at each of us in turn with bright blue eyes. 'Names, first of all?'

What was this, a game of twenty-one questions? 'By the goddess, you're demanding. We were clearly having a massive org –'

'Wicked, don't you dare. That's explicit,' whispered Prince Hugo, sighing.

They didn't know me yet, or how crude my mouth could be. But they would soon learn. I ignored him and continued, 'I'm Wicked, the next leader of the Roth witches, and betrothed to the leader of the Ajanid clan, if you want to know my life story. This is Princess Frost of Icefall, and Prince Hugo of Windspell. I believe they were forced to flee the palace, and your cabin was the safest shelter they could find. As for me, well I'm still figuring that out.'

Princess Frost just watched me with awe-filled eyes. Was she usually this quiet? These royals may have been obedient and loyal to their kingdoms, but in my experience they weren't silent either. Could a witch have cursed her as well?

Only time would tell.

Their leader let out a breathy laugh. 'We are warriors, witch. We know who they are. Wait, you're betrothed to Greyson Marks?' The charming devil's eyes widened with fear, but he covered it by trying to act amused. 'I really like her, boys. She's a fierce one.' He turned to me and asked, 'So what is a powerful witch like you doing with a glass body?'

Planting a hand on my hip and glaring at them as if I couldn't care less, I answered, 'Honestly, I've been asking myself the same question all day.'

'What is actually going on here?' he said.

'Tell us your names first, soldiers.'

The leader rolled his eyes. 'Very well. We are soldiers of Icefall. I am Harlow, and these are my brothers. We work on behalf of the king's army, while Marcus and Ryan worked for the royal palace guard. But Ryan does not seem to be with you, Marcus.'

The guard filled him in on what had happened in the palace, right up to the moment the prince and princess had stepped through the mirror, and later returned.

Harlow then went to the sleeping king, who was resting in one of the soldier's beds after a rough couple of days. 'Does the queen know of your current location?' he said. Then he gestured for his brothers to let the royals go, with a quick apology. 'Sorry, we just needed to see that you weren't ... under her spell. I will admit we have travelled to the palace, and seen the new guards that have taken over.'

'Not yet,' said Prince Hugo quietly. 'We were hoping it would stay that way.'

'What about you, Princess?' he said, glancing at Princess Frost, who just stared back at him. 'Any words for us?'

She shook her head. Either she wasn't in the mood to talk, or there was something wrong with her vocal chords.

When she pressed her finger to her lips, it became clear that it was the latter.

'Do you belong to the winter queen now?' I said.

The soldier sighed and nodded his head sadly before finally answering my question. 'Technically, yes. There's nothing we can do about it. But since the king is still alive, we still have a chance of restoring peace to

Icefall.' He took a deep breath, his muscular chest heaving. 'I am Harlow, lieutenant of the First Order. The royal army, so to speak. These men are my brothers.' He pointed at the man behind him, 'Griffin,' then his hand moved on again as he said, 'Titus, Liedan, Cassius, Rowan and Idris.'

So what had Titus and Cassius been doing as royal guards? Perhaps they had changed their work for a short time.

'It is very good to meet you,' said Prince Hugo, stepping into his princely demeanour once again. 'I am sorry for the intrusion. My beloved and her stepsister were –'

'Certainly makes my orgy comment look a little inappropriate, doesn't it?' I interrupted with a wink, earning myself a snarl from both the prince and princess.

'Alright,' said Harlow slowly. 'I'm sure we can find somewhere for you all to sleep as long as you promise to take care of the place, and you don't get in the way.'

'Thank you so much, Harlow. Brothers,' said Prince Hugo with a wide, beaming smile on his face. Harlow didn't seem to appreciate the label; I didn't miss the way his eyes widened when the prince spoke it. Perhaps he wasn't used to being referred to as an equal by a prince, or just hadn't worked out that this was all a part of the prince's need to impress. But the prince himself seemed blissfully unaware. 'We appreciate your welcome.'

'Don't fear, friends. We are loyal to our true royalty,' said Harlow with a smile. In that same moment, the soldier forced me outside.

I slammed my fists against the door, then sank down into the snow. 'Fine!' I screamed, shaking my head as desperation took over. 'You royals will pay!'

The plan began with gathering bottles of water and wine and putting them into a large leather bag we'd found in the corner of the cellar.

We hadn't technically stolen anything before, not for keepsakes anyway, besides causing havoc around the farm and taking some things which we'd planned to put back eventually, but we would now if it would give us some sustenance when we broke out.

He also kept a few food items in storage down here in the pantry, meat and rice and vegetables. We'd been down here for a day or so by now, and our uncle hadn't yet returned even to yell at us or threaten to hurt us for his own pleasure.

We kept ourselves busy by telling each other stories of our days with Mother and Father when we were young, and all of the things we wished to do together when we finally left. None of us entertained the thought that we weren't leaving. We wouldn't let ourselves become that desperate. Hope would remain with us for as long as we could keep hold of it, and I didn't intend to release my grip on it anytime soon.

We relieved ourselves in empty plastic tubs, having created a small wall of privacy out of some old umbrellas and blankets that we'd found. Any waste was emptied into the drains through the tiny window in the corner of the cellar.

Unfortunately, at four and six years old, only Seager and Mora were small enough to climb through it, but we also didn't want them to leave in the dark when we didn't know if our uncle was watching.

Or perhaps he was too intoxicated to even care if we tried to break out. Who knew?

When dawn finally rose, we prepared Seager and Mora, opened the window and gave them each a lift up. They were the smallest of our sisters, but they were our only hope at this point.

Tears welled in their eyes as they hugged us goodbye. 'I'm scared, Wicked,' Seager said as I handed her the first bag of water, and Mora the second.

'I know sweetheart, but you will have each other, alright? You both have to be brave. You remember where Greyson lives, in the little forest by the big tree, the one with all of your little trinkets hanging from it?' She nodded her head, laughing when I reminded her of all of the little pictures they had drawn only a few weeks ago. 'You go to him, and you tell him where we are, and he will get us out. Go now, quickly. He will keep you safe. I love you.'

She climbed out, and I took Mora into my arms. 'I know you are scared, my love, but you have to look after Seager, okay? You know how she loves to wander off. Do not let her leave your side. Promise me.'

'I promise,' she said meekly, and I kissed her cheek before letting her go. She climbed up after Seager and together we watched them running for the hills, their small hands linked at the fingertips.

Mora was a good child, and I knew she would keep Seager in line.

'What if they get hurt, Wicked?' said Lunar, her voice trembling with fear. At sixteen years old, she was the closest to me in age, and as much of a role model for the little ones as I was. It often felt like Lunar and I were the parents when they weren't around. 'Or lost, or ... by the goddess, I can't believe we just did that.'

'Seager loves Greyson,' I reminded them, as well as myself. My beloved Greyson was so good with the little ones, but especially Seager. He'd found a family in my sisters and I that he'd never really had for himself before. 'They will remember where to go, and he will keep them safe.'

'I hope you're right,' Lunar said nervously.

🍎

When Greyson finally arrived, he brought a monster with him.

Uncle Burgess came ploughing through the cellar door with Greyson's throat between his fists. His gaze met mine from across the room, eyes full of love and sympathy, and I wanted so badly to run over and embrace him, but I was so weak with the lack of food and energy that being trapped down here had caused.

I was also terrified that if I spoke a word out of place, my uncle would hurt one of my girls.

'You think you're all so clever, don't you, my little nieces? Here is your shining silver steed. You are never going to get out of here, alright. So you'd better accept that. Tomorrow you will work the farm, chained to a post if necessary. Your little sisters will be the first to drop with all of the labour I am going to put you all through. When your work is done, you will return here.'

'You're not going to get away with this,' Greyson growled, but my uncle just tightened his grip on his neck, so much that his face grew red.

'We will never return,' Lunar spat.

Then, against our agreement, she began to chant one of our powerful spells. We'd decided not to use our magic because we were still learning, and it could be dangerous, but she'd gone back on that promise. Not that I could blame her for wanting to help, but she hadn't thought things through properly, and that made me worry for her. 'Lunar,' I whispered in warning, but she continued more loudly.

If this spell worked, our uncle would soon be a toad. Not that he wasn't one already, but his physical form would match his slimy soul. A sigh left my lips as my other sisters began to join her, so of course I followed suit, hoping that good fortune would be in our favour if we worked in numbers. It was a spell we'd barely used, so I wanted to curse at Lunar for being so reckless, but her heart was in the right place so I said nothing.

'What are you witches doing?' said our uncle with uncertainty in his tone. 'Stop that, right now.'

The chanting only grew louder.

He was done for. In his rage, he let go of Greyson and charged for me, his ugly features blood red and eyes bulging, and forced Greyson to thrash against his bindings. But he took my throat into his hands instead, horror coiling through me as he pressed a knife against my skin, then called behind him.

One of his workers, a middle aged, shy man with a receding hairline and rounded features, came forward. In his hands were the bound wrists of Seager and Mora.

Blood boiling, I screamed at Uncle Burgess, 'You sadistic bastard!'

He laughed darkly, and snapped back, 'Bold of you to say so with a knife to your neck. Either you die, or your sisters do.'

'Fine, kill me – ,' I tried to say, but Greyson had stopped the words from leaving my mouth by placing his hand over it.

My sisters continued with their spells, but we weren't practiced in using our spells for reality, only for our lessons, so to our dismay, nothing was happening.

Our uncle only laughed louder, pressing the knife against my throat as my beloved tried to reach me and my sisters cried in fear. 'One by one, I will kill you,' he said slowly, as if enjoying the taste of the words.

'Doesn't that defeat the objective of having workers?' I yelled. Only minutes ago he'd been speaking of working us to the bone. I had the feeling that he was just trying to scare us into submitting to him like good little girls who he could use as his slaves, to be seen and not heard. Well, we weren't the type to sit still and look pretty, so he would be gravely disappointed.

He traced the knife lightly across my skin as if in answer, and my sisters cried out as I began to chant a new spell, one that had only ever worked to help my save my animals, put them to sleep so I could heal them without them feeling any pain.

He might not be a toad, but he would sleep for long enough to help us escape unscathed.

My sisters' safety, and that of Greyson and I, was all that mattered right now.

'Stop that!' my uncle hissed.

When I continued, gesturing at my sisters with my eyes, urging them to leave through the open door, he removed the knife from my throat, lowered it and plunged it hard into my stomach. The pain was like unlike anything I could ever have imagined. The blade burned as he twisted it inside my gut before tearing it out. As I screamed, my sisters sobbed, clinging to each other in fear as the man sneered in my face. My hands felt for my middle, and came away slick with blood.

'This is your fault,' he whispered. 'Now watch your sisters die.'

'Sir, you must stop this,' Blanc said, speaking for the first time since he'd arrived.

Seager knelt at my side as he let her go, but Greyson grabbed her and Mora and pulled them behind him. Then he did the same for the others as they carried on chanting the sleeping spell, picking up from where I'd left off. Bravely, considering the consequences that doing so had brought me.

Our uncle barked a deep laugh. 'Blanc, I have never heard you speak quite so much.'

The assistant gathered my sisters and led them into the farmhouse. Greyson seemed to watch him with suspicious eyes, but there was also a little admiration there. Neither of us had expected the man to try to help like this. 'I won't let you hurt another,' he shot back.

But their words were becoming quieter as the world shimmered around me, stars flying across my vision as I peered up at the ceiling.

One of my sisters was leaning over me, pressing something soft against my stomach. It was Lunar, I realised, with her almond curls falling around her face and bringing out her dark brown eyes. I couldn't help but think how pretty she looked, the very image of our mother.

A wave of nausea hit me suddenly, but my sister held me to the floor as I heaved, loudly casting a healing spell. Bless her heart.

Greyson flew into action as our uncle approached Blanc. Venom burned in his eyes as he raised the knife. The thing about mage warriors like him and his brothers was that they required a certain trait to power their spells.

Something I knew about Greyson, that he was unaware that I had discovered, was that his trait was envy. It was more of an emotion than a trait, but it had become a big part of him. He envied his brothers for their magical skill, his father for his powerful position as leader of the Ajanid clan, and me for my loving family. Soldiers through and through, there was no love between his large clan.

I knew he used that magic to throw my uncle across the room, push that knife through the air and plunge it deep into his heart.

25

FROST

One thing I knew, I was mute and afraid in the witch's cottage, the next I was back in the cabin that belonged to the guards.

Oh, and if things were not complex enough already, Winnie was made of glass, and she had been taken over by the witch that she claimed had begun to control her conscious mind.

What was worse was that there was no way for me to scream at the seven warriors or defend my stepsister as I would have done before. I hated that Hugo was forced to speak for me, and that I had just found myself a new friend and she had been taken from me just as quickly.

In the palace, I did not very often find new friends so, despite her mother's downfall, I was willing to move past those issues and be friends, sisters, even.

But I had ruined that for us when I was tricked by the wicked witch's intentions. *Wicked's intentions.* God, it was all so confusing, and I knew by Hugo's facial expressions and the way he shivered beside me that he was thinking the same.

Now, Winnie was made of glass with the witch's identity within her body, and the warriors had also sent her away. It was all my fault, and there was no way for me to even apologise.

'Frost, you need to focus on getting your kingdom back,' said Hugo. He was the best friend I had ever had, but right now he was not really speaking in my best interests. He may have cared for me and my kingdom, but he refused to understand why I needed to help my stepsister.

In my mind it was true that I needed to help Winnie, no matter the cost. So I ignored him and the warriors and ran out into the snow, ignoring Hugo when he followed. 'You are not yourself, Frost. Look, this is not even your fight.'

How dare he try to gaslight me like that?

In his eyes, I was being irrational, simply because he did not know what I was thinking, or what I was going to do next. Spinning around, feeling the rage and frustration building within, I slapped him hard across the face.

'What was that for?' Hugo's eyes were filled with hurt, and tears rolled down his face as a hand rose to his cheek.

It was as if he did not realise how controlling he could be, how condescending, even. I doubted it was intentional, and knew he did not have the brain capacity to be vindictive, but it was still too much for me to take, and I only wished he would stop.

'I do not understand you, Frost. I was just trying to help.'

No, all he wanted to do was talk down to me as if I could not deal with everything myself. I appreciated that he wanted to be helpful, but he was going about things the wrong way.

I ran into the snow, searching for the girl made of glass, unable to even scream her name. I sank to my knees, only to feel Hugo hauling me over his shoulder. It did not matter how many times I tried to fight him, kicking and scratching at his skin, he would not let me go. But after a while of fighting him, he released me, as if realising how hopeless it was, and when I turned around to face him, he was gone.

'You will catch your death out here.'

In the place Hugo had been standing was Harlow, the leader of my father's army. His eyes were full of concern, and questions that I could not even begin to answer if I tried.

Raising a finger, I pointed at the door. 'How could you send her away like that? How dare you?' my eyes read. I did not need to say the words.

It was clear that he had understood, because I saw the cogs stirring within. The regret, and the shame. Maybe he had already been feeling that way, without him having to see the look on my face. 'I will send a few of my brothers after her, alright?' He gazed hopefully into my eyes and relief crossed his face when I nodded. 'Good. Now, go and get some sleep.'

I sank down under the covers, trying to avoid the anxiety that stirred within me.

When I woke again a few hours later, Harlow was at my bedside.

He helped me to sit up, and began making decisions for us all, despite the fact that I was still half asleep. I rubbed the sleep out of my ideas as he gazed upon me with warmth behind his eyes and said, 'We'll go soon, but first we should train you some more. If we come across any of the queen's guards, you'll need to be prepared with even the basics.' He ran his hands down my arms consolingly, but I shoved him away, and he backed off. He had understood the message that I did not want to be touched. Good.

Then he led me to the rug before the fire where the others were gathered and eating breakfast. He handed me a plate of eggs and sliced bacon and I sat down and began to tuck in, slowly, not wanting to rush although I was ravenous.

I had not eaten this much since the morning of the wedding, as we had been making do with only the small rations we had found in the cabin.

But Harlow and his brothers had soon directed us to another parlour, one that we had not even noticed. His words registered as I ate. But could he not see that I already knew the basics? I was no warrior, but I had spent years of my life training with his fellow comrades. But then, I supposed he was right in the fact that we were up against *magical* soldiers, and that watching them in action could make even the most confident of fighters fall to their knees in fear.

I gestured for my father to join us, my intentions probably clear in my eyes.

'Absolutely not,' Harlow whispered, watching my father as he began preparing himself for the journey with weapons and armour. 'I will not risk the monarchy like that.'

My father peered at the soldiers with a regal smile on his mouth. 'I appreciate your concern, General Harlow, but I am experienced in combat and I can hold my own. I will become restless if I do not move around and make good use of my surroundings. I would like to join you.'

Before they could protest, he was already pulling on his armour and helping me into mine. Being here was a risk, and I was my father's only heir, and yet he was happy to train *me*. Perhaps this was different because I was not yet the queen, but in some ways, I was their only hope.

I only wished I had the voice to stand up for my father, as he was a powerful man and would not enjoy being seen as weak or someone who must be protected by remaining in the cabin. But, clearly, he could look out for himself.

My father had seemed lethargic since we had brought him here, no doubt a consequence of the enchantment that had been held over him by his wife, but now he seemed energised. Enthusiastic, even.

Seeing him like this refreshed me, filled me with a new hope that I had not thought I would experience for a long time to come.

The others began to file out and formed pairs, and Harlow's words went ignored, much to his frustration. His heart was in the right place, so I could not blame him for it. He was only trying to protect his king. But he also understood the hierarchy he must conform to, because eventually he bowed his head and answered, 'Yes, of course, Your Majesty. I apologise, I was only trying to act in your best interests.'

My father laughed softly. In his steel armour, with his white-blonde hair curling around his ears and a defiant expression on his face, he looked like more of a king than I had ever seen before. 'I could see that, my boy. You and your brothers have done my daughter and I a great service, and for that I will always be grateful. But I am not unconscious anymore, and I will take it from here.'

We formed our places, every one of us wearing armour and practicing with swords and spears.

I loved watching my father fight, so full of purpose. It pleased me to see him happy. Gone were the days of practicing hand to hand combat before we moved onto more advanced training.

Seeing the queen's men had reminded us that time was not something we had to our advantage. And I had shown Harlow and Marcus that my skills were better than they had first thought, so they began to show me some things I did not know, and only improved on the work I had already put in with the boys at the palace.

'She's got some fight in her,' Marcus said with a grin as I slid my sword past his with a new ferocity, the blade scraping against the middle of his armour.

I could not respond, but my smile would have told him everything he needed to know.

When we finished up the fight, with his sword lying on the ground several feet away, I helped him to his feet and he said breathlessly, 'Come on, girl. I want to see you take down the lieutenant.'

It felt good to be so productive. Not that I would be able to take the queen down in a fight if she appeared to us tonight, but it was progress. Who would have known that all of those nights sneaking out to fight with the guards would become so useful?

The others formed a circle as Harlow came to stand before me with a hand outstretched in greeting.

Boy, would this be fun.

We stepped quickly into action, and the sound of steel crashing against steel could be heard again, the adrenaline in my veins overpowering the noise of the soldiers' cheering in the background.

My limbs ached and my ribs felt like they might shatter from my earlier fights, but still I moved and swiped my blade across his. I learned more moves in that one session than I had in years.

For the first time since leaving the palace, a small glimmer of hope shimmered inside my heart.

Winnie was not herself, but the while the witch was in her glass body, it was the least I could do to look out for her. I needed to keep the witch in my sights for now, ready for when this was all over and Winnie could get herself back.

What was it about her being missing that made me care for her safety more?

She was still the daughter of the woman who had killed my father, and a stranger. But she had saved my life so quickly without even hesitating, and I had been so cruel to her. This would be my way of changing everything for her. I had to keep her safe.

First, that meant I needed to find her.

Together, the boys and I headed out of the cabin, through the forest, and away from the path that led to the Icefall palace. The place that had always been home to me. Walking down a long road, every one of us cloaked and disguised, we searched between the trees for the witch.

Harlow scanned the forest where Winnie had saved my life, and then we walked that open road in the sunshine. Despite the sun's light that bore down on us, the air was still bitter and I was forced to slip my gloved fingers into the pockets of my cloak.

Anyone who stumbled upon us might think we were the queen's guard herself, or so I hoped. That way the people should not intercept us on our travels.

After some time, we came upon a small gated village crowded with little thatched-roof houses, and between them, a small market square where merchants sold their wares to potential visitors. This road was clearly well travelled, and the people here seemed happy.

Visitors regularly passed through, asking questions and buying their stock. There were stalls with the most beautiful handmade jewellery, gemstone rings and pendants in bright colours that caught the sun's light, gold bracelets and more. Others shouted about fruit and vegetables, or silk and cotton dresses and bags.

These were my people, the residents of Icefall that I was supposed to protect. Tears welled in my eyes, but hope rose in my heart.

Despite losing my place in the palace, I somehow knew I was supposed to be here, to see this part of the world that I would one day rule. Watching my father's gaze as it skimmed through every small detail of the village only reminded me how important it was that we restored peace to Icefall. Because this situation with the queen was only temporary.

There was no way I was going to give up what was rightfully mine now.

'They are beautiful, are they not?' my father whispered, linking an arm through mine and taking the words right out of my mouth. 'Our people. They are the reason we must fight for our palace, our throne, and our home. One day it will be yours, my love.'

If only these people knew their king was in their midst. But perhaps it was better for us to see our world this way, to empathise with them so that we might serve them with more compassion and pride.

'Let's take a break and gather some supplies,' said Griffin, leading us through the marketplace.

We split off, each eyeing up different stalls. I walked around, purchased a few pretty pendants from a large merchant with a bald head and a long white beard, wearing overalls and knee-high boots. 'Hello miss,' he said, in a heavy eastern brawl. 'Anything you like the look of?'

Before him was a table full of glimmering stone rings and multicoloured bangles of shining steel, bright stone pendants. He pried, 'Have you travelled a long way? Maybe a bangle so you can ... my stars, that looks familiar. I have one just like that here –'

He had caught sight of the necklace at my throat, my mother's locket. I was a fool, and I should have hidden it beneath my armour. I dug it under my cloak, but it was too late. He scooped up a pendant that was very similar. Not an exact copy, but ... no, it was the same, but clearly faked. I studied the other pieces, and realised they were all copies of the jewellery that was often worn by my mother.

'Can I see that, miss?' he asked, his eyes widening. But then they hardened, and he stared at me more closely. 'Or should I say, Your Highness?'

Wanting to break away from him quickly, I placed a few golden coins down before him and picked up a heart-shaped amethyst pendant for Winnie and a diamond ring for my own keeping.

I ignored the merchant, who was now screaming at me to answer him, until Harlow and Griffin came over to block the man's path to me.

'You and your guards think you are safe here, Princess?' I ignored him and walked away, heading for the place where Liedan was scanning through rails of pretty gowns and overalls, oblivious to the commotion. 'Well, you should never have come to Ulrah. These villages will never support the cruel king and his reign. He doesn't care for his people, he is selfish and –'

Harlow was now on the other side of the table, holding the stocky merchant high in the air with his throat between his hands. My body was filled with a sudden warmth at the sight, leading me to wonder what was happening to me. When Hugo had defended me, all I had felt was a soft affection for the prince.

But this feeling was new, and it startled me. I would not have known what to say, even if I still had my voice.

'How dare you speak to your princess like that? She wasn't even going to tell you who she was, she was going to be a polite guest for your stall and pay you in riches, and this is how you repay her, disrespecting the father who was, just last night, slaughtered in his marital bed?'

My father glanced over, realising, as I had, that the guard was trying to protect his identity from those who seemed to detest him so much. But then he looked away, and the other guards began to shield him, blocking the merchant from recognising him for who he truly was. My cover may have been blown, but at least my father would be safe.

The man's eyes were wide as saucers as he stared between Harlow, Griffin and me. 'The ... the king is ... dead?'

'Now, don't you feel silly?' Harlow eyed him with a death glare. There was something enticing about the rage that burned behind his eyes, and the thought that it was all for me. A blush crept into my cheeks, and my gaze fell to the ground. 'Apologise to the princess, this instant.'

The merchant's dark eyes were cold as he spat back, 'Never. She is just like her father, and she will never be a good queen.' He stared down at me, and spat at my feet. Harlow squeezed his throat, and he finally let out a rasping, 'Alright, alright, I am sorry.' He restored the air to his lungs and regained his footing before answering, 'I am sorry the bastard king is dead. He was useless to Icefall anyway. All he does is take our good money and use it to add to his own wealth.'

Not true. These people knew nothing of the things my father had sacrificed for them. What a fool.

Harlow swung a fist, and then the merchant was on the floor with blood pouring from his nose. Harlow and Griffin pounced on the man until other residents ran over to break them up, while others watched with horrified stares.

My father was the one to tear the soldiers back, still disguised beneath his cloak.

Then it was all over, and we left the square through the village, frightened residents watching us from their houses.

'You swearing loyalty to your betrothed?' said Harlow, glancing down at the ring on my finger and grinning widely. 'Shouldn't he be buying that for you, and not the other way around?'

I glared back at him, wishing, not for the first time today, that I had my voice to scold him with.

Holding his hands up in a mock surrender, he laughed. 'Alright, I apologise. It is a pretty ring for a very pretty lady.'

His reference to Hugo suddenly dawned on me. Was he truly teasing me, or might he be jealous?

What a strange thought. He knew I was betrothed to a prince. Courting between a princess and an army general was no normality, and he should have known that.

'If you were wondering, he's definitely flirting with you,' said Marcus, confirming my thoughts with a smile. 'Don't let him get to you, he's got a soft heart really. He just likes to act tough.'

I shrugged.

'I would certainly ignore him,' said Hugo, appearing from behind me with Titus, Liedan and Cassius. I could not help but laugh, although no sound escaped my lips. 'He is simply jealous that I have the hand of such a beautiful princess.'

'Yes, I truly envy your marriage of convenience,' Harlow shot back, casting me a knowing smile. 'While it is clear to me that the princess doesn't see you in such a way.'

'As if a princess would align herself with a soldier,' Hugo retorted.

I had never seen him so worked up, his hands clenched into fists at his sides. They began their battle of testosterone, shoving at each other's chests with force so that my father and the other soldiers were left to tear them away from each other.

I had only ever known Hugo as my betrothed, and I would never become used to the thought of other boys fighting for my attention. So I stormed away from them both and chose to cast my attention elsewhere.

Looped over Liedan's arm were the laces of some new leather boots, and a heap of glimmering silk dresses. Did he have a lady back home to please? I wondered to myself with a chuckle.

The other soldiers had acquired some cloaks, and a few baskets of fruit and meats that we could fill the cabin with.

We resumed our search, with the soldiers politely asking the villagers if they had seen Wicked or her glass frame anywhere around these parts.

As expected, they just stared at us like we were insane or told us to leave and not come back. This was especially disappointing for Griffin, who was clearly the most excited to see their reactions to the glass girl walking through the village. 'Someone must have seen her,' he insisted. 'I mean, it's not like you see a walking glass statue every day! Wouldn't you want to tell someone? She'd become the product of public gossip.'

We passed a few small children playing chasing games. They watched us with nervous expressions, but a few of them even approached slowly. 'Princess!' cried one little girl, clutching the leg of my leather trousers as we passed through. Like the other children, she wore a cotton dress which was dirtied with mud and grass, as if she had been playing, and her long hair was braided over her shoulder. The girl's mother, a tall copy of the child with long dark curly hair, ran over and apologised before leading her away. But the girl insisted, 'Mama, it's the princess!'

The mother narrowed her eyes, but shook her head and apologised again when I offered her a grin. 'No Sharly, it's not. Come now, let's go and play.'

But the girl was persistent, and shoved her mother away when she tried to lead her into the house. 'I know it's the princess, Mama. She's a witch just like us, isn't she?'

A witch? Fear drummed through me, and I had to remind myself that she was just a child and children loved to play games.

She had made up the story...

As that thought processed in my mind, I remembered the creature I had seen before I had jumped into the river and the way it had spoken of my mother wanting to call me home. I had read a book in my palace library a few years ago about a creature called the Guardian, who protected the Roth witches from harm, and it was black like a panther, but with golden scales.

There was no way that my mother was a Roth witch, was there?

No, I would have known if that were true. She would have told me. She would never keep a secret like that from me.

Harlow offered, 'We are sorry to have troubled you. We are just passing through, looking for our friend.' He was staring at the woman, but she was now gaping at me, transfixed.

Being a Roth witch in Icefall was no crime, and in many cases it was celebrated. My father had always admired the witches and the work they had done for Icefall. Were the people of Ulrah all witches, and if so, why would they hate the king? More importantly, what would have caused a witch like my mother to hide her true identity from her husband and child?

'You speak of strange enchantments, and you do resemble the princess,' said the mother, taking me by surprise. She moved closer, pressed a hand against my face, and I realised she was blind. So how could she see what I looked like? 'It is you. It begins.' She took me by both shoulders, and began trembling violently from head to toe, leaving me wondering what in Icefall was happening. 'It has begun!' She gripped my face with both hands, and fear clamped my heart once again. 'Beware the false prince. Beware the heartless queen. Beware the witch with the devil's tricks!'

The witch's words about seers having foretold a story of two princesses washed over me suddenly.

This woman was not just a witch, she was a seer who had seen my future. But all I could think about as Harlow dragged me through that village, were the words spoken by the little girl: *She's a witch, Mama. Just like us.*

Back at the cabin I was a mess, unable to stop thinking of everything the seer witch had said.

'Beware the false prince. Beware the heartless queen. Beware the witch with the devil's tricks!'

We were no closer to finding Winnie, and the hope I had felt earlier had faded far too quickly.

There was nothing I could do but to cry, and let Hugo hold me. As someone I might grow to love as my betrothed, or as my best friend, I needed the support.

So I laid there in his arms as night formed a black sky, and let him kiss the tears off my face.

26

WICKED

'GIRLS, I AM GOING TO SHOW YOU the spirit realm of the witches. It might be strange for you, so you must promise to stay close.'

Mother's expression was full of worry, the kind that appeared when Lunar and I ventured too far through the Winter Forest when the sky was dark, as she led us into that familiar spot where Lunar and I so often played.

We loved the big tree and the trinkets that hung from its branches: keys and jewellery, small paintings of flowers. It was the only tree that anyone had decorated, and Lunar and I had always been drawn to it, but now we could see why. It meant something to our mother, which made it a great treasure.

'Wicked, you must keep hold of Lunar's hand at all times, in case she strays.'

I did as I was told and wove my little sister's fingers through mine. Then we followed Mother through a wide and gaping hole in the tree's trunk. I was determined to keep my only sister close, and be her guide, although I wasn't much bigger than her myself.

'Mother, no! I don't want to go!' Lunar cried, tears trailing down her small face.

Her fear only refuelled my own, as who knew what was out here in the dark? Wolves, bears and ghouls? Beastly creatures that would swallow you whole. This place was the thing of nightmares.

I tried not to be too scared as I needed to be strong for my only sister, or Mother would scold me.

I wouldn't be the wonderful big sister she so wanted me to be. I must never be Wicked, she always said. I must always do my best to be good, to be kind, or I would lose everything. Lose my mother and father, and my little sister. But Mother couldn't see the pressure that put onto my shoulders when I was barely strong enough to keep my own head up. But still I went on, as I always did, because I was resilient.

'Come, Lunar,' I said, singing to my sister as I so often did, knowing how it calmed her.

'Well done, Wicked,' Mother praised me as I brought Lunar through the tree and into the spirit realm: a world of darkness and greying, fading light.

Mother led us through the forest, and when I turned back I saw that the entrance we'd come through had disappeared. 'What is this place, Mother?'

There was no colour here, only greys, blacks and whites. Cloaked figures passed, some headless or with gaping wounds in their faces, some missing limbs or even floating above the ground.

We came out of the forest through a small clearing. Before us was a tall hill that hosted an enormous building made of crumbling stone. Its eerie presence sent a shiver up my spine.

'This is the witching world, child,' said Mother, with a hand resting on the small mound that was her stomach. 'Our home, the spirit realm of the witches. This is where we will come when we die. You see that building up on the hill? That is Urda's home, child, the goddess we love. You must be good, Wicked, remember that, or you will end up here before your time.'

Lunar began to cry again, so Mother took her into her arms. 'That there is the House of Roth.'

The first place I ran to was the frozen lake. Snow fell around me, coating my glass frame like a pretty white paint. But I kept moving through the trees, my legs leading me there as if they knew the way.

There was an opening here somewhere, a way to enter the House of Roth, the witching world.

The memory came to me in a flash as I wove through the snow. The entrance to the witching world was within the largest tree in the Winter Forest. I hoped that there, I might find the old witch, the one who had trapped me in this glass prison.

She must be here somewhere.

In the meantime, I was determined to see myself as I really was. Myself as I was in the future, or was it the past? To get my old life back, and my own body back. I knelt before the lake and stared at my reflection, at the icy blue surface of my transparent skin – my arms, the face which wasn't my own, light curls falling down over my shoulders.

I was peering at a stranger, something mystified and magical and completely unbelievable. And yet, coming away from the reflection and then back to it only brought back the same image.

It wasn't disappearing, as much as I wished it would. I was living a nightmare, and there was nothing I could do about it.

'Hello Wicked,' said a male voice, one I'd never heard before. 'Aren't *you* the fairest of them all? Why do you wear my daughter's face?'

I spun around as if someone new had appeared behind me, but this person was nowhere to be seen. Except ... I gazed down into the lake again, and there he was. Soft features and warm blue eyes, with spectacles perched on his head. 'Who are you?' I asked, with fear creeping into my voice.

'I am Farn Braxton, Mayor of Cranwick.' He paused, adding a smile before continuing, 'You are made of glass, but you have my precious child's face. Tell me what happened to you.'

'You knew my name, so surely you already know?'

He peered back at me with a thoughtful expression on his face. 'I recognise souls, I see them in auras. My daughter is also missing somewhere in Icefall. You are a witch of Roth, one of its leaders, I sense that in you. I know nothing else about you.' A trace of suspicion flickered there when he said, 'Did you harm my child and take her body, and have it enchanted somehow?'

I shook my head, frustrated that he would dare to make such accusations when he'd just claimed to sense souls. If he were so good at seeing who a person was, wouldn't he be able to see the memories, mistakes or regrets that stained them?

Or maybe it was more complex than that, and he couldn't actually recognise anything. 'I did no such thing. I don't know how long I've been in this body, or what has happened to my own. I think it's been a few days, but sometimes things feel real and I feel myself, while at others ... I'm as lost as your daughter was.' I laughed coldly as I realised what had occurred here, and who this man was. 'Your wife has married the Winter king, did you know?'

He shook his head sadly. 'She hasn't been my wife for a few years now. She planned this mew marriage behind my back, and told me she went to a witch to negotiate her terms for her plans, but I knew nothing else.' His eyes lit up. 'Was it you she spoke to?'

The queen told her husband nothing of her plans, but the king seemed to know everything. Didn't that show how much she truly loved this man? That didn't seem fair at all. I raised an eyebrow, and ignored his question. 'Do you know what occurred at the palace on their wedding night?'

His eyes widened just a little as if he were pondering my question and the meaning behind it. 'No, I know only of my daughter's departure, and very little of her mother's plans.'

'The king was almost poisoned to death as she lay beside him on their marital bed.'

His mouth dropped open. Anger radiated from him in waves, as if he thought I were playing a prank on him. If only that were true. 'Almost? No ... You're lying, trying to distract me from the truth of my daughter's fate. Tell me the truth, witch.'

'I don't know why I'm even speaking to you.' I moved to my feet and peered up at the sky.

This wasn't why I was here. The tree must have been somewhere close by. Curse this man for distracting me from what I was here to do.

'No, don't go!' he cried before I moved away completely. 'Please. Perhaps I can help you. Just tell me all that you know and I promise I will help you in some way.'

'How will you help me?' I couldn't bear to be tricked by this stranger, this mayor of the Mirror Village, and yet here I was, speaking into the lake.

To the father of the girl whose body I'd clearly been placed into.

'You are lost, are you not? Away from the witches that cursed you and my daughter. I can sense souls through reflections, it is a part of my magic. A gift that was bestowed upon me when I became the mayor of the Mirror Village. I will take you to them, if you help me.'

'I know how to access the witches, so your help isn't needed,' I lied, shaking off the feeling that I should follow him because I no longer wished to feel indebted to another person, and also because I feared that he might try to trick me.

'You're lying. I know where those witches live, in fact I can take you to them myself –'

'Really? Because I heard a rumour that you're sick, and your ex-wife, now evil queen, was searching for a healing potion for you, but gave her physical heart to the witches instead. Which is probably why she is now evil.'

His bright eyes widened, and his mouth dropped open in clear astonishment. Today was obviously a strange day for him, too. 'She did what?'

'If you know where the witches are, shouldn't you know this? You see all, after all.'

'I know only of their location,' he said with a sigh. 'Please, Wicked. We can help each other.'

'Very well.' I shook my head and sighed, thinking of all that I knew. I recalled what I'd heard about Leraia and Winnella as well as Princess Frost and Prince Hugo. When I was finished, the mayor of Cranwick – much to my surprise – stepped through the ice like a stairwell had been provided for him.

'Thank you, Wicked,' he said, casting me a soft smile. 'Now I will assist you in return.' He wasn't alone as he limped up the steps. 'Oh, please meet my nephew, Barchester. He's been looking after me while all of this is going on.'

The young man behind him stared at me, wide eyed. His mouth dropped open as he took me in, and then he looked around the forest with a look of awe, before returning his gaze to me. 'Uncle, what's happening? Winnie is made of glass.'

The mayor turned to his nephew and frowned. 'You heard everything she said, yes?'

'Sorry, Uncle,' said Barchester, almost shyly. I studied him – he was handsome, tall and lean with curious eyes. He wore a polo shirt with a bow tie, pointed toe leather shoes and spectacles like his uncle's. 'Hello, Wicked. I suppose I'm a little ... distracted. Nervous to be leaving Cranwick.'

'What did you both have to sacrifice to the witches to be able to leave?' I asked them.

'Nothing,' said Barchester innocently. 'My uncle has ways of getting around the witches' rules.' His expression was blank, as if he were afraid to give his opinion of his uncle's position.

I raised an eyebrow and the mayor gently smacked his nephew across the arm. 'Remember who you are speaking to, boy.'

'Sorry,' Barchester stuttered again. 'I suppose I got distracted by her glassy, witchy beauty. Honestly, Wicked, it's a little hard to take in that you have my cousin's face, and that it's made of ... '

'Glass,' I finished for him when his voice trailed off. 'Yes, well now you know why, so please take me to the witches. As they are, in the present.'

The mayor smiled and offered me his elbow. He linked my arm through his and stepped back under the ice. I shook my head and backed away, but he just pulled me against his side. 'Look, you left that cottage and something – no, someone – led you to the frozen lake. It's safe, believe us.'

I shook my head. 'No, I'll shatter. I'll –'

'I'm risking my daughter's body here. Please trust that I know what I'm doing.' His smile was earnest and real, but I didn't know how to believe him. 'I understand that you're confused; everything that you are has been placed into my daughter's body and cursed. But you can do this.'

I sighed, but something in his words made me trust him. 'You're right. Nothing makes sense. My memories feel like they're muddled up with someone else's – with Winnie's, possibly. I can barely remember my spells, my memories ... it feels like I'm looking down on myself from far away.'

'I'm sure it does, but look, you helped me and I promised to help you in return.'

'My uncle never breaks a promise,' said Barchester softly, shyly, with a light trace of a smile. 'You can trust in him. I always have, with my life. So has Winnie.'

'We have many scores to settle,' said the mayor with a smile. 'Come with us.'

So I placed my faith onto his shoulders, took his elbow and stepped down under the frozen water. 'Very well.' My heart was racing and pounding and beating – made of glass or not – as I was enveloped in the blackness of the stairwell beneath the ice. The magic swirled around me like a blast of wind, almost knocking me off my feet. 'What is this place?'

It was dark, almost pitch-black, but there were little lights everywhere, dotted alongside a narrow canal with boats spread out along the water.

Barchester helped me step down into one of the boats, labelled *The Mirror's Best Friend,* and I offered him my thanks.

'It's known as T*he Mirror Canal* or *The River Between Kingdoms,* depending on how you choose to look at it. Only authorised souls have the right to use the passage.' The mayor smiled down at me with a new warmth behind his eyes. Perhaps this was because I wore his daughter's face, or because he was beginning to favour me now that I'd told him everything.

Whatever his reasoning, I returned his smile. I looked around at the other boats, at their strange names and the suited people that manned them. *The Old Dog* was one, as was *The Headless Queen.* I wondered who they all belonged to, and from where these souls roamed. 'Couldn't Leraia have taken your boat out instead of making such a sacrifice?' I asked Farn, who was watching me now from the head of the boat.

'It's only accessible for me. Even if I'd given her permission, she would never have made it past the witches patrolling the borders, and she knew it.'

'But you can go anywhere you please?' I said, frowning. 'My apologies if this sounds rude, Mr Braxton, but how is that fair on everyone else?'

He shrugged as I took my seat on the small bed and he moved us away. 'No apology necessary, it is a fair point. I never asked for this life, I was simply born into it. Winnie will one day be the mayor of Cranwick, as will her son or daughter, and theirs after that.

'Look, it is my boat. But even I am held by certain restrictions: I may only travel if it benefits Cranwick, or if my family is in danger. But I must always make such arrangements with the witches first, and they have to approve my application each and every time. It's always a long process.'

I frowned. 'How do you think they will feel about receiving you today?'

He sighed. 'Oh, I am only taking you close to the border. Their cottage is in a forest not far from there. But I must go after my wife, stop her from destroying Icefall.'

'I thought she was no longer your wife?'

'She may have married someone else, whether she murdered him or not, but she is and will always be my only love. My daughter's mother. No one will take that away from me.'

But Barchester turned to his uncle and sighed. 'That wasn't part of the plan, Uncle Farn. She literally has no heart, she will kill us.'

There were so many questions in my mind that I wished to find answers to. 'What about healing you? The queen wanted to find a healing potion here? Come with me, and we will settle that score together. Along with my curse, and your daughter's.'

'I hate to say it, Uncle Farn, but the witch is right.'

'Very well,' said Mayor Farn with a heavy sigh. 'I will take you.' He seemed to think for a moment but was clearly in agreement. 'Prepare for a long ride, it's quite a journey to the other end of the canal.'

Barchester leaned back. 'So, Wicked. Tell us about yourself.'

27

FROST

In the comfort of the Winter Forest, Hugo and I laid together just as we used to in the palace gardens, listening to the birds singing in the sky, and feeling the wind on our skin.

This was a peaceful place, and I refused to let it be tainted by the fact that this was where I almost died. Winnie had saved my life, and for that I would always be grateful. Soon it would be time to get her back, but first we would enjoy the cool night air.

'You look beautiful, Frost,' said Hugo, stroking a strand of my hair away from my face. 'You always do. I am so fortunate that you will be my bride when all of this is over.' It amused me that he was still thinking of our alliance with everything that had happened.

Clearly his verbal battle with Harlow had riled him up, and their words had slipped beneath his skin. My father had arranged for our eventual marriage, so now he was here, as trapped and afraid as the rest of us. And yet my best friend was still focused on our future plans. But that was

Hugo. When there was a task he needed to fulfill, he would always stay committed.

And now, that task was me.

I let him kiss my cheek and brush his lips against the skin of my throat before he pulled away, wearing a sad expression.

The sight broke my heart. So I turned to him and pressed my lips against his, hoping it would trigger something within me. Butterflies, or a love that had been hiding beneath the surface. This was a little taste of what our future together might be. Hugo was handsome and the kindest person I knew, and he understood me better than anyone else in this world.

These last few days had cast him in a new light, one I would never have expected. Perhaps one day, I could learn to love him.

But there were still many more issues left to deal with, first. The biggest one being taking down my wicked stepmother and taking back my kingdom.

Hugo had gone to bed, and the others were gathered around in the snow some distance away, having their own midnight training session.

The cabin was quiet as I slipped out. I stepped forward, and found most of them circling Harlow and Marcus who were sparring in the centre. Harlow was clearly winning, and the others were watching and laughing. Worse, my father was among them, revelling in all of the testosterone.

It dawned on me for the first time how stupid they had been, so close to the cabin, putting their king at risk by making such noise. It was not truly envy that burned within me, but rage at these silly boys who believed they could act so rashly with their monarch and not suffer the consequences. Were they trying to draw the queen's enchanted guards right to our door?

I stormed ahead, unsheathed the sword on my hip and lunged for Harlow's waist before flipping him over my shoulder and slamming him hard into the snow. He had been so focused on Marcus backing away from him and plotting his next move that he had not seen me coming. Rumbling laughter and applause echoed through the forest, and the boys wore matching grins of admiration.

'Your Highness,' said Harlow, moving to his feet. His eyes were wide as saucers as he looked up at me. 'Where did you learn a move like that?'

Somewhere amidst the chaos, Hugo had appeared. I must have woken him before I left the cabin, and he had come looking for me, only to find me here with the others. 'Frost has always been a go-getter. She is also rather close with the palace guards, who may have taught her a thing or two.' He looked me up and down, missing the fact that Marcus was one of those soldiers, along with his brother Ryan. 'Frost, what are you doing here? I thought you were sleeping, you are not supposed to be –'

'I've heard the rumours,' said one of the brothers, interrupting the prince's words and taking us by surprise. Liedan, I believed his name was. He was tall and lean like his brothers, but much quieter, with long dark hair. He was handsome – they all were. 'But even a practiced warrior princess could do with some more training every now and again.'

I folded my arms over my chest, annoyed that they were out here so late and making all of this noise, but Harlow seemed to mistake it for me feeling left out because his face crumpled with guilt. 'I'm sorry, Your Highness. We should have invited you.'

I rolled my eyes, wishing, not for the first time, that I had my voice to tell him where to shove it. Grabbing Hugo's hand and gesturing to my father to come with us, I strode away from them.

'A few more weeks of training, and you will be brilliant!' Harlow called out from behind me.

Hugo and I exchanged a nervous glance. 'Weeks?' he shot back. 'Think of all the damage Queen Leraia could do to Icefall in that time! We have a few days at the most.'

I nodded in agreement, thinking of all the ways I could get my kingdom back. I did not want to kill the heartless queen to do so, but I needed to be rid of her so that she could never leave Cranwick again.

But there was no way to make such deals with the witches of Roth when I could not even speak. Everything was hopeless without my voice.

I would need to make use of what I did have in the meantime: determination, willpower and the need for success. Love and passion for my kingdom.

For Hugo, my best friend.

For Winnie, who had become like a sister to me in recent days. She had to be there somewhere. I would get her back, if only I could.

It would take time to train, but we would work quickly before I travelled back to the palace to take down the false queen.

The others had returned to their sparring, but as we walked away, Harlow ran over. I cast Hugo a look, and he linked an arm through my father's and led him to the cabin to give Harlow and I some privacy.

'Your Highness, I want you to know that we will look after you for the next few days, and then we will go with you to the palace,' said Harlow with a grin.

I could only give him a curt nod and a smile in response, but he seemed to understand.

Then his expression became suddenly wary, eyes wide with a new fear as he said, 'You must be careful, Your Highness.' He peered around him as he spoke, as if he were afraid that we were being watched. 'I have heard whispers that there is a soldier roaming these woods looking for you. He could be anywhere. Don't trust anyone, even us seven. We are the king's men, after all. The queen's now, I suppose.'

'Where?' I mouthed, hoping he would read my lips and understand.

'I don't know. Like I said, don't trust anyone.'

I pointed the tip of my sword at his chest as if to say, 'You?'

'Anyone,' he repeated, before stalking away. 'I imagine the queen will want your heart if hers is really missing.'

'It is not missing,' I would have said if I were able to speak. 'She gave it away.'

'Come on,' he said, gesturing for me to come inside. 'I promise we are not going to hurt you. I just want you to keep your wits about you, and always pay attention to your surroundings. You don't know who may have been persuaded by the power your stepmother possesses, should she wish to give it away to get you back.'

He did not need to tell me twice.

I went into the cabin after him and climbed into the bed they offered, and fell quickly asleep, dreaming of warriors in the night.

After another long day of combat training, Harlow and his brothers decided we needed some time away from the cabin and the secluded forest, so we took another expedition through Ulrah to find Wicked.

After all, there was no way she could survive on her own for very long in that fragile state.

My father had decided to stay behind with Titus, Griffin and Cassius this time, but Hugo chose to come with us, and I was pleased to have him beside me even as he began to point out all of the birds in the trees and their species.

I zoned out of the conversation, but hearing his voice calmed me. Because, with the queen's intentions unknown and looming over me, it was difficult not to feel panicked. So his soft smile and often childlike enthusiasm was all I needed.

Although the chances of finding the witch were slim, we kept moving because it was necessary. Because she was taking over Winnie's body, and it was important that we found her and brought her back safely, or there was a chance that Winnie would be lost to us forever. We tried a few villages along the river, knocking on doors and asking for sightings, hoping not to run into any more witches. But there were many in the villages around Icefall's capital, so it was more than likely that there were seers and healers here.

I could not get the thought out of my head that I was one of them, even if I knew they were lying and trying to trick their way into my head.

Witches had proven themselves to be less than trustworthy, and I refused to believe I was one of them. But in all of these villages: Ulrah, Zebiah and Marn, the children all stared at me with strange smiles on their faces and followed me through the streets as their parents observed with awe-filled eyes. They ran toward us through the narrow cobblestone streets, while the adults lingered in doorways or stopped their farming in the fields as we passed. Perhaps they did not get visitors very often, but even so, there was something off about the way they were looking at us. About the way they stared at me, compared to the others. I did not need to wait long to understand why.

'Papa, it's the witching princess!' a little girl cried out.

'It's her, the one who is going to save us!' said a small boy.

In their eyes, I was not just a princess, I was a witch, and my mother was, too. In their eyes, I was either something to fear and detest, or perhaps to some, someone who could protect them from my cruel father. The merchant had spoken of my family with such hatred, and it was impossible to know how many more people of Icefall felt the same. In Zebiah, the village closest to Ulrah, Hugo quizzed a few residents about Wicked's appearance but they just stared blankly at him. However, as soon as he brought up my heritage and why we were here, the atmosphere changed completely, and they all came rushing over to tell us everything they knew.

As far as I had always been told, my father had always helped the witches, and brought them closer to Icefall, promised them they would be safe. But any mention of the king from one witch had the others on their knees and trembling.

'He uses us,' said one mother, clutching her child to her knee. 'Exerts our power for his own riches, makes us conjure up silver and gold from stone just so he can continue to live in his special palace. My sisters said so. He used to be kind to us, only ever tried to bargain with us so that we, too, had something to gain from the deals he wished to make. But now, he uses us until we are weak and exhausted. His men are the ones that capture us, but we know who is really behind everything.'

The shock of these words brought tears to my eyes, and I sank to my knees. It could not be true.

I wished I could argue on his behalf, and tell them that it was not my father they had to fear, but his new wife. He was kind, and she was cruel. He was good, and she was evil.

Perhaps in her time in our kingdom, she had been painting this new image of my father to make him appear as the monster that she truly was herself.

But if they really believed that of him, he would not so easily gain their trust back.

I was glad that he had not come with us this time, as hearing them speak of him like this might just break his heart into pieces, and I could not bear the thought.

Hugo threw an arm around my shoulders, and his face was creased with sympathy. He did not need to hear me to speak to know what I was thinking, nor did the soldiers who brought me back to my feet and held me while I cried. 'Forgive us,' said Hugo to the mother, while rubbing my shoulders with a hand. 'This is not the king we know. He was kind, and welcoming to all people, and –'

'Was?' said the woman, her mouth falling open. A new smile crossed her lips, and she laughed with the others around her. People started to rejoice. 'He is in the ... past?' When Hugo nodded, she gestured for more of her friends to come over.

Witches beamed, smiles widening their lips. They were on their knees, thanking the skies that they were now safe and free from his wrath.

I could not do this any longer, I had to get away from this place. All I felt was hollow inside. My father was not as cruel as they claimed. It was an illusion that *she* had created, I was certain of it. He may have isolated himself from me, but he was not the kind of king to torture witches, or to hurt his own people. So why did their reactions seem so believable, and cut me so deeply inside?

With tears rolling down my face, I ran. But Harlow took me into his arms and held me, reminded me of why we were here. In their excitement, the witches of Zebiah had spilled a lead. Many of them had seen a strange figure passing through that night, her skin a transparent hollow blue. Like ice.

Like glass.

She was headed toward the long road that led to the autumn kingdom. Toward the canal that took the witches to the Mirror Village of Cranwick.

It had been a long day of endless combat training, and a draining evening of searching the villages for the witch, so we all climbed quickly into bed and sleep overwhelmed us all within only minutes.

I was in dreamland for some time, tossing and turning, in and out of sleep, when I heard a low voice saying my name, 'Princess Frost!' Somehow, it reminded me of the witches in the cabin, but also of Vencin, their strange cat-like guardian creature.

My feet were on the ground within a few moments, and I found myself moving toward the noise, still sleepy and in a daze, desperate to seek out the owner of the strange voice. My feet led me to the forest where a fire burned, and several naked figures danced around it, loudly chanting a strange rhyme.

What were they doing out here in the middle of the night?

Darkness calls to light,
Sings a song through the day,
Birds echo in the sky bright,
Tell me child, lead the way.

'Princess Frost,' the voice said again as I crept closer, fearful eyes watching the dancers as they pranced around the burning flames. 'Join us.'

And there he was, the panther-like beast, watching me with those piercing golden eyes. Vencin. 'Hello, Princess. You finally decided to seek us out, even if it was in your unconscious mind. But that is perfectly fine. We are glad for your company.'

The witches had stopped dancing, and the air was now silent, the fear dimmed to a mellow flicker of smoke. Some were elderly like the witches in Elder Wicked's cabin, while others were younger. Wisps of white hair fell around their faces as their gazes met the floor. But then they began to change, circled me silently and came to kneel before me, eyes wild and eerily dark. 'Princess,' they said in unison.

Not a single one was Wicked, or my mother.

Nor did I recognise any of them from Elder Wicked's home or the neighbouring villages.

But they were all watching me with doting expressions, as if I was important to them somehow. Where was my mother? I had called to them in my dreams, and them to me. So where was she?

'Princess,' they said again. Were they expecting me to respond?

'Celebrate with us,' they said, before the witch in the centre reached out a hand and pulled me against her.

Then, as one item, they moved to their feet, and the fire returned as we began to dance. In a circle around the fire, around and around and around, while the Guardians watched the trees, scanning for danger.

The witches must have had some powerful enemies to need such protection. What was I even doing? I had left the cabin so quickly in a sleep-like trance, and I could not remember the walk here. I tried to break away from the witches, but the one closest to me grasped my wrist and we spun faster, the witches chanting and singing over and over.

As they threw their faces to the sky, I realised they were praying. Worshipping the full moon, which was now a radiant circle of blood red light against the blackness.

The blood moon.

This was some kind of seance, and I was right in the middle of it.

As we danced I studied their faces, and everything washed over me in a flash. *Marin, Alisa, Talia, Violeta, Marissa, Lia and Noella.* Sisters, between the ages of sixteen and nineteen, all Roth witches.

They were raised on a farm close to Icefall. Wicked was their cousin. How did I know this?

'We know you, Princess,' they said in unison, as if answering my inner question. 'And you know us, as well. You are one of us, and you always have been.'

If so many witches were trying to persuade me that I was one of them, it must be true.

No, I thought as my body began trembling violently, this was all too much for me to take in.

'Your mother is watching you closely. She is so very proud,' they said.

If I was not already broken from the events of the recent days, that would have pushed me over the edge. I did not hear much else before my heart began racing too fast, and the blackness took me.

28

FROST

'COME HERE, LITTLE BIRD,' said the soldier approaching me with a wide and charming smile on his mouth.

He was handsome, and somehow familiar to me, with a firm jaw and soft curls that fell around his ears, and I fell instantly under his warmth. The kind eyes, and the smile that creased his full lips, enticed me. He beamed down at me, and ran a hand through my short dark hair. He whispered, 'You will be okay, Princess.'

Then his fingers curled against my cheek, and he quickly brought his lips to mine. I found myself breathing in his warmth as he said, 'I know everything is frightening right now, but you will make a grand queen, Leraia.'

Leraia? No, that was not right. The happy daydream quickly dissipated, and the moment was gone. Something was terribly wrong. I moved closer to the soldier with my sword raised.

Just as he plunged his sword deep into my chest.

A hand reached in and I screamed as it tore out my ever-beating heart.

I sank to my knees in the snow by the lake in the frozen forest, and looked up again into the face of the warrior who had taken my heart.

But it was a new face this time, and it was no longer a soldier. No longer Lieutenant Harlow.

Hugo beamed down upon me now. 'Yes, Frosty,' he whispered, casting me a proud smile as he held my heart in his hands. 'This will do nicely.'

It was just a dream, I told myself as the fear sank in.

But when I glanced around the room, around the cabin, Hugo was nowhere to be seen, and the soldiers were still sleeping peacefully in their beds.

A warm fire roared, the flames licking at the hearth. Through the window beside my bed, the sky was dark, the blood moon high in the sky and casting a strange scarlet light over the room. How long had it been since I had left the cabin, and found myself dancing in the forest with the witches?

Or had that even happened at all?

My hands flew to my chest, where they found countless bloodied bandages. I screamed, although no sound came out. My knees buckled beneath me, and suddenly I feared that the dream was not actually a nightmare, and that my heart was gone.

Harlow rushed over, saying softly, 'You're alright, Frost. You tried to claw your own heart out, but it's still there, look.'

Relief washed over me like a wave, but to my horror it did not last. He opened the bandages, and I glanced down again and a second scream burst from my throat, although no sound came out.

'Frost, there was something there before. I'm so sorry … '

How in Icefall was I still alive? My heart was gone. Hugo had betrayed me and was undoubtedly on his way to take my heart to my evil stepmother.

But in my confusion, there was something I had not even noticed. At my bedside now, alongside the warriors, a girl chanted words I did not understand, her enchantment slowly sealing my body back together. Her slanted cat eyes were familiar to me, but I could not understand why. Perhaps I had seen her in Elder Wicked's home, or elsewhere.

Her dark hair bounced above her brow, and fell in a sharp line at her jaw. There was something eerie about her stare, but I was beginning to find that this was typical for the Roth witches. They were an intense bunch.

'Hello, Your Highness,' she said softly, her voice quiet as a mouse. 'I'm Elora.'

A child witch. Where had she come from? She did not seem much older than Hugo and me, maybe a year or two younger, but there was a youthful enthusiasm to her smile as she drank me in.

I had closed my eyes for only a moment, then opened them again, and there she was.

'Now, you sleep. And you will see everything.'

Hugo was riding through the snow with a leather satchel hanging from his shoulder and a great beaming smile on his face.

No doubt, that satchel contained my heart, which he had taken from my chest while I slept. Just as Leraia had given hers away, mine was lost.

'Don't trust anyone,' Harlow had said back there in the snow. 'Anyone.'

Not even the best friend I was betrothed to. Had the soldier sensed the truth, or was it merely a coincidence that my best friend's betrayal had happened not even a day after his warning?

Hugo's men soon joined him. Where had they been hiding? Had he not been alone? 'I have it, my friends. Now, we ride to the palace.'

I had never seen the prince so full of pride. There was no remorse in those cold eyes. He had acted on his own accord, no doubt so he could take my stepmother's power.

The Windspell prince had quite literally stolen my heart.

But what was worse was that he could so easily give our location away to the queen, and her guards would be here within the hour.

'I am so sorry, Frost,' said my father, taking me into his arms as I began to sob. 'If I had sensed his character, I would never have betrothed him to you.'

How unfair it was that he felt the need to apologise to me for something that was not his fault.

How could he have known Hugo's true intentions for me? How could anyone have seen the monster that laid beneath his princely charm?

29

WICKED

THE CANAL BETWEEN WORLDS WAS A DARK PLACE filled with long and narrow boats in different colours and designs. Reds, browns and blues. They were all named strangely: *The Devil's Keep, The Rose Watcher,* and *A Bridge Over Seas* to name a few.

People lounged on little chairs while eating pots of soup or drank wine and ale when they weren't turning their boats away and setting off for faraway destinations. This place was both strange and familiar, but the terminal filled me with hope at the thought that we were going somewhere, even despite the circumstances.

Mayor Farn was speaking to me about something, but I didn't hear him because a new voice appeared inside my mind, deep and hollow, as if it belonged to an elderly person.

A witch, perhaps? Could it even have been the witch that cursed me, the one I was hoping to find?

'You are doing well, Wicked. Do not fear Farn Braxton but do not trust him, either. Come to us, and we shall end your enchantment,' the voice was warm despite its hollow sound, and full of something like admiration.

'Is it you?' I asked.

'I am you, Wicked, and you are me. But who I am is beside the point. I am going to show you a memory now as I realise that your mind is a little muddled at the moment.'

If only she knew how muddled it really was. Or, maybe she did if she were saying that. *'That is the understatement of the century. So you are me when I am older?'*

Much, much older, it seemed.

'I told you, it is beside the point.'

So it was true, then.

With those words, the setting changed. I was still in the tunnel between kingdoms on a boat riding across the water, but I was no longer with Mayor Farn and his nephew.

Now I was with Greyson, my beloved.

'You have been here before, child. You will see.'

I did see, much to my surprise, and once I had, it was strange that I hadn't recognised it at first.

Greyson and I had travelled through these tunnels for years, with him or his brother Eric navigating them. Often while Eric drove, Greyson and I would lay down in the small bed and make love to each other there.

When Greyson drove and Eric slept, we would talk from the head of the boat about our daily errands, our families, patrolling the waters, and make sure no one unsavoury was here. Once, Greyson had even held me over the side of the boat to see if I was tough enough to climb back up.

I threw him into the water.

An ache stung my chest now when I thought of him. I wondered what he was doing now, where he was, or who he was with.

'Pay attention to the memory,' the older version of myself snapped. 'It's only meant to help you on your journey.'

'How? I don't know what I'm doing? How is Greyson going to assist me with my current plans when I haven't seen him for so long?'

But the voice no longer answered my questions.

Instead, Greyson leaned in and brushed his lips against mine. I'd missed him, how he felt. Missed his long dark curls and those warm brown eyes. I pressed my fingers to my lips after he turned away.

In this moment, I wasn't her. I wasn't made of glass, and I looked like myself.

This was truly one of my own memories.

'The Old Witch should take us right down stream toward the Icefall Mountains,' said Greyson, offering me a smile and stroking a finger through my red hair.

That name murmured inside my heart. How I'd loved that boat. How had I forgotten its name?

How had I forgotten the tunnel I'd roamed through so many times?

How had I forgotten everything I used to be?

Greyson leaned in and kissed me again before calling out, 'How much longer now, Eric?'

'Why do we need to go to the mountains?' I asked, my mind filling with confusion. I remembered feeling it, wondering what Greyson had planned for us all.

'There are diamonds there, Wicked. Jewels beyond our imagination.'

His face instantly lit up. 'We won't have to worry about your coven or my clan anymore. We can escape, just as we always wanted to.'

And I remembered now, like I'd merely unblocked the memory, how much I loved him, longed to go with him, to be with him and build our lives together. But something had happened on that trip, something that I couldn't remember, that was clearly still locked away inside my treasury of lost memories.

I would see it all soon, I only needed to keep watching.

'Only a few hours to the mountains, Grey,' said Eric with a chuckle. 'Go on you two, get some rest.'

'You know I don't rest when Wicked is around,' said Greyson, casting his brother a knowing glance which his brother quickly returned.

'Oh I know. Don't worry, I'll be on look out. Have fun.' He laughed, and I blushed crimson.

'Did you really need to embarrass me like that?' I said as he laid me down on the bed and curled up beside me, kissing on my neck, my arms, and my cheeks.

Every inch of my body burned with pleasure at his touch.

The memory was gone, and I was back in the boat with Mayor Farn and Barchester, more confused than ever about what I'd seen.

I was unable to make sense of my jumbled memories, but longed for Greyson, my love, now that I remembered in detail how wonderful things used to be between us. How much he cared for my family and me. 'How long will it take to get to the witches' house?' I asked, thinking of everything I needed to do now to make things right. We needed to move quickly.

'Only half an hour or so,' said Mayor Farn through his exhaustion, running a hand through his short hair. 'I know you're desperate, but be patient.'

If he thought I was desperate to find the witches, he didn't know the half of it.

A sigh left my lips before I could stop it. Couldn't he see that this wasn't me?

Unfortunately for him and his nephew, patience was a virtue I didn't possess.

Unfortunately for me, these memories were washing over me more quickly now with each moment that passed, like something inside me had been unplugged and everything was now becoming clearer.

When we finally reached the mountain caves on the edge of Icefall, Greyson led us into the blackness with his sword raised, but I stopped in my tracks, sensing the wolf's steps from somewhere close by. 'Greyson? Eric?' I called out, but they were already too far ahead, excited to find the jewels that were so well known to the mages in these parts.

It wasn't just wolves, either. There were rumours of giants roaming this area as well as elves, orcs and even the fae. Fairies watching from their small homes in the trees.

This place was dangerous, and I'd seen it first-hand, but the boys wouldn't believe me.

Memories clouded my mind then, reminding me that something terrible had happened there that day.

'Why is this important, Wicked?' I asked this elder version of myself. If she was so determined to show me these memories, she needed to make the message clearer. But this elder version of myself was stubborn. I supposed, now that I was thinking about it, I shouldn't have been surprised.

'Watch, and you will see,' I was told.

I walked into the cave, my legs moving of their own accord, like a film only showing me what I'd already seen and done.

'Come on, Wicked!' Eric called out playfully, encouraging as ever. 'Or do your legs still hurt from your session on the boat?'

'That is none of your business, Eric Marks!' I replied, reeling at the audacity of his words. But I heard Greyson chuckling behind him and knew this was one of those moments I'd cherish forever, where I truly felt at home even if it wouldn't last.

But I hadn't yet known the truth; that fate would soon take over again.

I took Greyson's hand and he and his brother led me through the darkness. I chanted a protection spell so the wolves wouldn't see, hear or smell us within these caves. If only I'd known what other dangers lurked within, I might have cast more enchantments.

I might have saved their lives.

Now their fates were clear to me, and I was forced to hold back a scream. It was like a fog had fallen over me but now it was all slowly beginning to clear away, like it'd always meant to.

Deep inside the mountain caves was an enchanted waterfall guarded by a pack of enormous, snarling wolves. There must have been a dozen of them, a whole pack, pacing and growling at the magic they clearly sensed nearby. Greyson approached with his sword raised but I called out, 'Don't! They can't see, hear or smell you. There is no need to harm them.'

Looking back now, I realise I probably shouldn't have said that.

He sighed as if I were taking away the fun of their journey. 'Look at that water, it's clearly magical. Do you think it heals people, and stops them ageing?'

'The possibilities are endless,' said Eric, stepping past two of the wolves and dipping a finger into the water. 'Oh, goodness ... ' He looked up and pointed high above the waterfall to the roof of the cave where there were hundreds of sparkling jewels. 'Greyson, look!'

'It's all we need to get away! Pass over the bags!' His brother threw him the satchels and Greyson's eyes lit up in green and blue as he spoke enchantments only he and his brothers knew in their sacred tongue. They were beautiful words, and the mages' work came clear.

But using magic drained the mages, and each jewel Greyson pulled down made him a little more exhausted. Still, he moved one after the other through the air, and into his satchels. Eric took a few as well.

I focused on the wolves, who were now intent on the brothers as if the magic they were using was lessening the protective enchantment hanging over them.

I gathered some of the sparkling water into my bottle only to look down and find a male face watching me. He was young, only a boy with light brown curls falling around his face, and kind eyes. 'Bring me that water, Wicked,' he said, although I'd never seen him before. How did he know my name? 'Please, I am very sick. In fact, I am dying. If I use too much magical energy to protect my family's village, it will kill me. You will help me one day, Wicked. I know you will. I don't care how long it takes, just bring it to me, please.'

'Who are you? And what are you talking about, trying to protect your family's village?' I had so many questions, and they all appeared in my mind one after the other. But he'd disappeared, and then there I was, left with only Eric and Greyson and the wolves for company. The wolves that were circling them now, ready to pounce. They took too many of the magical jewels, and they were exhausted.

I tried to place another enchantment over them, but it was too late.

The wolves pounced and feasted. Greyson and Eric's greed had been the death of them.

I ran from the cave screaming, seeing only the boy's eyes.

'That was Mayor Farn, wasn't it? What kind of fortune telling is this?' I yelled, my face soaked with tears.

Where was the satchel full of jewels and magical water now?

What had I done with it after that day?

I had the sudden feeling that I knew where I would find it.

'You know what you must do now, child?' said the older Wicked.

The memory faded, and I was back on the boat with Farn and Barchester. It finally dawned on me that this memory had granted me with a lesson, and a purpose. All of the memories my elder self had shown me had led me to this moment.

My life with my sisters, with my parents and my beloved, it was all much clearer now.

'I think I know where the potion is to heal you. You spoke to me as a boy in an enchanted pool of water. But I need to meet with the witches, and with my elder self, to find it.'

'I've been waiting for this day for years,' he said with a bright smile on his face, and tears welling in his eyes. 'I knew this would happen one day, that I would find you. I just didn't expect you to be wearing my daughter's face when you came to me.'

Despite everything, a smile crept across my lips. 'Or, a face made of glass?'

He laughed softly. 'Yes, exactly. What changed? Why the urgency?'

'A good lesson from my elder self.'

30

FROST

PRINCE HUGO WAS A STRANGER BEFORE HIS MEN, overwhelmed by pride as they strode into the Icefall palace grounds. Then they stepped down and announced to the guards waiting there, 'I have what Her Majesty has asked for. Take us to her.'

If he had not already stolen it, my heart would have shattered into thousands of pieces in that moment.

I still was not truly sure what I had wanted with Prince Hugo. A peaceful future for both of our kingdoms, and perhaps a love that would grow over time.

But whether it was a platonic friendship and an alliance or a marriage that could one day end with both of us falling in love, Hugo had been my friend first. The one person I could count on through everything – my mother's death, my father's abandonment and eventual demise, and then the destruction of my kingdom.

Whether or not I had loved him as a future husband, I had adored him as a friend, and as my biggest supporter. But he had betrayed me, and taken my stepmother's side.

He was as good as dead to me now.

'Yes, of course, Your Highness,' said the guard he had spoken to. 'This way.'

They were led into the palace through a more subtle entrance meant solely for royals and nobles, while their horses were taken to the stables to rest. I watched Hugo and his men storming through, excited to gift the queen with what he had taken from me.

Surely it was no good to him now, broken as it was, or maybe he merely saw himself as the queen's messenger. A new way for him to climb the royal ladder more quickly. How fortunate he would be now. I hoped it made him happy.

And then, in my blissful need for revenge, I hoped that one day that happiness would be ripped away from him, just as our future together had been.

'What happened there, Hugo?' asked one of his brothers, his voice barely louder than a whisper. 'You were gone for longer than expected.'

'There were some complications with some witches, her stepsister and the warriors, but I am here now and that is what matters. I look forward to receiving my prize.'

'Good luck, brother,' said Hugo's friend.

Arrogance and hunger for power radiated from him in waves as he stood there grinning at his friend.

This man was not the best friend I had always admired; he was a stranger.

An enemy.

'Thank you, Marlo,' he said with a regal smile. 'Witness a new day. Soon, I will be the king of Icefall.'

As if being the heir of Windspell was not enough, he wanted Icefall as well. Fear crept through my chest at the thought that he might have been planning this since we were children.

I woke, sweating, and staggered into the back of my bed, unable to stop screaming even though no sound came out. What foolish choices he was making!

If he had married me as planned, he would have become the king of Icefall anyway.

Now he was going to ... marry my stepmother to get there more quickly? Rage bubbled in my veins as I remembered all of that bile he had spewed about me being the true queen of Icefall, and how my stepmother was merely a placeholder to me finding my footing on my throne. It had clearly all been just a ploy to get me to believe him.

To help him betray my trust.

'What of Windspell?' said Marlo with a curious smile, which Hugo quickly returned.

It was false, and completely unexpected, and it made my stomach flip. 'I have my plans for them as well. My sister will face my wrath, as will Father. As for Mother, well I do not have to worry about her interference.'

What was he talking about? His mother was a strong-minded soul, and she would never let him betray her kingdom like this, whether he was her only son or not. His parents and his sister were good people, and good rulers, and they were as much of a family to me as my own. Hugo was no better than my stepmother now, willing to harm his own family for power.

This Marlo did not even care to stop his friend's cruel plans. Anyone in their right mind would have done something, or at least tried. The kind prince I had always known and loved had become the villain that would ruin what was left of my life forever. Perhaps if Leraia had not done it, Hugo would have killed my father instead and married me to take his place on my throne. My kingdom was already in turmoil, but he had just made everything a thousand times worse.

They were introduced at the door of the throne room and walked inside. Queen Leraia was sitting on her throne, entertaining herself with a high stack of books as servants brought her food and drinks on trays. Her dark hair was braided into a neat bun atop her head where a silver crown was placed, with roses woven through the steel. She was wearing my crown and one of my mother's gowns.

Crimson, like blood, like her lips.

Like my stolen heart.

'Your Highness, my dear huntsman!' she exclaimed, putting her books to one side and stepping down to meet him. 'Do you have what I asked for?'

'Yes, Your Majesty,' said Hugo, beaming with pride as he opened the satchel and the small enchanted box where he had placed my still-beating heart.

'Oh, wonderful!' she said with pure delight on her face. 'Bring in the prisoner.'

Hugo stepped aside as the young witch was brought to her knees before the queen. I had seen her inside Wicked's house. When had she been captured?

What about the rest of them?

'Cast the spell, witch. I want that heart inside my chest right now.'

Whimpering, the witch fell to her knees but slowly began chanting the spell and the heart – my heart – in Hugo's hands, disappeared before our eyes.

The queen collapsed, and a soldier caught her in his arms. Her eyes fluttered closed.

'What happened?' Hugo cried when the queen remained limp. 'Someone help her!'

'She will be fine,' said the witch as the soldiers restrained her. But they paused when she added, 'Just give her a few minutes and she will be good as new.'

They waited, pressing their blades against her throat as my stolen heart was settled into Leraia's chest.

She had given away her own, and taken mine.

When Leraia woke, she smiled at the Autumn prince. 'Well done, boy. Prepare for the wedding, my king!' She laughed. 'We will have a marriage of convenience, just as you were supposed to have with the girl. Then I will be rid of you, as well.' A wicked glint appeared in her eyes, and Hugo began to beg.

His eyes were solemn as he pleaded, 'No, no! Your Majesty, you promised that we would be united in eternal matrimony, sharing our power between us as equals –'

She had sold him the dream. He truly thought they would be together forever, wearing matching crowns and ruling the four kingdoms.

What nonsense.

She laughed in his face. 'You are a boy. Did you really think we would live happily ever after? Don't be silly. Your title is all I want from you.' She nodded once, and her guard forced him to his knees with a sword against his throat. 'Have Frost's body brought to the palace. I want her to be encased in glass, a statue to be displayed in the palace grounds. Just like the garden statue of that mother she cares for so much.'

'Her body?' said Hugo, practically stuttering the words.

'You heard me, Prince. You killed her, so bring me her body.'

'I did not ... '

It dawned on me then, that perhaps he had not wanted me to die. Could he have sought out the witches himself, found a way for me to live without my heart, just as she had for so long? It did not take away the destruction he had caused, not in the slightest, but it did offer a new perspective.

But it also meant that, if it were true, he was in deep trouble with the queen.

Confirming my thoughts, her eyes burned, and she took a step closer to the prince. There was no way he was getting out of that palace alive now.

Even with everything he had done to me, I had to force myself to keep watching them speak.

'What do you mean you didn't kill her?' said Leraia, edging closer to Hugo, who took a nervous step backward.

Then slowly, as if eyeing a wildcat who was about to pounce upon him, he reached for the sword at his belt. The queen's guards circled him. He was surrounded; he would never get himself out of this. 'I gave you her heart, Your Majesty, just as you asked.'

'Are you trying to tell me that she is out there somewhere, alive?' Her anger seemed to fester when the prince merely stared back at her with fearful eyes.

I had never seen him so afraid. But for the first time, I thought he deserved it.

'Well, boy? Answer me!'

Hugo stuttered, 'She will not come for you, I promise.'

Oh, is that right? I thought, now seething myself, more than ever before. I will come for her and then I will come for you, Hugo.

'You did not complete my request.' She called out to the guards, 'Kill him, and find me some of your best warriors who will bring me the girl's head!'

I could not help myself; fear thrummed in my veins when she spoke those words. I had to make sure that did not happen, and somehow, deep down I knew that meant I would have to take her down. I did not want to stoop to her level, but we had to be rid of her one way or another, even if it meant using desperate measures.

Hugo gasped before screaming, 'No, Your Majesty! Let me go, and I will get her for you! Please, do not do this!'

But there was no way he would ever win this. His time was up. Within minutes, with just a single gesture from the queen, a guard plunged a sword into Hugo's chest, killing him instantly.

I woke, screaming silently once more, to find Harlow and the young witch at my bedside.

If only someone would tell me that it was all a dream, that Hugo was not dead ...

The witch just held me as I sobbed against her chest, soothing me. 'Shh,' she whispered, and her voice was so soft, like a lullaby, that I found myself listening intently. 'It will be alright. Look, don't tell my grandmother, but I think you deserve this. You've been through so much already. I'm so sorry, Frost.'

I stared up at her as she raised her hands, chanting a new spell before focusing on me again. She was looking at me with so much concern while stroking my hair away from my face. It finally dawned on me how much had actually happened in such a short amount of time.

It was as if I had been running through the motions on survival mode, and now it had all come crashing down around me.

'Thank you,' I mouthed, only to clear my throat and at the same time, realised my voice was back. I had never liked how softspoken I was, but in that moment it was heaven to my ears. A true miracle, that I had these witches and their magic. 'Thank you.'

She laughed. 'My grandmother can be quite brutal at times.'

Her grandmother? She had called her that before, but I had brushed over it, so overwhelmed by everything. That meant that one of the witches I had seen in her house must have been her mother. But more importantly, she had healed me. She had been raised by the witches, and possessed powerful magic of her own. Magic that could help us in our fight against my stepmother.

Not for the first time since I had arrived here, hope fizzled in my heart. It was small progress, but progress all the same. Every door that had slammed in my face seemed to lead to another that could take me to new places.

I moved to my feet, determined to use this new hope to push myself forward, to keep moving. 'Come on, we are going to the palace.'

'In the middle of the night?' said Harlow, shaking his head and staring at me like I had grown another head. 'Surely not?'

'I am going to kill my stepmother and get Winnie back.' It had not felt right to me before, but now, I had never been so certain of anything.

I needed to do this to make things right for my friends, for my father and for my people.

'And your heart?' said the young witch with a smile.

'That, too.' I moved to my feet, but my legs were not as strong as they usually were.

'Slowly,' said the witch, helping me back onto the bed as I collapsed. 'You've been asleep for a few days, so you might feel a little weak at first. Princess Frost, I fear that with no heart, you might not be able to move as carefully as you usually can –'

What would happen to me now that my heart had been stolen? 'Three days? And the prince left … Elora, where are the others? I have to … Who knows what the queen has done since he left?'

If what I had seen was real, Hugo was dead, and the queen would soon know where we were.

'What will you do when you go to the queen?' said Elora, watching me with a curious expression. It was clear that she admired me and my determination, but she was also afraid. 'You saw how powerful her magic is. It's too soon.'

'But I am losing time. I have lost Hugo, and I may have no father soon. She has taken everything from me. I cannot sit here and do nothing.'

'I know, but –'

There was only one thing I could think of that would help me make things better. If I did nothing, I would grow restless. I needed something to throw my energy into while we prepared ourselves to fight.

Where better to start than with my true heritage? If my mother was truly a witch, magic was already in my veins, and it was something I could use. 'Then train me, and teach me magic,' I insisted. 'It might not be enough to defeat the queen, but it is better than nothing.'

She eyed me nervously. 'I would, but I am still learning myself.'

'Show me what you *do* know.'

'I suppose I can try.'

We set to work, with the young witch leading me through some simple levitation spells. 'I need to aim higher than this, Elora,' I said when she told me, over and over, to repeat this process. 'It is not enough to defeat my stepmother.'

Elora sighed in frustration. She looked at me as if she were dealing with a small child. 'You must always begin with the basics. If you cannot focus enough to handle a simple levitation spell, how will you throw an oncoming soldier across the room? Send a sword flying away from your head and back at your enemy? The devil is in the detail, Princess.'

As much as I did not want to admit it, I knew she was right.

After a few hours of training, we headed back inside, exhausted. It had been a good day, full of strength and resilience. Great progress, and glimmers of hope that waited for us some distance away.

But, deep in my chest, I knew those glimmers were sadly not enough. We did not have time to sit around and do nothing. I had to keep moving, or I would lose all hope forever. My father was safe here, in the care of the soldiers and the witch. He would be okay, and I would make things better for us all.

While everyone else was sleeping, I took what I needed from the wall and slipped out into the night, but not without first kissing my father goodbye.

31

WICKED

'This way,' said Mayor Farn, leading Barchester and I away from the canal, and up a nearby tunnel that sent us out onto a narrow road overshadowed by trees.

'Is he usually this abrupt?' I asked the boy with a chuckle as I moved slowly on glass legs, with Barchester kindly taking my arm for assistance.

'Yes,' said Barchester, smiling. 'But don't worry, he's a good man, if a little tiring at times.'

He cast his uncle a long look, and I wondered what he was thinking. Maybe wondering, for himself, how he'd ended up in this strange predicament, having to chase after a glass witch to get his cousin back.

If I were him, I probably would have freaked out, too.

'What was that?' said the mayor, turning back to face his nephew.

'Nothing, Uncle.' Barchester raised an eyebrow at me when his uncle strode on, much faster this time. He eyed me closely, and flashed me a grin. 'Can you slow the pace a little? She can't walk very fast.'

I narrowed my eyes. 'She has a name.'

Barchester chuckled. 'Sorry, Wicked. You never answered my question back there on the boat. Who are you, really?'

He was ridiculous, but I had to admit that I was enjoying the company. It felt good to have someone actually show interest in me again, rather than looking at me in fear simply because I was a witch. 'Honestly, I'm not sure I know,' I answered. 'Sometimes I think the old witch only placed fragments of my identity into Winnie's mind, or body, or whatever.'

I recalled the memory that had come to me with Eric and Greyson, and the others I had remembered of my time with my sisters and my uncle, and his mouth dropped open.

'Wow, that is insane.' He was quiet for a while, pondering my words. 'Well, as lovely as you are, I need my cousin back. And I'm sure you want your own body back as well. There is much to be done to get there.'

I laughed, and not for the first time I realised I was starting to like this boy, even without Winnie's consciousness inside my mind. 'It would be good if things started making sense for us again.'

He shook his head and smiled. 'Well, if it means anything, I think you're pretty cool.'

'Thanks. You're not so bad yourself.'

He chuckled shyly, before asking, 'So, tell me about these mage warriors. I bet they're super-hot, right?' He raised an eyebrow, and I found myself laughing along with him.

I could have guessed that there was something different about him. In the four kingdoms, it wasn't common to meet someone who was so openly committed to their own gender. For some of the royals, it wouldn't be seen as acceptable. Oceanwell, especially. Icefall, Blossomheart and Windspell were more open to different types of people. So Winnie and Barchester were both refreshing to meet, although this was the first time I had come to admit it to myself.

'They are certainly powerful from what I do remember, often arrogant and a little greedy. You might have liked Eric; he was an extravagant soul to say the least.'

He laughed. 'Oh, I love extravagant!'

'I would have guessed as much.' As we walked, I listened intently, but the only sound to be heard, other than Barchester's laughter, was the howling of wolves somewhere in the distance.

We were close to the Winter border, an enchanted place full of monsters and more magical creatures than you could imagine, and edging nearer to Windspell with every step.

Prince Hugo's kingdom.

There was a tingling within me, a foreboding sense that I somehow knew only witches possessed.

Something bad had happened to him, I *felt* it.

It was like the untangling of my memories was also opening up the magic inside me.

Perhaps if it didn't work out with the witches, I would remove the curse hanging over me, myself.

'Are you two coming?' Mayor Farn called out from further up the road. He waited at a junction, and then turned left into a wide-open field before taking us into another part of the snow-covered forest, overlooked by trees filled with icy branches.

'Windspell is a day's carriage ride that way. The witches live in a small cabin close to the border. Can you see it from here?' He pointed to a high bridge where a stream of elderly witches patrolled, watching over the world below. 'Well, they live this way. But we have to keep moving. Come with me.'

A sudden thought occurred to me, and a feeling of unease crept in. 'Will you get into trouble for being away from Cranwick without permission?'

He shook his head and smiled. 'I think you'll find that since my family is in danger, it counts.'

He couldn't have been any more correct, and although he was

speaking on a personal level, his words hit home for me as well. There were so many questions left unanswered, and only time would reveal the truth. What had happened to Hugo?

Where was Princess Frost, and would Winnie – and me – ever be truly free again?

Why hadn't I thought to slip through the portals to find the witches, as Princess Frost had?

No, the answer to that final question was clear: first, I'd been afraid I might shatter if I fell, but also, how would the witch react to me if she found me that way? At least if I knew where her home was, I would know how to get back to Icefall without becoming trapped or having to dive through another mirror, ending up goddess knows where.

We continued walking, endless steps through the ground, which was now half snow and half icy slush. We walked between the mountain roads under the great raging stone.

'I thought you said they live in the forest?' I asked Mayor Farn, who was now walking through a nearby tunnel like he'd been here hundreds of times.

'I suppose I lied,' he said, with a low chuckle. 'There are reasons the witches live away from the rest of the world.'

I stopped, frowning up at the rock wall above me. 'And how do you trust that I won't speak of their location to another soul?'

He turned back to face me and gave a sad smile. 'I don't, but the witches have their ways of keeping you silent, should you become trouble for them. There are rules everywhere, for anyone, even if you don't know you are restricted by them.'

With those words he turned and walked away, beckoning us to follow. 'Come, it's just down here.'

He turned right into a hole in the mountains, into an open space. We passed through the gap in the stone, into a small dimly lit street twinkling with little glass lights encased in glass containers, the street eerily quiet.

A black door stood over me. I'd seen it before, but where?

'You are close by, child. I can sense you.' The elderly voice appeared inside my mind again. Then the door opened and I stared into a face I knew well.

The witch who had cursed Winnie and me.

My own face, only now soft and wrinkled with age. 'Hello, Wicked.'

The words I wanted to say vanished from my lips as Farn and Barchester charged through the open door. Real and true, this was the face of my future.

Seeing her now only made everything feel more real. And there she was, holding a very familiar satchel over one arm, the one containing bottles of enchanted water.

'We told you, Wicked,' said Mayor Farn, taking my silence as confusion. 'The witch is you, and you are her.' He supported me with an arm before taking the bag from her hands. 'I told you that you would help me one day, witch.' His raised finger was now pointed at the elder version of me. 'Barchester, take her.'

'What are you doing?' My eyes narrowed as they settled on the man and his nephew.

It was at that moment that I realised the man had been using me and my memories.

What a fool I'd been. There was the enchanted water that his wife had promised to bring him.

This was a man determined to survive.

But he could at least have bargained with me, and tried to help me find my body in return.

What would she and her sisters do to him now? Within seconds, they were on their knees, thick golden rope binding their wrists and ankles. 'You have no such authority to make demands, Mayor Farn,' said the elder witch, eyeing him with a cold stare.

In a blink, he was on the ground clutching his throat. The satchel was back in her hands, and the mayor and his nephew lost their composure.

What had he expected, trying to negotiate with such a powerful witch? It was hopeless.

It was an exceptionally cold day, and my sisters had chosen to spend it exploring the Icefall mountain caves, with hopes to find an enchanted well, the water said to hold both healing and anti-ageing qualities.

What could be better than that for a coven of young witches who only wished to prove themselves to the parents who expected so much of them?

It was only meant to be a day of fun and freedom for us girls, while our parents were away on a trip, but as you might have expected, it didn't end that way.

No such luck.

Seager was only two years old, and loved to wander. We needed to keep an eye on her so she couldn't fall into any danger, but the girl had always been sneaky, and talented at getting away from us all when we were occupied with other things. You wouldn't believe the amount of times Lunar and I were forced to pull her out of trees, streams and lakes because she'd run off and gotten herself stuck.

We told her to stay close, and not to leave without one of us. She and Mora ran across the stone floor of the cave, chasing and spraying each other with bottles of the well's enchanted water while the other girls watched on and Lunar and I attempted to control them, thankful that they were still in our sights.

Deep in these caves roamed a pack of wolves. Our adventures to this place had always ended eventfully. Three times we'd been here now, but this was the first time with my young sisters at my side.

For hours I had been telling them of the darker parts of the cave and trying to steer them away from the venture, but Marthy's paintings had pointing her toward this part of the world. My sister had a talent for telling the future with her paintings, but she always said they led her brush, as if she were possessed by something. Or perhaps it was just her magical niche, just as mine seemed to be leadership and healing.

She was on the ground with her sketchbook, painting the well and the bright crystals hanging from the dark walls. She and the others were far too stubborn to stop them when they wanted to begin something new, so Greyson had promised to come along with us and become our great protector.

We would be in safe hands, I was certain of it, as long as we stayed together.

Vielle was admiring Marthy's work over her shoulder, and Sara and Corani were splashing around in the well.

'Wicked, watch this!' Corani squealed excitedly, before sending a wave of the special water crashing to the ground, soaking both Marthy and her drawing.

'Don't waste it,' Lunar scolded.

'Corani, you ruined it! How could you be so … ,' Marthy's words trailed off as the magical water caused one of her hand-drawn crystals to materialise, glistening in the light of the well, above her page. 'Oh my god, do it again!' she squealed, taking the jewel into her hands and studying it closely.

Corani was ready to kick the water again when I held my hand up, halting her in the action before she lost us the water. 'That was amazing, Marthy,' she whispered, climbing out of the well and coming to join Marthy and the others.

'Is it real?' said Hera, coming over with Everly to examine the crystal, but Marthy tore it out of her reach and shoved it into her satchel.

'Very real,' she answered. 'And it's mine.'

'Fine,' said Hera, with an edge of disappointment in her tone. 'Draw me a unicorn instead, then. I want a unicorn.'

'No, give me a trident,' said Heaven, eyeing her sister with awe-filled eyes. 'I want to –'

'A mermaid,' said Alis.

'A star!' said Mora and Crescent at once.

'Make me rich,' Lunar muttered, although I sensed the bitter sarcasm in her tone. 'Wicked, where is Seager?' Her voice held a nervousness that made my stomach twist, especially when I realised she was right.

Our smallest sister was missing. I scanned the cave, frantic and terrified, when I finally found her in the corner beside the well. She gripped a vial of enchanted water in her tiny hands, and she wasn't alone. A new opening I hadn't spotted revealed the snarling heads of three large wolves, slowly approaching my baby sister.

One minute she'd been running around before our eyes, while the next she'd disappeared amidst the commotion of Marthy's artist revelation.

'Wicked!' she screamed. 'Big dog! Big teeth.'

'Hold on Seager, don't make any sudden moves.' Lunar gasped aloud, and the girls fell silent as the wolves moved closer. 'Hold on,' I said again as Seager began to cry, reaching out her arms to me.

She wanted to run to me and curl up against my chest, and it was all I could do not to yell as she screamed, intending to dart past the beast.

'Do something, Wicked,' Marthy whispered.

Behind her, the other wolves were circling us all. I began to chant a simple levitation spell we'd known for years, and one that even the smallest of the girls could do. But I had used it countless times, so I was the most equipped. Lunar spoke a similar spell that sent the wolves flying away from Seager and across the caves, and Seager fell into my arms at once.

The wolves sped forward, rage powering their attack, but one by one we ran from the cave with three large vials full of the enchanted water in our hands.

'I think It's safe to say we won't be going back,' said Lunar, clutching Mora to her chest. That was probably a lie, especially judging by the look of longing on Marthy's face as we left.

But no matter where we ended up, I promised myself from that moment that I would always do what I could to protect my little ones from danger.

'You tricked me, witch. You said you were helping me.' There was no hiding the bitterness from my voice as the witch hauled us inside, and traitor Farn and his nephew were nothing but liars who'd used me for their own gain.

I reached forward to take hold of the satchel which contained the bottles of water meant for Greyson and Eric that would heal them when I found them one day. Because I refused to truly believe they were dead and gone. If the satchel was here in the witch's house, they were out there, too, and I would find them. But the witch's grip was far stronger than mine, and her eyes were dark as she stared back at me.

'You want it, and your freedom, Wicked?' said the witch. 'Well, what are you willing to give up?' She stared into Winnie's glass eyes, and down at the body I'd been forced into.

'Remove her identity and her body from mine, witch,' I said. The memory had brought the spell right back to me, reminding me of the terrifying moment when I'd almost lost my little sister.

Within moments a grin was on my face and the satchel was in my hands. No sacrifice needed.

Another spell forced her and her sisters to her knees, now bound in thick ropes themselves. A grin spread across my lips when she tried to break away, but couldn't. Who was the better witch now?

Another spell freed Winnie's father and cousin. As the witch tried to tear herself free, casting an unfamiliar spell, but failing when my enchantments appeared stronger, she finally asked what *I* wanted, as if she didn't already know.

I needed only to cast her a pointed look for her to say, 'Very well.' She grinned as she began chanting the spell. She was speaking from the old tongue, the old language that I hadn't yet learned. 'I will punish myself no more.'

I glanced down at the uniform I always used to wear: the white cotton shirts; black leather trousers and belt, armed with my potions and Greyson's sword; my nails, which were always painted black; both arms fully tattooed with detailed stories from my coven. My auburn hair fell down to my back in thick, fierce curls.

'You're not so bad after all, Elder Wicked.'

She merely smiled darkly, eyes glinting in the light as her ropes frittered away into ash, along with her sisters'. She and the others were watching me with a look of admiration, I realised, when she said, 'Good luck on your quest, child.'

There was no other feeling like the bitter satisfaction that coursed through me in that moment, knowing that for the first time, I had won against the witch.

32

WINNIE

Everything around me, I saw as if I were peering through a glass window. Nothing made sense as I raised my hands, only to find myself in a small cabin.

I somehow knew I'd been here before but I couldn't remember when or what exactly I recognised about it. Arms wrapped themselves around my shoulders, fragile as they were, and pulled me close.

That lavender scent ... I had felt that before, had loved it as a child. How did I know that? The thought appeared and then vanished in a blink.

'Winnie!' a voice cried, male and familiar. Two men were watching me, one much older, the other with a smile that I both recognised and ... didn't. I had the strangest feeling that I knew who they were, but I couldn't remember where I had seen them before. 'Why did you do this to my daughter, witch?' the older man was saying to the elderly woman – the witch – with one arm still around me. Gentle but firm. 'She has done nothing to you.'

His daughter. This man was my father?

I studied his face, hoping that something about him might bring back my memories of him, but I felt nothing. It was as if my mind was full of fog, and nothing was fully visible. It seemed to have been that way for some time.

'It is all a part of the grand plan, Mayor Farn,' said the witch with a knowing smile. 'Your daughter will be well; she may just feel a little confused for some time.'

Confused? She didn't know the half of it, and frankly, neither did I.

'Well, if we have your permission, I'd like to take her home.'

Home. Where was home? 'Daughter ... ,' I repeated quietly. 'Father ...' Nothing made sense. The world around me was new and vast, and it filled me with a sudden terror that made my body shiver.

Glass. My fingers were blue and transparent, and tapping them against each other gave a tinkly little sound, like nails against a mirror. This was the thing the man had accused the witch of doing.

I was made of *glass*.

'Let me help.' The young woman at the witch's side began chanting a spell. Behind her, I realised there were others watching us. They seemed to resemble the witch in their features. I didn't think I had seen them before, but I couldn't be certain.

But looking upon the young witch who'd spoken, I saw that she and the elder witch wore the same face, only the decades between them were clear. They may have been as related as the others, grandmother and granddaughter, perhaps, but they were identical, and I realised there was something else going on here.

'You couldn't have done that before?' said my father, incredulous.

The girl just scowled back at him and shook her head, sighing. 'No, I told you that I couldn't remember many of my spells. A few were brought back from the memories this witch gave me.' She offered the elder witch a knowing look, studying her closely as if she were as intrigued by her as

I was. 'But Elder Wicked removing her identity from me … unlocked a lot more. Now, if you'll let me concentrate.'

Elder Wicked looked upon me and smiled proudly. 'Go on, child.' She spoke as if she were nudging a young apprentice, or a granddaughter.

My father held his hands up in a sign of surrender as the young witch returned my memories.

The curses she'd put over me and Princess Frost, my village curse, my father and cousin being here, my mother's darkness, all came flooding back, and I staggered to one side, forcing Barchester to catch me in his arms.

'Beautiful work, Wicked,' said the elder witch.

'Go to Hell,' the young Wicked snarled, and it hit me that they were more than related.

Could they even be copies of the same person?

Did the witch who'd cursed me really place her youthful self into my mind, or was I hallucinating once again? Now, here she was, out of my head and back in her own body, while mine was a walking statue just like Princess Frost's mother in the palace garden.

'You psycho,' I hissed. 'How could you do that? Do you know how strange this has all been for me? I've lost my own consciousness, and spent my days with a weird prince and several witches, while one has been stuck inside my head. I have been losing my freaking mind, and you must –'

Elder Wicked only grinned. 'As I said, child. It is all in the grand scheme of things.'

'I'll show you the grand scheme of things … ,' my words slipped away as I pounced on the witch, my fingers reaching for her throat.

'And she's *back*,' Barchester commented from behind me.

'You're not helping, Barchester,' said Dad, and he slunk backward, falling silent. 'Winnie, stop,' my father cried, coming over to tear me away from the witch.

'All is well now,' said the elderly witch with a smile, and practically ignored my rage-fuelled attack as my father held me against his chest, stopping me from charging toward her again.

How I wanted to rip her throat out for what she had done to me and the princess, but Dad had always been good at calming my temper when I struggled to contain it.

'I'm feeling generous,' she continued. 'Go and defeat the evil in our kingdom! But Winnie?'

'Yes, Wicked?' I said meekly, suddenly exhausted.

She smiled, clearly pleased. 'You must be the one to defeat the evil, not Princess Frost. You are the one who started everything. Your mother is the queen, and it was your mother that changed the course of Icefall's history, not hers.'

Her words made little sense. After all, I wasn't the princess whose life my mother had destroyed, although she had changed mine for the worst as well.

This wasn't my fight. But when I thought back to my time with Frost and Hugo and their friends in the cabin, I realised that maybe she was right and I was just as important in all of this as they were.

To end this war, I would have to destroy the mother I had always loved, who had cared for me when I was sick, who had shared with me her body, mind and soul. I wasn't sure I was brave enough for that, good enough, or strong enough. 'You want me to kill my mother?'

'Stopping your mother will also end the curse over your village.' She said these words as if she were talking about giving out her shopping list for me to run errands for her, and at the same time, handed me a violet-coloured candle. 'Take this. Farn and Barchester, your time here is done. Be on your way.' She gestured at the closest mirror, which now showed the open door to my home.

Tears welled in Dad's eyes. I ran forward and took my father and my cousin into my arms. 'I love you, both. I'll end this, I promise.'

And I would do it without killing my mother.

After all, I realised, the witch had said I needed to stop the queen, not necessarily destroy her.

With tears in their eyes, they stepped through the mirror.

The elder witch turned to me and said, 'To use a Babylon candle, you must –'

I took the young witch's hand and smiled, thinking of the palace and not waiting for her elder self to finish speaking.

33

FROST

THE BLACK SKY WAS LITTERED WITH TWINKLING STARS, fuelling the adrenaline in my veins as I prowled through the forest with my voice back in my mouth and magic within my veins.

I had been foolish to try to run before, but this time I felt that things would be different. With a sword in my hand, and hope in my heart. Winnie and Elora had made that feeling possible, along with the soldiers and even Hugo for a short time.

The forest was familiar to me now, almost as recognisable as the palace I had grown up in. I now knew these clearings like the back of my hand, and headed for the palace, reciting Elora's spells in my head. I strode out through some trees, and grinned up at the shining moon as I found myself right where I needed to be.

There was the palace, its little towers silhouetted against the night sky.

Tonight I would make things happen, and work toward destroying the queen who had hurt us all. I was alone, but it was better that way. No one else could be harmed by Her Majesty's wrath. Besides, it was me she had been searching for.

Revelling in this moment of being alone, I swung my sword, and at the same time, I practiced the spells Elora had shown me. Levitation spells, transformation spells, and control spells, I used them all. My skill was improving, I realised, as I watched a small flower become a mouse that ran off into the bushes. Then, as I moved my blade, a rush of wind sent it high into the air.

Only to come crashing down into Vencin's tail.

The Guardian did not yelp, or even move away from the sword. It slipped through him as if he were not there at all, or as if he were made of no substance.

'Why are you alone?' he said inside my mind, his earthy voice sending a shudder through me. 'I hope you are not planning to take the castle yet, child.'

All traces of the excitement I had been feeling vanished as the creature looked upon me with his slanted golden eyes. It was replaced with rage. 'Leave me be, beast.'

His laughter echoed, the sound shaking my mind's inner walls. 'You are not ready. More importantly, you should not do this on your own.'

Who was this creature to tell me what was right for me? 'How dare you –'

I could have sworn I heard him heave a sigh before he cut me off, 'I speak on behalf of your mother, Your Highness. I am her personal Guardian, and she has been watching your movements very closely. Your companions, as well. You have the protection of the House of Roth.'

My mother. This creature knew my mother. 'I do not understand. My mother is dead.'

'Yes, she rules the spirit realm of the witches, child. My words are her own, relayed to you.'

This was ridiculous. If it were so important to her she would have shown herself to me personally, not through this creature. 'Well then, tell her that I love her, but she is wrong and I can do this myself.'

'You need not to, Your Highness.'

Then he faded into nothing, before I could try to argue again. But I soon realised he was right, as behind him, through the trees, were my friends. Harlow, Marcus and Elora, and a few of the others. My father was not among them, so perhaps Titus and Cassius were caring for him back at the cabin, while the rest had come looking for me.

They were all prepared, wearing their armour and bearing the swords we had trained with. And Elora was not alone, either. She had brought some of her coven with her, and they all grinned at me.

Tears welled in my eyes as my heart grew suddenly full of love and emotion stirred at the surface. How could I have wanted to do this alone when I had so many who cared for me? Who wanted to fight with me against my stepmother. Who would, no doubt, have laid down their lives for me and my father if the opportunity arose. I supposed I was far from used to such friendships, and it was too easy to hold my guard up and push people away.

But I did not want to do that anymore, because I cared for them, too. Every one of those smiling faces now held a special place in my heart.

Harlow was the first to come forward, and bow to me. 'I am sorry for what you went through with Prince Hugo, Frost. You deserve so much better. But you didn't need to leave the cabin alone. We would have come with you.'

'Thank you.' What a fool I had been to believe in Hugo. Looking back now, it was impossible not to see how blind I had become by my love and devotion for him, and for his friendship. 'I know it was the queen leading him astray, but I still cannot picture him in the same way. All I see is that heart in his hands, my heart, and the pride in his eyes as he handed it to the queen.'

How happy he had been, elated for his future as the king of both Windspell and Icefall. 'Even if it did lead to his own demise.' I would never know if his intentions were real, or if he were truly beneath the queen's spell in that moment. That was what would always hurt me the most.

'He was weak to let her overpower him like that.' He wrapped an arm around my shoulders, and I leaned into his embrace. 'You're one of the bravest people I have ever met, Princess.'

A blush crept into my cheeks. If only he knew the effect he had on me. 'Says the warrior himself.'

'I wasn't always a warrior. But yes, I have met some very powerful soldiers. But, Princess, I'm not talking about physical strength, but the resilience to keep training and fighting through it all. None of them have gone through half as much as you, and yet if they suffered even half as much, I fear many of them would crumble too quickly.'

'I appreciate your kind words, but they are not necessary.' Elora had said something similar back at the cabin. But there was no way I could sit still and wallow, feeling sorry for myself over a situation I could not control. We needed to keep moving. 'Shall we go and get my father's throne back?'

'For you, they will always be necessary, Princess. I want you to know just how special you are. Let's do it.'

Harlow's smile was almost as bright as the moon. I would be lying if I said it did not send a light blush into my cheeks.

'We can help us get there more quickly,' said Elora, gesturing to the six witches she had brought. 'And before you ask, no we are not going to travel through a mirror.' She held out a candle, and a grin spread across her lips as the other witches brought out their own. 'These are my cousins, Your Highness. Meet Viera, Alanis, Briella, Carya, Mary and Crystal.' They wore wide smiles as they looked upon me. 'They each have different magical abilities that they can use against the queen, and are all happy to help you with your own spells as you are still learning.'

'Thank you, Elora. How do you propose we travel?'

'With these.' She held out her handle. 'To use a Babylon candle, you must picture the place you wish to be transported to as you blow out the flame.' One by one, the witches began to light their candles. 'I suggest we all create a circle, because we don't usually transport this many people at once. It will feel a little strange, but just push through it.'

We formed a large circle, and then, we left.

We were there in a blink, landing in the palace gardens, in the shrubbery beside my mother's statue.

A few of the guards came out of the bushes covered in thorns and roses, while the witches were standing together, laughing amongst themselves.

I moved slowly to my feet, and brushed myself off. My head was spinning, and my leather pants were covered in leaves and a few thorns, but at least I had not ended up in a tree, or fallen into my mother's statue. The statue itself was shattered into thousands of pieces, and all of my drawings, my little trinkets and my letters were scattered across the ground. The other statues were left untouched.

The sight broke my heart, and I fell to my knees in despair. Elora's face was also drenched with tears as she knelt down beside me, wrapping an arm around me. Perhaps she had a love for the queen that many did, despite not being a member of Icefall herself. My mother was a brilliant woman, dazzling and kind to all she passed, so of course she would have touched the heart of the witches as much as those of her people.

It was then that it hit me.

My mother was a witch, and she now ruled the House of Roth, according to the Guardian.

Could she have come from Elder Wicked's coven, and somehow be related to Elora as well?

It was all too much to think about, so I left the girl to cry, throwing an arm around her and letting her embrace me. She spoke a few soft words, and it took a moment to realise she was casting a spell.

Slowly, the statue began to reform, and the letters were tucked back into their original places. 'I'm sorry, Your Highness,' she whispered. 'Hopefully this helps ease your mind a little.'

I draped both arms around her, and pressed a kiss against her brow, still unable to hold back a sob.

The statue that had always brought me such comfort had been restored, and it was all thanks to the young witch. 'Thank you, thank you.'

'That's beautiful, Elora,' said Harlow, coming over with Marcus and the other guards to comfort me. His eyes were bright and thoughtful as he turned to me and asked, 'Are you alright? Ready to proceed? We need to form a plan before we storm in there.'

'Yes, I am ready. I have something in mind.'

We formed another circle, and it dawned on me that the witches were casting an invisibility spell over us as we talked, as a few guards passed us but did not seem to be able to see us.

I could not help but feel comforted, knowing that these witches would have considered such crucial details. With the guards and with the witches, we were in good company. I began to run through the ideas I had in mind, and listened to their suggestions as they gave them.

The stillness in the palace did not last for long, as soon, even from the gardens, we could hear screams coming from the throne room. We ran toward the noise, the witches maintaining our invisibility as we entered through the ballroom doors, Marcus and Harlow casting orders to their men as they began cutting down guards, our invisibility giving us the benefit of the element of surprise.

The queen's men were everywhere, but we were faster, and stronger. Like them, we had both bravery and magic on our side, even if the sources of our magic were different. For now, the queen was nowhere to be seen. Her men lay strewn about the ballroom, but we charged onward, grinning when they called out to each other, only for another to be attacked when they did not know we were coming.

When the guards did not attack with their swords, the witches transformed them into rodents or threw them into the air with their levitation spells.

'Stay close,' Harlow whispered, taking my hand as we left the ballroom and headed into the long corridor that would lead us to the throne room.

Feeling his fingers entwined in mine filled me with a comfort I had not felt since my embrace with Hugo before his death.

There were far more guards here, so we would have to work quickly, but when they knew what was happening, there would soon be more. But it felt good to know that I was not alone. 'Wait, Harlow, look!' My heart pounded as we crossed the hall toward it, only to stumble into a new statue.

Winnie.

Or Wicked, in Winnie's glass frame.

I tried to remember where I had seen Winnie last, until I remembered with horror that we had sent her away from the cabin. How we had searched for her, with no luck. Now, she was in as much danger as we were. It was our fault she was here.

We should never have sent her away.

Wicked staggered sideways as I wove my fingers through hers. Around her, guards were still falling from Marcus and Harlow's swords, guards who were unable to fight their invisible opponents.

Wicked stumbled from side to side, and screamed as Marcus took her into his arms, although she appeared terrified as she could not see him.

Our good fortune was not long-lasting, as the queen left the throne room, clapping her hands together in mock applause and staring at every one of us. To my horror, it became evident that we were no longer invisible. In fact, her magic seemed to be blocking the witches' own enchantments.

'How very clever,' she said, coming to stand before me. 'How are you still alive, little princess?'

'Frost,' Wicked whispered, her eyes wide like saucers as she stared at me. Her voice sounded like Winnie's. Was it possible that my stepsister was back in her own head? If that was the case, where was the young Wicked?

I stormed forward, taking both mine and Wicked's swords and spinning them in my hands, the way I had seen Harlow do with his brothers. I concentrated on the queen, who, despite wearing a copy of my face, had barely changed at all.

'I wanted to be the fairest of them all, you know,' she said, stepping down from the dais and approaching me slowly. 'I told my mirror man to give me the name of the fairest heart in Icefall, the most beautiful, and your name left his lips. He said your innocence was stifling, that your beauty came from your bravery and resilience. What a load of rubbish, honestly. But I must admit, I rather think it suits me.'

Her mirror man being her husband, and Winnie's father, Mayor Farn. Did he truly mean so little to her that she had removed the title he had held in her life for so long?

Of course he did.

Even her new husband, my father, meant nothing to her. Which was why she had not yet mentioned him, or asked if he was even still alive.

I could not help but feel a shiver crawling up my spine as she stared into my eyes. My own rage-filled expression was staring back at me. She had not only taken my kingdom, my father and my heart, but my image as well. But her greed would get her nowhere.

One day soon, she would fall.

We would win.

'You have taken my throne, and I am here to get it back.' We were not ready, not even close, and yet here we were. We would never have been ready, even if we waited and continued to train and fight. She could have done so much more damage in that time, so I told myself that the moment was right.

'And how do you intend to do that?' she asked, smiling between mocking laughter. 'I have the throne.'

The witches circled her, and slowly she backed away, until we were in the throne room. Despite her bold and confident façade, she seemed exhausted; her face was sickeningly pale and there were deep circles beneath her eyes.

But her throne had been transformed, I realised, during my absence from the palace. It was now made of glass, the very source of her magic: her vanity. Mage sorcerers' magic came from their greatest strengths, or in her case, their greatest weaknesses. It seemed to be a cruel trick of fate that the thing that made them a monster was fuelling their power. How unfortunate for the rest of us.

Why should the cruel, the selfish and the greedy be the ones to take it all?

As she sat down, her features became restored, her skin healthy and shining, her eyes piercingly dark, her dark hair glistening in the light.

As I locked eyes with Elora, an idea came to mind. I hoped she would understand what I planned to do from that look alone.

If she did not now, she soon would.

I began to chant a spell that she had taught me, shattering the glass throne beneath the queen and forcing her to fall down onto the thousands of tiny shards. As she laid there, her gown ripped and her body bleeding from the mess, Elora's cousins set to work again, transforming her men into goats and pigs so that Harlow and Marcus could cut them down.

'Princess Frost, that was brilliant!' Elora whispered, and I could not help but agree.

The queen had not known of my magic, so she had not known to block it.

I had finally caught her off guard.

However, Elora's smile quickly faded, because where the queen's men were dying, there were plenty more to come looking for them.

We would not have much time.

Together, the witches spoke a powerful spell in a language I did not recognise. The old tongue, the type Elder Wicked must have taught them.

'They're turning her into an old hag,' Elora whispered in translation. 'Taking away her precious beauty. Or yours, since she has your face.'

The queen, bursting with rage now, her face reddening more with each moment that passed, charged down the dais, brushing off the glass that was now poking out of her body.

Slowly, she began to transform into an old woman, her hair white with age, and wrinkles beneath her dark eyes. Boils appeared on her chin, and her teeth were rotting yellow and black.

Before she could reach me, Harlow and Marcus formed a wall between us.

Then around the witches, who were still chanting, continuing to transform her. But, despite their good efforts, the queen took hold of Wicked's glass form and held her tightly against her chest, and when she stared into her transparent eyes, seeing her reflection once again, the witches' good work disappeared.

My stepmother announced with delight, 'Oh, the little princess possesses magic, how special.' She laughed wickedly. 'Unfortunately for you, I have my very own mirror right here.'

She gestured for the guards that remained, and they forced us all to our knees. There was no fighting their magic. Harlow and Marcus fought against them, but their swords no longer seemed to affect them, as if there was a magical barrier between them and us.

The witches continued to enchant them, their voices increasing in volume and pitch until they were screaming, and tried to force the queen to fall, but one look at Wicked's glass frame returned her power instantly. We had been so close, but we were swiftly losing the battle against my stepmother.

What had Elder Wicked been thinking when she transformed Winnie into a walking glass statue? I could not imagine what good that was supposed to do for our cause. It seemed only to benefit the queen.

'Take them,' she ordered, and one by one we were hauled away. 'Put the girls in the tower. I have special plans for them.'

I mouthed to Wicked before I was dragged from the room, *I am sorry, I will get you out.*

She only stared back at me with disappointed eyes, and then looked away.

34

WICKED

PRINCESS FROST WAS MY GRANDDAUGHTER.

Or perhaps not mine exactly, but Elder Wicked's. The memories came flooding back, and suddenly I knew everything the elder witch did.

I hadn't birthed Queen Rosa myself, nor would I have been old enough to, but I felt the memory as if it were my own. Elder Wicked had given me, as her copy, her clone of sorts, things that I wouldn't have even happened yet. For quite some time I had gone back and forth in my mind, wondering why she would do that.

Now, as I looked upon her, her intentions became clear and everything clicked into place.

At first, Elder Wicked hadn't recognised Princess Frost as her granddaughter, and perhaps she'd even been cursed not to remember her by the queen herself.

Now, though, I understood. I had a purpose, and that was why I was here. She had a chance to relive her youth through me, and I had a life, to become a teacher and a guide for the princess and her stepsister.

Not only that, but Princess Frost wasn't Queen Rosa's only daughter. The young witch who had chosen to help her, Elora, was her half-sister, younger than her by a year. She'd been raised by the witches, Rosa's sisters. Her father was a lord, a summer fling for the late queen. A short affair.

There was so much to tell the princess.

I left the witch's house, and walked endlessly back to the winter cabin, excited for the first time, to see the princess and her friends and tell them everything I had learned of her heritage. How elated she would be to discover that she had a powerful coven of witches behind her.

But when I finally arrived at the cabin, she wasn't there.

Worse, the king slept while his guards lounged by the fire with a few of the coven for company.

But where were Winnie, Frost and Marcus and Harlow and the others? The timing couldn't have been worse. I hid behind a nearby tree as a carriage pulled up close to the cabin, and out streamed a line of soldiers bearing carved wooden staffs.

The queen's men had found us, and the king was vulnerable. I had to warn the others before the guards found him. I sent a mental message to the witches inside, and then to Titus and Cassius: *'Queen's men are coming. You have to get the king out now!'*

Then there was no way for me to get out, but *up*. Climbing the closest tree, I spotted an opening, a way to stay hidden while also giving them a better escape, a higher visual for myself.

I shimmied along the branches and threw myself into the next tree, and the next, before jumping onto the cabin's roof.

They had better not have fallen asleep. 'They're at the front, entering now! Leave out the back!'

But just as I sent the message, more men swarmed the exit doors.

They were surrounded.

'Wait, don't. Shit.'

'What then, Wicked?' Alis demanded, one of my – Elder Wicked's – elder sisters. *'They're here. Where are you?'*

The shouting was coming louder now, along with the sound of swords clashing with staffs. *'On the roof. Hit them with your spells!'*

'You think we didn't think of that already?' Alis snarled back. 'They have blocked our magic, Wicked. You must help us.'

These mages were powerful if they could block such ancient magic. But they didn't know I was here, and I had to use that to my advantage.

I called out a spell that sent two of them crashing into each other. Two more fell to the snow, and another placed his own knife to his throat.

'There is another,' a guard called out.

A swipe of the blade across his throat dropped him to the ground.

'Find her!' said one of the other guards, reaching for his friend's weapons and strapping them to his side. He looked up, almost seeing me, and I was forced to duck.

Titus and Cassius led the witches and the king away from the cabin, and relief swept through me, even as the king began to cut down his wife's soldiers.

The boys worked together while the witches reached for their swords and joined them, surprising them with their skills in combat.

They were finally escaping.

But what I hadn't noticed were the other two guards approaching Titus from behind.

The soldier didn't see them coming, but the king did. He dove between them, determined to get his guard away from the danger, and evidently not wanting to be the weak king who needed protecting at all costs. I shouted a new spell, but it was too late.

The first mage soldier's knife plunged into the king's chest, and he crumpled to the floor with a river of blood soaking the snow beneath him.

It wasn't enough, my magic or my warning.

Now the king was dead, and Princess Frost was officially the queen of Icefall. I hadn't been able to stop it, and I feared that she would never forgive me.

I approached The Mirror Canal where Winnie's father had led me while I was still trapped within her glass body, and roamed the canal, studying every boat.

When he'd brought me here, I knew nothing of this place and the way it worked. But my memories had brought me back, and reminded me of the days when my sisters and I would travel.

Seager and Mora loved to run alongside the boats when they were small, calling out their names and laughing at the various images painted on them.

Some showed drawings of small birds and prey, while others gave little inspirational messages or the occasional joke. Humankind were amusing to my little sisters. But I also knew how often witches roamed, using the canal to travel between kingdoms while others watched over the mirror portals. They were very private people, and not the type to initiate in daily conversation unless you caught them in a pleasant mood, and even then they would be short with you.

But The Mirror Canal was important to witches, even when they didn't like to travel close to others. They used these paths quite frequently, but not all of them were friendly like my sisters and me.

Some used it for darker reasons, to keep out of sight while hauling their captives to their holding places. Others were prone to starting violent altercations for the simplest of reasons.

Where else could Princess Frost and her friends have travelled to?

Maybe if I was fortunate enough, I might find more of Elder Wicked's sisters and cousins, maybe even her daughters, and they might lead me to her. Because she had to know what had happened to her father, even if it broke her heart all over again. She needed to know that s*he* was now the queen, her father's only blood heir, making the queen's reign void.

By sending her men to kill her husband, little did the woman know that she'd destroyed everything she seemed so proud to have built.

The kingdom that was never hers in the first place, now truly didn't belong to her.

She was both a monster and an imbecile.

Mayor Farn's boat wasn't here so I considered my options, roaming my fingers over the coins in the pocket of my cloak. Perhaps I should have gone back to the lake, found Mayor Farn and his nephew again.

But if the boat wasn't at its station, would they even have been there? Probably not. People came and went, shouting to each other and laughing with friends or greeting passers-by with a smile.

All seemed well and good until a large bearded man with broad shoulders and a wrinkled face caught me watching his boat, *Frog's Bones*, for a little too long.

In truth, I was just daydreaming about my days at the farm with my sisters, and wondering if I would catch any of them here. Until I remembered, once again, that those sisters were actually Elder Wicked's, and would have been almost as old as her by now. It was a depressing thought, reminding me, not for the first time and certainly not for the last, of how alone I really was in this world.

'Can I help you, Witch?' the man snapped, his voice pulling me from my thoughts, his tone venomous. Like my presence here was nothing but a nuisance to him.

'No, sorry.' I waved a hand and carried on, casting the man a polite smile, but he followed quickly, scowling. 'Sir, I didn't mean to disturb you, I do apologise –' Before I could utter another word, he'd hauled me off my feet with his huge hands around the collar of my cloak.

Clearly, it wasn't only the witches who were quick to start arguments.

'Are you a thief, Witch? Looking to steal away my boat when my back is turned?' His voice was deep and rough, but his hands were strong, and too close to ripping my head off.

'No, no, of course not. Please, let me go.'

His laughter rang through the hollow tunnel, but the ogre soon released me and I kept walking.

Pushing thoughts of him behind me, I took a long breath and reminded myself of what I was here to do. Find the princess, find some witches, and get out of here. But an eerie silence quickly took over the space, reminding me that I was heading into the territory of the witches who often used invisibility spells, and enchantments that masked their presence as they came and went about their business.

I was just thinking about the witches I missed when a voice broke the stillness. '*Wicked.*' It came from further down the narrow path, under one of the bridges up ahead. Thinking it might be the rude brute playing tricks on me, I ignored it. '*Wicked,*' it said again as I headed under the bridge, passing boats and reading their names until I found myself standing face to face with one of the Guardians.

Vencin, my dear friend. He peered at me through those angular golden eyes, his stripes glowing in the dimmed light as he inched closer on those thick, clawed feet. Of course, I should have known that the king of the Guardians would appear to me soon.

How hadn't I recognised that voice? It was buried deep somewhere in my subconscious, a sound that should have been instantly familiar. But then, I supposed it wasn't my fault that my memories weren't completely my own. Hadn't Princess Frost or Winnie mentioned meeting him recently?

'Ignore me no longer, Wicked,' he said inside my mind. 'Come with me. We must go to the House of Roth. Your ... daughter wishes to speak with you.'

'We both know she isn't truly my daughter, Vencin. She is my elder self's birth spawn. I'm her copy, remember? It's complicated, I suppose. Look, I have things I need to do ...'

The creature blocked my path, leaving my voice to trail off. 'You must speak with Queen Rosa, Wicked, no matter what you think of her.'

'She can come and find me herself if it's so important!'

Without another word, I spun around and stormed away. When I looked back, the Guardian was gone. If I were really so vital to Queen Rosa's cause, she could come to me. Because I was going to help her daughter as she hoped, but in my own way.

First, that involved meeting with a few crucial souls. It would be nothing but pure luck if I found them, but I had to try.

Some names on my list of old friends were: *Mala Stoker, Eris Bryles, Marisia Savant.*

These were just a few of the powerful witches I planned to find to help me defeat the queen. Cousins of mine, or Elder Wicked's. And thanks to Mayor Farn and Barchester, I knew I was heading in the right direction to find them. If they were still alive, that was, which was a big if.

Witches with such ancient magic also happened to know a few mage tricks, which was more than useful to me. Those who were practical in their subtlety would have learned to observe their enemy without being caught.

To defeat a mage, I must learn to think like one.

The hardest part would be finding them, and the harder part trying to convince them that we were on the side. If they were alive. Fingers crossed. Screw the Guardian, and Queen Rosa; I didn't need them.

I headed down the narrow path toward the end of the tunnel, by the docks, where I knew the witches' boats were stationed. The names I found there told me that I was getting closer to the mark.

The Witch's Head. Frog & Neut.

There were no boat owners down here, but as a witch I knew the signs of invisibility enchantments well: a few whispered voices appearing on the wind, the soft scent of rosewater and thyme, and glass jars full of eyes, fingers and toes, and various other organs which were often used for important spells, left lying around near the entrance to their side of the dock.

I was in the right place.

As I explored, it dawned on me that I may have to push past some of their boundaries.

I pulled back a few table covers, browsed their strange jars and acted as an outsider who knew nothing of their customs, only to be thrown to the ground by a sudden blast of ice-cold air. There, no witch liked a stranger touching their things.

Ignoring it, I moved to my feet and began to sing an old witch's rhyme, one that my mother used to sing to me as a child. One that any Roth witch would have known. It did the trick, because the icy air dissipated, and the old witch revealed herself.

She wasn't alone. Behind her were at least a dozen other witches, all resembling each other with their piercing eyes and the bold stares they cast me.

But I couldn't take my eyes off the witch who was clearly their leader. Like my elder self, her hair fell around her face in white locks, but her eyes were a piercing green. She was incredibly tall with a slender frame and long fingers that curled around her waist as she drank me in from behind her boat, her enchantment having been removed.

'I know you,' she said, her words taking me by surprise because I didn't recognise her at all. But her words explained everything as she said, 'You remind me of an old friend.'

She must have known Elder Wicked, or perhaps one of her many sisters. There wasn't a chance that she could be one of the twelve, was there? And, the others, too.

'What is your purpose here?' she hissed. Her stare was penetrating as she interrogated me, and yet, there was a soft amusement in those eyes, too, as if she knew I wasn't here to do any harm. As if she merely sensed my curiosity. 'Stealing from your own kind?'

Peering more closely at her, I knew I would have recognised those eyes anywhere. This witch wasn't Mala, Eris or Marisia. In fact, I had hit the jackpot, and this was Lunar, Elder Wicked's closest sister, the one who had practically helped her raise the others when their parents were elsewhere dealing with important matters.

My sister. But what was she doing here?

Behind her were a few of the others. Marthy, the artist, and Mora and Seager, the two smaller sisters who loved to cause mischief. They closely resembled their younger selves from the memories that had appeared to me in a flash. I'd been looking for the elder's cousins, but instead I'd found her *sisters*. Or at least a few of them.

With hope brimming in my chest, I began to tell them everything. Who I was, and all that had happened since the elder witch had placed my conscience into Winnie's glass body.

Lunar watched me with a thoughtful expression on her face. 'Well, that explains where Alis, Heaven, Crescent and Everly have disappeared to. But they should have told us if they knew.' She peered at me more closely. 'Foolish Wicked, thinking that only a youthful version of herself could save Icefall. Why clone yourself when you possess all of the ancient magic in the world for yourself? I don't understand my older sister sometimes, I must admit.'

'Neither does anyone else,' I snapped. 'And when I visited her, she barely told me anything. But how would your younger sisters know what would happen at the cabin?'

It suddenly dawned on me that Elder Wicked had mentioned Seers. Some of her sisters possessed future-reading abilities. Could Alis and the others have appeared at the cabin for that reason?

'Seers, I suppose that makes sense. But surely they would have seen the king's death coming, and known they wouldn't be able to stop it ... ,' I ran a hand through my hair as my voice trailed off, my frustration brewing.

'There is always a chance that the visions don't come true, child,' said Marthy, holding out one of her paintings.

Black and grey stained the canvas, and a drawing of over a dozen figures circling what appeared to be a small campfire. But there was so much darkness in the picture, and it didn't make sense. But perhaps the message would have been clearer to the eye of the artist herself.

'My own drawings sometimes predict events that don't turn out as we expect. Alis and Everly have visions appear to them in their mind's eye, while Heaven's visions only appear when she sings. But again, many of those have not come true or have shown them different endings.'

'So they hoped they could stop it from happening.' It was the only thing that made sense. I thought that maybe the soldiers had found them and brought them to the cabin, but maybe they had come of their own accord, hoping to be another kind of protection for the monarch.

'Yes, child,' said Lunar softly. 'Marthy's paintings have also predicted the death of the princess and her stepsister. But perhaps that, too, can be undone. We must try.'

'*We?*' I couldn't believe what I was hearing. These powerful witches, who at first had accused me of stealing from them, wished to help me.

'Yes, *Wicked*. Although we don't always understand our older sister's decisions, we have always trusted that she makes them for a good reason. You clearly matter to her, for her to keep you around, so you matter to us, too. We will help you find the princess and her friends, and restore peace to the kingdom of Icefall.'

35

WINNIE

The Babylon candle had brought me straight to the palace's throne room, moments before Frost arrived with the witches and the guards, who forced me to my knees beneath my mother's glass throne.

Maybe I should have waited for the witches to finish telling me how to use it first.

But there was no sense in dwelling on the past, as my time in Icefall had taught me so far.

I'd been forced to watch as they cut down the queen's men, only for her to restore her power when she sat back down on the throne.

The queen hadn't even known that Frost had magic, and honestly, it had been a shock to the system to actually see her use it. Frost had been granted the element of surprise at first, but then the mages had overpowered them.

Now, once again, Frost and I were trapped under my mother's thumb. I needed to speak to a mage or a witch, or someone with the magical ability to undo my curse. How could she do this to me, and to Princess Frost? To my father and my cousin?

It was pure sickness.

I stared out of the window, wishing there was some way I could leave this tower and find Frost and Wicked, who would surely know how to undo my curse.

The tower contained two small rooms, one being my new prison cell, the second no doubt holding Frost. Mine was basic, and only a little bigger than my bedroom at home. A large, gold-coated oval mirror hung on the wall, above a small bed with a soft woollen quilt and a few pillows.

Beside the bed was a dust-covered wooden chest. Standing over it was a wide window with a beautifully serene view of the vast Icefall forest that surrounded us. The snow-topped trees stretched on for miles, along the river and toward those outer villages where the smaller residences could be seen, little clusters of houses and marketplaces.

Further beyond, somewhere in the distance were the gates of Cranwick and my father and Barchester. I could only pray they were safe, and that they weren't growing sick with worry. It was only another bitter reminder that I still needed to get to the Winter Caves to find a cure for my father's sickness. Because with Wicked inside my consciousness, it seemed everything I wanted had been lost.

Now, it was time to get myself back. But first, I had to help myself and the princess.

Baby steps, one thing at a time.

I could hear the princess through the wall, and imagined her sitting back-to-back with me on the other side of it. The thin wall didn't hide the sound of her crying, and my heart broke for her all over again.

Remembering how the song had helped her in the forest, I tapped the wall once, leaned back and began to sing an old tune, one that my father used to sing to me when I was small. It brought tears to my eyes, reminding me of the days when he would lay me against his chest and gently rock me to sleep.

My father, who would always be my hero, no matter the distance between us.

'I missed that song. I haven't heard it for so long,' said a voice, not the princess's, but one I would have recognised anywhere. 'I have missed you, child.'

My heart thudded inside its glass cage out of pure shock. My father, who I had just been thinking of, had appeared, as if I had manifested him.

When I turned and stared into the mirror above my bed, there he was. Those eyes, and the warmth in his smile broke my heart, and only reminded me of home. I was filled with longing for the family that had once been so dear to me. Those days felt like a lifetime away now. 'You look beautiful, Winnie. Can you see me, sweetheart?'

It was dark around him, but there he was. 'Yes, yes Dad,' I answered, my voice soft with emotion. 'Where are you?' The light was dimmed and lit only by shimmering crystals. Behind him was a wall of stone, filled with the pink gems. The background was an image from a distant memory. A dream? I had definitely seen it before, but I couldn't remember where or when. 'I recognise that place, but I don't know why ...'

His voice trembled, full of urgency as he said, 'It's a cave, Winnie. There are wolves here, and a well containing water to heal my sickness, to end the curse over our city –'

Something like hope stirred in my heart. It was the caves that we needed. He would no longer be sick, and I wouldn't have to worry about his health anymore. But I was too afraid to believe it, knowing there was a possibility that it was too good to be true.

'So what are you waiting for? Get a bucket-full and go home!' I cried.

His eyes welled with tears, and one rolled down his cheek. 'You don't understand, Winnie. She has us caged up here, and there are wolves –'

Hot rage set my blood on fire, forcing me to clench my fists at my sides. My hope fizzled out as quickly as it had come. 'She? And, we? Who is there with you?' That last question was a stupid question to ask, I realised slowly. Of course it was my mother that did this to him. Who else?

It was so unfair, such a kick in the face to leave him there, so close to the magical water that could heal him, and not let him take any of it.

'Winnie, it's me!' My dear cousin appeared in the mirror, jubilant as ever despite the circumstances. 'Oh no, she's coming, Uncle Farn! Winnie, we have to go but we love you –'

'Barchester, no! Dad, come back!'

I wanted to cry. But then Barchester's words began to sink in. My mother had them locked up in the caves, the one I'd seen through Wicked's memories, but she was going to them.

She'd left the palace.

Seizing the opportunity, I scoured the room for anything strange. Hidden doors, or anything else that might lead me to Frost's room. But no such luck.

I shook the door handle, but it wouldn't budge, so I searched the room, and breathed a sigh of relief when I found a small steel nail poking out of my bed rail. Slipping it into the lock, I turned it and prayed I would be free. When the door opened, I practically ran into the tower. 'Frost?' I called out, pressing my ear against the door. 'Are you in there?'

'In here,' she answered from the door I was facing. 'What are you doing? How did you get out?'

'Never mind that. We don't have much time.'

Using the nail, I turned the lock on her door and slid it open.

Frost leapt into my arms, and we held each other for a moment before she said, 'Winnie, look. Your mother did not quite think things through before bringing us here.' Her face was pale, the skin beneath her eyes pink and swollen as if she'd been crying. She handed over a large book, bound in leather. 'Why would she leave this in my room?'

I skimmed the pages. They were diary entries, maybe, or a series of letters to someone important.

The book itself was the ancient type, the pages worn with age. On the bed laid several other books, all of them containing pages that had been ripped out.

Skimming over them all quickly, I soon realised they were spell books, but not the kind used by witches. They were covered in detailed sketches of plants and herbs, drawings of ingredients used for magic by the powerful Ajanid clan.

The mages: the witches' enemy.

And as it turned out, we'd hit the jackpot when it came to learning more about my cunning mother, because inside one of those books was a single note containing a plan to destroy the king of Icefall, and then his daughter.

But first, his wife.

That explained the princess's tear-stained face and the circles beneath her eyes. She'd already been processing the details.

I dove for the basin in her room and retched into it, my body trying to rid itself of all of my stomach's contents, but nothing came up.

My mother's destruction hadn't begun with courting the king; she'd also killed Queen Rosa so she could take her place. 'Frost, I am so sorry ... I ... I don't even know what to say.'

She placed a hand on my shoulder and stared into my eyes, but I couldn't meet hers without staring at the floor. Shame seeped into my veins like a vile poison. I hadn't even committed the crime, but I felt ... dirty ... to be the daughter of the woman who had.

Completely broken.

She offered me a slim smile in response, but I didn't have the strength to return it.

No one would know how it felt to be the daughter of a murderous mage.

An evil sorceress, and a monster.

'We have been through this,' she whispered, with her hands resting on my shoulders. She didn't take her pretty blue eyes off me as she said, 'You are not your mother. You are my stepsister, no matter what happens, but most of all, you are my friend. I just wish it did not take losing you to make me realise it.'

Her words warmed my devastated heart, but I broke down into sobs and let her hold me as I cried. Her friendship meant so much more to me than I had thought it would. After all, we hadn't even known each other for long. 'Thank you, Princess Frost.'

Her lips spread into a grin. 'Now come on, let us get out of here.'

I followed her, believing with my full heart that I would destroy my mother for everything she'd done to Frost and her family.

And to the kingdom of Icefall.

By the time I was finished with her, my mother would pay.

Our luck soon ran out.

Just as I was finished inserting the nail into the keyhole of the door, footsteps sounded on the other side, quickly climbing the stone steps beneath us. 'Shit! Get back into your room, Frost, and play along!' I whispered frantically. 'If you try to escape, she will hurt you, and I can't bear the thought of anything happening to you. Please.'

Although everything within her clearly screamed to fight against my words, she ran back into her room and closed the door behind her.

I darted back into my cell room and climbed into the bed, just as the door slipped open and my mother crept inside. She sat down on the edge, peering at my face while I pretended to be asleep.

Despite everything she had done, her beauty still struck me. She wore Frost's face, but it still seemed older, and the girl's features didn't suit her, like a filter that didn't quite fit. Her raven hair had grown and now fell down her back in thick curls.

She was Frost, and yet ... she wasn't.

She rose to her feet. She was much taller than the petite princess, and held a regal stance that only a queen would. With the princess's heart inside her chest, she stormed across the room, blasting cold air into my face. She wore a pale green gown in the finest silk, embroidered with black velvet patterns that swirled like tree vines across the skirts.

She rushed over and cupped my glass face in her hands. 'Winnella, my dear girl. What have those wretched witches done to you?' she said, finally deciding to wake me instead. I shook her off and pushed her off. She drew herself away from me, clearly hurt by my rejection. But then she persisted, 'We're going to get back at them, my girl.' She spoke as if my glass form hadn't benefited her back in the throne room. Restored her magic, and her false beauty.

'What are you going to do to me?' I growled through gritted teeth.

I had told Frost to play along, purely because there was a higher chance of my mother lashing out at her and potentially fatally harming her. But I hoped that my fragility would be a form of protection in itself, and that she would need me and my glass form too much to do anything to damage me.

She took a long and slow step backward, with the audacity to appear hurt, as if she were the victim here. 'Why are you looking at me like that? Like you ... hate me. Like you are afraid of me.'

Was she serious?

Of course she was. How naïve could she be to still think I would be fully comfortable around her after everything she'd done.

'Because, Mum, I'm not sure I could ever hate you, but I *am* afraid of you. You're a monster. You slaughtered Prince Hugo, left Princess Frost without a father, stole her home, her heart and her face, and now what ... you're going to be rid of me, too? Or keep me here as a prisoner for the rest of my life?'

She winced as if I'd slapped her, then clapped her hands together and brushed my words aside as if they weren't important. She seemed to gather herself, her rage overflowing, but her regal composure had taken priority. 'Those are all just tiny details, darling. You must sit at my side. Eternal power until the end of days, and you will be my heir, so that when the time comes, you will be queen.'

I backed away from her, only to fall onto the bed. I considered her words, disgusted, but thought that perhaps I could use this to get out of here and return Frost to her palace, and her father to his throne. She wanted to use me for my curse, so that she could have endless magic without having to sit on her throne, but I wouldn't let her.

Still, anything was better than being locked up here. It would be better to work with her, and find a way to free us all. I sat upon the bed, and peered up at her almost thoughtfully. 'Alright, Mum ... I'm sorry.' I paused again as if considering my words. 'What did you have in mind?'

You might have thought I'd suggested the decorations for my birthday celebration. Her smile almost seemed the same, other than the widening curve at her lips. Her eyes were bolder and the light reflected in them, making her appear even more eerie.

I swallowed hard as she answered, 'I suggest a grand ball where you will be announced as my daughter, my princess and heir. My people will meet you officially, and I will tell you my plans for you after that. We will bring the princess as well, and they will believe we are a happy family for a time. Then I will announce the king's death, and be rid of his daughter. Come along now, child.'

That wasn't quite enough. I could get more from her if I kept going. 'But Mum, I should know everything before the ball. What if someone questions me, and I stumble?'

She smiled serenely. 'Don't you worry your pretty head about that. You will know everything, soon. For now, we have a ball to prepare for!'

She spun around and stormed away, her heels clanking against the tiles. I followed, wondering what exactly I was getting myself into. I would play along with her little game until I knew I could get away, back to Frost and Wicked, and my father and cousin.

She would never have me; she lost me when she gave her heart to the Roth witches and attempted to kill the king.

'You'll love being a princess, darling,' she said, offering me a smile which I only half returned. But every flicker of it was poised like porcelain. False. Not for the first time, I felt as if I was watching a stranger as she cackled and said, 'It's like all of your childhood wishes are coming true.'

Oh, how she thought she knew me. In a way, she always had, but I felt like a different person now. Those were the days, when I was wrapped up in fantasy stories, dreaming of princes and princesses, sword fights and magical adventures across the seas. I would read, and often write my own stories as well, wishing I was the character I was narrating.

Now that everything was more real, and no longer just a story from a book, I detested her for everything she'd done and was still doing to my stepsister. My friend. Not to mention Hugo's death, and the downfall of the Winter kingdom.

And all of that was after she'd chosen to leave Cranwick behind.

'What about Dad and Barchester?' I asked, unable to bite my tongue for any longer. 'What about the curse on our village? My childhood dream was for our people to be able to travel freely – for our freedom!' I might have over-stepped, and suddenly I realised this may well become my downfall.

But, to my relief, my mother seemed to admire my new boldness because she smiled. 'Put them behind you child, as I have.' She spun around, and raised her arms above her head. 'This is my home now, my life, and yours.'

How dare she? I forced myself to swallow my rage, to keep moving. Too much confrontation would only be harmful to mine and Frost's cause. So I'd play the part, for a while, as I had told Frost to. I'd prove myself worthy of my mother's time, of her planning and celebrating. 'Very well,

Mum, lead me there.'

She kept walking through the corridors with more confidence than I'd ever seen in her before.

This palace, this role, this power had transformed her into something ... else. I couldn't help but wonder what would have happened if I'd never followed her through the mirror. Would things have stayed the same back home, or I would have spent my days, miserably pining after the mother who'd abandoned us? A shiver coursed through me at the thought.

But then I remembered that I would have never met Princess Frost or Wicked. I wouldn't have learned the truth of my mother's past, that she was a sorceress with dangerous schemes beneath her belt.

But everything was different now, and I would just have to accept that. So I studied the false queen, because that was all she was now, no longer my father's wife or my beloved guardian.

I watched her movements as she glided through the halls, elated by the destruction she'd caused. 'Will I continue to sleep in the tower room, Mum?' I asked, the label spoken through gritted teeth, a little relieved that her back was turned to me.

'Of course not, my darling,' she said, turning to face me. 'That is no room for a princess.'

We continued for what felt like an hour, but was probably only a few minutes, until we entered the suite. 'Wow, it's lovely.' I entered, and took in the wide window with yet another grand view of the forest. The chest of drawers and the bed fit for a queen, sheets and blankets adorned in velvet red. There was even a writing desk where some stationery had been set up. 'Who did this room belong to?'

She laughed bitterly. 'Does it matter? It's yours, now.'

'Please don't tell me it was Princess Frost's room, Mum. I couldn't bear that.'

Her smile faded quickly. 'Of course not, that is mine now.'

I stared at my reflection in the mirror, and I could see right through my body.

I was just another walking reflection, and yet somehow the maid had managed to make my glass body glisten by dressing me in a sparkling blue gown. My light blonde hair fell motionlessly down to my shoulders, but she'd also placed a small floral crown on my head, and tied it down with a thread of dark blue ribbon.

My glass eyelids were painted with dark wings, and my lips were as red as the flowers in Princess Frost's palace gardens.

I no longer felt like the daughter of Cranwick's mayor, but like my stepsister instead. I felt like a princess, and I looked like one as well.

'You are beautiful, Your Highness,' said the maid almost nervously. I heard the way her voice trembled as if she were afraid of me. But more likely, of my mother.

But her fear still stung, and I hoped this would end once she and the other servants realised my intentions for them were good. 'Thank you, you've done a wonderful job. You may go, Ma'am. I need some time to myself.'

'Of course, Your Highness.' She curtsied and left the room, offering me one last smile before she went. I watched the door as it closed behind her.

Fear drummed through me at the thought of everything I needed to do to convince my mother that I was on her side, while also helping Frost and the others. 'Dad? Barchester, are you there?'

A flash of terror flickered in my chest. What if they didn't come? Could I really do this alone?

Yes, yes I would, because I had to. No matter what happened, my mother would be defeated.

Then there was my cousin, a face that brought me so much comfort and relief that I instantly relaxed, knowing I could do this. How I'd missed him.

'Wow, Winnie, you are stunning. So elegant, the queen of chic.' Typical Barchester, of course the first thing he'd be concerned about was the gown hanging from my shoulders, and not the fact that my entire form had turned to glass. But the relief within me dissipated as Barchester inched closer and whispered frantically, 'Look Winnie, something has happened. You need to be careful. Your mother –'

'Barchester, quiet!' I heard Dad saying. He sounded terrified. 'She's coming.'

'Who is coming? No, don't go, not again!'

But he vanished, leaving me frightened, watching him go. It couldn't be my mother, as she was to attend the ball. Could it?

The maid returned with two guards bearing the staffs of the mages. So, not only was my mother to use their power for her own vicious intentions, but she clearly saw them as our shield of protection as well.

What bargain had she made with their leaders to get them on her side? It would have needed to be a high price as I wasn't sure they'd ever spent much time with any of the four royal families before. But I couldn't focus on that because I was still reeling from Dad's frightened exclamation. So, when the guard turned back to me, I barely looked in his direction.

'Your Highness, we are here to escort you to the ballroom,' he said, a tall soldier with raven black hair. Did he know Greyson? 'I must say, you look wonderful.'

I supposed it was time to forget about Dad and Barchester for a while, and focus on the here and now. 'You possess magical abilities, yes?' I asked, choosing to try my luck before we left the privacy of my room.

'Of sorts ... Ah, yes. But we aren't permitted to offer you –'

'Undo this curse, please.' I shoved my glass hand in his face. 'I am becoming rather sick of it.'

'I'm afraid I cannot do that, Your Highness.' '

'Can't, or won't?' I asked with an eyebrow raised. There was something he wasn't telling me, something that none of them were. 'She told you not to touch me, didn't she?'

Of course it was Mum.

In this form, she still held such power over me. I was restricted, barely able to move without fear of my body shattering into pieces. 'Take me to her.'

He nodded curtly, with relief in his eyes, as if he feared me broaching the subject anymore. 'Yes, Your Highness.'

36

WINNIE

We made our way there, then entered the grand room to a herald's introduction.

Just like the day of the wedding, chaos had erupted within the room, an atmosphere full of excitement and happy chatter. The dance floor was full of people swaying to the music and talking amongst themselves, colourful gowns catching the light from chandeliers that hung from the ceilings.

When I walked into the room, the world seemed to stop moving.

People who'd been drinking, eating and dancing now stopped to take in the sight of me, and many gasps sounded as I walked the floor to Mum's table. I mean, I couldn't blame them. If I saw a walking statue, I would have stared as well.

Clearly, nobody in this room had known that the queen's daughter was made of glass. But wasn't that the whole point of this grand ball? For my mother, at least. Here, she could parade me around the palace and show me off like some kind of prized goat, while Frost had to play along and act for her benefit, or risk coming to harm. Because that was just what mothers were supposed to do for their children.

Everything about this situation was a disaster, but how could I slip my way out of this one? I thought that maybe I could start making some powerful friends. Mum wanted me to mingle at this ball, so that was what I would do. Hopefully it would all be useful later, when she saw my true thoughts on everything she was doing, and had already done.

My focus quickly turned to my mother, and the attention of the room seemed to follow my gaze.

'My friends, meet my daughter and your Royal Highness, Princess Winnella. My heir.' She was a sight to behold in her gown, with the golden crown sitting on her head, the intricately detailed surface woven with white and blue roses. Her gown matched the flowers in a shimmering sea blue. One of Queen Rosa's old gowns, no doubt.

There was nothing original about this persona she was trying to create; she was copying everything she knew of the previous queen, and still somehow hoped to appear better than she was. She was naïve to think that would work. The people may be uncertain about King James and Princess Frost, but they had adored their queen. The tales told of a charming mother and wife who cared for her family and her people above all else.

At her side was Frost, watching me with a sad smile on her lips. Her wrist shook, and I spotted a small steel chain looped around it. Her lip trembled, and I sensed that she was trying not to cry.

How unfair.

Seeing her that way made my blood grow hot, and I found myself digging my fingernails into the palm of my hands, searing into my skin so sharply that blood was drawn. That was a first.

'And of course, my stepdaughter, Princess Frost,' my mother added as an afterthought.

I decided to use her motives to my advantage, faced the ballroom and more importantly, the other royals and nobles who were backing away from Mum and I, whispering amongst each other as they cast glances at us all in turn. Fear, terror and rage flickered in their faces as they drank in my mother, who was laughing with three of her mage men as if they were the best friends she'd ever had.

The stares of the other royals made me want to turn and run from the room, but I held my ground and lifted my chin before walking the ballroom with confidence, as if I did this every day.

I nodded curtly and offered them little smiles even when I saw them avert their gazes when I passed, obviously uncomfortable. Because I was different, and because I was associated with the cruel queen and all that she'd done. Because my body was now made of glass. Enchanted, cursed, and doomed.

Screw them all.

They didn't need to know anything about me or why I was really here. Of course they would presume I was a subject of my mother's destruction.

Of course they would be afraid of me.

Well, damn their opinions. I would prove myself useful in this little game, and they wouldn't even see me coming, because that was just what princesses should do.

The nobles all lingered on the dance floor in little groups, the women holding champagne flutes and laughing with their friends or standing close to their husbands, while the younger royals danced together, swapping partners every now and again.

As I approached, the dancing stopped and the twin Summer princesses, Princess Piper and Princess Martha, laughed in my face. 'If it is not the glass abomination herself,' said the tallest, who I presumed was Piper. 'Should you not be somewhere over there, scheming murders with your mother?'

I ignored her, but her sister's words came before I could say a single word. 'Piper, get away from her, she is dangerous.' She pulled her sister against her side as if she thought she could defend her much better that way.

'Dangerous?' Piper snarled. 'One shove and she will shatter!'

'Bit of a contradictive statement,' I muttered. Couldn't they see how ridiculous they were? There was no substance between them. They were practically one person in two identical bodies. 'So I'm a murderer, but I'm also fragile.'

'I think you hit the nail on the head right there,' said the cow.

'Right on the bullseye,' said Martha, showing me that any trace of personality she possessed would only have been an imitation of her sister's.

If they didn't stop talking, perhaps I would show them how dangerous I could really be. But thankfully I didn't need to, because to my relief, Aurelia, the Autumn princess, gathered the Spring princess to one side, and led me away from the Summer fools, taking my hand in her other one.

'Ignore them,' said Princess Aurelia as she linked an arm through mine, casting me a sweet smile.

Who made these porcelain princesses? They were unnaturally beautiful, like something out of a beauty magazine, and yet they were intelligent, kind and graceful all at once. Designed and taught to contain literal perfection within their fingertips.

'Do not worry, Artemia and I have heard all about your mother and what she has done, but we can sense that you are as much of a prisoner here as Princess Frost would be if she had not ran away. And those two just love to gossip for the sake of it. But they are not a good judge of character like we are.'

The Autumn and Spring princesses laughed as they walked me through the room, greeting their parents and friends and introducing me like they'd known me for years. I knew I was in good hands if I stayed close to them, and even caught Mum watching me with a smile from across the room.

For an instant I even forgot everything she'd done, and was reminded me of the early days when I brought new friends home from school, even if those friendships didn't stick when they realised I was the daughter of the mayor. The outsider, and the outcast.

Barchester was the only friend I needed, but Mum never saw it that way. Now I understood that it all had to do with what she thought of her own image. She would be proud of a popular daughter, one who only thought of herself and how she looked to the rest of the world. But I quickly realised that this was her way of living through me, outpouring her expectations of her younger self onto me. Her regrets and failures became my future goals as far as she was concerned.

'A lot has happened since I last saw you, that much is clear,' said Princess Artemia. The Spring princess looked at me with curious eyes, but a smile still graced her full lips. 'Tell me everything.'

'That's the understatement of the century. Honestly, I wish I had the time but I think my mother is going to cut my head off if I spend too much time gossiping.' I appreciated their kindness, but this wasn't their fight.

Her laughter was like a breath of spring, soft and light. 'I understand, and I will not keep you for too long. I simply admire your sense of humour in such ... dark times.'

'You have heard the news then?' So perhaps I didn't need to tell her everything, after all, and she was just asking for confirmation of what she already knew.

'I think even the underwater and sky kingdoms have heard the news, Winnella. You are very much the talk of every kingdom these days.'

A few of my mother's men passed by, so the princesses gathered my wrist and led me through the doors into Frost's gardens.

The fresh air and the floral scent of earth only reminded me of her, reminding me of how trapped she was. The chain looped around her wrist was linked to one of the mage soldiers, who were constantly watching her, making sure she stayed in line.

'I have to ask,' Princess Artemia whispered, 'what is going on with Princess Frost? Everyone is terrified for her, and she looks so scared –'

The princess had practically read my mind.

A stream of guards had followed us into the gardens so I masked the quiet conversation with joyful laughter. 'Artemia, it's so lovely to speak with you!'

There was something they could do, I realised. But it wouldn't be easy.

The guards dispersed, so I whispered, 'I intend to keep her safe, but I need your help. Yours, and any friends you may have in this palace. My mother is watching me very closely, but you may hear something that I cannot.'

'You should know that we are both here for you,' said Princess Artemia. 'She murdered Aurelia's brother, and I fear that my best friend is next. We will help you escape.'

Was it true? Would she kill the princess of Windspell as well as her brother, or was she safe? It was impossible to know.

Prince Hugo had been killed for defying her orders, but Princess Aurelia hadn't had any real contact with my mother yet, as far as I knew. Still, it was good to be on the safe side and be cautious, so I couldn't blame them, but how could they help us escape when the guards were observing my every move like this?

It didn't seem possible, but I would take all of the help I could get. If I could assist Prince Hugo's sister as well, then I would be doing Frost a favour in a different way.

'If you are truly against the queen, Winnella, we will work with you and get you out of here safely. Here is what I have in mind.' Princess Artemia inched closer and whispered her detailed plan into my ear, spreading hope through me at the thought that I might help Frost again, and be able to defeat the queen.

With the assistance of a few other princesses, we could win against my mother's brutal schemes.

With an organised outline in our minds of how the escape plan would go, we headed back into the ballroom because the guards were now getting closer, no doubt listening to every word we had to say, all of which would be reported back to my mother.

We found ourselves standing before the mage clan's leader, Greyson Marks. But my new friends were led away by their parents as the mage leader approached me, urging them to leave us to talk privately. There he was, with snow white hair and the same bright eyes I'd seen upon that lake when I'd first met Frost, even if he wasn't real at the time. Just a figment of Wicked's imagination.

But why was he here, with her? He was the man from Wicked's memories, and her dreams. Her beloved. He must have been under my mother's spell, or it didn't make sense. Why would he participate in her ballroom games?

He stepped forward, bent down and planted a kiss upon my hand. 'It's a pleasure to meet you, Your Highness.'

'I thought you were dead,' I said with widening eyes. My mother laughed, and others joined her as if it were the finest joke they'd ever heard.

Greyson chuckled. 'Far from it.' He raised an eyebrow, and I saw the glint that appeared in his smile. It was almost as if he were enjoying this conversation. 'We have never met before, Your Highness. How would you even know of me?'

'I have friends in magical places.' If only he knew the half of it. 'But we have met before.'

Even if it was in my hallucination.

'Who might those friends be?' Greyson asked, walking closely behind me and politely linking an arm through mine.

Wasn't this what gentlemen did when they were at a ball? I suddenly felt like I was in an episode of *Bridgerton,* only it wasn't a handsome prince I was walking with but an old man.

My mother tore him away with just a tug of his wrist, and I wondered if he were as much of a prisoner as I was, or if he was somehow playing her. 'My daughter has been very busy as of late. Come and sit, and I'll show you everything she has been doing.' She turned to me with hardened eyes as I was forced into a chair, and Frost was quickly pushed down into a seat on the other side of my mother. 'You too, Daughter. We will see all of the betrayals you have committed against your own mother.'

Despite everything I felt about my mother, those words sank into my chest like a blade and twisted, tearing me apart from the inside. Because she was the traitor, and yet I *had* been working against her. I'd known that she was aware of it, but I never thought she would try to humiliate me like this.

'Of course, Mother,' I said, speaking the title through gritted teeth. 'Show me.' It was the worst thing I could have said or done.

My mother's newest prisoner was brought in and thrown down before the nobles and royals. Right there, restrained with chains, was Elder Wicked.

I ran to her side and knelt before her without thinking, only for my mother to pull me back to my feet. Would her cruelty ever end? 'What have you done?' I cried.

This witch had cursed me, placed her conscience into my mind and made me into a glass statue, but I still couldn't help but feel something for her. She and the other witches cared for me and Frost, I could see it in the sadness behind her eyes as she looked between Frost and me. The princess met my gaze, and tears rolled down her face as she took in the witch.

What were we going to do?

The queen's eyes pleaded with me almost kindly, and they were brimming with tears as she said, 'I have done what is best for you, and for our people. You have to believe that.' She almost seemed sincere. 'She cursed you, didn't she? She is the monster here, not me!'

She still believed she was the victim, and now she was trying to make everyone else take her side. She reached for me, and tried to take my hands in hers, but I tore them from her grasp. Her eyes were red with rage and despair, deep circles appearing in the skin beneath them, as she screeched, 'Guards!'

Ten out of ten for performance, I thought. Those tears really hit the spot.

Her guards forced Elder Wicked to her knees, and one of them held a blade against the witch's throat.

'No, Mother!' the scream that burst from my lips caused my throat to burn.

There was no playing her little game, or pretending to be at her side now. The witch who'd been helping me was innocent, and kind and a great and powerful being. And she could help us end this.

We couldn't lose her.

The queen snarled down at me. 'We will finally be rid of the witches, one by one. You deserve freedom, and power. So much of it.' She raced forward and took my hands into hers. 'You deserve this, the chance to finally destroy them.' She tugged me closer against her side. Couldn't she see that the witches were my friends? 'You make the choice, child.'

She was right in the fact that the witches had been the cause of my torment for years, the reason I had felt so trapped in Cranwick. But I wasn't my mother, and I couldn't hurt the witches for revenge. I had a temper sometimes, but I wasn't cruel like that. It wasn't in me to kill someone with intent. My mother knew that the witch's death was an accident. She couldn't seriously believe I could do this.

Wiping the tears from my face with the sleeve of my cloak, my voice returned barely above a whisper as I answered, 'I choose to let them go.'

She sighed heavily and released me, disappointment once again clear in her eyes, and in her body language. 'You must see that they will only hurt you, my love.' Her tone was pleading. She wanted so badly for me to take her side, but that would never happen.

I ignored her and turned away as Elder Wicked took me in for the first time, her eyes narrowing as she glanced between the queen, the mages and me. 'Go, Winnie. Flee this place right now. You don't belong here; you are worth so much more.'

She was right about that. But escaping wouldn't be as easy as running away right now.

Besides, there was an organised plan that we needed to see through first, all thanks to the Spring and Autumn princesses.

Greyson approached Elder Wicked and pressed his hand to her cheek, causing several gasps to appear from around the room. 'My love,' he said, helping her to sit up properly. The affection in his eyes broke my heart. 'What happened to you?'

'She did,' said the witch, her voice rough like gravel as she called out my mother. 'You should leave her; sever whatever connection you have.'

What connection would Greyson have had with my mother?

Elder Wicked continued, 'She is only here for herself. She killed our daughter, remember?' Greyson stared back at her wide eyed, clearly confused. 'You really don't remember, do you? She has tainted your memories just like she did to me.'

'Your daughter?' I stared between the queen, Greyson and the witch. 'Who ... ,' my voice trailed off, but the question hung in the air, leaving everyone reeling, wondering what she was talking about. 'Mother, explain yourself.'

The queen spat at Elder Wicked's feet, and many people around the room grimaced with disgust.

My mother refused to answer my question or even speak to me directly, but she hissed, 'She is vermin. Stupid witch, forcing my daughter to speak to me like I am nothing.'

She smacked the witch hard across the face, leaving a large red mark and forcing her to reel back in pain. Her brutality turned my stomach, and I found myself bent over, dry heaving over the ground.

'You are nothing,' I shot back, wiping my mouth and staring back hard in her face. 'Nothing to me, and nothing to my father and Barchester. Nothing to Icefall. Nothing to anyone.'

She raised her hand as if she were going to hit me, but then that hand clenched into a fist and she pulled away. A sob heaved from her chest as she, too, bent over retching, with tears dripping down her face. Then she hissed, 'How could you speak to me like that, Winnella? After everything we've been through together? I am your mother, and you are my child.'

'I wish I wasn't,' I spat back, and watched her reel backward, as if I'd slapped her.

She reached for me, but I turned away.

'You deserve it,' said Elder Wicked, and her face twisted, lip curling in disgust. She fought against her chains, and the fury that burned behind those eyes was white hot. 'You deserve everything that's coming to you.'

'This monster,' said my mother. She moved closer, staring down her nose at the witch. She didn't even look my way. 'Greyson, kill her, since my daughter refuses to obey me.'

'No!' I screamed, an ache forming in my chest at the thought of witnessing another act of harm against the witch I'd come to care for. Despite the curse she'd placed over me, and everything she'd done, I felt in my heart that she wanted to help us. She cared for the princess, and she wanted to end my mother's reign.

As the mages responded to their queen, the leader seemed to keep them restricted, frozen like statues. Then he smiled at Elder Wicked before turning to me and saying, 'Go. My men will follow you, but not for *her*.' His stare flickered between my mother and me as he spoke those words.

He'd been the reason why the queen had guards. Some of them were Greyson's mage men, from his clan. Now, they were turning away from her, on his orders. This was progress, even if we were still stuck here. He was going to get Elder Wicked out of here.

'No!' my mother screamed, her plans failing.

'Who is your daughter?' I asked Elder Wicked, almost in a whisper.

'Queen Rosa, Princess Frost's mother.'

My body could have shattered by the sheer pounding of my heart inside my chest in that moment.

A few important truths dawned on me then: the witch who'd cursed me and Frost was my stepsister's grandmother, Greyson was her grandfather, and finally, what was so much worse, Elder Wicked's words dawned on me. 'She killed the Winter queen ... '

My mother hadn't only killed my friend's father for her throne, but her mother for her position in the king's life, as well.

Which explained the sorcery books.

Which meant that my mother had been orchestrating her evil schemes long before she gave her heart away to the witch.

There was so much more going on here than a few silly curses. God, that was the final straw.

'Yes, child. Look, we don't have much time. But tomorrow the queen is planning a parade for you both, to show you off as her daughters and reveal her plans for the kingdom. I have a feeling that my sisters will come to you then, so be alert. They will wish to rescue us all.' She pressed a kiss to my forehead before Greyson's men led me away, a few of the others holding back my mother as she screamed my name and struggled against them.

'Tell the princess your plans. Work together. Most of all, Winnie, I must apologise for how I treated you. I didn't know who you were, that you were the girls from the prophecy, until it was too late, until I had already committed a curse that cannot be undone. Please forgive me. But know that it was all part of the grand scheme of things.'

'You keep saying that, but it doesn't make sense. Did you plan for this all along?'

She shook her head, and answered none of my questions. Her cryptic words left me full of frustration as Greyson's men led me away, and the witch said, 'Good luck, child.'

I turned back before I exited the ballroom, and called out, 'I forgive you, Elder Wicked.'

For the first time her eyes were kind, and her grin was the last thing I saw before I left.

37

FROST

THE MONSTER HAD ME BOUND IN CHAINS, and paraded me through the ballroom like a pet on the end of a lead, while Winnie was treated as Icefall's beloved princess.

But the queen had not fooled my people yet.

Royals and nobles I knew and respected well watched her with fearful eyes, and Winnie with disgust. There was no chance that I would ever blame Winnie for her mother's choices, because none of this was her fault, and I knew by the glances she cast me from across the ballroom that she was not enjoying herself as the Summer princesses seemed to believe she was. They eyed her closely, as if she were nothing but the enemy.

But the Spring and Autumn princesses looked upon her with sympathy in their eyes, clearly understanding this ballroom game more than the others. We could use this to our advantage, I hoped.

The more allies, the better.

The mages were cunning. Only Winnie and I could see the chains binding me to the mage men, meaning that in the queen's eyes, the nobles would have seen me moving freely around the ballroom.

But one of those mages followed me closely everywhere I went. If anyone asked why, the warriors told them they were there for my protection. But those who knew me would have known.

I strode up to Princess Aurelia, who stood with her parents, and curtsied low. 'It has been so long!' I cried, pulling her into a low embrace, the chain biting into my wrist when I strained slightly too far. 'I am so sorry for your loss. Hugo will be greatly missed.'

They did not need to know how he had betrayed me, not when they were grieving him. It would only change how they saw him, and I did not want that for them.

'And yours, as well, my beloved daughter-in-law.' The Autumn queen gathered me into her arms, and I breathed in the earthy scent of her embrace. 'Thank you, Princess Frost. We will not speak of him here. Come to us later tonight after the ball, and we will bring you safely to Windspell. You are still as much of a daughter to us as Aurelia is, although our beloved son is gone. But we fear it is not safe for you here.'

If only it were that simple, and they could just whisk me away forever. I would be safe in Windspell, but Icefall would still be in disarray.

My father deserved to have his throne back, and his palace, and my kingdom. My people deserved a kind and loving ruler in their palace. Someone who would treat them with dignity and respect.

Before I could answer, the mage guard tugged my wrist and tore me away from the Autumn royals, but Princess Aurelia whispered, 'You will always be my sister,' before they led me across the ballroom.

Their words brought tears to my eyes; happy tears for the first time.

Winnie had a plan, it seemed, as I had seen her speaking with both Princess Aurelia and Princess Artemia, the princess of Blossomheart. We could do this, with all of the love and support we had received so far. It showed us that people believed in us, and wanted us to win.

It was more than I could have ever wished for.

But as the queen sat us down, and Elder Wicked's beloved was revealed, my hopes began to dissipate. It became clear that she had something in store for us both, when Elder Wicked was brought to her knees, and the queen claimed that Winnie had betrayed her. Then Greyson turned against the queen. Seeing his beloved must have broken the spell the queen had over him. If my magic worked, I would have done something to break her free.

But the fact that this powerful witch could not use her magic spoke volumes of what the queen had done. How was it possible for her to remove our magic like this? It made everything so much harder.

We needed to find some way to weaken the queen so she could not block our magic for any longer.

Because to fight her, it was necessary.

'Princess Frost, you should meet Winnie in the dungeons tonight. She will tell you everything.'

Greyson nodded once before scurrying away, barking orders at his men, who stormed away from the queen.

Winnie was gone. Where was she going?

'Not so fast.' A tug of my chain made me turn around, and I wished I had not. The queen pulled me against her chest, with her dagger pressed against my throat. 'Stop right there, Greyson Marks, unless you want me to cut your granddaughter into pieces.' Her dagger glinted in the light, revealing a hilt engraved in gemstones, as her words settled in my chest. She grinned as I met her eye.

Granddaughter. If she was right, this man was my grandfather, and we were blood.

Reality crept over me as I realised that Elder Wicked would have been speaking of my mother earlier. *She killed our daughter, remember?*

Queen Rosa, my mother, was the daughter of Elder Wicked and Greyson. I had known my mother was suspected to be a witch, but this ... this was too much. Queen Leraia had killed my mother, and destroyed everything good in my life. This was just another secret to be revealed, leaving my chest numb.

But still my knees sank beneath me, leaving Queen Leraia to take my head in her hands.

'Rosa ... married the king.' Greyson's eyes were wide as he took me in.

How had he not known? How long had he and Elder Wicked been apart for him to be so unaware of everything my mother had achieved in her life?

'I warned her not to, but I never saw her again so I always assumed ...' He raised a hand, and the queen was blasted across the room as if by an enormously strong gust of wind. So there was no magical block on his power.

Interesting.

Then he stood me behind him, and freed me from my chains.

Elder Wicked reached for him, and two of his men led us to the dungeons while three others contained the queen inside a steel cage. 'Go,' said Greyson. 'Winnie is waiting for you in the dungeons.

'She has a plan for you both, and your friends are down there. Free them.'

He threw me a small sword, and offered me a smile. 'You should get moving, *Granddaughter.*'

Winnie was in the palace dungeons as Greyson had predicted, and she was not alone.

She had freed the guards already, and they were on their way out of the dungeons through the exit Winnie had taken before, Greyson's men having freed them. Greyson led Elder Wicked out, and Winnie moved as if to follow them, but instead she closed the door behind them and turned to me.

'Good, they are free,' she said.

'We should go with them then,' I said, pushing her toward the door. 'Come on.'

'No.' She blocked the door, even as I tried to move past her. 'We are in the best place to do this here. Elder Wicked is free, which was more than I planned for. We have to go through with the parade, and make the people believe we will save them. We cannot do so much good from the Winter Forest, Frost. Think about it. We came here for a reason. I know you did.'

I studied the girl closely, remembering her timid nature the day of the wedding, amazed at how far she had come since then. How far we had all come.

That felt like a lifetime ago now.

As much as I wanted to protest against her words, I knew she was right. 'Alright, what is your plan? Play along.'

She filled me in on everything she hoped to do, and I gave her a few of my own ideas as well. Soon enough, we had a vaguely distinguished scheme. We were the best team we could have been.

But as you might have expected, our hope did not last for long.

'You all believe you are so clever, don't you?' There was the voice that sent a chill through me every time I heard it.

I turned to face the queen. She was covered in scrapes, and her dress and her hands were torn and bleeding, but she was here before us. She must have clawed her way out of the cage. 'Well, I hope you know that I will break you down until you both submit to my plans for you.' She moved closer, and whispered in my ear, 'I intend for you to join your mother and father in the spirit realm, little princess.'

'Only my mother is there, so you are severely mistaken,' I growled.

She cackled. 'You may believe that if you wish. I may not have succeeded the first time, but he is there now.'

'No, he is not.' I refused to believe it.

But as Greyson reappeared, he and three of his men now bound in chains, I suspected it was true.

Still, I would not let the reality sink in, or I would break down. It was not true. 'You are lying.'

The dark glint in her eye told me everything I needed to know, and yet it filled me with terror. 'Perhaps you will meet him very soon, Princess.'

My knees buckled beneath me, and I screamed with rage and heartache as Winnie threw her glass arms around me. I howled as I never had before, sobbing between screams as everything inside me shattered. 'No, no, no. You are wrong, you have to be.'

But the queen's smile was wicked as she stared back at me. 'You are both mine, until I decide I am finished with you.'

A chain reappeared around my wrist, and this time, Winnie's did as well. 'Come along now, Daughters. We have a royal parade to prepare for!'

Daughters. As much as she wished my people would believe she cared for me, and that she had replaced the new, kind and loving mother I had lost, it would never happen that way for her.

For so long she had been a wolf in a sheep's clothing, but now her outer layers had been peeled away, leaving something dark and rotting beneath.

38

WICKED

BACK AT THE CABIN, I was surrounded by witches.

It probably shouldn't have been as overwhelming as it was, considering the memories I already held of them all.

But they still weren't really my experiences, and I hadn't really lived them. Just as she hadn't been through my own; the days I'd spent with Princess Frost and Winnie and the others, becoming their magical protector.

Even if they had spent a good portion of that time having sent me away. I knew that in time, we would be friends.

The thirteen sister-witches, now including Elder Wicked herself, were gathered in the soldiers' cabin, debating what to do with the king's body.

Today was the palace parade, and we were planning to catch it and get the princess and her stepsister out, but first we had some things to deal with. The kings' body; the boy soldiers and aligning them with our schemes; rescuing Mayor Farn and Barchester from the Winter Caves, and then we needed to find some disguises for the parade.

Because now that we knew the queen could easily block our magic if she chose to, we couldn't let her even suspect that we were there. Which meant we needed to blend in.

The sisters were sitting in a narrow circle before the fire, with Elder Wicked's daughters behind them. The older sisters were almost identical, both in appearance and nature. Lunar and Elder Wicked were used to taking charge but they were always kind, and the younger ones clearly respected them for it.

'We should think about a burial,' said Elder Wicked. 'But we will need to get the girls out of the palace before then.' She glanced around at her sisters, and her five daughters, the boy soldiers Titus and Cassius and I, who stood close to the king's corpse.

It was laid out on the floor in a wreath of flowers, roses, sunflowers and tulips, his hands gently resting at his waist, ringed fingers interlinked. Knowing that his daughter would never see him alive again brought tears to my eyes. How heartbroken she would be when she came finally returned.

'Heaven, it's happening again,' said Elder Wicked to her sister, having noticed that her sister Marthy was now painting frantically, as if she were possessed by something other. 'What does her painting depict?'

I didn't wait for Heaven's answer. My stomach twisted when I remembered how Lunar had said that her artist sister could foresee the future through her work. Remembering some of the dark paintings I had seen – Elder Wicked had seen – from her before. Blackness, dark monsters and murderous souls.

Always death.

'Nothing good,' Heaven had answered while I drifted off into my thoughts, causing the others to gather around the witch. 'We can only hope she is wrong.' She peered around, her sisters all nodding and murmuring in clear agreement.

She was right. This one showed two girls kneeling before a crowd, beneath the raised hand of a taller woman, who was clearly the queen. Their throats were slit, and their wrists chained together, but they smiled, practically grinned at the people beneath them who watched with love and admiration.

Behind them was a dark carriage with blacked out windows. *The parade.*

It was so much darker than Marthy's other paintings, and more daunting, knowing that the parade was soon to come. My only comfort came from the thought that not all of the stories within her paintings had come to life.

Elder Wicked rose to stand close to the king's body, and ran a hand through his hair. I'd almost forgotten that, for a time, this man had been her son-in-law. Family. But the late queen had lived a busy life as his bride.

Memories came rushing back. Days spent in the palace with them, Queen Rosa appearing distracted, no doubt by her many duties. These memories always washed over me as if I were a stranger watching them, because although they were happening in my mind, they didn't feel real.

'Who would like to watch over him while we travel to the Winter Caves?' Elder Wicked asked. 'Bearing in mind that the queen and her men know where he is, so you may encounter them again. I would like to rescue Mayor Farn and Barchester, and I wish to bring all four of my daughters, as well as Lunar and Marthy. Anyone else who wishes to come along is welcome. That includes you, boy soldiers.'

'Why does she keep calling us that?' I heard Cassius mutter.

'Because you are boys,' I answered with a snigger, 'and soldiers.'

They looked up from where they had been examining the king's fallen armour. Titus was working on repairing it when the witch called to them, while Cassius was stitching his ripped uniform back together.

'I will stay with him,' said Titus. 'He did lay down his life for me, after all.' His eyes were solemn as he spoke, as if he were reimagining the tragic moment.

Elder Wicked offered him a respectful nod. 'Good choice. And you?' she said, turning to Cassius. But before he answered, she seemed to change her mind and cut in, 'You must stay with your friend.'

'No, I have to go. To the palace, when the time comes. My beloved is there.'

Somehow I knew the witch he was speaking of was Elora, Princess Frost's younger sister. I'd seen the way they were looking at each other when they were together in the cabin.

'Very well,' said Elder Wicked.

'Give my regards to the others,' said Titus. 'I would like some of the witches to stay. We can prepare the disguises before the parade.'

Then it was decided. Elder Wicked and I would go with her four daughters, Flora, Verity, and twins Maeve and Morgana, along with Sara, Corani, Vielle, Heaven and Alis.

The others would sew clothes for us all, marking the witches in the cotton garments worn by many of the residents of Icefall's poorer villages.

We would blend in, and when the time came, hope that the stories told in Marthy's paintings would be far off the mark.

Then we would bring the princesses home, and bury the king.

When we entered the Winter Caves later that morning, the wolves were howling.

At first I feared they sensed that we were coming, but as we walked through the caves, nostalgia settling over us, we realised that it wasn't us that the wolves were reacting to. They were chained, their bodies gravely thin due to clear malnourishment, and all of them wore striped wounds undoubtedly caused by lashings. As much as I didn't want to be eaten and feared being around them, it hurt my heart to see the beasts being treated this way.

'Poor buggers,' Flora agreed, watching them with the same concern that waited behind my eyes. 'Look, the mage men are there. Handsome devils, aren't they?' She laughed as her mother cast her a look of scorn. 'What? Who are you to judge me for appreciating their beauty?'

'Yes, and look where it got me,' Elder Wicked snapped back.

'It got you five wonderful daughters, didn't it?' Flora's sister Verity argued.

'Beautiful, and talented,' Flora agreed.

'And modest,' their sister Morgana commented.

'Quit the bickering, won't you?' Elder Wicked said with a sigh, casting me a look of indifference and a sly smile as she inched closer to the mage warriors who were clearly here to watch over the caged Mayor Farn and his nephew. 'We need to get them out of there without being noticed. If they block our magic, it's over. Remember that.'

'Yes, Mother,' they answered, one by one.

'Yes, Wicked,' said her sisters.

'Let's act accordingly to our abilities,' said Flora, the eldest of the five daughters.

As it turned out, each of them were special, and Elder Wicked had chosen them to come here for a reason. Like her aunt Marthy, Flora was clairvoyant, which meant she could read the future through images, although hers were often through smaller sketches rather than paintings.

Verity was clairaudient, as I was, along with Elder Wicked, meaning she could hear spirits and communicate with others through their mind's voice.

Rosa had been clairsentient, so she could sense clear feeling, easily reading others' emotions.

She and Maeve shared this ability, while Morgana was claircognizant, so she could experience clear knowing through regular premonitions that appeared to her. She'd always made the joke that they never came when she was hungry, although this was probably because she wasn't as focused as normal as she was too preoccupied with her stomach's rumblings.

'We need to act quickly or they will feel our magic,' I said, taking Elder Wicked by surprise as I led them all toward the cage, skirting around rocks so the mage men wouldn't notice me coming.

'That was already implied,' my elder self said sharply, her tone both condescending and rude.

Oh, boy. She didn't want me to have any authority over her witches?

Well then, she shouldn't have brought me here in the first place. I wasn't here to step on her toes, but I refused to be disrespected.

'Verity,' she and I said at once, both of us having the same thought that we could take a similar approach to mine and Winnie's escape from the palace dungeons before this had all begun, and ask Verity to control their minds. Maybe send them crashing into each other, make them end themselves, or even order them to unlock the cages. But surely that would be too easy, and if more men were on their way, we were in trouble. We needed to be more subtle.

Perhaps I should have suggested it in her mind to not anger the elder witch. But maybe that wouldn't have mattered anyway.

'I know what to do,' said Verity. 'Both of you, keep your prides to yourselves. We don't need your temper tantrums right now.'

'Who in Roth do you think you are talking to, Verity?' Even to her adult daughter, she could play the role of the scornful mother.

'Come on, Mother. Can't you see that there are more important things to focus on?'

'Of course there are, but that gives you no right to undermine me. I am your mother, and your High Priestess of Roth, and you will listen to me. Not her. She has my memories, but not my decades of experience.'

Her words stung, but I refused to let them sink in. Verity was right, we needed to keep going. And suddenly, there were so many ideas forming within my mind that I thought I might burst. 'Here is what we should do.' I began to explain my plan, watching it playing out before my eyes, and then turned to Verity's sisters and her aunts.

'You don't know how we work, Wicked,' Verity argued, studying me closely as she talked. 'Like my mother said, you don't have her many years of experience.'

'I don't, but I do have the thought behind those memories. I understand why she acted in the ways she did, because she is me and I am her, although at the same time we are not. You must let me prove my worth to you,' I answered quickly, with my arms folded over my chest, my feet suddenly itching to get me away from here and put our plan into action.

'Ignore her,' Elder Wicked said slowly, her words getting my back up again.

Couldn't she see that I was just trying to help her and the other witches?

'I have a better –' She was about to explain a better plan, one that she thought was best, when we heard a few of the mage soldiers arguing with each other as they whipped the wolves.

They were preparing to pull the chained creatures toward the prisoners. We were losing time. 'Sorry, Elder Wicked,' I said, 'but we don't have time to form another plan. We'd better get on with it, or Winnie's father and uncle will become wolf food.'

Her eyes burned with clear rage, her pride more powerful than any other emotion she felt, but I ignored it, a new satisfaction pouring through me as the witches began to nod in agreement, knowing there was no other choice.

There were at least a dozen mage guards, I realised as we began to move closer, making sure to remain hidden behind the stone pillars inside the cave, allowing Elder Wicked and her sisters and I to approach the cage so the mayor and his nephew might see us. Hopefully, without the mage men doing the same. But as we edged further into the cave, the captive wolves began to growl, scenting us although we couldn't be seen.

Unfortunately, this alerted the mage men to the new threat. It wouldn't be long before we were either attacked by them or eaten.

One line was all I needed: *I am on my way.* I sent the mental voice into each of their minds and grinned as they began to squirm. The queen's voice, one they would have recognised instantly.

Then came the best part: the transformation.

Flora cast the spell that would make me appear to them as their majesty, the woman they followed with no hesitation. The witches watched with awe as I twirled, wearing Princess Frost's face but the queen's tall and slender frame, and a sea blue gown with glistening gemstones covering the heart-shaped neckline and bodice.

Tragically, I had never felt quite so beautiful.

'I must admit, it's brilliant,' Elder Wicked praised, to my surprise. Then she brought her daughters and sisters over, and said to Flora, 'Can you remember the faces of her men?'

'I'll try,' Flora answered. Then, concentrating, she began to alter the appearance of the other witches.

But we weren't quick enough. One of the queen's men came around the side of the pillar we stood behind, a skinny wolf in tow. Somehow, the beast worked in his favour. Perhaps the lashings had broken them down.

'Who are you?' he demanded. Then he noticed me, and he bowed, tearing the wolf away from me. 'I'm sorry, Your Majesty. I didn't expect you so soon.' He and his men studied the witches behind me. Elder Wicked and her sisters hadn't yet transformed. Only her daughters now resembled some of Queen Leraia's guards. 'You brought the prisoners?'

Shit.

We were so close, and now if I didn't convince them they would become suspicious of our intentions here. Praying that Elder Wicked and her sisters would forgive me, I answered, 'They escaped the palace so they believed they could fool me, but I know better.' As I spoke, Flora whispered an enchantment that would alter my voice, and to our relief they hadn't blocked their magic yet. Perhaps only the queen herself could do that. 'I will deal with the prisoners myself.

'I believe I may have spotted a trespasser outside the caves. You should go and search for them. I don't want them anywhere near my precious conquests.' I grinned as I peered around at the transformed witches, as if I were her and proud of what I'd done.

One of the guards eyed me with an uncertain gaze, but he seemed to want to obey. Perhaps he was too scared to go against her rules, despite his clear suspicion. 'But, Your Majesty, are you sure?'

'How dare you question my intentions? That was an order,' I cut in, and felt satisfaction brewing as they nodded and went off to do my bidding. It would buy us some time, but not long, so we needed to move quickly. My own voice returning, I smiled at the witches and said, 'That was quite fun.'

'Wicked, that was wonderful,' said Sara, Elder Wicked's sister.

'I'm sorry I doubted you,' said Verity sheepishly.

'As am I,' said Corani.

'Agreed,' said Alis.

'Sorry,' Vielle apologised.

Elder Wicked said nothing, but her stare told me everything she was feeling: admiration and shame at herself for not wanting to go along with my ideas. She knew I was right, she was just too stubborn to admit it to anyone else.

'Let's move,' Vielle continued. 'They will be back soon, and I'd rather not be on the front end of those wolves.'

'They look so hungry,' said Heaven, always thinking of the poor animals. 'Maybe we can come back for them later.'

'Not the priority, Heaven,' Lunar snapped. 'Too much is at stake.'

'You think I don't already know that?' said Heaven.

'All of you, quit it!' Elder Wicked snarled. 'Wicked, what's next on the agenda?'

Was she actually asking me? That was progress, and it only fuelled me as I moved on.

'Don't look so excited. My old mind needs a rest every now and again.'

That was her pride speaking.

She enjoyed watching me lead, I just knew it. I was sure that it reminded her of her youth. But I would take any feedback I could get.

In case we stumbled into any other guards, the transformed witches gripped their undisguised ones by the shoulders and shoved them forward.

'You'd better not be locking us up,' Elder Wicked warned, her growl barely above a whisper. 'Tell me your plan, Wicked. We need to be able to work together –'

'There's no time. Just trust me,' I said quickly. Then in their heads, I said, *'They're coming. We'll get them out, and swarm them.'*

And then it all began.

They knew we were here, and that surely meant that they knew I was an impostor. Heaven and Alis worked on the cage's lock, while Sara and Corani led Elder Wicked to the place where the wolves were chained, and slowly chanted a control spell.

The wolves nuzzled against Elder Wicked as their chains were removed from the post.

By the time Mayor Farn and Barchester were freed, the transformation had worn off, but it didn't matter as, of course, our plan had been unsuccessful anyway. They ran to us, Barchester clinging to Elder Wicked as if she were his own grandmother, but she seemed to calm him before pushing him off her.

'Thank you for coming, Elder Wicked,' he said. 'You're the best.'

Clearly uncomfortable, she brushed him off, making Mayor Farn and the rest of us laugh. 'We're not out of here yet, boy,' she said, not hiding her grimace. 'Don't thank your gods yet.'

'Oh, I'm not religious, but sure,' he said, not fully understanding the meaning behind her words. 'Thank you. Those wolves have been eyeing me up like a gourmet menu for days. I thought I was going to be nothing but bones before you showed up.' He eyed the wolves with fearful eyes, and jumped away, but the wolf just sniffed him.

'You are welcome. Now, come on.'

By the time we headed back to the cave's only visible entrance, we were surrounded.

Which was just perfect.

Cassius moved with his sword, fighting alongside the witches as the mage warriors advanced on us. Barchester and Mayor Farn were each handed a sword and told to do what they could as the mage guards continued to circle us.

'Erm, I'm no good with weapons,' Barchester cried, practically throwing the weapon to the floor. 'Can someone take this for me while I go and hide?'

Mayor Farn laughed and brought his nephew closer, and began to show him a few quick sword techniques, although I had no idea where he would have learned them. Perhaps, like his daughter, he was a big fan of stories of legend. But using one wouldn't be the same as reading about one. They would have to move quickly, and work together.

Elder Wicked began to chant in the ancient tongue, sending a wave of the guards crashing into the walls of the cave. But it wasn't enough.

'Let them loose,' I told the others mentally, hoping they would understand.

'No, it's too risky,' Verity answered. 'The wolves are too hungry. What if they eat us instead?'

It was a good point, but desperate times called for desperate measures. 'The control spell won't last long anyway, and they will turn on us. Do it.

We will have to hope luck is on our side.'

One by one, the witches released their wolves. The mage men tried to run, but the wolves were faster.

One by one, the wolves began to feast.

Then we fled the cave, with Winnie's father and cousin safely at our side.

39

FROST

My stepmother wore my dead mother's blood-red ballgown and my face to the Winter Parade, and the people were stunned. You could see their eyes widening as our carriage rode through the streets of Marellia, Icefall's capital, mouths dropping open with confusion and fear.

'She's mad,' said one dark skinned man, cradling a baby against his chest.

We rode through the long and narrow cobblestone streets, alongside little thatched roof cottages, some of their windows broken or even frozen off due to the constant cold.

The queen smiled and waved at everyone she passed. She expected the same of Winnie and I, nudging Winnie every few moments and constantly checking our faces, ordering us to smile to our people.

But my stepmother did not know how the people hated her, or perhaps she did, but chose to ignore it. They only stared back with cold eyes.

They had loved their monarchy, once.

The last time I had come to Marellia on a parade like this, I was a baby in my mother's arms, and my parents waved while they held me with love and joy. The people cheered and applauded, threw blue roses at our carriage and sang songs of admiration, old tales of princes and kings in castles.

They had celebrated my arrival as their beloved princess. My father had always loved to tell me countless tales of our lives in the palace, back when the people loved him.

Before Queen Leraia had come crashing into our world, and destroyed everything.

The energy here today was ice cold.

'She's evil,' a woman said, her voice barely above a whisper, but somehow I knew the queen had heard it.

Horror churned my stomach as the woman was torn from her place and thrown to the ground with a mage warrior standing over her.

Queen Leraia had only needed to nod her head in her direction.

Then the man who had called her mad was taken as well. One by one, people were led from the doors of their homes and forced to their knees for speaking critically of their false queen.

Anger was hot in my veins, and my fists were clenched at my sides. But my wrists were still chained to the carriage, as Winnie's were.

I could not move, nor could she. 'No, Mother!' she cried beside me, but it was too late. I could only watch helplessly as people were deemed as treasonous and beaten by the mage warriors.

Then the queen stepped down from the carriage and grabbed the first woman herself, raised her hand and unsheathed her jewelled dagger. In an instant, the dagger was across the woman's throat, and then she was gone.

The crowd clambered away from the queen as Winnie and I stared in horror. Queen Leraia faced the crowd, and took the fallen woman's golden hair between her fingers, tugging her face upward. 'Let her be an example to anyone who wishes to defy me. Your king is dead, and my daughters and I are all that remain. I am your queen. One day, when I am gone, my Winnella will take my throne. But for now, you will succumb to me, or you will pay the price.'

'The king is not dead,' someone cried bravely, but they did not know what she had done.

'Do you dare to call me a liar?' In moments, they were beneath the hand of one of her men. Her face scrunched up as her rage took over, making her ugly. That was my face, but it was not. Her heart had begun to make it something new, and no doubt my heart in her chest as well.

There was no saving her.

'You are wrong.' I held myself tall as she turned to me, and allowed her to take in every detail slowly. Let her think what she wished of me. I did not care.

'Frost, no!' said Winnie.

My stepmother's rage contorted her features further, but at least her attention had been diverted from the woman who had just spoken. 'My father is certainly dead, I believe you on that although it breaks me,' I said, speaking clearly so that the entire crowd could hear me. 'But you are not our queen.'

I felt every pair of eyes in the crowd searing into my skin as I spoke with pride, 'The very moment you killed my father, you made your precious reign void. Only a blood heir can truly rule Icefall. I am that heir, despite the fact that you ruined my life.

'You killed my mother, took my father, my heart and even my face, but I will not let you have my kingdom, my stepsister or my friends.' Then I faced my people, levelling my voice as I spoke, 'I am your queen now, and I promise to always care for you. You are the voice of this kingdom. Take a stand against this monster. Throw up your hands and –'

The people began to protest, many agreeing with my words, others shouting against them.

The commotion did not continue for long, and the world swayed around me as a deep searing pain seeped into my chest. My vision blurred, and my entire body grew cold with violent shivers.

When I looked down, my hands came away slick with blood. Poking out of the front of the gown, out of my empty chest, was the blade of a jewel-studded dagger.

Stars shone before my eyes, and all I heard was Winnie shouting my name before I crumpled to the ground and the blackness overtook me.

Part Three

THE LOVED, THE BRAVE & THE WISE

40

WINNIE

SUDDENLY, IT ALL MADE SENSE why the witch had said I must be the one to stop my mother destroying everyone around her.

Frost was far more vulnerable to my mother's rage, while my glass frame, and her love for me, seemed to carry its own level of protection. Of course, for Frost to speak her mind to my mother, and to my people, she would lose her life.

Frost dropped like a stone, and my mother appeared victorious.

I fell with Frost, my heart breaking inside my chest. My mother now believed she'd won, and even reached for my arm in excitement. She still cared for me, and believed her own lies, the justification she'd claimed that she had done everything for me.

Her false words had swallowed her whole. My mother beamed, right until the people began to protest, just as their princess had urged them to.

They shook the carriage and chanted curses against her while she hid herself behind her mage soldiers for protection. How brave she'd been until now, how elated. Now, she'd become a coward. She had taken everything from Frost, but now she would take my friend from me as well.

Frost was more than the princess to me now, more than my stepsister, even. She'd become the sister I'd never had, and now I was going to lose her. I cradled her in my arms as the people rebelled, and the mages tried to ward them off.

My mother peered down at me with rage-filled eyes as I held Frost tightly against my chest. 'Let her go. She's the enemy, Winnella.'

'It's Winnie, and you're wrong. Why would you do all of this, Mum? You were once so good.' She used to be a devoted wife, and a loving mother. She was a good mayor's wife, caring for the people of Cranwick and seeing her duties through with the utmost competency.

If only I could plead with her, and somehow make her take it all back. But everything she'd destroyed was so permanent, there was no bringing back the king or the Autumn prince, taking back her marriage to the king, no stopping her from stabbing Frost, no way to bring all of those people back to life.

And worst of all, she had no remorse for anything she'd done. How could I forgive her when she wasn't even sorry? She truly believed everything she had done was justified, to get her to where she needed to be. The sad truth was that so far, she'd succeeded.

She was a queen, full of magic and power, as she'd planned.

Even as she reached for me, tears rolled down her face. 'Winnella, how can you say that to me? I am your mother, and I love you so much. I have plans for us. I am trying to protect your future, and our life together.'

With my heart now racing, and tears rolling down my glass face, I screamed, 'I can't believe you're still so wrapped up in your own lies. You are doing this for yourself, and yourself only. If you truly loved me, you wouldn't have left in the first place.

'You wouldn't have given your heart away to the witches and murdered the late queen! You would have stayed and worked things out with Dad.

You would have been my mother. But instead, your greed got the better of you, and then your vanity.' I kissed Frost's brow, and rocked her from side to side, praying she would wake up.

My mother's eyes were wide, as if she hadn't quite anticipated how much I knew of her endless deceit. The destruction she'd caused for everyone in Icefall. 'How did you –'

My eyes burned with rage as I shot back, 'I know everything, Mum. You could have healed Dad another way, stayed, but you wanted to leave, didn't you? You'd been planning this for a very long time.'

Her face twisted and she appeared heartbroken. But if she thought she would receive any sympathy from me now, she would be sorely mistaken.

'Please, Winnie. Come with me, and we can talk everything through properly at the palace.' Her words actually sounded sincere, but I knew better than to fall for her tricks.

I laughed in her face. 'You're delirious! Mother, I'm sitting here with my dying friend in my arms.'

She spun around, and then nodded once to her men, and they began to help her back into the carriage.

But I wasn't finished with her yet. I knew now what I needed to do. Lying Frost down, I rose to my feet, tore my mother's dagger from Frost's chest, covering the wound with my cloak and watching as two men rushed forward from the crowd to stem the bleeding. They nodded to me, urging me on.

I darted forward, and drove that blade hard into my mother's back.

Before she could turn on me, I ran to Frost and scooped her up into my arms.

It was in that moment that I realised I recognised those two male faces. They followed me, and my father held me in his arms, a hand stroking Frost's hair away from her face.

'Hello, Winnie.' Tears stung my eyes as Dad and Barchester tore me and Frost into the crowd, and I sobbed with relief.

How could they have escaped the Winter Caves? I didn't care, because they were here with me.

A shrill scream sounded from behind me, and there was my mother, held down by Elder Wicked herself, with her own blade still in her back.

Then I realised that the elder witch wasn't alone, and she was surrounded by witches. Her sisters, and some younger witches that may well have been her daughters or nieces.

'Winnie, you will come back to me!' my mother cried. 'You wouldn't leave your mother forever, I know you wouldn't.'

Hadn't the dagger in her back told her how I felt? But she was persistent, I'd give her that.

'Quick, let's go,' said Dad, leading me away.

The people continued to protest, and the streets were in chaos. The witches fought to restrain the queen, while others were cutting down mage warriors. When there were only a few left, my mother slumped forward, unconscious, and they threw her into the carriage. The crowd continued to chant.

'Kill the false queen!'

'Save the Winter princess!'

'Shatter the girl made of glass!'

Their screams stirred hope in my heart, but some of those words stung.

As she was contained, I realised what I needed to do. Still holding the unconscious princess in my arms, I turned to the people and called out, 'Your queen will be safe, your true queen, Queen Frost! She is a witch, daughter of the late queen of Icefall.

'Queen Rosa. I know you might not believe I care for her because the monster in that carriage is my mother, but Princess Frost and I have been through a lot together and she would want me to help her people when she cannot. I promise I will do that, on her behalf. But for now, I need you to help her.'

I began to explain everything that had happened to us since I came to Icefall, of the witches we were working with, and of my father's curse. 'She loves you as her people, so I love you as well. Help her, help me, and I will be eternally grateful to you.'

'How can we trust you?' a woman called out. 'You might lie, like the false queen.'

'Prove your worth!' her husband retorted.

'Are you joking?' another woman yelled to them both, coming to my defence, much to my surprise. 'She just stabbed her own mother in the back! For the princess, and for us. And she's glass, like the curse she speaks of, isn't she? She speaks the truth, I'm sure of it.'

If it wouldn't have made things weird, I would have leaned forward and kissed that woman.

Wicked came forward wearing a beaming smile. She chanted a spell, and Frost's chest began to heal. 'The queen took Princess Frost's heart, so a young witch placed a healing spell over her,' she announced to the people, who watched her hands with confusion. 'It has been keeping her alive although she has no heart. That spell is the reason why she is still alive.'

Frost began to wake up, and glanced around with fearful eyes. She stared at the people who watched her with wide smiles full of love and relief that she was still alive. 'What happened?'

'The queen failed to consider that her own choice saved the life of the girl she was so determined to kill,' Wicked answered. 'What an imbecile.'

With a grin, I turned to the people of Icefall. 'So how about we go and get your kingdom back?'

41

WICKED

THE PALACE STANK OF DEATH.

When we entered on Princess Frost's order, the stench of something putrid pierced the still air, making every one of us gag. It was like rotten egg, blood, faeces, urine and bile all wrapped together into one vile and reeking mess. It was worse than anything I'd ever encountered before, and it forced my stomach to twist uncontrollably until I retched on the stone ground of the dimly lit tunnel that led us into the lower floors of the palace.

There were no bodies to be found yet, but the smell was unbelievable, horror lingering in the atmosphere at the thought of what we might encounter here. To Cassius and Winnie, it would have been only a sickness in their stomach, a nausea, but for us witches, it was so much worse.

It was like, despite the fact that the queen was no longer here to block it, the palace itself was rejecting our magic and making us ill. But for this magic to still be here when she wasn't ... this was a very dark and ancient magic indeed.

I could tell, by the way the others fidgeted and squirmed uncomfortably, that they felt the same.

As we moved, we struggled not to inhale the rancid air, but the acid threatened to rush into my mouth. 'There is powerful magic at play here,' I said quietly, tearing a strip off my cloak to cover my nose and mouth. 'Hold your breath.'

We soon reached the corridor that led us to the servants' quarters and the kitchens.

With a piece of cloth tied over her eyes, so that if she woke she couldn't use her reflection to heal herself, we brought the injured and unconscious queen through the door.

We couldn't risk her seeing Winnie and using her as her own personal mirror again.

'It's disgusting,' said Winnie softly, tugging her shirt collar up over her nose. 'We have to keep going. Maybe it'll fade as we go.'

'Can't ... breathe,' said Princess Frost from beneath her cloak. 'Would ... rather be ... stabbed in the chest again than suffer this.'

'Don't be dramatic, Princess,' said Cassius, proving my earlier point that he wasn't struggling as much as the rest of us.

Her Royal Highness turned on the soldier with her eyes blazing, forcing Winnie to tear her away from him, muttering, 'Ignore him, Frost.'

We pressed on through the dimly lit halls of the palace's lower floors until we reached the dungeons. The stench was thicker down here, as if the scent of death came from some souls that had only just departed this world, the presence of their bodies still lingering, choking, in the air.

Elora was down here somewhere, as were Greyson and his men, and the boy soldiers. Griffin, Marcus and Harlow and some of his brothers.

The darkness cloaked us as we stepped inside, and Flora spoke a spell that would reveal any hidden dangers to us, and gave us the light to see our way through. Cassius took out the guard before he noticed us. But as we entered the dungeons, our friends were nowhere to be seen.

In fact, in that instant, I was completely alone.

Winnie and Princess Frost and everyone else had disappeared, which made me wonder if the prisoners were truly missing at all. The world around me flickered and shone, and I felt suddenly dizzy. My knees buckled beneath me and I fell, smacking my head hard against the stone floor. When I sat up again, the world was still spinning, and as I lifted my hand to my head, it came away slick with blood.

Shit. I needed to find someone to help me, to head back to …

That was strange. I couldn't remember where I was going, or what I had been doing before I ended up here. What was wrong with me?

'Wicked?' the voice was faint, but I would have known it anywhere.

It was a flickering light in a pitch-black room. I glanced around but still, there was no one to be seen.

He was nowhere to be seen.

'Wicked.'

A light appeared in one of the cells at the back of the space, revealing a figure with raven black hair and the soft blue eyes I knew so well. Kind eyes. He was tall, his dark hair falling down his back in light waves, over his muscled frame.

'Wicked, come to me.'

There he was. But how was this possible?

Had Wicked given me my love, after all?

I walked toward him, a swell of emotion bringing tears to my eyes. I hadn't seen my beloved in so long and yet there he was, right before my eyes.

It all felt too good to be true. But it wasn't. He was here, and I could touch him. He was real.

'Wicked,' he said again. 'How I've missed you, my dear.' His hand rose up to my bleeding head, and his face crumpled with concern. 'What happened to you, love? Who hurt you?'

'I ... I don't know, Greyson. Something strange is happening to me. I didn't think ... I didn't think I would ever see you again.'

He spoke a spell, words I hadn't heard for quite some time, and then just like that, the blood was gone. My head was healed. 'There you go, all better.'

He leaned down and his lips grazed the skin of my forehead, and I felt calmer. Both in my mind, and in my heart. Then he turned away from me, lifted his hand and beckoned me forward.

I moved into the cell, only to find it empty.

He was gone, and I was alone. I spun around as the darkness and confusion swarmed me. 'Greyson, no! My love. Come back.'

'Wicked?' I faced the voice again, but this time it was Princess Frost speaking.

There she was, alongside Winnie, Cassius and the witches. The world still spun, but everything came flooding back. Why we were here, and what we were planning to do. The magic spell that had been cast over the palace. I ignored it, because whether this was all real or not, I wanted to see him again.

But no matter how many times I glanced around, frantic, Greyson wasn't there. Could I have imagined him as the result of some kind of hallucination?

How cruel a thought that was. How I'd missed having him beside me, embracing me and kissing me deeply. My love for him hadn't disappeared, it had only been buried beneath all of the other confusing memories inside my mind. What a cruel trick the palace had played on my mind.

'What's going on?' Princess Frost placed her hand on my shoulder but I turned away, hearing the sound of Greyson's voice again, and didn't answer her. 'Wicked, you can talk to me.'

'No, I can't. I have to ... go.'

'Wicked.' He was there once again, standing right behind them, and staring into my eyes with a concerned expression on his face.

Relief swept through me, bringing a smile to my lips. It wasn't a trick, and I hadn't imagined him.

'This way.' He drifted out of sight so I followed.

I no longer felt any of the others around me, but moved after him until I saw him on the other side of the hall, my feet moving of their own accord. 'I'm coming, Greyson,' I whispered, following the light to the end of it. 'Slow down, I'm almost there.'

He'd disappeared again, and the thickness in the air was extreme by now, so much that I bent over and retched until the remnants of my stomach's contents spilled on the stone floor. Once I recovered I continued to move, removing my cloak and covering my mouth with the cloth of the hood to stop the sickness from returning. My feet still pushed me onward through the dark tunnels, until I found myself in a narrow walkway, surrounded by hundreds or thousands of skulls.

Human skulls ...

'Wicked ... ,' the voice had become increasingly shrill by now, and as I walked through that tunnel I took in the sight of the skulls which had been lodged into the walls, their eyes like blackened pits, their surfaces broken and chipped. It all made me feel more than a bit sick, and yet somehow, I felt I had seen it before, like an overwhelming sense of de ja vu. 'Wicked ... '

'Where am I?' I called out, my voice echoing through the darkness. I kept walking, but this was a maze of which there seemed to be no end. 'Greyson?'

'Wicked,' his voice appeared again, but now he was nowhere to be seen. 'Wicked ... '

'Where are you? What's going on?'

'Look where you are, Wicked,' the voice replied, its shrillness increasing, causing a shiver to crawl up my spine. 'Look what you're surrounded by.'

'Tell me, Greyson.'

Then at the end of the corridor, he appeared. Young and radiant, with his raven waves falling around his shoulders. He came closer, and I tucked the satchel containing the jar with the queen's heart over my shoulder, away from him.

I still didn't know what was happening, but it was like there was a fog hanging over my mind, stealing away my concentration and making it difficult to focus. But he was right before me now, his skin almost glimmering in a dark blue as if he were made of some watery substance, and his eyes ... Tears slipped down my face as he reached closer.

'Kiss me, Wicked.'

'I love you. How I've missed you.'

When he brushed his lips against mine, a flash of light shot up into the ceiling and all around us, causing the eyes of the skulls to shimmer like stars.

I awoke on the ground sometime later, in a grand room with golden walls. But there was no way of calculating exactly how long it'd been. I was lying on some kind of podium, overlooking a wide seating area where a dozen hooded figures faced me.

Once again, Greyson was nowhere to be seen.

The figures stared me down with hard eyes. 'Hello, Wicked,' said the one in the centre, her voice deep and hollow. 'Do you know where you are?'

I looked around at the high tapestries on the walls which depicted the terrors suffered by the Roth witches for centuries. I drank in the faces in the crowds around the room, watching me. Only their dark eyes could be seen beneath the hoods of their cloaks, pale sagging skin over large noses, and broken and blackened teeth behind full lips.

Witches.

'I'm in the House of Roth ... ,' my voice drifted off as I recognised the eternal realm of the witches, and realised that in Greyson's ghostly kiss, my life had ended. 'But I'm not supposed to be here, I'm not ready yet. I must help the princesses, save them from the cruel queen's destruction ... You must help me, please.'

It was impossible to stop the terror and fear from creeping into my voice. There was so much I still needed to do – this couldn't be the end. It wasn't right.

'You're here for a reason, because you were tricked by a spell caused by Queen Leraia and her mage warriors. Please tell us what really happened, Mother.' She removed her hood to reveal Queen Rosa's face. The late queen. How much she resembled Princess Frost in her pretty blue eyes, the thin curve of her nose and that thick dark hair.

She left her seat and walked up onto the podium, coming to stand before me. As she came closer, I realised that she didn't look like a corpse or a ghost. Her complexion was paler than what would be considered normal, but she seemed real.

Alive.

'Mother. No, you can't call me that ... I'm not, ' I fell to my knees as my voice trailed off, and she ran forward up to gather me into her arms, where she placed her hand on my cheek. Something about her affection felt wrong, like it wasn't meant for me. 'Elder Wicked should be the one to see you.'

She smiled, and a single tear dripped down her face as she planted a kiss on my cheek and said, 'You're right, Wicked, it's not your time yet. Go home.' Then she wrapped her arms around me, and sent me away.

When I woke again, I was in the Icefall palace dungeons. On the ground, with Princess Frost, Winnie and Elora staring down at me. The soldiers were behind them, along with Winnie and the witches we'd come with.

A heavy wave of tears rolled down my face, and it was hard to breathe through heaving sobs.

What a fool I'd been. These brave girls had rescued the prisoners while I ... died and came back to life, all because I chose to follow Greyson's ghost.

And yet, they still cared for me. Comforted me, and held me as I cried.

'Wicked, what happened?' said Elora, just as I faded out of focus.

My eyes closed and I began drifting away again, thinking only of Greyson's face. I didn't deserve them or their kindness.

I'd failed them.

'Wicked ... '

42

WINNIE

'What's wrong with her?' said Frost, staring down at the young Wicked who'd collapsed and fallen unconscious on the dungeon floor.

One minute, she'd wandered into one of the cells, crying out for Greyson but ignoring him when he responded, and the next she'd dropped like a stone into a pond.

After so much time apart, we were all so relieved to be together again. My father and my cousin were back with me, and now we had broken Greyson and his brothers, and Marcus and Harlow and the other soldiers, out of their cells as well.

My father took the enchanted water from the witches and drank it with a beaming grin. I was so glad he had it, but I couldn't help but feel like a terrible daughter because with so much going on at the palace, it wasn't me that had brought it to him.

After all, it should have been me. It was a big part of why I was in

Icefall in the first place.

But I had to keep moving. My goals had changed. When I first came to Icefall, I was a different person, trapped in Cranwick and wanting to break free, and depressed and angry at the world for it.

But if I dwelled on the past for too long, I wouldn't get anywhere else. And there was still so much to lose, so much to do. Not only that, but the witches were on our side, and we had new plans for my mother, who now laid unconscious at our feet.

Hope began to spread, lifting our moods and weaving a subtle excitement through the air, despite the foul smell and the darkness of the palace.

Things were finally looking brighter for us all.

But then Wicked had shown signs that she was hearing something, and disappeared from sight.

'I think my mother has a plan for us all,' I said, glancing down at her frail, sleeping form. 'Or at least, she did before ... ,' my voice veered off, but I didn't need to finish because I knew they would understand.

'What do we do?' said Flora, who knelt down beside Wicked and pressed a palm to her cheek. 'We can't leave her here, but we already have to carry ...' Her eyes flickered to my mother, and her mouth turned upward in disgust. The usual response to my mother now.

'It won't be for much longer,' I said with a sad smile. 'We have plans for her, remember?' I turned back to our friend who was laid out beside her on the ground. 'Wicked?' I reached down to stroke her hair just as her eyes opened. 'You're okay.'

Her head was still bleeding, but Elora had bound it with a strip of cloth, a makeshift bandage, and we would heal her when we returned safely to the cabin. The witches didn't seem able to use their magic, despite my mother not being awake to block them. Perhaps it was the palace itself, or some of her previous spell lingered.

But nothing explained the horrid smell that still remained in the air, turning every one of our stomachs so we had to try and block it out.

Tears poured from Wicked's eyes, and a smile creased her mouth. 'I followed Greyson, and he ... he kissed me.'

My gaze flickered to the mage warrior who was watching her with a confused expression. But the witch wasn't looking at him. Her eyes were glazed over, as if she were daydreaming.

'Then I went to the House of Roth. I died, and I saw Queen Rosa, and it was wonderful.'

Maeve and Morgana shared a concerned look, while Flora shook her head. The other witches began to whisper amongst themselves, words of disbelief and shock. Elder Wicked gently stroked Frost's hair as tears started to fall down her face.

'You saw my mother?' Frost whispered. 'How? The spirit beast has been telling me for days now that she wishes to speak to me, but she won't show herself. But she did, to you.' She folded her arms over her chest, understandably angry and clearly jealous.

'Rosa is gone, that's not possible,' said Flora, taking Wicked's hand. Flora's sisters and aunts murmured in agreement with her. 'I think this magic on the palace is built to play tricks on us.'

My thoughts, exactly.

'I just told you that I died, didn't I?' Wicked cried. 'You don't believe me?' The hurt was clear in her eyes now. 'I promise you, I saw her. She's on the Witching Council, in fact she's their leader. I was so happy to see her.' Although she seemed happy, the smile still visible on her face, there was something solemn about her expression.

'Wicked, I didn't kiss you, for a start,' Greyson said, and her eyes met with his and she frowned as if seeing him for the first time.

'It wasn't you,' she said. 'I mean ... it wasn't you as you are now. You were younger, my age.' She stared at the floor, and then up at the others, who were still watching her as if she were mad. 'Now I see why you're all looking at me like that. It sounds crazy, but you have to listen to me. I kissed him, and I ended up there. And then I saw her.'

Frost and Elora both knelt down beside her. 'You saw her?' they both said at once, staring at her with wide eyes.

But the words seemed to be registering for them more now, for all of us. It made sense, in a strange way. If this was the palace playing tricks on us.

If this was my mother's doing, of course the spell would hit us in the worst possible way. In a personal way. So, to bring young Greyson back to young Wicked, of course that would have smacked her right in the jugular. That would hurt. The spell wanted to kill her, so she'd ended up in the spirit realm somehow, but the witches had decided it wasn't her time yet so they brought her back.

When I explained this theory to the others, understanding seemed to resonate through the crowd.

'How did she seem?' said Frost, eyes wide like saucers. A single tear dripped down her face as she reached for Wicked's hand and held it in her own.

'Warm, kind and affectionate. As beautiful as you, Frost.' Frost's tears came harder as the witch spoke. 'She sent me back, said it wasn't my time yet.'

Wicked's gaze dropped to the floor, especially when Morgana's eyes burned with a sudden rage. I had been correct. 'And yet, it was hers?' Morgana said. 'You get to live, but she doesn't? How is that fair? You're a literal copy of our mother. A freak of nature.'

Wicked's eyes widened in horror, and her hands flew to her mouth as if the witch had slapped her. A series of gasps sounded in the air. How many of them felt the same about Elder Wicked's copy?

'I'm real, and I'm alive,' she snapped. 'It's not my fault I'm here or that the queen murdered her, so don't you dare blame me for that. I just died, for goodness' sake.'

'Yet, you came back,' Morgana shot back.

Tears dripped down young Wicked's face as she stormed off down the hall. Unable to help myself, I hissed, 'It's not her fault. Elder Wicked copied her and placed her own identity into my body.'

To my surprise, Wicked stopped and turned back to listen to me. But Morgana scowled at me like I was nothing more than an irritating child. I supposed, in her eyes, I wasn't much more than that. I was no witch like them, after all.

I was just the daughter of a monster.

'I know, I was there. I just don't think it's right.' Her gaze flickered to Wicked again, and she said, 'She isn't natural.'

Before I could say anything else, Wicked stomped off and didn't return. Anger boiled hot in my veins as I snapped, 'Well, you can hardly blame her for that, so cut it out.'

Morgana's frown deepened as she fixed her glare on me again and snapped, 'You're not even a real princess. Why would I listen to anything you say?'

'Mor, stop it!' said Maeve.

But her twin sister stepped closer and leaned over me. 'Go back to your cursed little village, and never come back. You're nothing more than the spawn of evil, which makes you nothing to us.'

Frost ran after me as I slipped out of their sight, heading back into the main hallway leading to the higher floors of the palace, but I pushed her away.

Nothing she said would change my mind. The witch was right, I wasn't important to them.

I would never be truly welcome here.

'Winnella.' The sound of my name echoed through the empty halls.

My anger still burned within me as I remembered how Morgana had spoken to me back there so I thought that perhaps I was hallucinating it.

Then it appeared again, but this time it sounded different. Familiar. Frost had followed me, and she was standing a short distance away, watching me with a strange expression on her face. Who had spoken it the first time?

I hadn't quite made it off the dungeon floor when I'd heard it, the tone distinctly familiar, but I wasn't sure why or where I'd heard it before.

At least, until I finally turned around.

There, ahead of the others, was the Winter king, my stepfather. He was wearing the soldier's uniform that he'd worn at his wedding to my mother, and his hair was dishevelled, his complexion a sickly white, paler than the princess's herself. The queen had told us that he'd died, not in his bed all of those days ago as we'd first thought, but recently, at her hand. How could he be here, standing before me like this?

'Frost ... ,' I said, and pointed in his direction, waiting for her to notice him.

'What?' she said, and only stared ahead with a confused expression. She was looking right at him, but her face didn't change. She didn't seem to notice him. 'What are you looking at? There's just another door there. I think it leads to more cells.'

She couldn't see him.

Wicked had sounded mad at first, but now it seemed that it was my turn. The palace truly was playing cruel tricks on us. But he was so real, so vivid. Something was very wrong with me. 'No, can't you see your father? He's standing right there.'

Tears welled in her eyes, and rolled down her cheeks. Guilt crept into my chest when I saw the heartbreak in her eyes, but there was nothing I could do about it. 'Low blow, Winnie.'

She spun away from me, and was about to storm back to the dungeons to join the others.

'No, please, Frost. I promise you I'm not lying to you, he's really standing there ... '

She turned back around, cast me a scornful look and raced off down the hall, leaving me behind.

But the king was still watching me.

I hesitated. If this was a hallucination, wouldn't Frost be seeing her late father, not me?

It didn't make sense.

'Winnella, come with me.' King James was still staring at me. Like his daughter, he strode off, but he gestured for me to follow.

Alarm bells were ringing inside my mind, but a small part of me wanted to see where he would take me. Surely it was silly, after all Wicked had followed Greyson and died. But my feet had a life of their own as I began to walk after him.

'Come to me.'

It wasn't like Frost was going to come back for me any time soon.

Taking a deep breath, I followed the king's ghostly form, wondering what the hell I was getting myself into. I told myself I wasn't going to end up in the House of Roth like Wicked, and that I knew what I was doing. I wasn't going to kiss him, or make any wrong moves. I would be vigilant, careful and calculating. Because if this was a trick, I wasn't going to fall for it. But maybe it would answer some questions about whatever the hell was going on in this palace right now.

'Where am I?' I followed him into a dark corridor, and the choking smell grew in its strength.

I felt the sudden urge to turn back, tried to tear myself away and run for the dungeons where I would find my friends again.

But he grasped my wrist and tugged me toward him until I found myself standing at the edge of a small child's bedroom.

Here, there were two small beds, a small doll's house and several other clothes and toys, and the grand window that revealed the view of the Winter forest we'd come to know so well.

The sight only brought me back to myself again, reminding me of everything we'd done in that forest, of the friendships we'd made and the schemes we'd designed together.

Horror coiled through me as I stared at those little beds and the children sleeping in them.

The *babies*. One with short raven curls, the other fair-haired.

The ghost of King James Winter of Icefall watched me from the doorway and nodded his head. 'They cannot see you, child. Go on, take a closer look.'

'Who are they?' I inched forward, and peered over the cots, stared down at their small sleeping faces. They must have been around a year old.

When I looked into the blue eyes of the child on the left, when I saw the small mouth, pale cheeks and dark curled hair, I knew deep in my heart that this was Princess Frost as a child. As for the other girl, her features were similar but they were still her own, her eyes almond shaped and more of a grey-blue.

Were they twins? Who was she?

'Ask yourself that question,' said the Winter king, peering at me closely, with a knowing smile on his lips. There was something about that smile that unnerved me, and a shiver crawled up my spine.

'Frost and Elora?' I asked quietly, afraid to know the answer although it was beginning to dawn on me that there was something deeper going on here. The reason why I'd been led here, and not Frost.

He chuckled bitterly. 'You and I both know Elora was never mine. Besides, you should also know that she is one year younger.'

'I don't understand,' I said. But, wasn't that a lie? I vaguely remembered being told of Elora's story, how she'd been raised by the witches after Queen Rosa had a short affair with a lord, and fallen pregnant.

Of course I knew what I was looking at, I just didn't want to believe it. Because a revelation like that would rip the ground out from beneath my feet.

With everything I had already learned about my mother and her secrets, that ground was already full of gaping holes. Soon, I would fall through.

'Did you know who I was when I came to the palace?' I asked softly, although I wasn't sure I wanted to know the answer.

Because if he did, why act like he didn't know me? Why continue to treat me like a stepdaughter even after we'd left the palace?

He cast me a sad smile. 'Of course not, child. But I never would have forgotten you, so I fear she must have enchanted me to not know you when I saw you. She may have sensed that there was a chance you may meet me again, and taken precautions. I never stopped wondering what happened to you, or if you were even ... alive. We never stopped searching for you, our girl. But it was not until she sent her guards after me and I saw my beloved Rosa again that I realised what had happened. Her spell must have worn off after death.'

If it were true, this was no hallucination after all. He was showing me the story of my own reality.

Tears welled in my eyes. 'Are you saying you think she ... took me from you?'

'Keep watching, and you will find out.' He vanished, and I screamed, but neither of the girls stirred.

I really was as invisible to them as he'd said.

Shortly afterwards, a far younger Winter king entered the room with ... Queen Rosa. She was beautiful, with Frost's pretty eyes and dark hair. Her silver night dress showed off the curve of her plump, rounded belly. There in her womb was little Elora.

Queen Rosa and the king went to each of the children, to Frost and I, my *twin sister,* tucking us in and stroking our hair before leaving the room.

Outside the window, it was clearly snowing. Sometime later, although

I don't know how long it was, the window blew open after a strong gust of wind and a cloaked figure entered the room. After checking the room was almost empty, she slipped down her hood, revealing her face.

Queen Leraia, my mother, or so I'd always thought. She crossed the room, studied both of the girls before quickly reaching for the child with the blonde hair and slipping her under her coat as if she weighed nothing, then disappeared back through the window as if she'd never been there at all.

It all felt like a distant dream.

But it made sense, didn't it? I sank to my knees in desperation as the world crashed and burned around me. My mother had stolen me from the Winter palace. I was truly Elora and Frost's sister, their blood sister. A princess of Icefall.

As if the queen's destruction wasn't enough already, this was the worst of it. Not only had she killed her sister, married her sister's husband and killed her niece's betrothed out of spite, she'd also stolen her child. I was Elder Wicked's granddaughter, although that was no surprise now, and Queen Rosa's daughter.

Which also meant I was part witch.

The ultimate revelation.

This changed everything.

Elder Wicked had cursed me.

Was there a chance that, like the king, she hadn't known who I was when I came to her that day?

What of my poor father, the man who'd raised me? And my cousin and best friend, Barchester?

Questions spun within my mind, and as I knelt on the ground, it was hard to breathe through the sobs that burst from my lips. Dizziness rushed over me, and my whole body felt cold inside. How the witches had teased me that I was no true princess like Frost.

Well, it seemed they were wrong. Everyone was wrong, even me.

'We searched for you for so long,' said King James, my father, who'd reappeared in the doorway. 'When Leraia married me, she chose not to bring you to the wedding. She probably would have never let me see you. If I had known, please understand that I would have called things off immediately, no matter how much my kingdom needed her kingdom's riches.'

'Because she killed you.'

He sighed heavily as if he also couldn't fathom all of the devastation she'd caused. I couldn't blame him for that. She'd stolen me from my family, my real family. Although I loved Dad, and he would always have been my father in my heart.

But I couldn't help but wonder what my life would have been like, had she not chosen to take me all of those years ago.

'Yes, exactly. Your real name is Ivy, to tell you the truth. You and your sister were both very dear to us.' He sighed again, and reached out a hand to me. 'As for Elora ... well, I never blamed your mother, truly. I was bitter and angry for a long time, of course, but over time I forgave her.

'Our relationship had turned sour a couple of months after you were born. I went away a lot on royal duties, and I often regret being so cold to her in my letters, but she became lonely, I suppose. She began seeing a lord from the south, Lord Dresden Falks, who also has mage connections, so I have been told.'

'I still can't contemplate that this is even happening ... I don't know what to say.'

His eyes were warm, and so like Frost's as he smiled at me. 'It's a lot to take in, but I hope I have shed some light for you, because you deserve to know the truth. Both your mother and I love you very much.'

My mother. Queen Rosa was my birth mother.

No wonder Frost and I shared the same childhood lullabies, the same one I'd sung to her on the fallen tree above the waterfall. No wonder she had felt like a sister to me since we'd met.

'Frost and I became close recently through the events that followed your attempted murder on your wedding night, but I never knew ... Are we twins?'

'You have sensed a connection for some time, I have been watching you both. You have been through the worst, but you always returned to each other even though you did not know how close you really were.' He glanced upward, as if remembering the time.

'And yes, you are twins. Both born January 1st. Fraternal twins, so not identical, but there are similarities. You are seven minutes apart – her older. I am so glad you are together again, and I hope you will always look after each other. I wish things could have turned out differently for us as a family.'

He was right, I'd definitely felt closer to Frost than anyone else in my life.

But I hadn't expected this, nor would I ever.

A new question appeared in my mind, one I desperately needed to know the answer to. 'Will I see you again?'

'I will visit you again in your dreams, soon.'

A tear slipped down my face, and I quickly swiped it away with the sleeve of my cloak. 'Thank you for showing me everything.'

He was so like Frost, my twin sister, as he planted a ghostly kiss on my forehead and said, 'Be well, my love. Go, avenge us. Get our kingdom back, and take care of your sisters.'

43

FROST

'Winnie?' It seemed to be one thing after another in this place since our arrival.

I had found Wicked a short distance away, having returned after the palace played its tricks on her, but then Winnie had also collapsed. She was convinced that she had seen my father's ghost, and had even tried running through a wall to follow him.

Had she actually knocked herself out, or was she also seeing things that were not there?

Queen Leraia had enchanted the palace, that much was clear now, but she had done it in such a way that brought Winnie back to us.

Could she be trying to bring us together again, just to destroy us all at once?

So many questions were brewing in my mind that it was hard to keep myself together.

Winnie slowly opened her eyes, and the witches and Harlow's

brothers crowded around us as I leaned over her. When she saw us, she coughed and tried to sit up slowly. 'Frost?' she whispered softly. 'I had the strangest dream ...'

I helped her sit up against me, leaning her back by my side as she told me what she had seen.

The memory of my father – our father – and our mother putting us to bed before Leraia snuck in through the window and stole my twin sister while she was sleeping.

Wicked had seen my mother, and Winnie had seen my father. It was hardly fair, and it could not be true. It was all a part of the magical tricks this palace was playing on us.

Trying to break us apart, and to lead us away from the parts of the palace that we needed to go to.

'No, I do not believe you.'

'We're all being tested, I told you,' said Flora, shaking her head. 'If you hear voices, ignore them. They're not real.'

'Was he calling your name?' said Wicked, returning to my side again.

I did not know where she had gone when the witches had insulted her. Perhaps, like Winnie, she had just needed some space. But she had come back, and that was all that mattered. She may have been abnormal to the other witches, but she was as much a part of this as Winnie and me. She belonged with us.

Winnie coughed and tried to sit up carefully.

I was surprised she had not shattered from falling away from the wall she had thrown herself into.

Perhaps that was just how powerful the enchantment was.

'Yes, consistently,' said Winnie. 'I tried to run away but he pulled me with him and made me watch this scene ... memory? I don't know, but it was so vivid, and he told me he was going to annul the marriage to my ... to the queen, but he never got the chance.' She sat up properly. 'I need to speak to Dad ... Mayor Farn. I'm so confused.'

'I'm here, Winnie. We will talk properly soon, and privately,' he said, taking her into his arms. 'I don't think now is the right time.'

'It does not matter, because it was just a hallucination,' I said. 'You may as well speak now.'

Winnie stared at me. 'You don't believe me?'

She could not be serious. 'Do you? After all, Wicked said she followed a young Greyson, but he wasn't even real. She also said she died as a result of her actions. How can you believe this?'

She shook her head, clearly confused. 'It just all seemed so … vivid.'

'Well, that is the power of magic. Look, let us just get out of these dungeons for a start. Perhaps we can talk about the rest of it later. Can you walk?'

Mayor Farn held her, and Barchester took her hand in his. She shrugged.

Flora and Maeve turned around. 'Let's move, and let you three catch up,' said Flora.

We made our way out, heading for the throne room where the queen was no doubt waiting for us.

How could Winnie think this was true?

'Surely we would have sensed something if we were twins? And they never told me about you or Elora. It does not make sense.'

'He thinks he may have been enchanted by the queen,' she said softly. 'And Elder Wicked and the others, too. That's a big part of why I think I believed him. It makes sense, doesn't it? Besides, we do kind of look alike.' She laughed darkly as the reality of our situation dawned on all of us.

I finally started to wonder if it could be true.

'Sorry I said you weren't a princess,' said Morgana with a bitter laugh. 'Looks like I was wrong.'

'Yeah, you were,' said Winnie firmly.

I could not help but chuckle at her audacity. Of course she was not the type to let the witch get away with a comment like that simply because she apologised.

'I find it strange, too,' said Elora. 'They never told me, either. I mean, Mother came to visit me sometimes, but I was raised with the coven, so I was always concentrating more on my studies. She never told me that I had a sister, or *two*. In fact, I never even knew she was a queen.'

'I never knew she was a witch,' I said.

But why would they raise us separately?

Even if Elora did not have the same father, she was still our sister. Perhaps Mother had thought it would be too painful for Father, having her around, especially after Winnie had been taken.

Had losing her caused issues between my parents? Or Mother simply believed Elora was better suited to the family she had come from. Tragically, there was so much we would never know.

'I never knew her at all,' said Winnie with a sad smile. 'Not that it was her fault, after everything we've learned. At least you both knew who you were. Sorry, I know I sound bitter, and I don't mean to be rude. It's just … a lot to process.'

'Of course,' said Elora with a smile. 'Don't worry about it. We have bigger things to focus on right now, and as your dad says, we can talk about everything properly, privately, when this is all over.'

Maturely spoken for a fifteen-year-old, I thought, although she seemed so much younger to me.

'Who *is* Queen Leraia?' I said, my eyes searching the palace walls as my thoughts continued wandering. Who was she, other than the cruel queen who had destroyed our kingdom? 'Where does she really come from?'

'She's the daughter of Greyson, and our mother's half-sister. Perhaps she dated one of the mage leaders in the past and thinks she still has some kind of standing with them,' said Winnie, clearly thinking it through. 'She may have done so before she met Dad … Mayor Farn.'

'So, why marry the Mayor of Cranwick,' said Elora, 'where she would be restricted in her movements, and as confined as the rest of them?'

'My dad has a good view of the palace through every mirror. Perhaps she saw him as her way in, to begin working on her cruel plans,' said Winnie, her eyes fixed on the floor. 'Then she stole me, killed Queen Rosa when we were eleven or so, and began courting the king a couple of years later.'

'How sick,' said Elora, frowning in disgust.

'I have the feeling we will find out the truth soon enough,' I said, wondering what would happen next. 'Both Wicked and Winnie have seen strange things in the palace already, and collapsed. Has anyone else noticed anything?'

Just as I asked, as if I had willed the darkness into motion with my words, it appeared that Maeve and Morgana were convulsing on the floor, with the mages surrounding them. What was happening here?

What were they seeing?

We let them wake up, then held them as they tried to calm themselves and each other.

'I saw Mother,' said Maeve, with tears rolling down her face. 'But she was in the House of Roth beside Rosa, on the Witching Council.'

'I saw the same thing,' said Morgana, taking Maeve into her arms. 'Verity was there, too ... '

'Thanks for the heart attack, girls,' Elder Wicked snarled. 'I would just love to hear all about my death, and my visit to the House of Roth.'

'What happened, exactly?' Verity asked.

'Don't tell us,' Elder Wicked snapped. 'I don't want to know.'

'It probably won't come true,' said Marthy, with her sketchbook in hand. 'Remember my parade painting of the princesses? Didn't happen.'

'Calm yourself,' said Flora. 'It was just a dream.'

'It'll be okay,' said Marcus reassuringly, and his brothers joined him in agreement.

'But what if it wasn't? Wicked went to the House of Roth but didn't see Mother. Winnie's dream was just as true, and she learned who she really was. They weren't dreams!' said Morgana, clinging to Maeve with fearful eyes.

This couldn't be real, or true.

It wasn't fair or right. But it did make sense. Too much sense, if I were honest.

'Frost ... ,' the voice was enchanting and soft like a melody, tearing me away from the voices of those around me.

Tears sprang to my eyes at the sound of it. I would have known that voice anywhere – it was the voice of my childhood, of love, comfort and nostalgia.

'Frost.'

'Frost,' said Winnie, this time. 'Did you just hear something?' She asked the mayor to put her down, and then she rushed after me as my feet began moving of their own accord. She called out, 'Everyone, it's happening again!'

But her voice did not sound quite as soft and lovely as my mother's. I had not seen her for five years, and how I had missed her. Although the witches around me tried to stop me weaving through the palace after my mother, I kept moving. The only thing I could focus on was her voice and the swish of her skirts as they disappeared down the hall.

She wanted me to come with her. She had been calling to me for so long now, and she loved me and finally wanted me beside her.

It was my time to see her again.

I followed the first voice to the entrance of the dungeons where we had first entered. Torches were hanging on the walls, lighting the way, but my gaze remained transfixed on the slim shadow of light and the back of a pale blue gown which my mother had worn so many times throughout her life at the palace.

With me, with us. How could I remember her, but not Winnie or

Elora? It made no sense.

The queen must have placed some spell over us as children when she took Winnie, because I would have known her as my sister. I should have recognised her when I first saw her on the day of the wedding.

I should have embraced her as a twin sister would. I should have sensed her, *felt* her here.

But I had not, and it did not feel right.

'Mother, I am coming.' I was captivated by the softness of her voice as it sang my name, the sound echoing softly through the palace halls. 'Mother, where are you going?'

'Frost, it's not real,' I heard Flora saying from somewhere in the distance, but my legs would not listen, nor would my heart. It was under the spell of the palace, and it triggered every movement and every thought of mine. 'Ignore it.'

But the sickness here was so strong, and it felt like it was consuming me from the inside out and forcing me to bring up what was left in my body.

'Come with me, Frost,' said Mother's voice.

I knew if I saw her this darkness inside would fritter away like paper in the wind, so I kept moving until I reached the throne room. The space was dark, yet the window was open. The room was illuminated in a blueish light, like the sea amid a powerful storm.

Sitting upon the throne, watching me, was my beautiful mother. Her hair was tied onto her head in a braided bun with a small black crown wrapped around it, black and blue roses woven through the detailed steel surface. Her lips were painted blood red, her eyelids a dark blue, and her eyes were cold.

And yet in that moment, she was more beautiful than I had ever seen her.

This was not the mother I remembered.

I told myself that this was some strange impersonation of who she had used to be, especially as she began to speak, 'Frost. You have failed me,' she said, steeping down off the dais and coming to stand before me. 'You are nothing. Your sister is far more than you will ever be.'

I could not hide the hurt that pierced my chest at those words, and I knew it was visible on my face. 'Elora is kind, Mother. But I did not even know she was my sister until – '

She sneered down at me as if I were nothing more than dirt on her pretty heeled shoe. 'I am not speaking of Elora, Frost. I am talking about Ivy, my beloved girl. My true heir.'

'No, no. I am the eldest, Mother –'

'Age means nothing. She is my heir at heart. I do not know why we even kept you. It should have been you that was taken, not her.'

This was not my mother. Those words were not something she had ever said to me before, and she had certainly never taken that tone with me when I was a small child. 'No, Mother!'

No matter how hard I tried to imagine that this was nothing but a nightmare, her words nestled themselves inside my chest and wove themselves through the cells of my heart like a tangled spiderweb which would never come free, or at least not until she ripped it from my chest. But it was not even there anymore, so how was this possible?

I did not even need to spin around to feel the disappointment on her face.

'I will avenge you, Mother. I will do this for us all, and you will see my value.'

When everything was over and I was back with those I cared for, we carried the unconscious queen to the tower, where we placed her into a tin box pierced with holes.

We made sure there was nothing reflective inside the room that she could use to heal herself, and that Winnie was far away as we worked, and then we left. The others travelled back to the cabin, while Marcus and Titus chose to stay with Greyson and his men, who would guard the queen's room.

As for the queen herself, we still were not entirely sure what we would do with her yet, but the answers would come in time.

First, our main priority was returning my heart to me. Everything else would follow when the moment was right.

44

WICKED

Here in the tower of the Winter palace, a glimmer of hope settled in my heart.

There was something strangely calming about the view from up here, the snow-topped rolling hills that surrounded the palace and the nearby villages of Icefall, the sun shining its light over the trees that reached high into the sky.

Here, we had a plan.

Princess Frost, the soldiers and the witches lingered behind me as I began chanting the spell that would remove Princess Frost's heart from the false queen's chest. We would do this. The princess would have her heart back, and her face, and then we would work toward her coronation.

She and Winnie, her twin sister, could live safely in the palace with us witches for protection.

They would no longer call me a failure.

The six mage guards knelt on the ground, Greyson and his men,

Harlow and Marcus and their brothers each standing guard behind them, holding a blade to their throats in case they tried anything. Their mouths and eyes were covered, and their wrists were bound. Although they struggled, not a single one had tried to block our magic, so it became clear that it was only the queen who could do so, after all.

And she was … well, otherwise occupied.

We had chosen not to bring Winnie into the room while we worked, out of fear that the queen used her as a mirror again.

'Very good,' Elder Wicked praised me softly as the queen began slamming her hands against the inside of the tin box she was trapped in. The elder witch wrapped an arm around Princess Frost the moment she took a deep breath and bent over, clutching her chest. 'Looks like it's working.'

Her words only made me more determined to keep moving. The witches gathered around the princess protectively as I chanted the spell more loudly, feeling it with everything in me and wanting us to do well. For the princess, for our coven, and for Icefall.

The banging inside the box increased, and now we could hear the queen screaming and thrashing as the spell took its toll on her.

It was working. I wasn't the only one speaking the words now, the witches had also joined in, and Princess Frost herself. Tears rolled down her face but she still cried out in love and hope.

Then the princess screamed and crumpled to the floor. I tried to run to her, but a sudden fatigue had begun to wash over me.

Hysterical laughter sounded from inside the tin box. 'Your witch sister already tried that, and lost her life in the process.'

My witch sister? Who could she have been speaking about? All of the witches were here, all of them alive and well … aside from …

No. Seager, Elder Wicked's youngest sister, was missing.

Always evading the group, since she was a child. I locked eyes with Elder Wicked, and she fell to her knees, clutching her chest just as Princess

Frost had done. But it wasn't because she was missing her heart, as the princess was, but because she was grieving her most precious sister.

The sister who was only a baby during many of those early memories.

Tears poured down all of our faces as Elder Wicked screamed out in pain, in the loss of her dear little sister. 'You murderous wrench!' she hissed, kicking at the box and pushing it over with all of her might, so hard that the laughter stopped.

I'd never seen her lose her composure like that before. She was the oldest sister, the one who always needed to be strong for them. This was her at her lowest point.

'How dare you?' she said, her voice barely louder than a whisper, and gravel deep with desperation.

'Do you know who I really am?' said the queen.

'A narcissist?' said Elder Wicked, her desperation gone, rolling her eyes as her wall began to form around her again. She had been good at putting up a front, but how long would it be until she broke down like that again? 'A cruel queen who only thinks of herself? A cold-hearted monster?'

I had to keep moving, and continue with my spells. So I spoke them even when my voice began to cut out, when my knees struggled to hold me upright.

'Well, I suppose so.' The queen laughed delightedly, like it was the best joke she could have made. But I heard her voice weakening, and took it for a positive. Like me, she was growing tired. 'But I am also a daughter of one of the strongest mage leaders in history. Isn't that right, Father?'

For some time, no one answered, but then Greyson spat, 'You are no true daughter of mine. My only children are kind and fair. Rosa, Verity, Flora, Maeve and Morgana. My five girls.'

'Six,' said the queen, her desperation now clear in her trembling voice. Not only was she tired, but heartbroken as well. 'You have six girls, father.' Her determination to be included was evident; to be loved. 'Only unlike them, I am a full mage just like my mother, Madame Ember.'

This was a diversion, I realised, a way to distract us from casting the spell. I continued to chant, pushing away the fatigue that threatened to force me from my knees to the cold stone floor.

If it took every bit of energy that remained within me, I would do this. The princess would have her heart back, and the queen would be destroyed.

But it was hopeless, and I couldn't help but fall silent as my words became faded whispers. The mages were blocking the spell, their defensive enchantments weakening every muscle in my body until my skin burned and my limbs ached.

And then there was nothing, and I sank to the ground, the fatigue spreading fire through me until I couldn't move. Stretching out an arm, or a leg, or even a finger was impossible.

Frozen on the spot, I willed my mind to keep trying. Told my body to keep fighting so that my mind would always be strong enough. I chanted the spell once again, ignoring the weakness it stirred inside my body. I continued, and I wouldn't stop until it worked.

Then Greyson and his men did what they should have done all along. He nodded once, and his men killed all six of the mages with tears in their eyes. Perhaps they had been brothers, once. Friends.

But they knew what had to be done.

'Kill them!' the queen screamed, her frustration clearly getting the better of her. 'All of them.' But she didn't know that her men were gone.

'There will be others,' said Greyson. 'When we're finished here we should find them, too.'

He was right. After some time, the door slammed open and more mage warriors filed in.

The witches began shooting waves of power against them, forcing them down the steps and out of the tower. Others were thrown through the tower window, scattering shards of glass across the room.

Even amid the chaos around me, I struggled for what felt like hours to remove Princess Frost's heart from the queen's chest.

The witches also continued as Mayor Farn and Barchester knelt over the unconscious princess.

'You will not win this!' the queen screamed, but by now the thrashing still continued so much that the box was shaking again. 'I will end you.'

'Fighting words for someone trapped in a box!' Elder Wicked snapped, making me and the rest of the witches laugh.

But I didn't waste my energy by responding.

There was far too much at stake.

Her men were dropping like flies, but more were appearing from behind her.

'Traitors,' Greyson murmured. 'Those three are my sons – her brothers.'

'How many children do you have, Grandfather?' Elora murmured, laughing a little to herself. The other witches joined her, probably wondering the same.

'Too many.'

'Father's been busy,' said Maeve with a smile.

'Thanks, Father,' said Flora, laughing. 'You're proud of us though, right?' As she spoke, her eyes were wide with love and hope.

'Most of you, yes.' His honesty was charming, and made me wish I had my own Greyson at my side.

A companion, and a friend.

Until I realised that the thought wasn't helpful at all, under the circumstances. 'Almost there, Frost,' I whispered as the queen's cage grew still.

Only seconds later, the darkness overwhelmed me, too.

45

WINNIE

When we reached the tower floor, steel bars were placed over every window.

It was happening. Since no one wanted to become the monster the queen was and kill her, we had a new plan to put into place instead.

Her tin box would remain here. One of our men would guard the door each day and night in shifts, so we'd taken down the names of all volunteers and created a fair schedule.

Queen Leraia was given the room she'd passed onto me, which was still damp and dusty.

But I had to wait outside as the beds were removed, along with every other cabinet, sink, and every other piece of furniture. Even the windows were covered with dark wood so she couldn't use the glass to break herself free.

Her deception had been pristine; no one had ever suspected that she could possibly be so cruel, or detect the plans brewing in her cunning mind for so many years. She'd stolen from her sister, first her child and then her life, then the king and his kingdom. She deserved everything that was coming to her.

This would be her prison for the rest of her life, trapped in this tin box and unable to break free.

Just as I was currently enclosed in a glass body, this was her new home for eternity.

'Aside from the guards, no one comes up here without permission from Frost, Elora and I. Get all three requests granted, but only for good reason. She can be dangerous if she breaks free again. Don't be silly about this.'

Here she would be, forever enclosed in her prison. Just like me.

They all nodded in agreement. 'Yes, Winnie.'

Hearing their voices like this made me realise what I truly wanted. 'You know what? Call me Ivy. It's the name my true parents gave me.'

I made the mistake of locking eyes with Mayor Farn as I spoke, and watched his face crumple, clearly heartbroken. Guilt seeped into my chest. I had hoped he would know I wasn't speaking about him when I said the words, but I supposed they were a little too close to home.

'No, Winnie. Please ... ' He began to cry so hard that one of the guards was forced to escort him, sobbing, from the room.

Scowling, Barchester ran after him, but not without casting a heavy glare in my direction.

'I'll speak to him in a moment,' I said, my heart breaking despite everything. 'But yes, you've all learned of my true heritage now. So, please call me Ivy.'

'Spoken like a true queen,' said Princess Frost, reaching for my hand. She still had a bump on her head from where she'd fallen, but it didn't make her any less pretty. She was practically glowing, clearly happy to have her heart back in her chest, all thanks to Wicked. 'I know this must be hard for you. I am sorry.'

'It's hard for us all,' I said softly, weaving my fingers through hers. 'I still can't believe I'm a twin.' Laughter burst from my lips, and then Elora wrapped us both in a hug as Frost and I began to cry happy tears. 'I'm so glad I have you both.'

'Me, too,' said Elora with a grin. 'No stealing my clothes, though!'

'I don't know about that. I quite like those trousers,' I teased, knowing there was no way I would be caught dead in a pair like that.

The kind of clothes worn by the people of Marellia. My people, because I was a *princess,* and next in line to the throne if God forbid, something happened to my twin sister. It was still hard not to feel like I'd fallen into one of my fantasy books, but honestly, I was just glad to have them at my side.

'They're not even mine!' Elora said, laughing.

Everyone was quiet for some time after that, or having their own conversations.

Until Greyson said suddenly, 'I still think we should have just killed them all.'

Flora wrapped an arm around his shoulders, holding him close. I might have been exaggerating a little when I said no one had wanted to kill my *aunt.* Greyson had demanded that we do it, so that she couldn't come back and hurt anyone else. But the witches had just reminded her that this was his daughter he was talking about, and what if, despite everything, he later regretted his decision?

Murder wasn't something you could ever take back. I knew that better than anyone. Even if the witch's death was an accident. Even if I had attempted to kill the queen at the parade.

'And stoop to her level?' I retorted, the image of myself killing the queen entering my mind and causing a shudder to rush through me.

Was it ever right to kill a murderer, or to become the one to order their execution?

It was one of those centuries-old debates that would always remain unanswered. Besides, this woman may not be my mother now, but she always had been in my heart, and I wasn't sure I was strong enough to kill her.

I had stabbed her in the back when she'd done the same to Frost, but that was out of pure rage, an impulsive decision. To actually process it all before doing so felt different, and wrong. 'No thank you.'

'Alright then. Now come on, we have a coronation to prepare for. Twin queens, how wonderful.' He wore a grand, beaming smile as he looked upon us both.

'At least, until one of us marries and produces an heir,' said Frost with a smile, taking my hand.

I stared down at our linked fingers in awe, imagining our father watching us from the back of the room with a wide grin on his mouth, glad we were finally together. My cheeks might have blushed crimson if they weren't made of glass. 'But I don't know how to be a … a queen. I didn't even know I was a princess.'

'Follow my lead. I have been building up to this my whole life. We will learn together, and probably make mistakes. But do it all at my side, okay?'

She was right, this would all be fine if we helped each other. I wiped my tears away and cast her a slim smile. 'Okay.'

'Let's go before we can never leave,' said Elora, and we walked away.

I told myself it was all for the better, but a tear still lingered on my cheek.

46

FROST

THE AIR WAS COLD BUT SERENE from the balcony of the palace's tower. The sun shone its light down on the mountains that surrounded the palace of Icefall and the Winter Forest beyond. From here you could see the Winter Caves in the far distance. The birds could be heard singing in the trees. You could watch the snow falling and reach out a hand to touch it.

It was the perfect place to clear my head and spend some time alone, thinking through what would happen next. Perhaps I would make this my spot, where I would come when things became overwhelming and I just needed a moment to process and breathe.

Soon, I would take my father's place on his throne. I would be the queen that he had always told me I would one day become. He always said he wanted me to be powerful and strong, kind but resilient and never the one to back down from a fight.

Like my mother, I supposed.

But why had they chosen not to tell me that once I had been a twin? That I had two younger sisters? Even the sister who had not been stolen by my mother's half-sister had been raised away from the palace, away from me. I would never understand their reasons now. I would never see either of them again.

But I knew they were always with me, and I could not let these questions ruin how I saw them.

I would have to remind myself every day that they cared for me, and for Winnie ... Ivy, and Elora.

Everything I did now would be to protect my sisters, and my friends. And my kingdom.

'Princess, are you alright?' Harlow found me on the balcony of the tower, staring out at the beauty before me, and deep in my thoughts.

He was still dressed in his fighting leathers, his hair falling around his ears. Like the view, he was incredibly beautiful as his lips spread into a smile then. 'Or should I say queen?' He laughed as he took my hand in his. 'You look magnificent, Princess Frost. I have always found you so.'

Although his words warmed my chest, there were questions brewing within. 'Thank you. But, why are you saying this now? You had plenty of chances back in the cabin.' Despite everything, his words had made me smile. 'I do not understand what you want from me, Harlow.'

His laughter lingered in the air, and for a moment he looked away. But then his eyes returned to mine, staring deeply into them as if he wanted to say something but did not know how to get the words across. 'I suppose I was afraid of you. You're a firecracker, Princess.'

'Is this all because I tackled you into the snow?' I said breathlessly, returning his laughter as the memory came to mind. 'I am not someone to be afraid of, unless you are my cruel stepmother.'

He ran a hand through his sun curls. 'Don't worry, I have no intention of becoming an evil queen.' His words brought a smile to my face, and I could not help the laughter that escaped. 'But I do want to tell you something about myself that I have been keeping quiet for some time now.'

I said nothing but nodded, waiting for him to go on, and wondering what he had to say.

'I want you to know that I understand your fear and hesitation to rule over your people, to take your father's place.'

His words were sincere, but I was not sure I entirely believed them. How could he truly understand my position? He was a soldier.

'And I would like to kiss you.'

'Do you truly understand? You are no princess, Harlow.' My cheeks grew warm as his mouth spread wide into a grin, his gaze falling to my lips. 'You are a valiant soldier, Harlow, but you are no –'

'Princess Frost, I am a prince,' he cut in, his words forcing the air from my lungs.

How was it possible?

'I am the heir of Oceanwell, Prince Harwin Summer. I have a younger sister and two awful stepsisters who would happily take the position if it were so easily handed over. But I have been avoiding my duties for some time. I have not felt ... ready for the responsibility. I know you understand how that feels. We are similar in that way, Princess Frost.'

The words were strong, and they would not register. 'So you have been galivanting around here as a soldier of Icefall?'

Did he not understand the consequences of his actions? If my father had found out, this beautiful Prince Harwin would be seen as a spy. A soldier from the enemy kingdom, trying to get close to the princess to take Icefall down. He would be sent to the dungeons, and possibly executed in front of my people.

But I was not my father. Soon, I would be queen, and it would be my decision what to do with him. 'Do you not understand that this would make us enemies, *Prince Harwin*? You could land yourself in serious trouble, and you wish to *kiss* me?'

It seemed unbelievable. A creature of the Summer world, of oceans and deserts, had disguised himself as a lieutenant in the coldest climate of them all. But it could be true.

Perhaps Winnie's revelation had brought this to light, made him realise that we should know the truth. Or he simply felt like telling me.

He laughed, the sound deep and rasping, forcing my stomach to flip over on itself. 'We do not have to be enemies, Princess Frost. Wars between kingdoms often occur for the silliest of reasons. Perhaps with our reign, we can change things.'

He was really selling me the dream, as Winnie would have said. Little butterflies seemed to be spinning around inside my stomach.

What was happening to me? I had never felt such things before, not even when I spent those lovely evenings with Hugo. As I remembered everything, it all came back, washing over me like a wave, remembering everything that had happened to the prince that had once been my beloved, and suddenly I could barely breathe.

But still Harlow continued, 'I had to break away to find some freedom. My mother, and my stepsisters, Piper and Martha, can be intense. Demanding.

'They are spoiled princesses through and through, but not ... not like you. You are kind of heart, as well as beautiful. Like my sister, Violet. The twins can be vain, like my stepmother. They want my throne.

'I have considered letting them have it, and I have not felt worthy. But you ... you make me feel strong. You and Winnie, you make me feel like I can do anything. Be anyone. I could be a good king, and I could do good for my people. But Princess Frost, I have never felt so *scared*.'

He chose to tell me this now, after everything that had happened in Icefall. What perfect timing. I had only just mentioned marrying and siring heirs for Icefall, for goodness' sakes. 'How do I know you are not lying? You have not told me who you are all of this time. How do I know you are not an impostor? A soldier with a sudden need for power?'

He lifted his wrist, revealing a dark tattoo: a circular crest with a wave passing over a small well. 'All of us royals have one. You can ask my mother to show you hers when we travel to Oceanwell. But first, I would like to ask for your hand in marriage.'

He knelt down on one knee, and my hands threw to my mouth, covering my face. In his hand was a small box containing a large diamond ring. 'I would give you this, Princess. It was my grandmother's. Passed down so that one day I will give it to the right person. That person, for me, is you.'

'Marriage?' I repeated, too stunned to speak fully and ask all of the questions that were brewing inside. 'Harlow, I appreciate your friendship and I have loved every moment of you training me, but I am far from ready for such a commitment –'

He laughed again, and it did something to me.

My newly returned heart was racing too fast, and my entire body felt ice cold inside.

'It is Prince Harwin, Frost. Harlow was just a fantasy. Tell me you do not feel something for me. I have been watching you. We have spent time together training, and I have fallen for you. But that is not the only reason I am asking you now. Typically, I would wait and ask you once we have spent time courting each other. But my father is sick and dying, and I will have to take his place soon. You are due to become queen of your own kingdom as well. Together, we could align ourselves and heal both of our kingdoms. Our happiness together could come later.'

I had already lost one marriage of convenience, and it did not seem right to jump straight into another after everything that had happened with Hugo. 'This is all happening too fast, Harlow.' Could he not see how much this was frightening me?

That I already had so much to deal with?

'Harwin.'

'What?' I asked.

'My name is Prince Harwin of Oceanwell.'

'You already said that. Well, you really changed your name to disguise yourself.'

Despite everything, the ring in his hand and the way he was staring up at me now, and my racing heart, I could not help but laugh.

He grinned. 'Join me, Princess Frost. Say you will do it.'

'You have awful timing, *Your Highness*. I will have to consider it.' With that, I stormed off the balcony, from the tower and back into the palace, leaving him kneeling on the ground.

We all took a seat in the Grand Hall, so we could plan what to do next.

I could not help but feel for Mayor Farn when Winnie had taken back her name as he clearly loved her. But I hoped they would work things out, as he had always been a great father to her. But she was clearly still struggling with coming to terms with learning who she really was, so I could not entirely blame her, either. It would only take time, but I would be there with her through it all.

My twin sister, and my fellow queen.

If Elora wanted to be, she was also welcome here as often as she pleased. Our parents were dead, but we would be there for each other as Winnie had promised our father when she saw him in her strangely enchanted dream, here at the palace.

'This place feels so much bigger than I imagined,' said Elora, looking around with her eyes filled with awe.

'Well it is the *Grand Hall*,' said Barchester, coming back in to sit beside us with Mayor Farn following closely behind.

'I was talking about the palace, not the room,' said Elora, rolling her eyes to the ceiling. 'I thought you'd be smarter, being the nephew of a mayor.'

'Elora, that's not nice,' Flora scorned her niece. 'Apologise.'

Elora sighed heavily. 'Fine. I'm sorry, Barchester.'

He just shook his head and shrugged before saying, 'My uncle wants to say something.'

We all faced him, and the mayor glanced back. 'I'm sorry for my behaviour before. I thought, at first, that we should speak privately, Winnie ... Ivy, but there is no time for that, is there? I will support you in your choices, whatever they may be.

'I thought ... my wife had always wanted a child, and when she told me she'd found a baby girl through an adoption agency, I knew she'd fallen in love with you and she seemed so happy, and well, I was thrilled. I'd always wanted to be a father, but we'd had issues conceiving for a long time.

'Well, she had gone so far as to create legal documents and hired a lawyer ... probably an actor, now that I think about it, and well, I believed her. Because nobody thinks their wife is capable of such a thing, right? So when I heard what had happened to you, it broke my heart all over again. I am sorry to all of you for everything she has done, but especially you.'

She shook her head. A tear rolled down her face as she said, 'I can't do this, I'm sorry.'

He hung his head, but it was clear in his body language that he was hurt. He stood up from his chair, said, 'I completely understand – ,' and began to move away but Winnie stopped him.

She inched forward, this time with a slight smile creeping across her face. 'No, no. Sorry I wasn't clear, I mean, call me Winnie. Ivy is too ... strange. Sorry, Frost.'

I grinned, my heart returned to my chest and full of love for both of my sisters, and my aunts and great-aunts. And my grandfather and his men.

A whole other family that I had not known even existed. I had never felt quite so fortunate. 'You are Winnie to me, anyway.'

She leapt into the mayor's arms. 'Sorry for the way I spoke to you. I suppose I was overwhelmed by everything. You'll always be my dad, no matter what.'

Tears fell down his face, but he was smiling through his tears. 'Don't apologise, Winnie. I love you, and I'm so proud of you, my dear girl.'

'I love you, too.'

'Oh, will you all stop making me cry already?' said Maeve, wiping her face.

'Pull yourself together, Mae,' said Morgana.

We began working out our schedule after that.

We arranged for the coronation to take place in a week's time, on our birthdays. There would be a ball with music and food and dancing, and the next morning our people could come and ask us for support for anything they may need.

When the conversation was finished, I pulled my cloak high over my head and walked through the halls. I walked beneath the arch to stare up at her glass statue, and took a seat on a nearby bench. 'I miss you, Mother,' I said, discarding the image that entered my mind, of her on that throne with the black and blue rose-crown, because that was not her, but her cruel sister's imitation of her.

'I am so proud of you and your sisters.'

I threw a hand over my mouth, and tears rolled down my face, as she was standing before me.

I closed my eyes, willing for her to go away.

This was not fair. How could they do this to me, whoever was playing this prank?

But when I opened them she was still there, draped in the soft red gown I had worn at Father and Leraia's wedding, the one she had adored so much, with her dark hair falling over her chest.

As she looked upon me now, I began to see the resemblance between her and her cruel half-sister, and how much she looked like her father, Greyson, and her mother, Elder Wicked.

How could I have been so blind for so long?

Behind her was Vencin, the black fur covered feline creature with golden stripes across his body, those eyes peering into mine. His mouth stretched open, and seemed to smile.

My mother's soft blue eyes were full of tears, but her smile was warm. 'I love every one of you with all of my heart. My dear girls.'

'You are not real.' A sob escaped my throat as I tried to blink the tears back. 'No ... '

Vencin had been telling me that she wanted to come to me for so long, but seeing her in that throne room had destroyed that glimmer of hope I had felt.

But now, here she was, ready to shatter my heart all over again.

'I am here, Frost. It is me.' She moved forward, barely a fingertip's touch away. Her skin glimmered transparently, and I wondered, if I reached out to touch her, would my hand fall through? 'I see you have found your sisters. You have seen your grandparents, and your many aunts and uncles.' She laughed. 'There are a lot of them, yes?'

My heart was beating too fast, my body trembling with fear, disbelief and something else: love. I had never thought I would see her again, but for a while I had even believed that was her true self when I saw her in my dream state when I entered the palace again. 'How is this happening?'

'That enchantment my sister placed over the palace, some of it still remains. It has thinned the veil between the world of the dead and the living, so I can visit you for a short while. It is how your father was able to show Winnie the past.'

That explained the stench of death. That *was* real, and not a hallucination.

'But you were on the throne ... '

She shook her head, eyes suddenly burning with rage. 'That was not me, that was Leraia playing dress-up.' She rolled her eyes. 'There is someone else here to see you.' She turned on her heel, and gestured for them to come forward.

They stepped through, and there he was, Hugo. The boy I had loved as a best friend, who I had always been destined to be with since we were only small children. I could not help but wonder in that moment, who Winnie would have been assigned to marry, if anyone at all. Was I their only heir, or would they have given us the opportunity to rule together?

'No, I do not want to see him. Leave, Hugo. I want my mother to come back.'

He inched closer, while my mother waited patiently behind him with her fingers interlocked over her middle. 'I cannot stay for long, so just let me say something. Please.'

I crossed my arms over my chest. 'You have precisely one minute.'

'I do not even have that. Look, she enchanted me. I am sorry I betrayed you, it was not meant to be that way –'

There was nothing he could say that would bring him back to me, and nothing he could say that would ever make me trust him again. 'You are lying. You were only thinking of the power it would bring you. Leave.'

'Frost –'

'Are you deaf? I said, go! You are not sorry, you only care about yourself.'

With a sad expression on his face, he turned and walked back through the curtain between our worlds. 'I am sorry, Frosty.' He vanished, and I broke down in tears.

Mother approached me slowly. It was so strange because I had not seen those soft eyes for five years. 'Oh Frost, I am so sorry.' She turned back, eyes clearly alarmed by something she had heard, and then she said, 'I have to go. But please know that I am always here, watching over you and the others. Do us proud, my girl. Look after yourselves.' She slipped back through the curtain and my head fell into my hands as the sobs burst from my throat.

Winnie found me there, saying, 'We removed the last of Leraia's spell from the palace ... Hey, hey, come here.' She pulled me closer, her glass cheek ice cold against mine. There was so much love and concern in those glass eyes that I just sobbed harder. 'You're alright. What happened?'

'I saw ... I saw Mother and Hugo.' I was barely able to get the words out through my anxiety and despair. 'I do not know ... Mother was right here, she said she loves me and that she was watching over me and Hugo tried to apologise, but I sent him away and I did not know what to do –'

'Hey, breathe.' She sat down beside me on the bench and wrapped her arms gently around my neck before pulling away again. 'How is it possible?'

'She said the veil between our world and theirs had been made thinner with Leraia's enchantment.'

Her mouth dropped open, and her eyes were wide. 'Well, that explains all of the creepy things we've been seeing. What strong magic her mages must have to be able to open the world to the supernatural like that.'

'I know. It was surreal, Winnie.' I wiped my tears away and inhaled deeply, calming myself as best I could. 'But I am glad it happened, in a strange way.'

A smile spread over her mouth. 'I'm happy for you, Frost. Us removing the enchantment must have affected it, too.'

'What do you mean?' I asked.

Her expression was thoughtful as she stared at me, eyes full of warmth. 'Well, she clearly couldn't have stayed long, or Elora and I might have seen her, too. What about the king?'

'I am not sure, he was not mentioned. Elder Wicked said she was on the Witching Council. Maybe they were forced apart.'

'Perhaps we'll find out, one day. Do you want me to stay with you for a while?'

'That would be nice, thank you.'

'Of course. So that's her.' She pointed at Mother's statue, and when I nodded, she went to take Mother's glass hand in her own. 'Funny that we're both the same.'

Tears threatened to fall once again, and I was sure it was clear in my voice as I said, 'You look more like her than I do, now.' I tried to laugh, but seeing her had somehow opened up the wound, preparing me for heartbreak all over again.

'Well, you got to see her, I didn't,' she said teasingly, with a light smile. 'I hope she's happy wherever she is. Father, too.'

'Me too.' I took her hand and held it. 'Thank you for being here, Winnie.'

She chuckled softly. 'Not that you deserve it, you're awful.'

I mocked false hurt. 'You are pretty horrid, yourself.' I wiped my tears away, thinking for the first time in so long that things would finally be alright.

47

WICKED

IT WAS SOON DECIDED THAT CORONATION PLANS could wait for a few hours. Elder Wicked and her sisters had lost a precious member of their coven, and it was time to bury her. We took a carriage out to the lake that divided Icefall from Windspell, where Elder Wicked and her family would often spend their time, taking boat trips or enjoying picnics.

It was slightly warmer than the Winter kingdom, but Elder Wicked and her sisters still enjoyed the cool Autumn air.

We'd found Seager's body in the palace dungeons, hidden beneath some cloaks as if they'd discarded her there.

Today, we would say goodbye.

'I can't believe we're doing this,' said Flora. She leaned against Greyson's shoulder as we rode there. She took Verity's hand, and Elder Wicked's sisters Lunar and Alis and their daughters all cried.

They were a close-knit family, a coven and a community in itself, which would make it harder for them to cope with the day's events.

Elora held two small girls close to her, Alis's granddaughters, Amaria and Analisa. Alis had dressed them in matching black dresses with tights and shiny shoes. Their red hair was braided at their shoulders, and their faces were stained with tears. 'It's okay,' said Elora, whispering softly to them. 'Great Auntie Seager is watching over us all. We'll see her again one day in the House of Roth.'

'*She* should have stayed there,' said Morgana, pointing a long bony finger at me. 'If Seager has to stay, so should she.'

'Wicked doesn't deserve that, Morgana,' said Elora. 'She is your mother in name and spirit, but she's also her own person and has earned her right to be here, so be quiet.'

Bless her heart. How I wanted to reach over and hug her, but I also didn't want to spook the girls she was standing with.

Morgana stared down at the girl with a scowl on her face. 'Don't be rude, Elora. Your mother wouldn't have let you speak to me that way –'

Elora returned her glare. 'You don't get to speak about my mother if you're going to be cruel, and to be honest, I know she would have said the same damn thing. In fact, she would have encouraged me to say it!' Elora was practically screaming now, and I felt a little warmth in my chest at the thought of her coming to my defence like that.

'Thank you, Elora. Morgana, let's give each other some space and not speak to each other for the rest of the journey.'

She rolled her eyes. 'There's plenty of space out there. Get out of this carriage and ride with the soldiers.'

There were plenty of us, which meant we needed a few carriages to transport us. Morgana gestured at the driver to stop, and the vehicle came to a halt. 'Go on.'

Elder Wicked held out her hand and snapped, 'Morgana, will you leave her alone already? She has done so much good for us all. Stop letting the green monster overwhelm you.'

The witch sat back, but her anger didn't diminish.

'Thanks, Elder Wicked,' I said.

Flora said with a smile, 'You're great, Wicked. Sorry about Morgana, she's always been a little more sensitive.' She eyed her sister scornfully, and there were some knowing glances passed between a few of the witches, clearly agreeing with her.

'I am not sensitive,' Morgana hissed, only further proving her sister's point.

'Thank you,' I said, ignoring Morgana. 'I appreciate that.'

Sometime later, Elora took my hand. 'Oh, look, we're here.'

I glanced outside, and there we were, surrounded by trees in the prettiest colours, auburns and reds and greens. 'I was born here,' I said, glancing around at the enormous lake where the boats were docked and some sailed on the water. Memories of my sisters and I playing in those fields when we were children came to mind, and then frittered away when I realised they weren't truly my own.

I, myself, had never done any of those things. Elder Wicked had, which made me feel like an impostor in my own skin. 'I mean, Elder Wicked was. You see that cabin?'

'Yes, that's our grandmother's home,' said Flora with a thoughtful smile. 'That's why we love it here, it always made us feel closer to her.'

'Tell us about her?' said Princess Frost, stepping out of the other carriage with Winnie and a few of the soldiers, including Harlow and Griffin.

I didn't miss the way Harlow was watching Princess Frost, and the way her gaze flickered away from him. Had something happened between them?

I would have to find out.

We all gathered around to hear Elder Wicked speak. 'Alright. Well, her name was Falcon, and she was admired by many. She was the leader of her coven just as I was always destined to be, as the eldest of her sisters.' We moved forward, prepared a small boat and the soldiers lowered Seager's frail body into it as she continued speaking, 'My mother had six sisters, all with different magical expertise.

'True to her name, hers was animals, more specifically, birds. It was like her mother somehow knew before she was even born. Perhaps my mother herself even knew what would happen in my future and named me accordingly.'

'Ironically, rather,' said Elora with a grin. 'You are the opposite of your name. Both of you.'

'It's possible,' said Lunar, smiling. 'Many witches often have premonitions about their future offspring. I've already had a few about my girls, Ruby and Jasmine. But I won't ruin their timelines for them as that would just spoil the fun.'

There was laughter around the space before Elder Wicked continued, 'Anyway, my mother was strong, and a loving mother to my sisters and me. We will all have memories of countless birds flocking around their home, empowering their strong mother.'

She smiled sadly. 'But my mother is not the reason we are here, of course. We are here to remember Seager, our dear sister. When she was held in captivity, she died trying to remove Princess Frost's heart from the queen's chest. She died a hero.'

Tears rolled down her face as her eyes glazed over, remembering her. 'We remember her playful nature. Always the first to get into mischief, but also the first to pull others out of it. Her smile, her laughter. Her love for art, and for music.

'We remember her as we send her on her journey to the House of Roth. May she find her way there safely. May Rosa and the other witches care for her as we have.' She wiped her tears away with the sleeve of her cloak, and said, 'Elora, whenever you're ready.'

Elora clung to my side, and began singing.

Far away you may be,
But always close to me,
Deep in my chest a pain sets,
One which will never truly rest,
It'll last long enough for my heart to break,
Come back to me soon, to quell the ache.

'Seager was the kindest sister I could have asked for,' said Flora. 'Other than all of you, of course.' There was some laughter before she continued, 'Her heart was enormous, whether it was in lending an ear or helping me through a tough time. When we thought Father had died, I was broken.'

Greyson was staring at the ground, clearly feeling guilty.

'But she was always there.'

'You won't know how many times I had to save her clumsy arse,' said Lunar. 'She was always falling out of trees as a kid, poisoning herself with too many sleeping potions or being a little too rough with the playfighting, but she was kind. The best musician, and the most creative person I ever knew. I wish you'd seen more of her, girls. You would have loved her.'

We set the boats alight and sent them out onto the lake as Elora began singing again.

'Goodbye, Great Auntie,' said Alis's granddaughters at once.

'See you soon, Seager,' I said.

48

WINNIE

AFTER THE REMEMBRANCE CEREMONY AT THE LAKE, we went to Elder Wicked's mother's old home and were invited inside by her niece Sasha, Marthy's daughter, who was still living at the cabin with her daughters and granddaughters.

We'd extended the invitation for the ceremony but they had politely declined, not feeling they deserved to be there. 'We haven't seen Auntie Seager in so long,' her niece said slowly. 'We will pay our own respects. We will have a stone set in the gardens with her name engraved.'

'That's a sweet idea, Sasha,' said Marthy, wrapping her and her daughter and granddaughters in a hug. 'I hope you have all been well. It's been a long time, hasn't it?'

'It has, Mother,' said Sasha. 'I have missed you dearly. You could have come to visit.'

Marthy cast her a sad smile. 'I'm sorry. A lot has happened in Icefall, and Elder Wicked and the rest of us, we've been quite busy.'

'You were always too busy for us, Mother,' said Sasha. 'Always too occupied with your painting, and your long journeys to find more serene locations to paint, to –'

Guilt flashed behind the witch's eyes, but she insisted, 'I promise you, dear, this time it is nothing like that.' It was sad that they had gone so long without seeing each other, but as Marthy had said, things had been intense in Icefall.

Now, we were inside the cabin, surrounded by squawking birds in cages, as well as other animals like lizards, snakes, mice, rats and several black cats.

There were three young witches in the corner of the room reading fairytale stories and pointing at the pictures. They were probably Sasha's grandchildren.

'Thank you so much for letting us come and see you, great aunt Sasha,' said Elora, polite as ever.

Breaking away from her conversation with her mother, Sasha patted the top of Elora's head like she were a dog or one of her birds. 'Oh, aren't you a dear?'

'We're so sorry for your loss, Sasha,' said Frost with a sad smile.

'Thank you, dear.'

I took Sasha in as she came over and enveloped me in a hug, clearly taking more interest in my glass frame than the others. 'I'm sorry, but you ... Mother said she foresaw this. Has it happened yet, have you killed the queen?'

We were all stunned into silence, but she was staring hard into my eyes and I was unable to move.

'You have, please tell me it's true.' She paused before saying, 'No, if you had, your curse would have disappeared. It's too soon, isn't it?'

'No, we have her imprisoned ... '

She glanced around as we took in all of Falcon's birds. Her chirping ones, and her bald eagles. Her parrots, mice, snakes and lizards. 'No, that won't do. She must die.'

As she was speaking, one of the birds began screaming, a high-pitched shrill sound.

'No, no. You must go. Destroy her.' She took the screaming bird onto her gloved hand. Hands flew over ears as the screaming echoed through the home, shattering every mirror. 'She will break free.'

I couldn't help but feel the fear seeping into my chest and causing my stomach to twist over on itself, and the butterflies that flew around inside me.

Had we made the right choice?

There was an eerie silence as the bird stopped screaming.

'We have guards watching her, and mage soldiers. She is restrained inside a tin casket,' said Frost, the words clearly getting to her as much as they were for me.

'No, it will never be enough,' said Sasha, shaking her head. 'She must die.'

'She must die,' said one of the parrots, its voice a high-pitched imitation of Sasha's.

Behind it, the other bird began screaming again, and then they were all shrieking.

'She must die,' said Sasha again. 'As for you, your curse will not end until she does.'

My hope dissipated in seconds. 'Someone here must be able to end it?' I said, the need for freedom creeping into my voice, not for the first time and certainly not the last.

'No, it's too powerful. But it will happen once she's truly gone.'

'I can't kill her, I can't ... '

She'd done so much evil and hurt so many, but I still couldn't find it inside myself to end her life.

Besides, I was no killer.

Did I even have the heart to do it?

Of course not.

'Imprisoning her was manageable, but ... someone else will have to.'

'Time will tell,' said Sasha, thinking deeply.

Then, it was as if the conversation had never happened as she smiled upon us all and asked, 'Tea and cake, anyone?'

49

FROST

WE MADE OUR WAY BACK TO THE PALACE, and Harlow held my hand on the ride home.

I stared out at the colourful trees and the boats that passed us by on the water. My thoughts festered with my rage and anxieties at the mess the queen had made. The only way to end Winnie's curse and fix Queen Leraia's destruction was to kill her. It did not seem fair or just that to save the kingdom from the chaos she had created, we needed to become her.

Murderers and monsters.

'What's the matter?' said Harlow softly, Prince Harwin, watching me thoughtfully.

I was still unsure how to speak to him since his sudden proposal on the balcony, and I still had not answered him, but I could tell somehow, that it was not his main concern, which was a relief because it was the last thing I was concerned about.

'I just keep thinking about the queen. Sasha seemed so intent on us destroying her, and I hated watching Winnie's face fall as she said it. She said Elder Wicked's mother Falcon had seen it coming, and knew more about everything than we did.'

He offered me a sympathetic smile. 'Your witches and mages are powerful. They will help you through it all. Besides, you are a witch, are you not? You are powerful, Princess Frost. Hold tight.'

'I know, but is it enough?'

That question would linger unanswered for some time. We had a whole team of witches and mages on our side, but the queen continued to evade our attacks. She had not been killed when Winnie had stabbed her in the chest during the parade. I had not either, but the enchantment that was keeping me alive when my heart was stolen had protected me from facing death then, so it was not the same.

Why was the mage sorceress so special that she could avoid damnation so easily?

For the rest of the ride, we stared out of the window. My thoughts were spinning, while Marthy sat quietly over her painting, not working for the first time since I had seen her. Her conversation with her daughter was no doubt still on her mind, stopping her from concentrating.

Elder Wicked and her other sisters crowded around, and were singing their old songs to distract themselves. Her daughters were sitting quietly with the soldiers, laughing and clearly flirting. I could not blame them.

We would do anything we could to not think of the queen's destruction for just a few hours.

As it happened, Sasha was right. The tower was empty, which meant that the queen and her mage soldiers had escaped. The tin box had not even shattered; it was all still in one piece, without a single chip.

'How did this happen?' said Winnie, finally stepping into the room. 'We removed the enchantment she placed over the palace, and we made a plan.'

Magic. It was the only answer.

'I hate to say it, but I told you so,' said Greyson, running a hand through his raven hair and sighing heavily. 'As a mage warrior myself, I know how her magic works and I knew it would be strong enough for her to break free. A tin box, although it's not glass, has some reflective qualities. We lowered our defences, and we planned for the future without taking every precaution.'

'We took precautions, we just didn't kill her!' Winnie said exasperatedly.

I could see by her clenched fists that she was close to punching something, but I really hoped she would not as I did not think we would be able to save her from that.

'I am sorry Greyson, but how is that helpful?' I said, pinching the bridge of my nose between my thumb and forefinger. He thought his lectures were useful, but they just made everyone more scared.

How was that fair?

'It needed to be said. We must remember our mistakes!' Greyson shot back. 'It's important in case the same thing happens again.'

A sigh burst from my lips. 'Look, we need a new plan. We will try everywhere they could have gone: the witching cabin, Harlow's home, the forest, the caves. This time, we will do it. We will kill her. I am sorry, Winnie.'

'You might be too late,' Greyson warned.

'Cut it out, Greyson!' I hissed. 'Unless you have a helpful suggestion, please stop talking.'

'Don't you dare speak to me that way, Princess. It's not my fault that you girls refused to listen to my advice.' Before I could say anything else, he stormed out of the room, leaving me watching him with my blood boiling.

'Don't make me do it, please,' said Winnie, her voice soft and quiet like a mouse. 'I couldn't do that ... I was barely able to put that knife in her chest ...' She was on the floor, curled up into a ball, her body language giving away how vulnerable she felt.

'Don't worry,' said Wicked, her voice filled with fire. 'For what she did to Seager alone, I'll do it myself.'

'Me, too,' said Morgana, for once agreeing with her mother's copy.

'Same here,' said Mayor Farn, to Winnie's clear surprise.

'No, Dad. I don't want you going, you're staying here,' she said. 'You too, Barchester.'

'Thank god,' said her cousin meekly.

'No, we're going, and that's the end of it,' said Mayor Farn. 'If anything happens to me, you will take my position.'

'Uncle, no! That was Winnie's role –'

'Everything has changed now, so you're taking it,' said Winnie, offering him a warm smile. 'My place is here now, with Frost.'

'I will do it,' I said, and I truly meant it.

After everything she had done to my mother and father, to Winnie and Elora and even Hugo, I would kill her. If that was the only way to keep my kingdom safe and free from harm, then I would do it. 'It feels right. Besides, I will not force Winnie to bear that weight on her shoulders.'

Then my voice took on a teasing tone as I said, 'They are very fragile shoulders.'

'Unfortunately so, but they haven't broken yet,' Winnie said with a grin.

'Alright, we should get moving,' said Greyson.

He returned a few minutes later with a clearer head. Then he gathered us all together and divided us into small groups, ignoring my defensive comments and telling me to stop being childish.

That only made me more angry, but deep down I knew he was right and there was no time for such petty bickering. 'You'll check the forest, you'll search the cabin, you'll go to the canal.'

Then he turned to a few of the others. 'Come on, we're going to the caves.'

50

WICKED

It was time to slaughter the cruel queen, no matter the cost. We would find her and end her for the final time.

Elora, Elder Wicked and her daughters, and her sister Lunar, all came along with me while many of the others had split off with Greyson, Princess Frost and Winnie.

We also had Cassius, Liedan, Griffin and a few of the mage men with us, talking amongst themselves. They didn't seem to want to be included, but I was determined for this to change.

We travelled by carriage to the forest, and I gestured for the three men to come forward. 'Come, tell us who you all are,' I said.

The tallest, the one in the centre, laughed. 'For what purpose? We only serve our clan.'

It wouldn't be as simple as that. 'We usually only serve our own coven, but times have changed and we are all working together in this fight against the evil queen.'

'Are we?' he said, smirking. 'You haven't paid us any attention before now.'

'As I said, times have changed,' I said with a shrug. 'We have always had our own ways, and you yours. Now we must help each other.'

'She has a point,' said Elora, crossing her arms over her chest in her stubborn way, causing her aunts and I to laugh and the mage men to sigh heavily.

'Very well,' said the one who'd spoken before. 'If you really wish to know, I'm Lucius, this is my brother Dennard and my boyfriend, Lance. Do you also wish to know our birth dates and the measurements for our manhood's?'

He was smirking so heavily, and his boyfriend and brother joined him in his laughter.

I frowned, ignoring his sarcasm and answering, 'That won't be necessary.'

'What is he talking about?' said Elora quietly, to me alone.

'Don't worry,' I said, trying to withhold a trace of my own laughter. It would have been impossible not to. How ridiculous.

'Look, we are here for Greyson, and we are loyal to his cause.'

'Do you know what that is?' said Elora with an eyebrow raised.

I admired the girl's wit, and her challenging nature. How she loved to help people but also keep them accountable. For a girl so young, she was so wise.

I was glad she had the company of the other witches, and that she'd been raised well. She was in good hands, and the perfect young witch to help her sisters in their fight.

The mage stared her down, analysing her with a fierce look which she quickly returned. 'To help people, of course. He is the best leader our clan has ever had.'

'I thought you only helped your clan,' Elora snapped back. 'He's their father, her beloved and my grandfather, so you should be loyal to us, too.'

He laughed. 'You think we don't know who you all are?'

'Just telling you,' said Elora with some frustration creeping into her voice.

'That won't be necessary,' he said mockingly. 'If you're part of our clan we'll take care of you, but otherwise we will act alone.'

'That seems like a lonely way to live,' said Maeve.

'It's a crucial one,' said Dennard, just as monotonal as his brother.

'Well, we are almost here,' I said.

'We know,' said Lance with a bitter smile.

What was wrong with these men?

They only served themselves, and that was fine, but to ignore someone you were supposed to be working with to help the good of the kingdom, and eventually the good of your own clan as well, they were fools. Selfish, ignorant fools. Karma would come for them, and hit them where it hurts, and I would be happy to watch. But for now, we had no choice but to work together.

It didn't take long for us to reach the frozen lake's edge, where we found a single blood-red apple sitting in the centre of the ice.

As if the mage sorceress somehow knew we would search for her here.

Following the fruit across the ice, we saw a girl lying upon its surface, shivering with the cold. 'It's a trick. She's not real.' But the girl began to sing, and I placed a hand over my mouth. 'It's the song Elora was singing at Elder Wicked's ceremony!'

'We were there,' said Lucius, his voice dripping with sarcasm.

I cast him a glare before looking around, panicked.

But Elder Wicked had clearly had the same thought. Her daughters and sisters were here, but ...

'Where is Elora?' she said, her voice laced with panic.

Our words had distracted us, and now Elora was missing. The girl was in danger.

My heart was pounding hard within my chest as the girl on the ice began to sit up. There was Elora, lying across the ice with wide and terrified eyes. How had this happened? Only moments ago, she'd been at my side. 'It's a trick,' I told myself. Just like the hallucinations at the palace, just like Winnie and Frost's ghostly encounters. 'She's not real.'

'Wicked! Help me!' By now the singing had stopped, and now the young witch was far away and screaming. 'The ice is breaking!'

She crawled backward as the cold water threatened to pull her under.

As she moved, she held the apple between her fingers, clutching it like it was her lifeline. She tried to move backward, but that water was coming closer with every second that passed.

I began chanting a spell I'd spoken a few times, a levitation spell. But the magic wasn't working. It was like the forest itself was rejecting it as the palace had when the queen's mage spell had taken over before, forcing us to see ghosts. Or the queen was somehow blocking our magic again. 'Mages, I need you.'

'If your magic doesn't work, how will ours?' said Lance, shaking his head. But he cut his palm and began speaking out a spell, only for the forest to reject it in the same way.

'Fine, I'm going.' I removed my cloak and boots so that I wore nothing but my leather shirt and pants. 'Stay by the edge to pull us in, if needed.'

'This is probably what she wants!' said Lucius frustratedly, looking me up and down as if I was nothing but a fool.

Perhaps he was right, and I was an idiot for putting myself at risk. But Elora wasn't going to get hurt while I was here. No way would I watch that and do nothing. 'Do I look like I care?' I was practically screaming now, but I couldn't help myself. They were making me so angry. 'Stay here in case we need help.'

'I'm here, Wicked,' said Griffin, offering me his hand as I lowered myself onto the ice.

'We're behind you,' said Cassius, as behind him, Liedan nodded his head. 'Right here.'

I crawled across the ice as my heart raced and my stomach twisted itself into knots, remaining focused on the apple in Elora's hand as I inched closer, trying to reach for her.

The ice was breaking beneath me now, and the bottom half of my body was almost in the water. Without allowing myself any time to think about it, I leapt, screaming, 'Elora!'

'Wicked, I'm falling –'

She was almost under the ice now, and I couldn't reach her. Tears rolled down my face as I clung to the surface, trying to keep my grip.

'Wicked!' She sank under completely, and I dived down head-first.

My body was so, so cold. I had never felt such pain before. But still I searched for her, grasping for an arm or a leg, anything, until finally I caught my grip.

I had something, her hand? I tugged it hard and rose to the surface, hauled her small body over my head, even as I began sinking, falling …

I let her go, reached for a hand hold. There was nothing, and the water was filling my mouth and my throat. My lungs.

'Wicked … ,' I heard screaming, but the voices were faint, and so far away that they could have been whispering. 'Wicked, where are you?'

I threw up an arm, tried to find something, but suddenly the darkness was everywhere, and I let go.

I knew somehow that I probably shouldn't have, but the pain was so strong, and the energy within me was fading with every second that passed.

'Wicked, don't leave me, please!'

I opened my eyes and looked around. I was lying on the snow, soaking wet, with Griffin and Elora leaning over me. I sat up, as a rush of icy water burst from my throat. Retching, I let it all out.

'Oh my god, you gave us as a scare! What were you doing, throwing yourself at the frozen lake like that?' said Griffin.

'Is … is Elora okay?' I said, but struggled to speak between bursts of water and bile.

'She's fine, what are you talking about?'

I stared up at Elora through sore, reddened eyes and saw that she wasn't even a little bit wet.

What was happening to me?

The darkness overwhelmed me again, and all I could see was that red apple in her hand and her cruel glint of a smile, like the girl had planned for this all along. But of course she hadn't.

This was *Her Majesty*'s doing.

51

WINNIE

WHEN WE ENTERED THE CAVE and found the queen smiling at us, surrounded by countless mage warriors, my hope faded and frittered away like ash. 'You tried so hard to be rid of me,' she said, peering around at all of us and taking our faces in, one by one.

I was suddenly thankful that Elora, Wicked, Elder Wicked and a few of the witches had gone to the forest, since they were sure to be in less danger there, but I couldn't help but feel more concerned for the man who'd raised me, and my best friend Barchester. They were human, and so they wouldn't even be able to defend themselves with any kind of magic.

As for me, well I might be part witch like Frost and Elora, but I didn't know any spells. I'd never been taught magic by a powerful coven. So in a way, I was as vulnerable as they were.

'Many of us mage warriors are strong, resilient and powerful in our own individual ways. Isn't that right, Father?' She approached Greyson, and grazed his chin with her black-painted fingernail. 'Yours is envy, isn't it? Our weaknesses are our biggest strengths, ironically. Father's magic is at its highest when he feels greed and bitterness.

'My mother's was her fire, which is saying something since her name was literally Ember. No, but she was bossy, confrontational and hot-headed, as well as beautiful. Like me, I suppose.'

Her laughter echoed through the cave. 'You were fools. Silly girls, thinking you could outsmart me. This day has been a long time coming. I hoped to keep you, Winnella, but you clearly have other ideas, so it's your loss.' She shrugged like it was nothing. 'Such a shame. We could have done so much together.'

She inched closer again and I pushed out at her with all my might. She staggered but merely laughed, lunged and took my throat in both hands before forcing me to stumble backwards, much harder.

I stumbled but caught myself on Frost's arm before I could fully hit the ground and shatter.

'So close!' she said, inching forward again. 'How easy it will be to watch you break into hundreds of tiny pieces.'

'Wouldn't be that satisfying for you though, would it?' I growled. 'Because you need my curse.'

She said nothing more of my curse as we walked further into the cave. Frost and I went to the well while Greyson and his loyal followers remained close, guarding us under his watch. 'I see you've chosen your side, Father,' said my aunt.

Dad sat down on the edge of the wall, staring into the water. Barchester followed shortly behind him, always remaining close, looking out for his uncle although I knew how scared he was inside.

The mages began forming a circle of sorts, under Greyson's silent watch. I wondered what their traits were, the sources from which they drew their magical abilities.

Leraia was trying to reach me again, but Frost and I followed Dad and Barchester to the well as we tried to think of a plan to destroy her.

Greyson had given us instructions but it didn't seem like Frost was ready to follow them. Perhaps she was afraid or didn't know if she could do that to me.

In that moment, I made the decision that I would take her place, even though I'd told them I would never have been able to do such a thing.

After all, Elder Wicked had said I must be the one to destroy her.

I cast Greyson a nod, gave Frost a smile and watched her eyes widen almost frantically as she realised what I was going to do, then took her knife and hid it beneath my cloak in my belt before facing the queen. 'You were always such a good mother,' I said slowly, feeling the others' gazes on me from behind as I moved forward. 'Caring, loving and kind. You were there through every injury while playing out in the garden, you were there when I lost my first tooth, when I had my first kiss, when I had my first crush on a boy. Well, until you planned to leave Dad, marry the Winter king and then kill him, of course.'

I shrugged, then began laughing, thinking back over the recent days and everything that had happened since then. How ridiculous it all sounded out loud. 'But I thought you were perfect, and I loved you dearly, which is why this betrayal has hurt so much. You ripped our family apart, but the bigger piece, the part that represents Dad, Aunt May, Barchester and I, is still strong. We will be just fine without you, Leraia.'

I watched her wince at those words, saw the way her face fell just a little. Just enough. 'You're nothing now, but a liar and a false queen. Keep your vanity, but it will earn you nothing.'

I stared hard into her eyes, even as my stomach twisted and flipped inside. I wouldn't let it stop me. My hand reached for the hilt of the blade, slowly, and pulled it out.

She kept her eyes on me, and held that stare. 'Silly child. You want to play princess? You can still be my guest if you like. Come with me. Rule at my side, and be my heir.'

I laughed, the sound taking over a bitter edge. 'I don't need you for that, I know who I am now. I am Princess Ivy Winnella Winter of Icefall, but you can call me Winnie. The girl you stole, and the girl you raised and then abandoned.'

'That's all a bit dramatic, isn't it?' said Leraia with a cold smile on her lips. 'You were never meant for them. You were always mine.'

'You're delirious. I am your niece, and you took me from my bed in the middle of the night. You decided you wanted me, and that was it? You are not human, Leraia. You are a creature from below the depths of the earth.'

'She's my sister,' said Frost, placing a hand on my shoulder.

'My granddaughter,' said Greyson, over my other shoulder.

'My daughter, in blood or not,' said Dad from behind him.

'My cousin,' said Barchester. 'Like a sister, and my best friend.'

'How very precious,' Leraia retorted.

'And I'm certainly not something for you to possess, or someone to follow in your footsteps!'

My satisfaction brewed within as the hurt flickered behind her cold eyes, as I raised the knife and dug it hard into her stomach, and then her chest.

Again, and again and again.

Then she screamed, her hands fell to her middle and came away slick with blood.

She lifted her scarlet hands, lifted them high and chanted her words, lifting me high into the air before throwing me back down hard.

They had no time to even think about trying to stop her. I glanced down at the floor and found my body in pieces.

At the same time, she crumpled to her knees, but only a glance into one of my shattered pieces restored her body, immediately healing her wounds and removing the blood as if it'd never been there at all.

'Oh, my darling, what did you think was going to happen?'

All I could see in my vision was broken glass and the queen's cruel, satisfied smile before the blackness came.

52

FROST

POOR WINNIE WAS BROKEN AND SHATTERED INTO PIECES.
I gathered a bucket full of the enchanted water from the well with help from Mayor Farn, Greyson and the others, the mage men and Harlow's brother Titus, and together we poured the enchanted liquid over the bits of glass that remained.

Nothing happened, and tears rolled down my face at the thought that after everything, I had lost her. My twin sister, and the girl who had become my closest friend within such a short amount of time.

Mayor Farn was broken himself, with tears in his eyes and his face contorted with rage.

He reached for Idris's sword and held it out before the queen, who merely raised an eyebrow in surprise. 'Farn, love? It's like that now, is it?'

'It most certainly is.' He raised the sword higher, forcing the mages to step between him and the queen. 'I can't believe I ever fell for you.'

'You saw how she heals herself, be smart,' said the mage warrior before him. I did not know his name. They never seemed to want to speak to us. 'Don't act irrationally out of rage.'

Mayor Farn just pushed the warrior aside. 'Then help me, or get out of my way. She killed my daughter, and I don't take that lightly.'

Queen Leraia cackled. 'I like this new you, Farn. Shame you couldn't have shown me a little more of that grit when we were married.'

'Not that you would have noticed it, anyway. I know how you planned for so long to take that throne, how you used me and my position as Mayor of Cranwick to get close to it. To her father.' He pointed at me, and the queen's eyes hardened. 'She will make a far better queen than you would have ever been. I am honoured to have loved her sister for so many years and to have raised her, but I'm glad they have finally found each other. Well ... ,' he broke down again.

The queen prodded his chest with a bony finger. 'You know, it's not only glass that powers me, Farn. I can use the water from that well, or see myself in the pupils of your eyes. Then I could pull the energy from them, and what would happen?' She leaned in close enough to kiss him, then quickly pulled away. 'Your mages are frozen, their magic unusable. I prevented your witches from doing the same in the Winter Forest. Do you wish to see?'

Panic stirred within me. What had she done to Wicked and the others? She held out her mirror, and through it, we saw Wicked lying, drenched, on the snow beside the frozen lake, which was now not so still, with the ice in broken pieces and the rest in rising waves. At her side, unconscious, were Elora, Cassius, Harlow and Griffin.

In Wicked's hand was a blood-red apple.

'You will never defeat me. I am far more powerful than all of you combined. Especially you.'

As she held Mayor Farn under her spell, suddenly the sword in his hand spun to face him, with the blade pointed directly at his chest.

'No!' Barchester darted forward, and Harlow's brothers followed him as he threw himself between his uncle and the blade. His screams pierced the air, but the blade had merely grazed his side, appearing far worse than it was.

The queen began to cackle, far more like the sound of a witch rather than a mage's.

Mayor Farn turned slowly away, and I told myself to focus. I possessed powerful magic in my veins, and I could save them. I began chanting a mage spell, reciting the words purely from memory. The mage soldiers behind the queen dropped to the ground unconscious, one by one.

The queen faced me, her mouth falling open with surprise. 'You're strong, niece, but it will never be enough.'

Her words only fuelled my rage, spurring me on. Mayor Farn's sword spun around again, aiming for him once more, but I chanted the witching spell that Elora had taught me in the wood, and turned it back to face her.

Kept moving, kept chanting.

'Interesting magic,' said the queen, laughing a little. 'Just like your whore mother.'

How dare she?

In seconds, that sword spiralled her way, but instead of aiming for her body as she was expecting, it knocked the mirror out of her hands, forcing it to smash into tiny pieces on the ground.

I pulled the hood of my cloak up over my head and closed my eyes so she could not use them as a weapon before sending that sword crashing into her body. When I opened them, I saw that blood was pouring from a wound in her shoulder.

She cried out in pain.

Then, everything happened so fast.

Every other sword flew at me and at my friends. Mayor Farn crumpled to the floor with a sword lodged deep in his chest, and Barchester began screaming as he took his uncle into his arms while the soldiers attempted to recover their weapons.

The mage soldiers, including Greyson, were frozen in time, unable to move or even blink.

As I glanced around, one of the swords caught me in the thigh before clattering to the ground, and I moaned in pain, attempting to cover the wound with my cloak. I bent down and quickly scooped it up, whimpering when I was forced to bend, sending pain shooting through my leg as blood spilled through my leather trousers, soaking them with the thick liquid.

My mouth began moving of its own accord, speaking a mage healing spell, and it was like I had been taught the words as a young child but somehow forgotten them, because it was like second nature using them. To my relief, the wound began to heal and my thigh became quickly dry as if I had never been hurt at all. I spoke the words over and over, hoping to heal Barchester's wounds, and his shocked expression told me it had worked.

When I concentrated on healing Mayor Farn, nothing happened. There was no removing the sword from his chest without hurting any vital organs, especially his heart.

Poor Winnie, and poor Barchester. I felt like a failure, and I feared they would never forgive me if I did not continue to try to keep him alive.

The soldiers were gone, and the queen had vanished amidst the chaos, just as Wicked, Harlow, Cassius, Elora and Griffin arrived with a few of the mage men. I stared at them, puzzled and probably in shock. In Wicked's hands was a single black crow, caged, but still wearing a tiny steel crown.

I peered at it, unable to process what I was seeing. 'It was the best I could do, sorry,' said Wicked. 'I caught her trying to flee, and managed to chant the spell just in time, but that should hold her for a while. What happened here?'

What an impossible question to answer.

53

WICKED

Princess Frost barely had time to explain as I saw Mayor Farn crumpled in Barchester's arms, and the scattered glass on the ground that could only have been Winnie.

The tears quickly began pouring as heavy sobs burst from my throat. After everything we'd been through together already, it had come to this.

It wasn't fair.

Winnie deserved to live her life happy and free from her vile aunt, alongside her sisters and not too far away from the man who'd always been her father.

And as if to rub salt in the wound, the crowned little crow was trying to hop around inside her cage. But at least she was unable to move. It felt good to see her looking so vulnerable, so helpless.

Even if the bitch was impossible to kill.

Mayor Farn reached for my hand, and then for Princess Frost and Elora's. His face had turned a deathly white, and seeing it only made the tears fall harder. 'Look after each other,' he said softly, 'and bring her back. You have all become so dear to me. I love you all like my daughters.'

'Hey, no, don't speak like that. We're going to stop this right now,' I said.

But the mayor just shook his head. Somehow, he knew what was coming. He pointed at Princess Frost. 'Only her magic works. The queen ... placed ... an enchantment ... ,' he coughed between words as his voice trailed off, and the blood poured harder.

'Heal him, Princess Frost, like you healed me!' said Barchester suddenly, panicked.

The princess seemed to be frozen on the spot, staring at the fallen mayor and the pieces that were left of Winnie, utterly broken.

But then, to my surprise, she began chanting words I didn't understand, and I realised this was her mage heritage speaking, perhaps words she'd been taught by her mother when she was very young.

As the daughter of a witch and a mage warrior, the late queen must have learned something powerful from them both.

Princess Frost continued chanting, harder and harder, frantically, but Mayor Farn's eyes were slowly closing. 'It worked on me, and on Barchester ... Why is it not working on him, too?' she said, trying to get her breath back. She began again, slowly at first and then more quickly, but she was just making herself more and more breathless.

I spoke a spell, but nothing worked at all, and even as Princess Frost continued, we saw Mayor Farn lying still. After everything he'd been through already, perhaps with the sickness caused by the Cranwick curse on top, death had taken him from us.

I pounded my fists against the ground. We were too late. Poor Barchester, poor Winnie.

The princess sobbed into her hands. 'It was not enough!' Flora took her into her arms, but the princess was overwhelmed with her own emotion, and even I knew it was best for her to just let it all out. 'I could have saved him, I could have done it! If Winnie comes back to us, she will never forgive me. What am I going to do? It is not fair.'

'No, darling, it's not,' said Flora, rubbing Frost's shoulders. 'I'm sorry.'

Winnie. I thought of the poor girl and glanced down at the pieces, and began gathering them.

Perhaps there was something I could do to end Princess Frost's pain, at least something small. 'Sorry, but they're wet ... ,' I touched them, and my tears fell onto the glass, 'what?'

They began to move, and Princess Frost climbed to her feet. 'He was a hero,' she said. 'He helped us pour enchanted water on them when the queen knocked her down. The same water from the caves, the kind that should have healed him.'

'What a brilliant idea.' As the pieces moved, we watched them forming themselves back together slowly like a jigsaw puzzle which had taken ownership of its structure. For a few minutes, they reorganised themselves into the right places, forming feet, calves, knees, then thighs, hips, stomach, chest and right up to the top of the head.

Before us now, was Winnie, only moments after her father had died in her cousin's arms.

The crow began flapping its wings hysterically as if the queen, even in bird form, was angered by the events happening before her. Good.

Winnie peered around slowly. 'What happened?' Her mouth dropped open, and she knelt beside Barchester, caressing her father's cheek. 'No, it's not true ... '

'He tried to kill the queen for you, Winnie,' said Princess Frost with a sad smile. How strange she must have felt to have her sister back, while also having to share the tragic news. 'He thought you were dead. He died a hero.'

Rage hardened her gaze. 'He shouldn't have had to though, should he? Where is she? Did you finally kill her?'

I held up the cage and saw that the bird was bleeding. 'Don't let her look into your eyes,' I said, throwing my cloak over the cage. 'She takes power from her reflection.' So her wounds had remained even through the transition. She must have been weakening. 'Alright, let's go back to my cabin and figure this out. What happened to them? Greyson?'

Flora spoke a spell that should have erased their stillness, but it didn't work. 'She has stopped our magic, somehow. But Princess Frost's still works.'

'Yes, she did the same beside the lake.'

'What happened there?' said Princess Frost.

'I'll explain on the way. Elora, gather the wolves. Frost, I need your help.'

I told her a few spells, but to our surprise, they didn't work.

'I think it was my mage spells,' said Princess Frost. 'Although the levitation one that Elora taught me worked fine.'

'Spells that don't require much energy might have slipped past her. Alright, we're going to focus on removing her enchantment. Repeat after me.'

It took us some time, but we finally did it and pulled our groups together before heading to the witching home in the carriage, with Barchester and Harlow carrying Mayor Farn amongst themselves.

Winnie was understandably silent, while Princess Frost and Elora continued sharing worried glances. I knew she just needed time so we wouldn't bother her. At least until we reached my cabin.

'Does anyone want to see Cranwick?' I asked.

Her eyes met mine, and we left the wolves and our soldiers behind before heading through the mirror with Mayor Farn's body in our arms.

Greyson and his men were guarding the crow, so we reminded them of her ability to restore power through her reflection, and made our way to Winnie's old home.

We went to Cranwick's river harbour and found a small sailboat where we said goodbye to Mayor Farn, just as we had done to Seager before. 'Tell us if it's too soon, but I thought it would help to say goodbye while he still looks like himself.'

She shook her head. 'It's alright. I still can't believe it, it's all happened so quickly.'

'I tried to save him, Winnie,' said Princess Frost, her voice barely louder than a whisper. She found it hard to speak through her tears. 'He should not have died. I am so sorry.'

Winnie wrapped an arm around her sister's shoulders, and planted a gentle kiss on her cheek. 'I know. It's okay, I don't blame you, Frost.'

Barchester took them both into his arms and we led them to the riverbed, where we placed him down on a boat that would lead him to the seas between the mountains.

'I love you, Dad,' Winnie whispered into the wind, and planted a kiss on his cheek. 'You're my hero, forever and always.'

'Goodbye uncle,' said Barchester, throwing an arm around Winnie's shoulders.

We all said our own goodbyes before it was time to head back.

🍎

'I can't believe he's gone,' said Winnie many times over the next few hours.

I knew such grief and how it felt, and so soon after such revelations about who she was.

She loved him like he was her father, and that pain would be with her forever, but I hoped it would at least get better over time. 'I loved him so much.'

Her sisters held her as she cried in their arms, and the rest of us remained close for support.

'He is still here,' said Princess Frost, with a hand stroking Winnie's blonde hair. 'Even if you cannot see him. I saw Mother, remember? And

Hugo, even if I did not want to.' She laughed, and it was clear that it had made Winnie laugh a little, too, because she smiled.

'True,' she said, stroking her sister's thumb. 'Aren't we lucky, seeing ghosts?'

'At least we know for certain that they are okay, and that they're watching over us.'

'Through every mirror, no doubt,' said Barchester with a shadow of a smile on his mouth. 'Actually no, that would be quite scary.'

'I heard you tried to sacrifice yourself for Dad, Bar,' said Winnie, reaching for his hand. 'You're so brave, and I couldn't be more proud of you.'

He flexed, making her laugh. 'Of course, I'm so macho, aren't I? Meanwhile you're over there, giving us seven years of bad luck!' he teased, earning himself a mock slap on the arm from Winnie. 'Honestly though, I'm glad he saved you, even if I get sick of seeing your face sometimes.'

'Alright, Mayor Barchester,' I said, smiling.

He didn't say anything, but the crimson blush in his cheeks told me that he was more than a little excited about the prospect.

'Right everyone, we need to find a way to get rid of this evil crow for the final time.'

'Hopefully without shattering me again,' said Winnie.

'I have an idea,' said Flora, going to the kitchen before returning with a tin of rat poison. She ground it down into small pieces, before placing it into a tray filled with bird seed. 'Perfect.'

Then I took the tray from Flora and quickly placed it into the cage before removing my hand in case the queen-crow chose to nip at my fingers. 'Nobody remove the cloak. In fact, we should pin it down,' I said as Elora headed to the bedroom before coming back with a box of nails, probably from her tool kit. Together, we worked on hammering the cage to the countertop. 'Now, we wait.'

54

WINNIE

When we woke the next morning, the cloak had already been removed from the cage.

It was empty, the poison had disappeared and the mage soldiers were nowhere to be found.

The witches all wore saddened expressions, and Flora was bleeding from a wound in her stomach.

Just when things had been looking up, everything was going wrong again. I'd been healed by the enchanted water and brought back together, my glass frame still cracked in a few places, and despite my father's death, we'd almost begun to feel hopeful again. But the queen was far stronger than we could ever have anticipated, as she continued to escape us as we tried to quell her evil.

And to make things worse, my father was gone, but there was no time to grieve him. We'd said goodbye with a beautiful ceremony that would always remain in my heart as a treasured memory, but that was all we had. Perhaps when this was all over, we would take the time to talk through our grief.

For now, we had to keep moving.

Frost rushed over and healed Flora's wound almost instantly. She seemed more refreshed after her long sleep, which explained why she hadn't been able to heal my father before he died. She'd been exhausted, and his injury was impossible to fix. 'What happened, Flora?' she said.

'Thank you,' said Flora, running a hand over her healed stomach. 'So, we have some bad news.'

We all took a seat, our hope fading instantaneously. So much had been counting on the rat poison working. On the bird staying here and, on ... the queen's death. 'Go on,' I said, reaching for Frost's hand, almost out of habit.

'We have a mole here, and we fear that it's Greyson. We woke at sunrise as we usually do, and everyone else was still sleeping but I felt restless so I went out for a short walk. When I returned, they were gone but the crow was alive and healed.

'When she looked into our eyes, she was able to take her power from the reflections in them and she broke free from her cage and resumed her old form. I tried to stop her from leaving but she caught me in the stomach with her dagger. She ... she killed Maeve, who tried to defend me, and Morgana ran out to avenge her. Morgana hasn't yet returned.'

Wicked fell to her knees. 'No, Maeve ... ' The pain was clear in her face. Even if she wasn't Elder Wicked, it must have been so painful to have felt all of her memories with each of them, each of her children.

She must have known how it felt to be a mother, even a copy of one. 'No, it can't be ... Greyson would never do that to me. To Elder Wicked.' She moved to her feet, eyes burning with a sudden rage. 'Very well. I'm sending you out to stop her, take Verity and Lunar. We will take the girls to the soldiers' cabin, and they will go with you. Defend them, and destroy her!'

'Yes Wicked, of course.'

Together, we began to wake the others and tell them everything that had happened.

To decide on a new plan.

In Wicked's hand was a Babylon candle. 'Come, stand next to me.'

We left, all of us fearing the queen's next move.

She had to be stopped.

55

FROST

It had been a long day.

While Elder Wicked and a few of her sisters went in search of the queen with Marcus, Harlow and their brothers at their side, we chose to take the evening to rest. No doubt we would have to face her again soon, and we would take all of the energy we could get.

Elder Wicked's daughters Flora and Verity, and Elora and Winnie and I, were curled up on the couch or on the carpets of Harlow's cabin while Wicked cooked us all some pheasant and rice for dinner. We feared that if something happened to us now, our whole cause would have been for nothing.

So we were to stay here while they left, and also did their best to look for Morgana, who was still missing. It was getting late, and the sky outside was dark. They should not have been out for so long.

They promised they would return if there was no luck in finding her, and we could always try again at dawn. For now, we needed to stay calm.

Elora was fast asleep with her head resting on my lap, while Winnie was staring off into space. I was reading a story about a cruel queen and a princess who was sent into an enchanted sleep when there was a heavy knock at the door, quick and loud, like someone urgently needed to speak to us.

Transferring Elora's head to Winnie's lap, I went to see who was there.

'Frost, no. It could be her!' said Wicked from the kitchen. 'Don't do it.'

'She does not seem like the type to knock,' I said, laughing, although it held a bitter edge. 'It could be them returning.' I crossed the room, much to Wicked's dismay.

'At least take this.' Slowly, a knife lifted into the air and came over to me, and I gripped it by the hilt, then slipped it beneath my cloak.

'Thank you.' I opened the door and was surprised to find an old woman peering up at me, bent forward and leaning on a wooden stick. Her face was wrinkled in every place, and her teeth were crooked, her nose large, with several warts above her mouth, but her eyes were both kind and fearful at once. She reminded me of Elder Wicked and her many sisters. 'Hello there.'

She took a step closer, and stuck her walking stick into the gap, leaning onto her other foot for support. 'Hello deary, thank you for answering. I'm afraid I'm very sick, and it's incredibly cold out here. Might I come in for a bite to eat and some warm milk?'

She seemed so helpless, so frail and gentle. I would want a stranger to help Elder Wicked or her sisters if ever they were in trouble. I turned around to find Wicked shaking her head at me. Winnie's eyes were also wide and filled with fear, but I saw no harm in helping the old woman. 'May I ask first where you have come from? Where do you live?'

Her voice trembled with age as she spoke. 'Oh, I understand your need for caution, dearest, but perhaps I can tell you inside. I feel as if I'm going to freeze if I stand out here for a moment longer.'

'No,' I said, firmly enough but not coldly.

THE GIRL BEHIND THE GLASS

The woman was studying me closely as I spoke, and I realised she seemed familiar. But I could not, for the life of me, remember where I might have seen her before. As I stared into her eyes, I felt suddenly sick and incredibly weary.

I could not move, nor could I remember where I had come from or why I was here in this cabin. Still, not meaning to be rude, I said, 'I am sorry, I am afraid I cannot do that, but perhaps I can help you in some other way?'

She took my hand, her many rings biting into my skin and causing me to cry out. 'Sorry, deary.' She released me, apologetically, and pointed in the direction of the woods. 'I have lost my bird. Do you think you could help me find her?'

'Your bird? Where did you last see her?'

She began walking away. She had been so determined to come inside, and yet she now wanted me to come with her. It had to be a trap, especially as she had mentioned losing a bird of all creatures.

I slammed the door closed, and cast the others a nervous look.

When the door was blasted open as if by a strong wind, a feeling of pure terror came over me. Then she was right in front of me, her dark eyes staring through mine. 'Come, girl.'

My legs began to move of their own accord, despite the scream that burst from my lips, even as every instinct within me told me this was a trick or a trap. My body was completely under her spell.

Out in the snowy forest, the old woman turned and I found her smiling, which was odd considering the predicament she had found herself in. 'She was somewhere over here,' she said, and continued moving, surprisingly agile for someone with a walking stick.

My heart told me to turn back and run, but my legs would not let me.

'Falcon, her name is. Can you see her?'

I glanced around but all I could see were trees and darkness as stars formed over my vision.

There was something familiar about that name, and I tried reaching into my memories to figure out where I knew it from, but I could not remember. 'I cannot ... I cannot see anything,' I said as a rush of nausea churned my stomach. 'I do not feel very well.'

I collapsed in the snow as the old woman knelt down beside me. I could not move; I was paralysed and any movement only made the dizziness worse.

'Would you like an apple, dear? Take it, you need only a bite.'

'Tha ... thank you.' My throat was so dry that I could barely get the words out. I sank my teeth into the flesh of the fruit and chewed slowly before swallowing, and was instantly sick in the snow.

It tasted vile, like it was mixed with something strong and chemical. My eyes began closing, and all I wanted to do was close my eyes and fall into sleep.

'There, much better,' said the old woman, her fingers coming down to caress my cheek.

'Sleep now, Princess.'

56

WICKED

I was cooking and waiting for Princess Frost to return, minding my own business, when there was a heavy knock at the door.

Winnie went to answer it but I called out, 'Leave it.' Who could be knocking this time? The others hadn't yet returned and Princess Frost was still nowhere to be seen, but they lived here. They should have felt welcome enough to enter. 'They won't need to knock, any of them.'

There was something strange going on here, and the fact that the princess still hadn't returned had put me on edge. A new anxiety had begun to take over me, causing my chest to tighten so that it was hard to breathe.

A deep ache unsettled my stomach as I began to chant a spell that would force the door open without any of us going near it, and then we waited.

But there was nothing but a blast of wind and snow and then a pure, if not slightly eerie, silence.

'Princess Frost?' I called out into the open air as I reminded myself that Winnie and Elora were still huddled together in an armchair, safe from harm. The princess would return soon, and the rest of them would find the queen or destroy her, or bring her here so we could all figure it out, together.

Elora woke up, clearly disturbed by the sudden noise and commotion.

The door crept open but no one answered my call. Not Princess Frost, or anyone else. Winnie and Elora walked to the door, but I moved before they could reach them and it slammed shut again.

Only to slide quickly open once more, sending a shiver crawling up my spine.

'Was that you, Elora?' I asked, afraid to move even an inch, and afraid of what might be out there in the dark forest.

Evidently frightened, the girl just shook her head. 'Who's there?' I called out, this time more loudly. When no response came, I peered through the gap, into the snowy forest. 'Hello?'

My gaze moved across the snow and came to land on something small and brown. Feathers and talons, and a large oval-shaped head. It was a bird of some kind: a falcon. Taking my knife, I crossed the snow and knelt down as the bird turned to look at me with its slanted, piercing golden-green eyes.

'Hello there,' I said, reaching out a hand to stroke the bird, gently. 'It's alright. You're safe now.'

It stared up at me with hard, yet curious eyes that seemed to see right through me, like they already knew me. I tried to turn it around but I was transfixed, unable to focus on anything else. It was like those eyes had me under a spell, and all of my movements from now on would be carefully calculated.

Slowly, the creature began to transform into an elderly woman with sagging skin over narrow bones. She clearly hadn't seen a full meal for a long time, never mind actually tasted one.

The naked old woman stole a cloak from the hook by the door, wrapped it around herself and ran off into the forest, gesturing for me to come with her.

She was somehow familiar to me, but I couldn't work out why. 'This way,' she instructed me.

She wasn't familiar enough for me to let her in, or to go after her. 'Well, *that's* not happening.' I slammed the door shut, and went to sit beside Elora, who was staring at me, wide-eyed, obviously wondering what the hell had just happened.

'Are you okay, Wicked?' she said timidly.

'Yeah, I'm –' I was forced to stop talking as, behind me, the door creaked slowly open.

Again. There was an eerie silence, until suddenly a bird squawked loudly outside the cabin, practically shrieking and forcing us all to jump out of our skin.

'It's like something out of a horror movie,' said Winnie from beside me. 'Where did Frost go?'

A sudden blast of wind tore me toward the door, and I screamed as my legs began to move of their own accord, as if they didn't belong to me. I wasn't sure how it was possible with everything we'd done to stop her, but this had to be the queen's doing.

'No, no! This happened to Princess Frost, but I'll be damned if it happens to me! Get the hell off me, sorceress.'

'Wicked, what's happening?' Elora cried.

It didn't matter how many times I tried to stop myself, my legs continued to move.

I chanted a spell that I hoped would remove the hold she had over me, but it was useless. I was torn from the cabin and across the snow, through the Winter Forest, as if possessed.

The woman ran ahead of me, smiling back at me from between the trees.

'Where are we going?' I cried.

She turned back and offered me a smile. Not answering my question, she said, 'I'm Falcon, it's great to finally meet you.'

'Mother ... '

I should have known by the eyes alone. It would have been the perfect hallucination of Elder Wicked's mother, who would have been long gone.

This bitch really wanted to get into our heads, and so far, she'd been successful.

Falcon laughed. 'No, dear. My daughters are all grown now, you must have me confused with someone else. Come this way, my coven wish to see you.'

I crossed my arms over my chest. 'Why? You don't seem to even know who I am.'

She chuckled almost pleasantly, like this was all just one big joke. 'Of course I do, sweetheart. I can sense that you are one of us.'

But she didn't know the specifics of who I was, or she would believe I was Wicked. 'I'm your daughter, Wicked.' How would I even begin to explain who I was to this witch if she was so determined not to accept my claim?

She shook her head, and a frown appeared on her face. 'No, Wicked is much ... much older. But I do sense that you are one of us. You are one of her daughters, aren't you?'

If this was the case, how was she still alive?

How old must she be by now? Too old to be taking me through the forest. It didn't make sense.

But still, my legs kept moving, controlled by something else. Someone ... else. I had been possessed. There could be no other answer for it.

'You must come with us, and be one of us. Truly, and completely.' She gestured to a gap in the trees. Her smile was wide as she asked, 'What is your name, dear?'

'Wicked.'

She studied me with a curious expression. 'Very well – she must have named you after herself. I haven't seen her in such a long time. Is she well?'

'Wouldn't you know, as her mother?'

She sighed sadly. 'I'm afraid we have … drifted, recently.'

'Where are you taking me? You seem confused, one moment you don't know who I am but the next you're convinced I'm your granddaughter?'

'I can sense the strength of your magic. I can feel it. That kind of magic only belongs to the ancient bloodline of Roth witches, from my maternal line.'

But she didn't know I was merely a copy of Elder Wicked. Would my bloodline have been as strong, since I was essentially a clone of the elder witch? 'How?'

I was only becoming more cynical with every question, and every word we shared. I should have understood everything, being a Roth witch.

That thought only made me feel like more of a failure, and like I didn't truly belong in the world I should have come from. But if this was somehow a trick, like in the palace, perhaps she was false and the *real* Falcon would have believed I was her daughter.

By the goddess, this was far too complicated.

'It is like … a thumbprint. A scent, your individual signature,' she continued. 'It's familiar. It's difficult to explain. Come along, now.'

I followed her through the forest, trying not to end up tangled in the trees, and found her a few metres ahead offering me her hand.

I knew this path, and alarm bells began ringing within me, but my legs kept moving.

'We're almost there,' she said, and stopped, waiting for me.

I'd nearly reached her by now.

When she smiled into my eyes, turned and leapt into the river, a scream burst from my throat.

But instead of remaining trapped in the high-speed river, she flew over it, now a Falcon again. She hovered above me, and reached down with her sharp beak and tugged at my sleeve, before gripping me by the hood of my cloak with those talons, and lifting me high into the air.

'No!' I screamed, but her talons gripped my shoulders, keeping me restrained upright.

I tried to grasp at the branches, but she was far too strong, and I was unable to take hold of anything.

She lifted me, and only released me above the strong current of the river, sending me crashing into the water. I flailed, chanting any possible spell, but it was like all memories of my magic had been wiped away. I could barely remember a simple levitation spell, let alone one I'd taught any of the other girls.

The girls!

They needed me, and yet I was here, about to float down the river to the incoming waterfall.

I clutched at tree branches, rocks and at the riverbank itself, but I couldn't reach.

All the while, the falcon flew above, taunting me as my demise approached.

57

WINNIE

Both Frost and Wicked were now missing, along with Elder Wicked's daughter Morgana.

And the witches hadn't yet returned with the soldiers or the witch herself.

'Where did they go?' Elora asked me quietly. She was shivering with the cold air so I pulled a thick blanket around her, but I was too afraid to close the door in case the others were in danger when they finally came back.

'I don't know,' I said so softly that it was almost a whisper. 'But let's read together and hope they won't be too much longer.'

We huddled together, reading through a book of fantasy short stories about faraway worlds, kings, queens, knights and ladies, and at first we were pleased with the distraction. It was supposed to be calming, and in Cranwick it would have been a great escape from my daily life.

But here, it was hardly an escape.

In these kinds of stories, princesses fought evil queens and came out victorious. It all felt far too relatable, and only reminded me of our failures so far.

'If you hear the door, leave it. Like Wicked said, if it's them, they won't need to knock.'

It was in that moment that Harlow and his brothers returned with a few of the mage soldiers, including Greyson. They were all cloaked from head to toe, but they wore the same ghostly complexions.

The cabin seemed to grow suddenly cold, any hope that might have lingered within it having faded as they'd arrived. 'Harlow,' I said nervously, as the soldier placed his sword down on the carpet beside his bed. I couldn't help but feel the worry creeping in, fearful that something could have happened to either of them. 'Have you seen Frost or Wicked? They went out not too long ago, and haven't come back. Do you know where they could have gone?'

Harlow faced me silently. Griffin suddenly retched over the sink and ran to the bathroom while Greyson, Cassius, Titus and Liedan were silent with their eyes set on the floor.

'What is it? What's happened?'

'In ... in the forest ...' said Harlow, barely able to get his words out.

My heart plummeted into my stomach, but still I rushed forward and eased him gently down onto the bed before he passed out.

I glanced at Elora before slipping through the open door, even as I heard him call out, 'No, don't ... '

But I was already on my way there, with a sinking feeling in my chest and my stomach already churning with fear. I ran into the forest and followed the footsteps in the snow, away from the cabin and toward the clearing where I was certain that Frost or Wicked might have run to.

But it wasn't them that I found, but something far more heartbreaking. Far more sinister. Hanging from the same tree, with their heads tilted to one side and two pieces of red rope tied around their necks, were Maeve and Morgana.

But Flora had said Maeve had already died, so I realised that Morgana must have brought her here and placed her there, perhaps so they could be together. How awful. Frost and I were twins, but we'd been raised separately due to our aunt's theft.

I couldn't imagine losing the twin sister I had spent every waking moment of my life with.

I dropped to my knees in the snow, and my heart broke for Elder Wicked and her family all over again. For Greyson and his men. Not to mention ...

'Ivy ...'

I knew that voice from my dreams. Somehow I knew it from my childhood. My mother, Queen Rosa. Could I have remembered her when I was only a baby? How it felt to be in her arms? Her face, her kind eyes, or even her smell? I searched the forest for her, wondering if I was dreaming or perhaps I'd passed out through shock at seeing my aunts' bodies hanging together.

'Ivy ...'

'Yes, Mother? Where are you?' I peered through the trees, but there was nothing. No noise but the sound of my pounding heart. 'Please show yourself.'

Then she was right in front of me, and at first I almost jumped out of my own glass body.

She reached out a hand but it went right through me. Her mass of shiny dark hair fell down over one shoulder, and her blue eyes pierced through mine as she said, 'I love you, my dear.' She was draped in a navy-blue gown with a high collar, long sleeves and a corseted bodice that glimmered with silver gemstones. Her dress swayed past her feet as she walked. 'How I have wanted to meet you.'

'And you, Mother. How is this happening?'

I couldn't make sense of any of it. She was so beautiful, with Frost's eyes and a trace of Elora's smile. My nose. She'd shown herself to Frost back at the palace. Or was that even her, but our aunt?

It was hard to recall what Frost had said then, as it all felt so long ago now. So much had happened within that time. As much as I wanted to see my mother, deep in my heart I knew she would never have called me Ivy. She knew my name was Winnie, the name I'd always known.

I knew better than to follow her now. But something pulled me under, and kept my feet moving across the snow.

'Never mind that. I have to show you something.' She turned and walked away through the trees. The forest had its own tricks, just like the palace had when we'd returned, and I refused to fall for them all over again. But it seemed that was already happening. 'This way.'

All I wanted to know was where she was taking me. If this was the queen's tricks all over again, I wasn't sure my glass heart would be able to take it.

I decided it was best to play with the illusion, rather than let it play me. 'I can't believe what happened to your sisters, Mother. I'm so sorry.'

She turned around and smiled sadly. 'They are with me, now. Do you see them?' I glanced at the tree again, but she pointed in the other direction. 'No, they are there, look closely.'

I followed her finger to the centre of the forest, where, as she said, the twin witches were watching me. There was something off about my mother, like she was only here to show me the truth. 'Have you seen Frost or Wicked, Mother?' I asked, emphasising that last word for effect.

Were they alright? If something had happened to them, too, I wasn't sure what I would do.

'Are they safe?'

She reached out and cupped my face in her hand, but this time her skin actually grazed my cheek and her fingers were ice cold. There was something wrong about her eyes, too. 'This was what I wanted to show you, Ivy.' She was not going to get away with this.

'My name is Winnie. As my mother, even passed, you would have known that. But you're not her, are you, Aunt Leraia?'

Her eyes widened, her nose flared and a scowl appeared on her face. She tried to compose herself with a blank expression, but it was too late. 'My dear.'

She pointed at the snow beneath Maeve and Morgana's feet and then vanished into the darkness with a wicked smile on her face. I could do nothing but go to the place where the ghostly witches had been standing and found my twin sister encased in a glass casket engrained with floral patterns.

Frost had been delicately poised with her fingers intertwined over her stomach, her dark hair falling to her shoulders. Her lips were painted red, and she was wearing the gown she'd worn at her father's wedding. She even wore a colourful floral crown.

And the queen had wanted to show me herself.

There she was, beneath the hanging tree.

Once I began screaming, I was unable to stop, even as Harlow and the others tried to force me away, to pry my fingers from the glass.

58

FROST

I GLANCED AROUND TO FIND THAT I WAS IN A SMALL BEDROOM with only a bed, a few pieces of chipped wooden furniture and an oval mirror on the wall with a rose-tinted edge.

The room was much like a closet in itself, and it was clear that it had not been cleaned in a decade because there was dust everywhere and there was a musty odour. The kind of room that had grown ripe with age. But as I peered into the wardrobe, I saw that every dress had been carefully cleaned and ironed.

The owner cared little for the cleanliness of their surroundings, other than their appearance.

Now, who did that sound like?

Where was I? The last thing I remembered was following the elderly woman into the Winter Forest, and then I had started feeling strange and she offered me an apple. Could it have been poisoned?

Was it Queen Leraia in disguise?

I walked to the door and came out into a busy corridor overflowing with uniformed young girls, all carrying books and satchels. It seemed to be some kind of school or convent, but I could not work out why I was here, or what it had to do with me. That was, at least, until I spotted the back of a dark head with long raven hair, and when she turned I saw those familiarly narrow features, watching the others pass her by.

As I took a step closer and looked around, I noticed a blueish bruise over the girl's right eye.

But it was unmistakeable: here was Queen Leraia in her youth. Not only that, but her belly was full and round. She was heavily pregnant.

I crashed into a girl, but she did not even look my way. Could she see me?

She gathered her belongings and stormed off, her cheeks blushing as if she were embarrassed.

No, clearly I was invisible. Who was Leraia's child, and equally, who was their father? She could not have been married to Mayor Farn yet, so it must have been someone else. I would need to dig deeper.

I crept closer to young Leraia, internally praying that she would not see me. But as I approached, she seemed to stare right through me.

Why was I watching this memory? Did she not realise that I did not care for her past?

Clearly not. It seemed that she was trying to teach me a lesson, and it did not appear that I had any choice but to observe and learn her truth.

I waited, and watched young Leraia crying in the hallway, wondering what I would see next, when an older woman wearing a pristine uniform stormed over to her and took her roughly by the arm. She was shoved into a small office and forced into the chair opposite the woman's desk.

Now, I had the slightest idea where that bruise might have come from.

'You are not supposed to be here, Leraia,' said the woman, staring down her nose at the young pregnant girl. 'You are no longer welcome.'

Leraia frowned defiantly, and even in her youth it was so very familiar to me. 'Why, because of the baby?' She shot the woman a dark look. 'I told you I would take care of that! As soon as he's born, his father's sister will adopt him. Please can I stay? I miss the clan, and I have nowhere else to go!'

The woman just stared out of the window, not even paying her the attention she would have been craving in that moment. 'You ruined everything. I have found someone else who will go ahead with the plan.'

What plan?

My heart began racing. This must have been where everything started going wrong for Leraia.

It was in that moment that her words clicked. His father's sister will adopt him. The baby boy was Barchester.

Winnie and Barchester had always been more like brother and sister than cousins, and Mayor Farn was his father. Leraia did not care about him, her own greed came first.

Perhaps I would find out why. Poor Barchester.

Did he know the truth, and did Mayor Farn know before his death? My heart sank again. Poor Farn.

But unfortunately, it was far too late for that.

'Who?' Leraia asked, eyes hardening and her familiar glare appearing on her face.

'It is none of your concern.'

Leraia stood up and slammed her fists down on the desk. 'Tell me at once, Mother!'

Mother. This was Ember, the strong-willed mage clan leader Leraia had spoken of. It explained the resemblance. The dark hair, and the similar eyes.

The woman rose and bellowed, 'Sit down! You do not speak to me this way.'

'Why not? You kicked me out of the clan. You more than deserve it!'

Ember was the image of her daughter with her arms crossed over her chest. 'Would you like me to terminate the child's father? Because I am more than happy to make this little problem go away.'

How sick.

She had threatened to destroy Mayor Farn.

Leraia's desperation was evident in her trembling voice as she pleaded, 'No, Mother! Please, just let me fix this. I will be the best Winter queen the world has ever seen. I'll do you proud, I promise.'

So, that was what it was all about.

They wanted a mage queen on their throne, a mage in the royal family. The original plan must have been Leraia. She had felt pressured by her mother to put everything together. Suddenly everything was slowly clicking into place, but it did not do anything to ease my mind, in fact it only made me feel rather queasy.

Ember just let out a dark laugh. 'Now you're pleading with me?' Her eyes hardened again. 'Well, it won't work. The process has already begun, we have a mage on the throne after all. A half-mage, half-witch, perhaps, but one of us. She is already with child like you. In the earlier stages, but she is on her way there, and it is his. Unlike yours, her child will be a true heir of Winter.'

My mother. She was Ember's new plan, and she was pregnant with Winnie and me at this time. Could my mother have been forced to marry my father, as Leraia may have been otherwise?

She had killed my mother, and taken the place that was meant to be hers in the first place. But first, she had taken one of her twin daughters. Cold understanding settled in my heart. Although I still hated Leraia for everything she had done, I was beginning to see everything more clearly.

Her reasons. But they did not excuse the countless murders she had committed on behalf of her mother's original plan.

Leraia's burning rage intensified. I had not thought that were possible. 'You chose my half-sister?'

If looks could kill, this office would have been a bloodied wreck by now, on both sides of the table.

'Mother, how could you do this to me?'

Ember cackled. 'You did this to yourself, you and your cursed little boyfriend.' Then she raised her hand and slapped Leraia hard across the face. 'You disgust me. Get out of my office.'

Tears stung Leraia's eyes as she ran from her mother's workspace, but Ember just laughed and returned to her books as if the conversation had never happened at all.

For an instant, I actually felt sorry for Leraia.

But then the feeling faded when I realised this was the moment when she must have planned to kill her sister, steal her daughter and her husband before killing him, as well.

She would do it all just to avenge her abusive mother and take the throne for herself.

59

WICKED

I SCREAMED FOR WHAT FELT LIKE AN ETERNITY as I was thrown down the river, ever closer to the oncoming waterfall where I would undoubtedly face certain death if I couldn't work out a way to get myself out quickly. 'Elder Wicked!' I screamed, hoping that somewhere close by, she and the others were watching out for me, ready to help. 'Greyson!'

What was I even doing?

There was nobody here to save me. I needed to do that for myself, so I clung to branches, rocks and fallen trees on the riverbank. Anything to keep me above water. Oh, how I wished I had a Babylon candle in that moment to take me to any place I pleased.

'Help!' The water forced me under, and I coughed as too much of it tried to enter my mouth. My throat burned, and it was choking me. It was the second time in only a matter of days that I'd almost drowned; I wasn't doing too well.

The end of the stream was in sight now, and the waterfall itself was only a few metres ahead.

Shit.

Watching me from the riverbed was Princess Frost. She was laughing coldly and smiling as I continued to fall, the heavy current pulling me under over and over again. At her side were Winnie, Elora, Harlow, Griffin and Cassius.

My new friends, some of whom had even become family in recent days. Yet, they all wore the same mocking smiles. 'Goodbye Wicked, we won't miss you! You mean nothing to us.' This had to be a hallucination of some sort, but it still stung. It still felt so very real. 'We will be glad to see you die.'

'Die,' Winnie echoed.

'Die, Wicked!' Elora practically sung.

All along, the falcon roamed above, teasing and taunting me as the river pulled me through the strong currents and down, down, down over the edge of the waterfall. 'I refuse!' I screamed, closing my eyes as I hit the air and awaited the bone-shattering fall that I knew was coming.

Everything happened so quickly after that.

Before I hit the water, or as I expected to, I was brought back up into the air and away from the river, across to the riverbed where I was gently placed down on the grass. I laid there, too afraid to even open my eyes, when I felt a soft tap on my cheek and finally took in the face of Elder Wicked's beloved, Greyson, who we'd even suspected was a traitor.

'What happened here?' Greyson asked, leaning down to peer into my eyes. 'Are you alright?'

I spluttered some water, forced myself to breathe and sit up carefully, but it was almost impossible, and I thought I might pass out. 'I ... I think it was ... but you already know, don't you?'

He was frowning hard, scrutinising me with an intense gaze. He reminded me so very much of the young Greyson I'd seen in my hallucination in the palace, and that thought was not helping things at all.

He was handsome, even for an old man. Or maybe his eyes still reminded me of how they used to be, and it took me back to the past. 'You're not making sense.'

'The queen … ,' my voice trailed off, and I retched more dirty river water, feeling my stomach convulsing as the salty taste met with my throat.

There was still so much I wanted to say to the man, so much anger that still remained within. I knew the others felt the same. He didn't even seem to know how much damage he'd caused. 'You released her from her cage while we were away from it.'

His eyes widened, and a sudden fury burned behind them. His jaw was set into a firm line. 'You're welcome for saving your life.' He stood up and walked away from me, not even bothering to deny the accusation. So it was true. He was as selfish as his daughter, a heartbroken shell of a man who'd betrayed us and used our purpose for his own personal gain.

But I supposed I should be grateful that he'd saved me from an awful death.

I stood up slowly when something else came to mind. 'Where is the falcon? Do you see her?'

He turned back, facing me with a hard yet curious expression on his face. 'What are you talking about?' He peered around, then up at the sky. 'You met Elder Wicked's mother. Your own mother, too, in a strange way.' He stared, and his finger followed his gaze, and mine followed the hand. 'There she is.' He watched the bird move with a calm smile on his lips.

It seemed he'd forgotten about my accusation, which was probably for the best. I shrugged, despite the fact that inside my mind was reeling as I was unable to contemplate what had happened. 'I don't know if it was really her or not as it could have easily been one of the queen's tricks. I saw Winnie, Princess Frost and Elora, laughing at me from the riverbank as I almost drowned.'

His eyes widened but he brought a hand to the thick grey-black beard on his chin. 'Yes, it was probably her playing with you, then. I believe she did the same to them.'

There was nothing left to do but to go. 'Take me to them, please.'

'Of course.' He glanced down sadly, before peering into my eyes. 'I care for all of you, and I'm so sorry for everything. So once I say goodbye, and once we get through all of this together, I will leave you. You will all begin your lives fully, and prosper.'

I nodded, but couldn't help myself and asked, 'Where will you go?' He just shook his head, but I refused to let this be the end. Even if he was a selfish bastard, he was ours. He was one of us, and we would always care for him. 'Please. I want to know you'll be safe.'

He smiled sadly, but it seemed to hold all of his worries as it didn't quite meet his eyes. 'Very well. I have a haven, of sorts, in the Winter Mountains.'

I laughed gently as my rage began to ease. He was doing his best to help us, and then he would give us the time and space we'd requested of him. It was the honourable thing to do, and I should have expected no less from him. 'You've had a palace in the mountains all this time and didn't tell us.'

Even though my words were full of tension, I cracked a smile and the mood eased a little.

He returned the smile; he seemed to understand that I wasn't so angry with him that I would banish him completely. 'No, I just returned to my roots. It is where our clan lives and prospers, but my men and I all have our own homes there.'

Suddenly I realised I knew this from my own memories of Elder Wicked's youth, and their relationship. I'd been there, or she had. Years, and years ago. 'Why did you run from Elder Wicked?' I asked. 'She missed you so.'

I'd held her pain, both in her eyes and in my own memories. How strange it had been to feel her love for him through my own emotions, remembering times that I hadn't even lived through myself. I still couldn't get used to the feeling much.

He didn't meet my eyes, and his gaze was solemn as he said, 'I had to. Ember threatened her life, and those of my daughters'. Seeing them again brought me so much joy.'

There was now one question bubbling within me. 'Is Ember still alive?'

His face was unreadable as he said, 'No.' He spun on his heel, and gestured for me to follow. I was reeling with questions and was certain he knew it because he said, 'I can feel your eyes burning through the back of my head, so go ahead and ask me.'

'What happened to Leraia's mother?'

He didn't turn, and carried on walking quickly, urging for me to keep up with his pace. 'First, you must know that Ember was a brutal and abusive mother. On countless occasions, she would have Leraia locked up in her tiny bedroom and beaten for hours on end, or if she didn't, she would have some of the soldiers do it on her behalf. Often for the smallest reasons, or at the smallest confrontations.'

His eyes were sad, as if he genuinely felt sorry for her. 'Nothing was ever good enough. Leraia wasn't even close to being her dream daughter. She blamed Leraia for every little issue in her life, and once the abuse began, it became a sickness. Leraia's jealousy for the other girls, and for Rosa in particular, was clear from the beginning, although personally I hadn't ever understood why.

'But Rosa became the perfect daughter that Ember believed she never had, but she was mine, so Leraia clearly felt this expectation very early on. It makes more sense to me now than it did then.'

He ran a hand through his dark hair, and his gaze was glazed over as he remembered the past. 'When Rosa was very young, nine years old or so, she suffered from panic attacks and seeing ghosts in the night. Leraia, despite her envy for her mother's fairer treatment of her, was always the one who tried to calm her down.'

This was a large part of her magical ability, I remembered.

He paused, as if thinking his words through before continuing again, 'They became close, and one day Leraia heard it from Rosa's lips that Ember had laid a hand on her half-sister, as she had done to Leraia so many times before.

'Leraia lashed out, burning many pieces of her mother's favourite jewellery, clothes and books, to punish her for what she had done. Somehow this brutality against her sister was far worse to bear than the countless times she had suffered herself.'

I listened thoughtfully, surprised, for the first time, to feel sorry for the queen who had caused so much devastation in our lives.

Greyson's eyes were sad as he went on, 'Well, later on, when Leraia discovered that she was pregnant and Rosa was married to the Winter king in secret – who Ember called a brutal, cruel man who struck out at Rosa despite her own early pregnancy – Leraia was furious and found her mother in her office.

'She'd told Leraia to go, said she wasn't welcome, but Leraia told her mother she was heartless for marrying Rosa off to a cruel man, let alone a king, and hit her with a lethal, heart-stopping spell, which she had ... learned from me. I hadn't known what she wished to use it for, but I thought that perhaps she could protect herself from any potential danger, so it was good for her to know it ... '

He stopped talking and began sobbing. 'So I'm partly to blame for Ember's death. I mean, I never really loved the woman, it was merely a passing romance, but I also saw her as a colleague, or a close friend.'

'Leraia killed her own mother ... ,' my voice trailed off as I tried to gather my thoughts again. 'Wait, you said she and Rosa were pregnant ... '

'Yes, with her son.' He was peering into my eyes as if waiting for me to figure out what he was trying to say. 'And Rosa, with twin girls.'

'Frost and Winnie ... What of Leraia's son?' I thought about it for a while before it all clicked into place. 'Barchester.'

His eyes were stone cold. 'Yes, she almost kept him, until she experienced a vision. Something I can never forgive her for, let alone the rest. She rejected him for who he is, for who he becomes.'

Just as I was beginning to see the queen in a new light. Just as I was beginning to see her softer side. 'Because he prefers males?'

Greyson stared at the ground as he answered, 'Our clan was never ... open-minded about that kind of thing, or at least Leraia's mother wasn't, and I think her beliefs were instilled in her through the years of abuse.'

I narrowed my eyes. 'And where were you during this time?'

He swallowed hard. 'I didn't know Leraia was mine for many years, as Ember was always very ... promiscuous. She was adamant that the timing was off, so I believed her. So I was oblivious to what was happening. I trained and fought with the mage army on behalf of the Winter kingdom, and the others, and I had other children to care for. Wicked's children, and mine.'

'You knew Rosa was yours, and believed Leraia wasn't. Didn't you ever see yourself in her?'

'That's my point, Wicked. I wasn't looking closely enough until it was too late.' He shook his head. 'I only discovered the truth when I overheard Ember telling Leraia that she must avoid me at all costs.'

'She feared you'd find out.'

'Exactly. So I'm a father of many, but Leraia really felt like she was one of mine. I'm sure that has affected her as much as her mother's abuse.'

We were only a few metres away from the forest, and from the others now.

There was Princess Frost enclosed in the glass box, her hands locked together, her thin frame covered with colourful flowers. Blue roses. Her dark hair reminded me so much of her mother's. Her eyes would have been the same, were they open.

'Oh, Princess Frost.' I knelt down beside her, close to Harlow, Winnie and Elora who had made a close protective circle around her. 'We will get you out of there, I promise you that.'

Tears glistened in Winnie's eyes as she smiled and took my hand. 'Why are you soaking wet? What happened to you?'

I filled them in on my trip through the river, and Winnie told me all about her experience with the queen and seeing Maeve and Morgana hanging in the tree above. 'We've taken them to the cabin to prepare for a proper burial,' said Winnie softly, with tears rolling down her glass face.

My heart broke all over again, and my body trembled with pure hatred for the sorceress who'd ruined everything. Very soon, she would meet her end, and she would deserve every last bit of it.

'Morgana must have seen Maeve and … I can't even imagine what must have been going through her head in that moment.' I shook my head. 'And Princess Frost? She must have seen something, too.'

Winnie shrugged. 'We should have stopped her, and called her back.'

'I told her not to go, that's right.' An old woman had been asking for help, and Princess Frost must have given into the trick, her kindness being taken as a sign of weakness. 'Has anyone seen the queen or felt anything strange since then?'

'No, I don't think so,' said Winnie.

'Wait, what's that?' said Elora, pointing through the glass at Princess Frost's interlocked fingers, where a slip of paper was nestled between the flower petals of a blue rose. 'Someone, open it!'

Greyson, Griffin, Liedan and Harlow stepped forward and quickly pulled the lid off the glass casing before lying it down carefully beside her on the snow.

'Take it, Elora,' I said as she began to gently caress Princess Frost's head. 'Read it out.'

It was clear now that it was a small slip of paper with four lines neatly written in ink.

'It's a song,' said Elora with wide eyes. 'More specifically, it's a verse of a story song meant for bedtime tales in our coven.'

'Do you know it, Elora?' Winnie asked encouragingly, nudging her on.

'Yes, and I think the queen realises that, too.'

Slowly, she began to sing.

Deep in the forest, I will sleep,
Dreaming of the life I have missed,
Hear me whispering in the wind,
Feel my heart in true love's kiss.

'True love's kiss?' said Winnie, scratching her glass head in clear thought. 'Well, that makes no sense. What is the queen playing at?'

Elora's eyes lit up suddenly, as if something had come over her. I dreaded to know what had just happened in her brain, and yet I was intrigued. 'Harlow, care to wake the sleeping princess?'

The soldier's cheeks blushed crimson, but he seemed to understand what she was implying. With a little hesitation, he leaned down and brushed his mouth against Princess Frost's. Then he whispered, 'I miss your fighting moves and that contagious smile, Princess Frost. Please do feel free to wake up and grace us with your wonderful presence.'

Despite his playful tone, there was a solemn concern etched behind his eyes that told me he was genuinely terrified for her.

We waited, surrounding the sleeping princess as Elora began singing again and Harlow continued to gently kiss her, only for nothing to change.

'Elora, get the enchanted water,' I said softly as the idea came to mind. 'It worked for Winnie, and it might just work for Princess Frost as well.'

60

WINNIE

WE GATHERED BY THE FIRE IN HARLOW'S CABIN so we could devise a non-destructive plan. Not for the first time, and certainly not the last.

We'd even considered bringing the glass casket with us, but it was far too heavy even for our strength or any of our magic combined.

It was obvious that we were much better off reconvening here in the warmth than by her side where the queen could harm us again.

On that same note, Greyson had placed a protective spell over the casket, and over Harlow's home, so we would be safe here for now at least.

When Greyson had shared what he'd revealed to Wicked about Leraia's past, I wasn't entirely surprised, but when he'd mentioned her defending Queen Rosa, I was cynical to say the least.

Leraia had recently killed Dad, after all. And as for Barchester being her son, well ... he was still in bed recovering from his fainting spell. He would come to us when he was ready.

I'd almost fainted myself, but thankfully I was sitting in the armchair. 'I still can't believe she would defend our mother back then, only to later take her husband, her child and her life.'

Greyson shook his head. 'Perhaps she was as much under Ember's spell as Prince Hugo was with her. Who knows?'

'No, I think there's more to it than that. If she loved Rosa once, why did she kill her? Why threaten to kill us, and Dad? What changed?'

'She gave her heart away, remember,' said Greyson, frowning. 'I can't make sense of it, either.'

'No, because nothing changed when we put it back into her chest. Well, except for her face.' Which had transformed back into her own. 'That was creepy enough in itself. She wants to kill us all now. All of the heartless things she's done have far outweighed the goodness of her youth.'

There was no good left in her ice-cold heart, and there was no saving her now.

'This is hurting my brain,' said Elora, shaking her head and pinching her nose between her thumb and forefinger. 'We should think of a new way to wake Princess Frost.'

I shrugged. 'You're right, Elora. She should be our focus right now.'

Suddenly, the bedroom door opened and Barchester and Liedan entered the lounge, hand in hand. The way they were looking at each other sucked the air from my lungs. Barchester seemed much calmer, like Liedan had made him smile or cheered him up. How long had that been going on for?

But the sight warmed my chest. It was good to see my best friend happy again, especially after he'd lost his uncle. His father.

'I think I've just thought of a way to solve our little sleeping princess problem,' he said softly, reached for my hand and led me through the door.

The others followed, if a little nervously. I had seen so little of him since my arrival in Icefall, and a well of guilt had been forming in my chest for quite some time, for both him and my father.

I had been so consumed by everything that had happened here that I had barely helped them at all. It hurt to see how much he'd grown and know that I hadn't really been a part of that growth.

But I made a promise to myself in that moment that I would do better from this point on.

'Come with me, *sister.*'

There was nothing I wanted more.

61

FROST

'YOU KNOW PART OF MY STORY NOW, CHILD? Do you wish to know the rest?'

Leraia's voice echoed through the halls as I followed her younger self to her small room where she deposited her things, and then returned to her mother's office. What did she think that showing me her story would prove? I did not wish to see her youth, and it certainly would not change how I saw her.

She was a brutal narcissist with a hunger for blood, and there would be no coming back from that.

'Why would I care to know that?' I said, my mind's voice speaking for me. None of the other girls seemed to realise what was happening, nor did young Leraia herself, who seemed to stare right through me.

That bruise was far more colourful now.

'I simply want you to understand me and my choices,' she said, her inner voice louder than it had been before. 'Or do you wish to remain sleeping for an eternity?'

Confusion stirred within me. 'I do not want to know who you are or see your choices. Your actions have had disastrous consequences for me and my family. How did I get here? I am not sleeping, I am perfectly awake in this –'

'Child, your body is encased in glass, just not in the same way as your sister's. Your consciousness, on the other hand, is safe with me.' I heard the smirk in her voice, the way she would have been smiling. 'Do you wish for it to remain that way forever?'

My mind tried hopelessly to digest her words. 'I am in your head?'

By now, young Leraia was in the office. 'That you are. Enjoy the show.'

'No, come back –'

But she did not answer, nor was there any physical trace of her lingering in the air. I was sleeping, so where was my body? What of my sisters, and my friends? I had no choice but to watch.

The heavily pregnant Leraia was bent over the desk, staring hard at her mother who was scrutinising her carefully. 'I know what King James is, Mother.'

What was she talking about?

Ember raised an eyebrow. 'Oh?'

'Yes, did you know?'

Ember's face did not change. 'I would never have put you into his hands, child.'

'You disgust me. You made it seem like I wasn't good enough for him, or good enough to be queen! But what's worse is that you knew, and you let her marry him. In fact, you arranged it!' She was clearly seething now, her face contorting with rage while her mother just smirked.

I could not understand Leraia's problem with Rosa marrying my father, the envy aside.

'I would never have given you to him, as you are mine.'

'Yet my sister is disposable?' She approached Ember, staring into the mirror on the wall as the fury in her eyes strengthened. I knew now that this was her restoring her own magic, bringing it back into herself.

The more I watched her, the more I understood her. But I did not like any of it, not one little bit. I did not want to see more of her inner mind, or be forced to watch her make the disastrous choices that she had, because it would only be a painful reminder of everything that I had lost at her hands.

Ember did not flinch. 'She is only a half-mage. You are mine. I purely released you from the clan for your own safety. Half-mage children aren't treated well here. Your sister would have known that, too, had I not covered her back.'

Could this be Ember's way of justifying her own abandonment of her daughter? Perhaps Leraia was just like her mother in that, just like how Leraia still sought Winnie's love and attention, Ember wanted Leraia to love and respect her as well, despite her torment.

'Oh, you mean my son? Don't try to trick me into thinking you did it because you care about me! You kicked me out of the clan. Don't you know how frightening that is?'

'His father is cursed, is he not? Your son is no mage.'

'You're lying. You don't care about me or my baby.'

Ember leaned closer, and cast her daughter a knowing look as she said, 'I'm not just speaking of his mage heritage. You know, I dreamt of his future.'

'Your dreams aren't real.'

'Oh, but they are. I slumbered and saw that you would do great things for your people, but only if I didn't let you have the throne as you wished.'

My earlier thought had been right, then. She wanted to justify what she had done to her daughter with false affection. False intentions.

'Who knows what the future holds? For your son, I see an unjust life, one that will not easily grant him children, nor will be seen as right by our god. He will not be inclined to women.'

Leraia shook her head. 'I don't care. He is my son, and I will love him accordingly. But he will be raised as my nephew if you put me on the throne in Rosa's place, Mother. Do that to me, not her. She doesn't deserve that.'

Deserve what? My father was always known as fair and kind, loving and gentle. What lies were they trying to spin about him? He was never one to show his emotions with those he was not close to, but my mother and I knew he felt deeply, and sensitively.

Winnie would have felt this as well, had Leraia not ruined our lives in this way.

'I told you, it is already done. They are married, and she is with child. Go and be your fated self, daughter. Now, get out of my sight.' She claimed she had done what was right for Leraia, but she was still angry with her. She still rejected her grandson.

She was simply changing Leraia's reality now, manipulating her into believing she had made these choices for her own good.

Just as Leraia had later done to Winnie.

Even if Leraia was not Winnie's biological mother, she had raised her for many years, and so it was clear that she had been unable to stop the cycle of abuse that her own mother had laid upon her.

She may not have laid a hand on my sister, but she had still emotionally tormented her, and carried on the cycle in this way. It would stop with Winnie and Barchester, I just knew it. Because they were different, as Elora and I were. As Wicked was.

Our generation would be the one to change everything.

'No, Mother.' Leraia stepped backwards. But this time she did not leave, but placed a hand on her rounded belly and began chanting words I did not understand.

I could only watch as Leraia's face changed from still and calm to an expression of shock and despair as her mother began clutching her chest before falling face down, slumped over her desk.

62

WICKED

I WAS ON THE EDGE OF THE HARBOUR, close to Mother's cabin, overlooking the boats that led to the Winter Canal and the river between the four kingdoms, when a familiar voice appeared from some distance away. 'Wicked, my love.'

I turned to face my beloved, taking in that dark hair, his curled facial hair and those piercing eyes.

My hand immediately fell to my stomach as he leaned in and kissed me. 'Greyson, I'm so very happy to see you.' He kissed me again, smiling so deeply that I was unable to look away.

'I should hope so.' His laughter filled my chest in a spiralling echo, with a new warmth which brought me great comfort and was instantly welcome. 'You said you had something to tell me.'

I gestured for him to join me on my picnic blanket, overlooking the wonderful view of the harbour and the mountains beyond.

It was one of our favourite spots to relax, when we could break away from our families.

He sat down, wrapped an arm around my shoulder and pulled me closer against him. Then I took his hand and placed it over my stomach, where a slight rounded bulge had already began to form.

Each time I'd seen him at the coven or in the forest in recent months, I was always far too afraid to say the words, and my body had been buried in thick woollen clothing, but now was the day.

I'd told myself to be brave, that it was the best time to share our precious news. 'I already feel her inside me. Isn't that strange?'

His eyes widened and I felt his love for me clearly as his smile widened into a beaming grin. 'Yes, I mean, no. I mean, I have no idea ... Oh, Wicked, that's wonderful news!' He pulled me into his arms before gently leaning down and kissing my stomach, which made me laugh. 'A little girl?'

'Our girl,' I said, kissing him again.

'Ours,' he said, plucking a rose from the nearby bush. 'Perhaps we can call her Rose.'

'What about Rosa?'

'Perfect. Wow, I still can't believe it. I'm going to be a father.' He tugged me into his arms again and gently began stroking my tummy as if he could also feel our daughter moving inside.

Then he asked, 'How do you know she's a girl?'

How did I explain it? 'I just ... feel it. Besides, you know boys are quite far-fetched in our coven.'

He chuckled. 'Well, I've always wanted a daughter.'

63

WINNIE

There was something evolutionary about how much Barchester had changed, I thought, as he led me into the forest toward Frost's glass casing.

'It makes sense, think about it. True love's kiss,' he was saying, with my hand in one and Liedan's in the other. 'Your bond has clearly become so strong, and you love each other as twin sisters should. It's a shame that it didn't work for Harlow, but their relationship is still blossoming.'

'What has gotten into you, Bar?' I asked, although he was smiling brightly and I knew he felt the teasing in my tone of voice. My gaze flickered to Liedan behind him as I said, 'You're a new man.'

He shrugged. 'I suppose I am what you might call a prince.' That smirk was both one that I wanted to scratch off his face and see grow at the same time, which was a strange feeling.

My best friend was so strong and so brave, and I couldn't be more proud of him. Watching him flirting and laughing with the boy beside him made me curious.

'This is Liedan, by the way. We've been …'

'Courting?' I said, unable to stop the amusement from creeping into my tone. 'How long has this been going on for? How exactly did this happen?'

'Oh, he just fell into my lap one day,' said Liedan with a grin. 'And he hasn't left since.'

'Get over yourself,' Barchester teased, before turning back to me again as I knelt down at Frost's side. 'So, how are we feeling, Princess Ivy?'

'Fragile, I suppose. We've lost so many people, and I feel for Elder Wicked and the others. I want to do something for them, but I don't know what. I feel kind of helpless, actually. Is this what it's like to be a princess who has no control over her kingdom?'

I took Frost's hand, thinking over all of the power we would hold between us on those thrones.

My fingers stroked her cheek as I admired her beauty. If only there was a way to wake her that wouldn't cause her any harm.

'Don't you want to be queen?' said Elora softly from behind me.

I shook my head. 'It's not the most important thing in my life. You all are. I only want what she does, and I know she wants me at her side when she becomes queen.'

🍎

As Wicked and Griffin arrived, I realised what was important: Frost. I hadn't wanted to act without them so we spent our time talking to my sister, telling her everything we would do once she was safe and well.

Once we took back our parents' kingdom.

Once we defeated our aunt, Queen Leraia.

Now that they were here, we could finally change everything if our plan worked.

I took Frost's hand and gently kissed her cheek, and then Wicked and Elora did the same. 'Sleeping as ever ... wait, did anyone else see that? Her finger just moved.' I kissed Frost's cheek again, willing her to wake up. 'Come on, sister.'

'I told you,' said Barchester, smirking. 'You love each other.'

'Yes, we do,' I said, finally realising the truth for the first time. 'As do Elora, Wicked, and all of our lovely new friends.'

64

FROST

I WAS NO LONGER IN LERAIA'S BEDROOM or in the home of the Ajanid clan, but in the Winter palace, and sitting on the throne with Winnie at my side and Leraia on her knees before us.

It took a few minutes to register that Winnie was wearing a crown and the pale pink ballgown she had worn at Father's wedding.

There was a sword through Leraia's chest.

She glared up at us as blood poured from her mouth, eyes and nostrils. 'You did this, Winnie,' she said, but then she seemed to stare into the reflection of herself in the steel blade, and her wound began to heal.

The blood was gone, and her eyes sparkled in the light. 'You girls never learn, do you?'

Slowly, I opened my eyes and found trees, a star-spotted sky and Winnie, Elora, Wicked and Harlow, surrounded by his brothers and Barchester. Greyson and his men were nowhere to be seen.

I sat up and glanced around. In my hands were several blue roses, reminding me of that day in the Winter palace when my father had married the queen.

Disgusted at the sight of them, I discarded them and cast them furiously into the bushes.

'Take it easy,' said Winnie, offering me a sip of water from a glass bottle.

I was relieved to feel the cold liquid as it slipped down my throat. I craved more, and so I drank until Winnie was forced to tell me to be careful. 'I had the strangest dreams, Winnie,' I said, finally realising I was lying in some kind of glass box. 'You should have seen it. I was in the Ajanid's home watching the queen in her youth. She was heavily pregnant with ... ,' I peered up at Winnie's cousin. My cousin, as well. 'Barchester, I am sorry, Winnie.'

He did not seem surprised.

'Yes, we learned that too, but through Greyson,' said Wicked, reaching for my hand and holding it in her own. 'Go on. What else did you see?'

Where *was* the mage leader? I told myself to focus, and that knowledge would come with time.

I inhaled before continuing, 'I saw Ember tell Leraia to leave the clan, that her pregnancy meant she was no longer welcome. They planned to make her marry the queen, but Ember put my mother on the throne instead. She was in the early stages of pregnancy, too. But it was so strange.

'In a separate memory, Leraia returned to Ember, told her she was wrong for giving Queen Rosa away to a cruel king, but my father was never even brutal or cold.' I paused as I watched their faces fall with fear and terror. 'I watched Leraia kill Ember with a heart-stopping spell.' Then I told them about my most recent dream, involving Winnie and I sitting together in the throne room with a sword through her chest, bloodied tears falling from her eyes.

'Wow, that is insane,' said Barchester. 'My birth mother is a real piece of work.'

Winnie gripped his hand. 'And that's all she is: biology. Aunt May is your mother, even if she wasn't exactly the best one. But you have me. You will always have me, Bar.'

He just smiled sadly. 'Yes, you're right. Now, we should probably get you out of there before she sees you.' He helped me to my feet, which were not really working, so Harlow scooped me up into his arms before I collapsed in the snow again. 'Let's get back to the cabin and do some real training before we have to face her again.'

We carefully moved back to the cabin, where I was placed into the armchair with a warm cup of hot chocolate with marshmallows sitting on top. 'Well, this is worth the strange forest slumber! Look at the size of these, and this is heaven in a drink.'

I laughed as the others warmed themselves by the fire, all wearing the same triumphant smiles. 'Thanks for doing whatever you had to do to get me out of there.' Peering around at my sisters and my friends then, I had never felt quite so blessed.

'Always,' said Winnie slowly, casting me a smile. 'We saw some strange things while you were asleep, too. All designed by the queen, of course.'

Oh, god. After everything that had happened in the palace, I was not sure I wanted to know.

But intrigue took over, and I raised an eyebrow and waited for her to go on. She told me she had found Maeve and Morgana hanging from a tree in the forest, then saw me in the glass casket and found Wicked dripping wet at Greyson's side.

Then she told me how Wicked had been brought out of the cabin by a falcon who was revealed as Elder Wicked's mother, then almost sent her to her death down the river before Greyson caught her at the waterfall. 'I am so sorry to both of you, that is awful.'

'Yes, it is,' said Winnie, inching closer to me and curling up at the foot of my armchair. 'But we're all together again. She keeps trying to break us apart, but it never works! Well, apart from Greyson and his men. Has anyone seen them?'

'Not since we went to the forest to wake you,' said Wicked. 'Come on, finish up your drink and then we'll go.'

It seemed there was always one thing after the other, and would be forever.

At least, until we finally ended this.

65

WICKED

Back in the cold air once again, we searched the clearing for anything out of the ordinary.

'While we look, I'm going to teach you both some basic spells,' I told Winnie and Frost.

It was vital that the twin princesses learned to defend themselves against the cruel enchantress.

Even if they only knew a few simple spells, it would be better than nothing. 'I fear it won't be long until we see her again, and you both need to learn to harness your magic.'

Winnie frowned. Genuine fear widened her pretty blue eyes, and her body trembled as she spoke, 'I'm not witch material, Wicked. I barely knew about any of this –'

'Nor did your twin sister.' I could only give Frost a smile when I pictured her training with Elora. 'You both have witch, mage and royal heritage, which will benefit you both greatly. But you need to learn to use it, or you could get hurt.'

Frost was still staring at the ground. 'I am not sure I feel strong enough for a mage lesson right now. I can barely walk without staggering.'

'Then heal yourself as you've done before.'

I wasn't going to let them destroy their chances before they'd even begun. I would whip these princesses into shape before the day was done, that much was a promise I was determined to keep. 'Let's get started. Repeat after me.' I called out a series of levitational spells, purely to warm them up, and was satisfied as they slowly raised tree logs and fallen branches before moving onto more complex spells.

I taught them how to heal themselves and others. I showed them the spells to send someone to sleep, to temporarily stop the heart, to trigger memory loss in the brain, and I told them how to kill, but reminded them to only use these spells when they were at risk of harm. As a form of self-defence.

Winnie began writing them down as if she were afraid she would forget them.

'You can do it, both of you,' I assured them. 'You must.'

The soldiers were ahead of us now, searching every clearing and peering into trees before coming to a halt beside the frozen lake.

'Wicked!' Griffin cried out, and pointed down at the ice. 'Come and look at this.'

'What is it?' Frost and Winnie joined them at the lake and knelt before it. 'What's happened?'

I joined them, and found a sight that broke my heart. Greyson was lying beneath the surface of the ice, and surrounded by three of his men. 'Oh, God. How could she do this?'

'After all that she's already done, I'm hardly surprised,' said Barchester. Of course, I had to admit that he was right. 'Well, I suppose we need an ice pick.'

'No, that would be too dangerous; we don't know how close they are to the ice.' I stared at Barchester, a new thought springing to mind. 'Do you know any natural, preborn mage spells to remove your grandfather from the lake? Anything you wouldn't have been taught?'

He laughed, and it held a bitter edge. 'I only just found out my birth mother is a murderous mage sorceress. What magic do you expect me to know?'

He could use his traits just like his mother and grandfather, but that would be difficult if he didn't know what they were, or the triggers that would help him access his magic. Like Leraia's vanity. 'Well, mage magic is blood magic. I suppose I'm clutching at straws here, but I have to try.'

'I'm not even sure how I would begin.' He scratched his head. 'Do you know anything about how the mage warriors use their magic?'

My eyes lowered to his hands, and I found myself unsure of how to ask. 'They use their emotions, and their traits. But they often use *blood magic*.'

His mouth dropped open, but he'd clearly gotten the message. 'Seriously? Fine. I can't believe I'm saying this, but give me a knife.' I passed him mine and watched him cry out as he sliced into his hand, gasping as blood spilled from the wound in his palm. 'This is how they do it in the movies, right?' He laughed bitterly, and closed his eyes. 'Alright, now what?'

Being a mage sorcerer couldn't be all that difficult from being a witch, right? I tried to remember Greyson's stories about his methods, the way he learned to be a mage warrior, and also stole one of our techniques. I could only hope it would help him.

'Focus on the feeling of the blood rushing through your veins. Do you feel it?'

'Yes, I see stars. But I guess that could also be from the blood loss.'

I had to force myself to ignore his comment, and focus on the positives. 'Good, good. Concentrate on that, and see the lake in your mind with one big crack through the ice, no little pieces.'

'How do you know this?' he asked, clearly terrified.

'I'm just following Elder Wicked's memories of her closeness to Greyson. He talked about his magic growth sometimes. Do you see it?'

'Yes, yes.' He seemed to focus, biting his lip and concentrating. 'It's shattered. Did it work?'

Disappointment crept through me, both for myself and the boy. 'No, sorry ... try again.'

He released a frustrated sigh. 'Ugh, all that blood for nothing?'

'Good, let your anger fuel you.' I wanted him to continue to work on saving Greyson, but maybe it was foolish of me to expect so much from someone who'd never used magic before.

'What if I have more of my father's blood?' he said, breaking down in defeat. He knelt down on the snow beside the lake, and ran a hand over the edge of the ice. 'What if I'm no mage at all?'

I couldn't lose him or his magic now. There was no way he wouldn't possess any magic, he had to at least contain a small trace in his blood.

We just needed to keep him moving. 'No, you will have at least a little, so use what you do have. Work with me, alright?' He nodded, and slowly, together, we concentrated. I took his wounded hand, and held it in my own. 'Together, okay?'

'We should all help,' said Winnie, reaching for my hand, and Elora and Frost to come together as well. 'Teach us the spell that will break it.'

'We'll circle you,' said Harlow. 'Keep a look out for anything strange.'

'Great, perfect.'

Out of the corner of my eye, I spotted dancing shadows. Queen Rosa, Seager, King James, Maeve and Morgana, Prince Hugo and Mayor Farn all watched from the gaps in the trees, wearing the same eerie smiles. I told myself to ignore them, and that they were just tricks of the mind. So when they began singing the melody that had inspired us to wake Princess Frost, I told myself not to listen, and was doing well until ...

'Anyone else hearing the grand choir?' said Barchester with his eyes still closed.

Deep in the forest, I will sleep,
Dreaming of the life I have missed,
Hear me whispering in the wind,
Feel my heart in true love's kiss.

'They're not here, it's just the queen playing games,' I said, more to myself for the added effect. 'Everyone, focus.'

Deep in the forest, I will sleep,
Dreaming of the life I have missed,
Hear me whispering in the wind,
Feel my heart in true love's kiss.

The ice hadn't yet cracked but we didn't stop, and much to my surprise, Barchester began singing along. I opened an eye and frowned at him, but he just smiled. 'Can't beat them, join them?'

'You are so funny, Barchester,' said Frost.

'Thanks, Princess! I take that as a great compliment, coming from the future queen of Icefall.'

She laughed. 'You are welcome.'

Deep in the forest, I will sleep,
Dreaming of the life I have missed,
Hear me whispering in the wind,
Feel my heart in true love's kiss.

By now we were all singing along to the melody, and I grinned at the feeling of joy that came from this strangely unifying moment. 'Look, it's working.' The shadowed figures around us, eerie as they had been at first, fell away like fallen leaves in the bitter wind.

And the ice before us had cracked, leaving us all smiling with relief and the satisfaction of knowing that we'd done it. Carefully, we pulled Greyson and his men from the icy water and laid them down on the snow as Barchester peered at his bloodied hand before saying, 'Well, isn't that something?'

'We did it together,' said Winnie, wrapping an arm around his waist.

'Not quite.' I would have known that voice anywhere and it was the one of my nightmares.

Of all of ours.

'Hello, everyone. It's adorable that you still think you can destroy me.' There was Queen Leraia, wearing a gown of silver crystal stones over a tight black corset, as she pressed the blade of a sword against her father's throat. 'Time and time again you feel elated and joyful because you believe you've won. But you don't know how powerful I really am. Except for you, perhaps, Princess Frost.'

She pressed her fingernail against the princess's cheek, then lowered it to her chin. 'Did you enjoy watching my memories, child?'

Frost gritted her teeth, as behind her Harlow handed her his sword. She raised it to her side, and brought it upwards, but the queen's hand moved to her neck, tearing her off her feet.

She didn't even scream, just cast the queen a dark smile, a beaming grin as the soldiers circled the queen.

As I approached from behind, with Winnie, Barchester and Elora's fingers all woven together.

Deep in the forest, I will sleep,
Dreaming of the life I have missed,
Hear me whispering in the wind,
Feel my heart in true love's kiss.

I caught Winnie's eye, and willed her to concentrate. She nodded subtly enough before chanting the deadly spell that would permanently stop the queen's cruel heart from beating. 'It's the end for you, *Mother*.'

The queen turned on her, dropping Frost and letting her fall to the floor as she tried to grasp for breath.

Barchester was staring hard at the queen as she coughed, as she gripped her chest.

But she ignored him. 'No, you wouldn't do this to me. Not my Winnie.'

Winnie just laughed bitterly. 'I'm sure your mother thought the same about you.'

The queen's eyes widened.

Greyson broke free and pushed the queen to the ground, forced her head down into the snow and away from the lake. 'Nobody look at her, don't let her find strength in her own reflection.'

'My son,' said Leraia, her voice muffled as she tried to peer up at Barchester. Then she blinked and Winnie dropped to the floor, unconscious. 'Anyone else wish to stop my beating heart? Go ahead!'

Barchester grunted, and pounced on the queen. 'That's my sister! How dare you?'

She laughed bitterly, even as he held her head up by the brand. He brought her down, and sent her crashing into the snow. Blood poured from a wound in her forehead as she stared into his eyes, and spat on the ground. 'She's not though, is she, my boy?'

He spat on the snow before her. 'I'm not yours, I never was. You're just cells and biology to me.'

He ran to Winnie, and I took over as Greyson pinned her down. I began chanting the spell Winnie had used once again.

Frost whispered a healing spell that quickly woke Winnie, and she sat up beside her sister.

At once, we all chanted the spell Winnie had spoken before. Winnie, Frost, Elora and me.

The coven of witches, and the soldiers who'd sworn loyalty to us all. No matter how many times the queen tried to lead us astray, or separate or break us, we returned to each other.

Although we were emotionally scarred, our willpower was strong. Together.

66

WINNIE

My strength grew as I continued chanting the fatal spell that would end the cruel queen's life.

The woman who, despite everything, had always been a mother to me.

Kind, fair and true. But I reminded myself, not for the first time, that everything was different now and it had to be this way.

For our future, for our *family*.

For my parents, the late king and queen of Icefall. And for Dad's memory, the only father I'd ever known. I'd barely known my true parents.

The queen, my aunt. Barchester was better off without her, as we all were. So I kept talking, the words becoming second nature as the others joined in. This was the moment we'd all prepared for.

'It's done,' said Wicked.

Greyson was still holding Leraia, but she was still. I couldn't help myself, I burst. I fell to the floor and buried my face in the snow. She was gone, so where was the happiness, relief and elation?

The others were grinning; celebrating, but my body felt frozen. I couldn't move, and I was so cold.

'Winnie.' Barchester knelt beside me, and threw his cloak over me. 'Darling, you're not made of glass anymore, and you're nude ... '

I finally looked at him, then down at myself, at the skin of my hands, my bare legs. Tears streamed down my face but I didn't feel them. My skin was numb, but I didn't care as I wrapped myself in Barchester's cloak. 'What? Oh, my god ... '

'It must have been a curse that would last through her life. Elder Wicked said you wouldn't change back until she was gone,' said Frost.

'Come on, let's get you some clothes. Someone deal with that?' Barchester pulled me to my feet, securing the buttons on my cloak.

Greyson and the soldiers wrapped her body in flowers and weeds and pushed her frail form into the glass casing that Frost had been enclosed in. 'Make sure her face is covered so she can't use the glass's reflection. We'll put her in the dungeons just in case,' said Greyson. 'No mirrors. No tin boxes. Come on, man. Be proud of yourselves, girls. Grandson.'

Barchester's cheeks warmed. 'Oh, he called me Grandson.'

Greyson merely shrugged. 'Well, you're family, aren't you? Even if she wasn't your mother, you would be.' I held him in my arms, and we returned to the cabin. 'Speaking of, didn't you have a coronation coming up?'

'I suppose we do,' said Frost, taking my hand and smiling. 'But the naked princess should put some clothes on, first.'

I laughed. 'Barchester's got me covered, literally.'

'You're not even funny, *sister*,' said Barchester, rolling his eyes and laughing.

It was hard to believe that it was over, but here we were. We had the rest of our lives to live, a coronation to plan, and nobles and people to meet with. We would meet with the Royal Council and prepare for a better relationship with the other three kingdoms. Barchester would eventually return to Cranwick to take Dad's place as Mayor, and I hoped Cranwick's relationship with the Roth witches would be improved now that everything had changed.

It would all come with time, but for now we were happy. I was no longer trapped in Cranwick, I had my freedom, and a *purpose*.

I would be a twin *queen,* but I was just happy to be at Frost's side. I had two sisters and a whole family of soldiers and witches.

No more evil queen, no more death and torment.

67

FROST

THREE DAYS LATER we were waiting for the ceremony to begin. Our people were informed and many cheered in the streets as we made our way through, waving and throwing flowers on the ground.

Yellow and blue roses, fittingly, which had been our mother's favourite for so many years.

I was still yet to answer Harlow's question, but perhaps that would come with time. Some things did not happen instantly, and I was a strong believer that love was one of those things.

If it was meant to happen, it would. But if it did not, I would not fall to my knees in grief, because I had more than enough happiness in my life now.

Two sisters who loved me, and a cousin, and friends and family. Witches, and soldiers, and mages.

Elora, Wicked and Barchester rode with us, and we knew the others would be waiting in the audience. We approached the palace and entered the throne room, hand in hand, to cheering and music.

Winnie and I took our places on the twin thrones they had placed together, and the minister spoke of a better future for Icefall.

A new arrangement, but one that would be adapted over the centuries to come. We would rule from one palace, and we would overcome the rest over time. New rules were put into place, so that when one of us married and allied with another kingdom to produce an heir, they would rule fully with their sister as a close royal advisor.

I had been raised as a princess, knowing that one day I would be queen. Winnie was just happy to be there with me. For her, I knew her new title was simply a new bonus and a permanent home away from Cranwick. One where she could be close to me and Elora, and keep Barchester safely at her side.

We recited our royal vows.

'I now call you Queen Frost Winter and Queen Ivy Winnella Winter of Icefall, daughters of the late King James and Queen Rosa.'

Cheers and screams erupted through the palace walls and outside as a new kingdom was created. 'To a better Icefall!'

People screamed and cheered, as we stood up and faced our people. Our *queendom*.

'For the future,' we said at once.

It was only just the beginning of the rest of our lives.

END OF BOOK ONE

ACKNOWLEDGEMENTS

Well, where do I even begin?

Since I published my first YA fantasy novel, *Steel Princess,* in July 2022, I have been blown away by the support. If you have read the Acknowledgements section of that one, you might have noticed that I mentioned writing and querying my books for over twelve years.

Well, that is true.

My Facebook, Instagram, YouTube and Twitter friends will have noticed my countless writing and querying updates, because I love to use social media as an outlet. But people I don't really speak to that often have popped up saying they read and loved the novel.

Being an author is wild, right? A good amount of the books I have written, I have shelved them and put them away for another day, so I actually wrote this one during Camp NaNoWriMo a few years ago. It's been in the back of my mind for a while.

During Covid lockdown, I decided to rewrite *Steel Princess,* but I always knew I would come back to this one eventually as well. I fell in love with writing it as my first fairy tale retelling, and always knew I would want to make it even better at some point.

Anyway, ignore my drifting and let's get into it!

As always, I have to start with my wonderful family. Robert, my rock as always. How have we been living together for a year and a half now? Doesn't time fly? Thank you for listening when I need to rant about my books, my publishing process, work or anything else in general. I know I talk a lot! But you're my favourite person to spend every day with. Also, thank you for the beautiful mirror that you designed for my chapter headings. I love it just as much as the tiara you created for S*teel Princess*.

Elliott, the best footballer I know, and always dancing around the living room, thank you for the laughter. Roo, the *Marvel* expert, I always love asking you about what you're getting up to on your games. I love spending time with you and your dad and brother.

Paul, Lynda, Emma and Pauline, and family up north, you have always shown support in my books since I met you and for that I will always be grateful. I love visiting you with Robert and the boys.

Mum, Dad, Izzy and Ellie, I always look forward to your updates in our family group chat, and I love that you're so supportive whenever I share my milestones with my writing and publishing journey there as well.

Mum, you have always been there to listen when I want to talk about a new story or plot idea, and are always excited when I reveal a lovely new review of my first book. I love our little lunch dates and how we always have something to laugh about.

Dad, thank you for always being there to offer plot ideas and always asking what I'm working on at the moment as I love discussing my stories with you.

Izzy, I have loved watching you become a wonderful mother over the last year. I will always appreciate the baby spam and a cuddle when you can come and visit. I feel like we've become closer since little Isaac arrived and I'll always thank him for that.

Ellie, I always look forward to your craziness when I come and visit, and I cherish our movie nights. Thank you for always being there.

And not to forget about Dusty, never too far away to offer a furry cuddle when you need one!

Rhiannon, my best friend of thirteen years and my biggest fan! Your love and support has been mind-blowing, and I can't wait to see the selfie of you holding up this one just like you did for *Steel Princess!* Our evening catchups are always great fun, and I love hanging out with you and your gorgeous babies. You're the one person I go to when I have big news, and I'm always here cheering you on with your endeavours as well. Couldn't be prouder, watching you as a mummy. I know it's not easy, but you're amazing with them. Thank you for all of the love.

My Uni of Beds Creative Writing buddies, Sarah, Tazzy, Harry and Pippa, isn't it strange that uni finished seven years ago but it doesn't feel like that long ago at all? My trips to Luton to visit you all for lunch and ice cream (always ice cream, be weird if we didn't!), always make my week. I wish I could see you all more often but life has a habit of getting in the way, eh?

Christiana, my favourite YA loving buddy, thank you for always coming to YALC with me. You blew my mind when we went together and I'd brought my proof copy of *Steel Princess* along with me, and you were encouraging me to tell people about it in the queues of different events! I will always value our friendship.

Keeley, always a WhatsApp message away if I need you, thank you for being there. You're my first choice if I have any gossip or laughs to share. You've always been supportive of my writing since we worked together at *The Works* and I couldn't be more grateful.

To my writing friends I've met through socials and my freelance editing business, *Hooked On Words Editorial,* Ally Aldridge, Roxy Eloise, Michelle Kenney, Katharine & Liz Corr, Brittany Moore, Ariel Johnson, Jonathan Dunham, Evangeline Parry, Sean Harby, Sophie Queen, Angeline Trevena, Julia Scott, Josephine Blake, Holly Hypes Books, Lorna House, Crab & Bell, Sabrina at Book Ends, thank you for showing all the support to *Steel Princess* and my writing progress.

To my wonderful cover designer, Josephine Blake at Covers & Cupcakes, thank you for my two beautiful covers. You're brilliant at what you do, and I love your enthusiasm for your clients' work. I also love talking writing through with you, and I'm so proud of you for your own writing goals as well.

To my editor, Katie Wismer at Ahimsa Press, a great BookTuber who has inspired me for years, I love watching your vlogs, and your feedback on my work has been invaluable.

To my character artist, Athena Bliss, you're so talented at what you do and everyone should book you. Thank you for the beautiful drawings.

To my map artist, Abigail Hair, thank you for another wonderful map! I love watching my world come to life through your work.

To my formatter, Julia Scott at Evenstar Books, thank you for the beautiful interior of this book. You're a talented artist and a great writing friend.

To many of my colleagues, for showing interest in my books and always asking about my progress, Dawn, Laura, Emily, Amy, Liam, Jenny, Cheryl, Rosie, David, Laura, Ranjit, Sam, Jo, Linus, Maaya, and Leonardo, thanks for always being there to cheer me on with my writing!

To anyone who has read *Steel Princess,* reviewed it or added it to Goodreads, thank you so much. I love finding new reviews, and can't wait to do all of that all over again for my second novel.

STEEL PRINCESS, AVAILABLE ON AMAZON AND KINDLE UNLIMITED!

Do you love fantasy books with magic, but also the odd futuristic element? Think Crier's War, Cinder or The Kingdom!

Silver is a bot who has been raised by a travelling community of humans. When her mother is accused of treason, Silver and her friends must partake in a series of virtual challenges to get her back.

Eden is a tinker who was taken from his family when he was small. When an opportunity arises to find them, he takes it, only to be kidnapped by pirates from the Steel City's magical enemy kingdom. He will have to face a few sirens, sea creatures and find out some family secrets of his own along the way.

ABOUT THE AUTHOR

April Grace has always lived in Milton Keynes, and now lives with her boyfriend and, a few nights a week, his two cheeky sons. She has been writing young adult novels for twelve years now, which all started when she decided to write stories on Wattpad while she was supposed to be working hard on modules for her A Levels. (But she did go onto study Creative Writing at university the following year, so it all worked out in the end.)

She has worked for a popular UK bookstore, has temporarily worked for Ingram Spark's Milton Keynes warehouse, was formerly the Head of Literature for a London based charity providing creative opportunities for young people, and now owns her freelance editing company, Hooked On Words Editorial. She loves both reading and writing anything inspired by fairy tales and mythology.

She couldn't be more grateful for all of the love and support.

Printed in Great Britain
by Amazon